Our love is endless, it will find you.

-From us to M Z

Zara Alam lives in London, likes Agedashi Tofu far too much, has a degree in Philosophy and Drama and another one in Psychotherapy. On the side, she studies Psychological Astrology, and then finally - needs to calm down. She does this by listening loudly to music, having Pre-Raphaelite pictures everywhere, watching adventure/fantasy movies, and eating too much dark chocolate...

The Endless Sea

By

Zara Alam

Published by Zara Alam, London.

Copyright © Zara Alam 2014

A catalogue record for this book is available from the British Library.

ISBN 978-0-9931203-0-5

www.zara-alam.com

Front and back cover illustrations by Zara Alam 2014©

To my parents, with love, love and more love.

I owe enormous thanks and gratitude to the following people, who have been completely responsible in many ways, for my happiness and sanity.

For sound technical advice and great discussions: Simon A. Brown.

For helping for so long: John J. Costello.

For enormous love and support, my darlings: Maha Khan, Mehr F. Husain, Marianna Goral and my wonderful, Mariam Uddin.

A special thank you to Marina Kastrinaki, not just for the love and hugs, and showing me the gorgeousness of Greek island life, but for also giving me a refuge to work in.

Lastly I would like to thank my brother, for always being there and just being so special.

The Endless

Sea

PROLOGUE

The black suited man stepped off the train, bearing quietly in his left breast pocket, a beginning; although he did not know it. The photograph was all he had found at the home of a young traitor who had not betrayed him or his masters, but instead, had quite elegantly ruined himself. Yet the man, known in his dark circle as Maurice had not lingered upon why he had taken the train from France to London in such haste, he had been instead compelled by a conviction; after one look at her face, the photograph had borne him on. Maurice himself maintained no resemblance to anyone wholesome, or whole in any way and stood tall, long faced and sallow, slim but with menace, proud of his work or at least the power that it gave him. And so, he conveyed bravely this seeming trifle to London today, for it was a picture of a woman's face, simply this, looking on through black lashes, yet gazing preternaturally, as though she could hear the murmuring of the sea. There was no malice or cruelty no, but persuasion in her glance nonetheless, as though she beheld with the power to possess; she looked on ardently with lustrous black hair, cut in a fashion thought modern, a long time ago. A girl or a woman it didn't matter, for it had affected Maurice; a man whose work could be described quaintly as that of belonging to the 'underworld,' and had driven him to rush to London, so close to the seeming annals of power, to a man who truly held such power, to whom he had to convince that this photograph had meaning; far beyond its value as a simple keepsake.

Perhaps he was too formally dressed Maurice considered as he watched from his Black Cab the London streets pass by, as trees persisted in bearing tiny buds aloft, as was their right to in the spring; yet as usual there was a chill in the air. But it would not do to be casual, especially as they pulled up to the Mayfair address he had been given, he was glad that he was ready for this seeming

Gentlemen's club. He felt at the dark mahogany entrance hall on giving his name and his intended purpose, intensely conspicuous; not for being French, but for not belonging to this world at all, and he pursed his lips, focussing even more on his goal.

He was led along wood panelled corridors, and past quiet rooms full of men sitting on old plush chairs and reading newspapers. Until as he hoped, he was left outside a small room, and waited for the usher to leave before he knocked.

It was not so hard when he entered, for Maurice had seen this grey suited man before, but once again, he was nervous; ridicule was imminent he knew.

"What have you brought me, Maurice? What is so important?"

"Sir, we found nothing at all at the young man's apartment, but one of the books fell to the floor while we searched ... and something fell out ..." Maurice paused now, knowing his difficulty.

"Yes ... so, what is it?"

Maurice took the photograph of the woman, whose fulsome mouth alone spoke opulently in the silence, and placed it before the other.

"That is it? That is all?" the other man asked him -yet still regarded it.

"Sir ... it fell out of a book ... of *poetry*."

The other man fell silent, and Maurice waited.

"But how could we even find such a person, there is no name, date, place, nothing ..." said the other man.

A wave of gratitude washed over Maurice, he understood (!) The powerful, morally defunct man in front of him was not yet so empty, he could *see*. Maurice was expecting to be laughed at, bringing with him as he had a small picture of the traitor's former lover at best, or something more tawdry at the least, but it seemed instead that the man could feel what Maurice felt.

"Don't you have a machine, a facial recognition machine, I mean a computer for this?" asked Maurice, hopeful.

"What makes you think she is English, she may well be French?"

Maurice faltered, he had no idea what had made him assume that she was English.

"And moreover," continued the other man, "don't these fantastical machines, I mean computers, exist simply on television and in the movies, to be honest I have no idea if we have such things ... but on consideration ... GCHQ, MI5, MI6...they all must, I imagine."

And so, both men knew what had to be done, she would have to be found and the other man, the Minister, gently took the photograph from Maurice; who within his tall frame had carried it so delicately all the way there.

"Thank you, Maurice."

Maurice nodded feeling so grateful and then ashamed as though the emotion was a weakness; but he knew he had been right and the Minister had given him validation. Now he faced the journey back to Paris alone, without her to guard, and back to his life as it was; doing the deeds of evil men.

Chapter 1

On the Friday that Lucian drove into London, the city had fallen into the lull of a late and opulent summer afternoon. The unfamiliar heat hushed the birds and bees and the weight of summer burdened the heads of sultry roses; making them heavy with their own voluptuousness. As English gardens sweltered, still, yet ardent with delight, nothing else stirred to break the spell of the day, and in this fevered calm, only lonely butterflies went about their business and fluttered colours past Lucian's windscreen, to catch his eye every time.

As Luc drove on through the summer silence, he felt sick with exhaustion and the imposing heat; at the close of his journey his mind was absent, as if it had been cast away and finally lost, for he was far too fatigued to use it any more. Yet, it was also an act of self-abdication, as though he'd left a great deal of himself behind in France, which he had left a day ago. And still, in this self-inflicted mental absence, he found himself curiously present, empty yet pure, as if thoughts and feelings were from another era, now old confetti that had drifted far away over land and sea, littering the long journey he had just taken; as if everything there was to feel had been felt.

Soon, he slowed down and looked for a place to put his car. He checked his papers for the address for the last time and then, for there were no words, he sat trying to fix his gaze beyond the iron gates that stood at the entrance of his new home. Slowly, he quietly stared at the alabaster terrace that had once been built for the Prince Regent's friends, as its stucco glimmered in sunlight. Corinthian pillars were abundantly erected along the long stretch of its exterior, and it silently towered with a regal gait that promised things that were treasured, a long time ago. It was steeped in grandeur, no doubt an ostentatious monument to the past and carried its years voluptuously, like an old heavy perfume. Many large anonymous doors studded the building, but there was absolutely no one in sight. A weak breeze rustled the surrounding trees meekly and for that moment it felt as though it was all only for him; and a surge of fear soiled the exhilaration like a spilled cup of wine.

Luc tried to proceed but he felt somewhat intoxicated; perhaps it was the long journey that made him feel as though his new home was silently adrift in that lavish haze, as a fog of summer had cast itself all over and was pervading his senses. As he set about moving in the contents of his life from his car, nothing else stirred to break the spell of the day; he could hear only his own breath and the enormous clunking of objects being pushed and dragged and bumped against the still cool walls of the inside hallways. The invading dust and heat came up with him over the soft vermillion carpeted stairs, at first blurring the sight of a diminutive grey flat, that he very much did not expect.

To his slow surprise Luc saw that he was faced with something small and sterile, and what he imagined to be 'Standard Issue'. It had been meanly arranged and was devoid of human comforts, completely at odds with its opulent exterior and like an exiled room of a mansion, it purveyed a type of purposeful neglect. However, as Luc continued his rhythmic trips back and forth during an unbroken hour of unloading, the sombre gloom of the new apartment was shattered by his menagerie of scattered cases, trunks and boxes. Luc's new home suddenly heaved with bohemia; clothes for all occasions, statues, huge encyclopaedias and old electric fans; it was as if by his sheer volume of colourful chaos and clutter that the resident old ghosts were shocked into flight. All around him he had kept fragments of his life: ornaments and geological rocks, a small gold statue of the Egyptian sun-God: Ra, an extremely heavy, black and white marble chess set, books in English and French, from Baudelaire to world politics, and a small framed photograph of his mother. At every university the luggage contents and unpacking ritual had been the same and now in his early thirties, far away yet from student days, such habits were still unchanged. From his new window he could see his tired old car; looking completely out of place amongst the glittering stretched out automobiles of the rich.

He lacked the strength to unpack and organise his paraphernalia, and tried to avoid looking at the ominous heaps of disorder waiting to be arranged, but he did not want to sleep yet. It was only late afternoon yet he was addled by his exhaustion and unable to think, so he remained standing at his window, bathing in the intense sunlight. It should have felt like a heartening solar fog, a radiance to feed his soul, instead it was an immediate solar brand and an unwelcome reminder of the same time last year. For he'd stood in that same shroud of light before, flooding through the stained glass windows of an old French church, casting down everyone's lashes as eight hundred mourners basked in a sunny day of death. Condolences and well wishers words had come to him kindly meant and whispered, and sometimes echoing about the church walls, but only the sun had touched him, it blinded and that was enough.

His mother, Beatrice, was gone. It was unexpected and premature, and at bitter odds with the life he had imagined for himself, especially as his career had finally started to move in the direction that he'd wanted for so long. As he'd sat government tests and held his breath with anticipation during many interviews in odd, poorly lit underground buildings, she'd waned in the spring and had been robbed deftly by the summer.

Thus, in the months leading up to this moment, he had done his best to be busy, driven and focussed by his new life to come, always determined only to reach London and his new occupation. And yet, now at the beginning, he was finally worn away, exhausted; and so the deliquescent haze around the house gently permeated his mind and left it no longer so empty and the languorous gorgons beneath gently beckoned, loosened his grip and set his mind out to sea. His thoughts then came up as vivid creatures from the deep, casting forth all the experiences of the day, making him in the end surmise that all that he had seen and driven through, everything London had offered in its sun-blessed glory, every new twist and turn had had in the end, the same constant meaning: for the venerated monuments to heroic battles and the grand palaces boasting red smocked guards, the abundant royal parks and the thick rose gardens dancing with mercurial butterflies, had all had a referential beauty; intrinsically because they were beautiful, they had resounded only with the memory of her. It was as though she was his pivot for joy, his axis for all things good.

Defeated, he set of for the bathroom, eyes blind and stinging from the sun. The plain white tile was as he expected, but the free standing roll top bath with legs of gilded lion paws, he did not. An elaborate wide golden showerhead towered over on one side, glinting as if ready for a dandy. His bathroom was plush and antiquated, but in a magnificent manner; if they were trying to purge his home of its opulence, judging by the rest of his new flat, they'd failed completely here, it was as though to be dull and plainly functional was not its natural state and an untame restriction to try to maintain at the very least. He placed his grandmother's towels over a free standing dark oak towel holder and out of curiosity switched on an Art Nouveau lamp that sat as an elaborately elevated orb, delicate metal leaves upheld a many coloured ball of glass, that softly released an impractical glow in shades of blue, violet and rose, casting itself all over and mingling pleasingly with the sunlight.

He took off his filthy clothes and glasses, stinking of too much travel and stood in front of three oak framed full length mirrors on one side of the room. He was still bronzed by the sea and sand although this summer's visit to the family home had hardly been a holiday, his father still lingered there now, with his wife in the deep soft earth. Lucian's body had been hewn and stamped out through years of frantic summers with cousins upon a French beach. The hazel eyes and sun kissed sandy hair were his mother's, his gait and strength that reflected back at him, he did not realise, were also hers. He stared at himself, a waking comatose, this human form, he stared until the hot water gave up wafts of beckoning steam and his image disappeared under the mist.

As though a place of deliverance; the bath was heaven. He lay there in steamy bliss and partial delirium for a very long time. His mind then reeled back to an acceptable empty place, like a dark cave that was an inlet of the sea, and he slept. There were dreams then of gladiatorial victories in a dusty ancient Rome and of a more recent cold grey steely Paris during World War II, no sight of London at all even though that was where he was sure he was. But slowly even the dreams disappeared and it became quiet, like the dark coiled beckoning sleep of the dead, his mind finally in a restful abyss, although strangely to him, a place full of promise. He was grateful that his total exhaustion had taken him whole, like a pledge to the devil.

It was only much later, when the sun had begun to melt away and left a half lit demon dimension in its wake, that he awoke with a start. The cold water mocked his reverie and he rushed away from it dripping wet, still too dazed to know where he had kept his towels. His bathroom had come to life in soft rose, violet and black shadows and so he bumped into the furniture until fully awake. It was still silent and until he could remember where he was, he stood motionless for some time; his glistening form looked like a new born creature, standing in a room on the brink of night.

Slowly, he regained himself somewhat, oddly realising that he felt anxious, switching on many lights was beneficial, except that it revealed the many mountains of his chaos. He took a clean shirt from the sprawling luggage and then ran his hands through his hair to regain himself and perhaps decide what to unpack first.

Then, as if a call to the oncoming night, from his window he could hear a baby crying, no, howling as if in protest, and as this was the first human voice he'd heard in hours, he rushed to see. A pale woman with black hair was trying to juggle the infant in her arms; a couple of suitcases were dormant by her side while she searched for the keys to the house next door inside her enormous black handbag. Luc was intrigued and conceded to put on his dirty jeans again before he quickly found himself running down the now wine dark carpet, hoping to catch her before she was gone.

As he descended to the street level, and breathed in the warm night air he was so pleased to see her that he had not noticed her true demeanour: which was that of the desperate and driven, or that she wanted to enter the property before anyone noticed her, or the fact that she didn't live there.

Chapter 2

The woman knew that they wouldn't question her, for she did indeed possess a key. She was convinced however that once she was inside, it was only then that she could think about anything else, even though she had no idea of what type of reception she would receive. Yet, reducing her life to the simplest task was proving impossible as her baby was crying as though furious with her, and her handbag had mutinied, swallowing up her prize. There was nowhere to put down her child and her somewhat ragged suitcases were surely betraying her. Trying to be inconspicuous she gathered all her poise and looked down furiously into her bag, which she then shook, she was now close to tipping it over the ground, or throwing it across the road in a temper. Thus, the approach from a stranger was enough for her to just contain a shriek.

Uncharacteristically, she lost the power of speech and simply looked at him for a moment. Heart pounding, she registered that he smelled of soap and that his hair was still damp, he was smiling and speaking to her, but he then looked somewhat concerned, Christine, before too long passed, understood that he was saying that he was her neighbour and asking her if she needed any help. She could imagine that her face must have looked very white with her black eyeliner smudged conspicuously about. She attempted a small smile and responded, "I just have to find my key."

Looking once more into her traitorous bag she let him linger, not sure of what else to do, but she felt strangely calmed in his presence, as if he validated her. Soon enough and with enormous relief she did find the key, which found the lock that opened the enormous black door ...

Chapter 3

Luc watched, as gingerly, the pale and black haired woman walked in to an entrance hall of a house and stood completely still with her now silent child clamped to one side. She then suddenly marched off and disappeared leaving Luc standing at the threshold, unsure of what to do. He wondered if it would be rude to leave as he had just introduced himself, or rude to stay as she had accomplished her mission. As he turned away hesitant, the sight of the two ugly suitcases squatting behind stopped him. At that moment she returned without her baby and reached forward as though to seize one of the bags, so Luc immediately obliged and helped her with the enormous item; they were heavier than his, if that were possible and shabby compared to their remarkable surroundings.

"My name's Luc, I've just moved in next door," he said mid carry. "First floor," he added as if to reassure her that he was telling the truth, he remembered how wary people from London were.

He could see her more closely now, she had longish straight black hair and palest skin, probably quite fashionable he considered. He stood inside after setting down the last bag and she disappeared once again. He truly did not know what to do at that moment, leaving would be strange, yet the door stood wide open, to frame the summer night behind. He noticed that he was in a huge entrance hallway, almost empty except for two human height, gold and green Art Nouveau lamps on either side. Each was the shape of a beautiful woman, holding a sphere of light that was being offered up towards the ceiling, or heaven perhaps; vines and leaves trailed their limbs, yet moreover, they stood triumphant, proud, and oblivious of spectators. As the decorative women paraded unashamed and naked on either side of him, underfoot, a marble floor gleamed and blinked a pearly beige. He could see facing to his left a corridor leading all the way to the back, where he caught sight of an apricot walled, ironically rustic styled kitchen and closer to him on the other side, was a grand staircase that wound rhythmically up and up, onto unlit floors. She then reappeared suddenly, with her more appeased child.

"My name's Christine," she said, smiling now and holding out a hand. "If you're new you've got to see the gardens here, they're lovely."

Luc backed away as he shook her hand and wished her a good evening. It was strange but he still felt unsettled, as though this was not the type of human contact he'd been after. The sumptuous decor of the entrance hall disappeared behind the big black door as she closed it. He returned back upstairs to his new grey home raking over what he had just seen, his mind alert, she was pretty, he considered, perhaps older than him and perhaps not, but definitely not his type.

Chapter 4

"In short, I want you to spy on your superior and feel about for this group we suspect, I can't give you any whys or wherefores you understand. They're a subversive group, that is all. You have done well and have been a consistent servant of Her Majesty's government for a few years, I realise that you're not trained for this and that this is not your job, but we are only asking you to keep your eyes and ears open," the Minister finished.

"Is there really no more you can tell me?" asked Gemma, her bravery secretly disappearing.

The Minister took in a breath, and looked at her critically. "Your superior's name has been linked in various ways from the past, such as socially, or from university days at Oxford, with three people who we shall say ... have done us a disservice ... here are their names." He wrote them down for her:

Dora Belgrave 55, of Armstrong Inc.
John McMahon 51, of Grimbaud Industries.
Elsa de Vere 47, of Axe and Shiffel.

As her eyes took in the list, the room actually swayed but Gemma did not show it, but nor did she have any voice left, for she knew that these people were all dead. She prayed that she would neither blush nor grow pale. Her dark oak and green velvet surroundings made her feel like she was at a stately home, perhaps that idea was not so far removed as she was at a private Gentlemen's club, and it occurred to her then, even in her wakeful yet shocked stupor, that it was odd that she had been allowed in; this Minister must have power indeed.

"Good," the Minister continued, taking her silence for compliance. "I will get details to you as and when of what to look out for etc. Send a message to me here using your office twice a week or so, to keep me updated. Oh and we have a photograph …" He placed the photograph of a woman before her. "I don't know who she is yet but we will start working on it on Monday, see if she pops up anywhere."

At the sight of it, Gemma's heart plunged, but she knew she had been dismissed, so she rose, parts of her numb, and was glad that she had said nothing more, her voice had been struck down besides; not for words but for a timbre that might have betrayed her feelings, and that would not do.

Outside, the Mayfair streets looked different; it was not that she knew the area particularly well, but perhaps enough to know that the old fashioned and expensive buildings had never seemed menacing before, or to lean in upon her as they did, even in the intense sunlight. And so, she dazedly trod the pavement, away from this last rendezvous; completely unable to think. But she knew that it was imperative that she got a grip upon herself. To calm herself then, she decided to enter a small newsagents, decorated in a sleek 1930's style and effusive with more products than the usual magazines, soft drinks, gum and cheap sweets that it also sold.

Her simple act of blindly perusing the bright and cheaply wrapped chocolate bars and what seemed to her now garish women's magazine covers did however help, enough so that she was able to turn to what she realised she actually needed, and picked up a bottle of mineral water. She held it close as she approached the till. Her hand shook as she tried to separate the correct change from her wallet, the cuff of her crisp white, long sleeved shirt quivered and looked bulky upon her unsteady wrist; but this formal attire had protected her from the fierce rays of the sun as she had walked away from that Mayfair club and that meeting; the meaning of which she was still too stunned to understand. After the transaction, she realised that she had to leave the newsagents, although she wanted to stay there and linger amongst the well preened shelves, and not think about what had just happened. But a voice in her head began: *It was all undone, all undone!* So she knew she had to address it, silence it, fiercely she thought if she must.

She could have taken a taxi she knew if she couldn't manage the Underground, but she chose to walk on in her smart heels in the heat, letting the recent events try to approach some semblance of thought, while currently they only vividly disturbed her heartbeat. She realised that she had been clutching the small bottle to her chest, so she tried instead to hold it by her side as a normal person would. Her cheeks had taken on colour and she could not think of where to go that would allow her to think, (instinctively knowing that her home perhaps was not the right place until she knew where she was in all of this) so she did at last hail a black trundling taxi cab and uttered, "Trafalgar square please," through now dry and red heat swollen lips.

The journey was short and soon sure enough she found herself surrounded by many hot and ambling tourists as she headed to the fountains where mermen and dolphins adorned the sides in stone, looking on strong and proud. Here, she felt safer and began to think. Her first urge was that she wanted to see James immediately, her leader; she wanted to tell him what she had been just asked to do by a government minister no less, to spy upon her boss: Sir John Balthazar - who like her, also answered to James. She was suspicious, how could they *not* know that she too was part of the organisation that they were sniffing about for - but perhaps they didn't. And the photograph! Oh God how did they get a hold of that? If they found out who the woman in the photo was, it would lead them back to James no doubt, and maybe to all of them. She tried to breathe calmly, it was London, but everything now looked different; the iconic tourist scene that she found herself in, had now the cast of the macabre, and the lions at Lord Nelson's feet only threw down long shadows. But she stayed still and sure enough her head cooled, calmed by the sight of the cascading waters, she knew then that she would have to play along, to become a sort of double agent, although none in her group were spies in the normal sense, all they actually did was to tell the truth to the world. Even if she told James what had just happened, she would still have to play along or the Minister would really guess everything. She felt then at once isolated, contaminated even and spotted one of the few remaining red phone booths in London where she sorely wanted to head to (her mobile now a dangerous thing) and phone James, so he could meet her somewhere and so she could tell him this sorry truth. But she would not. She knew that she may be being played, that they may know that she was in James' group after all, and even if not, she may be being kept an eye on. So she made a decision: under a blazing sun as she gazed into the waters straddled by strapping sea creatures, Gods and mermen, that she would say nothing and keep this to herself, until she was sure of how much the Minister knew, to keep everyone including herself, safe.

Chapter 5

It was hard to settle in; the weekend lay ahead of Luc full of possibility but was a seemingly bloodless beckoning, his canvas blank now, a virgin page, at once an appealing and unnerving fact. He woke early on Saturday morning, looked at his still terminally unkempt luggage and then shook his head with a sigh; he had accepted his chaos a long time ago and decided to ignore it. As he dressed, he realised that he was relieved that at least that a friend was coming to see him today. He had known James for all of his memory, since he had been born; their parents had been neighbours in Berkshire where he'd grown up in part. James and his sister Angelica were as family to Luc, though he'd never used those words. They had all been bound by proximity, time, camaraderie, and now the fond gaze of memory; such simple yet emphatic bonds that he appreciated now as a gift. Luc realised that they both had lost their parents through illness five years ago and that even though adults, they were now orphans almost like him, as he still had his father. He took some anguished comfort from this and felt also guilt; that he had not realised the gravity of the experience of it up until then, the gouging scope of it that the loss of a parent could be. Of course he had understood it intellectually, but he'd never foreseen the internal displacement, the hollow hell that had no instruction.

But he tried to then put his grief aside for that moment, as he was in a diminutive way, bubbling with excitement to see them; it was as though the emotion came forth from an unknown recess within, as from the bottom of a cauldron. Luc, James and their other childhood friend Mischa had been very close up until they had all scattered one year, off away in different directions for university. Even then, displaced, they had still met in the summers often at Luc's beach home in a small but picturesque town in the southwest of France, where Luc's mother had grown up. Luc's father was English and his mother had been French, but Luc was raised with no thought of barriers or lines drawn between the two cultures or languages, and had drifted in between them all of his life, geographically, mentally and emotionally.

The buzzer sounded, sending a thrill through him and also a shock of annoyance, as it was very rude and obnoxious sound. He immediately compared it to the experience he'd just had of the building next door, which probably had elegant sailing chimes he imagined. He was bemused as he thought of 'next door', it was technically true, but as it was a palace compared to his untidy little flat, he couldn't hold it in such close approximation. 'Next door' surely, was another world.

There was murmuring behind the door which alerted him to the fact that Angelica was with James. As he opened it, Luc smiled conspiratorially at them, as though he had won his new life by adulterated means and shouldn't have been there at all, yet he said nothing, as though containing himself; the doorway framed the last two important people in the world to him so perfectly that he simply valued the sight of them for a few moments; it was better than the shrouds of sunlight that he had been subject to yesterday, this simple, human, familial glory was superior, and he had not seen them since the funeral.

James stood, in a distressed deep brown leather jacket, jeans and rumpled dark blonde hair, he could perhaps have been more aware of his allure, his good looks, but that wasn't who he was. Anjelica stood even more blonde, though it was a pixie crop, a blue-eyed sweet faced goddess in a black t-shirt and jeans thought Luc, although, in retrospect he would realise that they both had looked a little fatigued and distracted, as with eyes of treated blue glass. They were not perturbed by the delayed greeting and in a few moments both men stepped forward and hugged, aggressively close, they patted each other hard on the back and then let go. Luc reached for Angelica and pulled her into the same style of embrace, yet trying not to break her ribs. He kissed her on both cheeks and then without thinking, rumpled her hair, even though she was now 27.

"Noooo," she whined loudly. "You *can't* do that anymore."

But they laughed, the three, still standing together, with a mirth that was not frivolous, as they stood absorbed by the unspoken gravity of the reunion, a whole year after Beatrice's funeral.

"I like your apartment," James commented turning his head to view all of Luc's things, showing his gratification that he had seen them all before.

"Well, it's nothing like next door," Luc replied intriguingly.

"What do you mean?" asked James

"I caught a glimpse last night, it looks like a palace. I suppose it should judging by the building -but then I end up with this," and he gestured about amiably.

"It's not that bad," Anjelica said distracted, still trying to reassemble her hair, "have you got a mirror though?" She asked as she walked into a ray of sunlight from the window, it blurred the sight of her into gold and silhouette.

"Yes, actually I like this part," Luc said leading her to the bathroom. They all went together and observed, as he then switched on the main light, which was the bare bones of an ornate yet paired down chandelier. He then proceeded to switch on his Art Nouveau lamp as well, with a back turned private smile.

"Oh, it's lovely," whispered Anjelica.

James agreed while eyeing the golden lion paws upon the bath tub.

"Shall we go and look around?" asked Luc, himself curious, realising that he hadn't seen the entire building yet or the communal gardens that the mysterious woman had told him about last night.

They left shortly, all as inquisitive as each other, they went to the bottom of the stairs, their denims and keen demeanour dissonant to the stately grandeur of the dark oak staircase and long stretch of vermillion carpet, and then down a badly lit corridor that made the carpet cast a reddish gory glare onto the yellowing walls, to the back of the building and its garden. There, there were large French doors through which a few steps would soon lead down into a very surprising and vast amount of flora and fauna to be tucked away in the middle of Regents Park, in the centre of London. From where they stood while still inside however, Luc could see that a tall wooden fence created a division to his right between what he believed was his part, from the 'palace's' garden next door.

As Luc rummaged in his pocket for the keys, he noticed something on the other side beyond the fence. Turning his head carefully to the right and tiptoeing, he caught sight of a woman sitting at a garden table. She had a cigarette in her hand and was wearing a loose summer dress in navy, upon which white printed flowers shone in the sunlight as they skirted her thighs and bare legs. She didn't look at her own garden, which looked equally as nice as Luc's; she didn't look at anything at all. Her dark hair billowed briefly in the breeze, oblivious of him and glinted ember red as the sun tried to gild it. She looked, unplaceable to Luc, she certainly wasn't the woman from last night, he noticed that she was barefoot, but it was her skin that left him confused, perhaps she was suntanned, or Italian … Middle Eastern … Brazilian? He could not guess at all, for her languor, manner and familiarity with the surroundings seemed utterly English to him. The single most striking fact was that she looked like she didn't care; about the lovely gardens, the beautiful summer's day, which were rare in London he knew, and more, for there was more, and if Luc had been alone he would have stayed there and tried to discover it. She brought the cigarette to her lips, it looked well framed by her hair that curled gently yet only lasted the length of her neck, but then she spluttered and coughed abruptly. Not a smoker then thought Luc, she recovered, not realising that she had an audience and continued to stare glassy eyed into nothingness.

By this time James and Anjelica were also on tiptoe looking at what Luc had been captivated by, as Luc came away from it and turned the key in the lock, Anjelica asked, "Who's that, I wonder?"

"Don't know," Luc shrugged, "maybe my neighbour." He frowned mildly. The image of her settled in him unbidden, like an echo reverberating, as if he had glimpsed a mermaid.

His own garden yet was full and blooming and did not lay out in a plain and modest manner. There was no obvious lawn but twists and turns and enclaves fringed with hanging plants, sumptuously obscuring one section from another. In summer it sang out in rapturous vivid greens and studded itself with heavy blooms and colours. Plants were in a state of prolonged ecstasy as the unusual hot summer had colluded with the lavish attention of the gardeners to make them lush and yielding beyond themselves. Luc was keen to explore it as he thought he saw a water feature around one of the turns and he was caught by small statues everywhere, most of them elegant women from myth and legend looking lost or startled. As they wandered further with the garden's meanderings Luc's heart grew more fond, as there were also statues of mermaids around the water fountain he'd found; they too, like the other statues looked as if they were unfamiliar with this time period. He had a feeling that the other apartments in his building must be sumptuous for the gardens to be as they were. He did not mind however, it was more simply an observation.

"I can't hear the city at all," said Anjelica, looking about as if searching for it.

"I know, I can only hear the trickling of the fountain, no cars, no nothing," said Luc.

"There aren't even any other people here today on a day like this," added James, looking around as well.

They found groups of wrought iron seats on pretty paved areas and a table placed in each separate alcove or section, sometimes in a mottled green colour, Luc supposed so that each occupant of his building could find their own private space. Yet, even as they settled somewhere, too soon it grew uncomfortably hot, so Anjelica asked, "What are your plans, Luc, I mean I know you start your new job on Monday, but did you need to do anything before? Also, what exactly is your new job again?"

"I'm going to be an analyst for a government department, on trade and stuff, it's nothing special ... but it's something I suppose, it's fairly low level, but my experience of European diplomacy and negotiation was what they wanted me for," Luc nodded to himself, after reeling off the official description. "Oh, and also for my language skills, you know, the French bit."

"It *is* special," said Anjelica, her eyes on him and tone quiet, and then added, 'just think, they let you *drive* here for it ... during a worldwide embargo on travel."

"And didn't it take you a million interviews to get?" added James. "Well done, mate." And he smiled at him.

Luc blushed against his wishes, but took their praise nonetheless. "I suppose I do need some things, bedding, kitchen things ... are things still OK here since the travel lockdown? I mean, are things still available?"

"You know it's only been two weeks but we haven't felt too bad with the effects yet," said Anjelica, "if it continues, then yes, I think things will start disappearing off the shelves, James agrees, but not yet ... I hope they can contain this virus strain where it is, I know it's dangerous but it just feels so far away, anyway, so should we go now?"

"And come to me after," added James. "Or if you like, stay the weekend at mine until you feel fully set up at the flat."

"What about you, still a genealogist?" asked Luc, trying not to smile.

"Oh ... yeah," said James, now failing not to smirk.

"I still don't get it," said Luc. Though he liked it for being rebelliously strange, he had imagined James however of being able to do absolutely anything he put his mind to.

"And you, Jelly?" asked Luc.

"She's still a holistic psychotherapist," answered James.

"Wow Jelly … she really grew up," he said to James.

Luc drank in their presence, his oldest friends, and he was relieved to be with them; last night he'd had a pizza delivered, having found a delivery flier impaled upon a cork board full of notices near the front door, and then curled up on his bare bed in his sleeping bag. He'd also felt unbearably alone, thinking that this new beginning was not as glorious as he'd imagined, and that this quest felt very meagre to him at its start. However, bumping into the strange woman next door had occupied his thoughts for some time as he'd tried to sleep; back in that drifting sea-state of mind, he could not place what was wrong, but had felt the incongruity of the episode nonetheless.

It seemed however that James and Anjelica were not going to leave him alone that weekend, and that Luc was to be a constant part of their everyday lives; and so it felt again like it did when they had been growing up as young men, a long time ago. Perhaps it was because James and Anjelica were both parentless now that they knew what it was that Luc needed, or perhaps it had always been like this; James and Mischa had both helped carry his mother's coffin, they had flown down to him as quickly as they could, Luc had been away from England for a few years now, but his bonds seemed intact with both of these men. And yet, he hadn't expected this welcome at all, he had been so focussed on the new profession and coming to live in central London, that he'd forgotten that this part of his life existed. Perhaps being an adult, in a very adult occupation working for the British government, made him expect to have to forgo that part of himself, the part that he associated with childhood, like a trade or sacrifice to the laws of time, or an unconscious sacrifice to Nature herself.

The irony of the now full and bustling weekend was that Luc had not had enough time to imagine what was to come on Monday; but it felt very agreeable to be somewhere new, untroubled and untainted. A new beginning away from his mother and father and history it seemed; apart from the presence of James, Anjelica and Mischa, who ironically made him feel like a young boy.

Chapter 6

Mer couldn't believe that she'd let Christine dress her. Christine had badgered her into wearing a nice summer dress and had conceded the deep navy colour when Mer had sighed and looked away. Mer had even let Christine paint her toenails a deep dark glossy red. She looked at her bare feet unmoving as she sat outside in the heat, they looked very alive, glimmering, brimming with something that Mer could not connect to in the slightest. She viewed them like traitors and even curled her toes up to hide them from herself, Christine hadn't forced her to daub crimson the nails on her hands however, as if she knew that that was asking too much. In retribution Mer had stolen Christine's packet of cigarettes, knowing that Christine would be rummaging about at work, at a loss to explain the disappearance. Mer didn't smoke, but she planned to. It was her task for the day.

She was glad that she didn't have to see anyone like this. The dress was too pretty, the nails too vivid, the day hideously bright, it was wholly too much, at least the dress and nails were dark she thought, too mockingly dark for the bright summery day that she sat outside in. Her garden flourished, it was all hers now after all. It was in a similar style to all the gardens for these buildings. Twisting and turning and embellished with alcoves and briars; the gardeners did a magnificent job. Her rose bushes thronged unevenly, perhaps there were too many of them, jagged amongst the softer flowers and plants that melded together, yet standing out proudly, as if well aware of their supremacy. They were not pretty, but emphatically beautiful, especially the unnaturally lilac blooms, and the heavy innocence of the white, but moreover, the English red; not like the tight, tacky, slick bunches of buds they sell in cellophane for would be lovers, the English reds bloomed in heartfelt abandon, fanning out in sumptuousness, each petal adorning the other as voluptuous layers created a self-contained glory, they were brimming with themselves -but again, wasted on her she thought. She was not even quite sure what day it was, but muted voices from the garden next door made her feel it that might be a Saturday or Sunday.

She took some matches and struck one in a dramatic but contained manner. Holding the cigarette in her mouth, she brought the flame to it, and made that part brief, to quickly let out the smoke and not yet inhale. She tried again, this time taking in what she could, paused and then inevitably spluttered, no downright hacked and coughed. She thought dimly that if in company she would have been embarrassed, but she was alone and so didn't care, no, she wouldn't have cared anymore anyway. Her hand hung languorously by her side, cigarette dangling, she would not give up on it.

In front of her a large glossy flier had been placed on a little round garden table with an impromptu rock fixed upon it, to stop it fluttering away in the breeze.

'CONNECT TO THE ARTS'

It had emblazoned as its headline, and boasted a year long course helping one to explore all aspects of creativity, achieving a recognised certificate upon its completion. Christine, as usual, had come out with guns blazing to 'fix' Mer as her mission. Mer sighed knowing that it wouldn't stop, that Christine never stopped, especially now that she was living with her. Mer was uncertain as to how that had occurred as well … but today Mer and her cigarette did not care. The flier fluttered away under the stone, restless, and gleaming sickly in the sunshine. The course was being held very close at the nearby Regents Park Institute and was on Thursday evenings. If Mer could groan she would have, it was too much.

She thought about the fact that she already knew about art and that she had a degree in Fine Art and Art History, *and* worked in an art gallery, or rather she had worked, but no more. She gave that up. She'd given everything up. Yet her mind rallied; it was good, unspoiled, fresh she thought and literature, painting, drama, all those things that had ended as soon as schooling had, a part of her felt drawn to that. It seemed a bizarre idea, but attractive, like going back to where it had all gone wrong, to the source and to start again at school like a new beginning. But, she would have to work for this, read things, even write an essay or two -she could always drop out she hedged. That helped. The cigarette had created its own self-suspended column of ash still attached to itself, untroubled and unsucked. She looked at it wistfully, the packet was full, she'd try again.

She didn't have a watch, she ignored the phones, all of them, she'd left her mobile somewhere in the house. She was pleased with this, free, no one could bother her now, apart from Christine, and she frowned briefly. She considered that it was because of a recently imposed worldwide embargo on travel, that her parents didn't know that she'd thrown out her husband for no good reason after only six months of marriage. Her parents were in New York, the husband was gone and Mer was in her garden, in a new house that her father had given her as her wedding gift. A distant part of her squirmed at the fact, that the entirety of this had to be confronted eventually. She glanced at her packet of cigarettes and was so grateful for the embargo, it had created something: a mighty disconnection that perhaps served only her, if nothing else, it had created stillness, and she so prized it.

A disease was trying to be stopped short, nipped in the bud in the far off lands that it threatened, so that for two weeks now no one could travel. Thus there weren't as many tourists that summer in London and the stock exchange quivered dangerously, the media was screaming, fearing global economic collapse if the embargo continued, but for Mer, it had created her own personal stasis, a most wonderful thing.

Today would be curious, Christine would come back home, working on a Saturday, but in her line of work in the media that wasn't unusual and her baby Marina would come back as well, probably from some emergency Saturday day care that she'd been bundled to, the baby was sweet, Mer half smiled. But no, she could not face dinner plans, or to think about them. Christine could and would have to fend for herself. She had her own key, which Mer had given to her to keep as her 'emergency person', which it seems that Christine has used for her own emergency.

As she tried again however clumsily to smoke her cigarette, Mer thought that it had been the warmest summer since childhood, when she had been sent home pale from school one day with a suspected case of sunstroke, leaving Christine looking on from a desk beside her, who dare not be ill as her place was there by scholarship. It did not sit well for Mer this heat, everybody was so cheerful, she did not begrudge them that but felt alien, like a traitor, displeased and disgruntled with perfection. So she hid as best she could, in her little palace, yet now, due to Christine's abrupt arrival her hermit status was deeply under threat.

It had all began on that sickly hot day she remembered, when she had been standing barefoot at her second floor window and watching an appealing stranger unload his car. So much had come out of it! Such wondrous things and he'd seemed, or would have seemed so sweetly attractive to her, but little resonated. She had been drinking that day and hated the fact, reprimanding herself once again. She had liked the loosened connection with life that the vodka gave her, leaving her an undone clasp. She knew it wasn't to last and she'd been right, after that day her three weeks of drinking during the day ended, and the internal toxic ebb and flow that engendered numbed limbs by the evening, were shortly over. She had a secret regret however, she was annoyed that the vodka had enfeebled her that evening, so that she had had no idea how to react or know what to do when faced with Christine. The second floor room in which she'd stood, boasted chequered black and white flooring and an enormous powerful glinting chandelier, a most petite ballroom yet large enough for a grand celebration. When Mer and her husband had moved in, it had presented itself decoratively and a red chaise longue perched suggestively in the corner had delighted her imagination; Mer had taken pleasure in the sight but her husband had wanted to abandon the chair as he didn't want anything to be second hand. They never reached agreement upon the décor however, for it had been such a trifling and unhelpful problem, as Mer had found her very marriage an alien landscape, and could not even recognise herself within it.

Since her husband Zafar had left, she had been free to do nothing but rattle about the house and languish. She did not want to go back to work, or speak to her husband who had angrily walked out, hoping it would shock some sense into her, she did not *want* and she was content with that. That night, when Christine had broken in, Mer had fallen asleep near dusk on the red chaise longue and woken to hear distant sounds of clattering and splashes of water. She had never before been afraid in her new house, but she was gripped with alarm momentarily and was too inebriated to successfully manage the situation being thrown at her. Yet, she crept down the two flights of stairs clinging to the banister, trying not to make a sound and the soft thuds of footsteps and mild clattering became clearer, as if there were thieves in the kitchen. Mer's kitchen was at the back of the house on the ground floor and faced the garden, which at night could well mimic the snarl of the forest, an easy entry point- but Mer continued, feeling no choice in the matter, she reached the foot of the stairs in the gleaming hallway and there were two enormous and shabby black suitcases. No!!! He has come back, No! She was ready to burst, she could not fathom it, she should have changed the locks she thought. She crept still, along the cool passageway and saw a figure at the sink, washing up, dark hair and the slim outline of a woman who was cleaning fervently. It was Christine. Oh thank God it was Christine she thought, but the suitcases ... Mer's mind was a marmalade fog, loosened and lulled by Vodka. She managed a weak call from behind the door frame, "Christine?"

Christine spun around half shocked herself, still with the washing up gloves on and ran to Mer to put her arms around her, careful not to clamp her sodden hands upon her and in this embrace she whispered, "Please can we stay here?"

Mer pulled away and replied, "Of course. But what's happened? The baby is here too?" She noticed, so many questions, they pulled away like threads from a woolly brain.

"It's not good." Christine shook her head.

Mer knew her well enough to ask her then, "Christine, what've you done?"

But Christine only shook her head again. The alarm in Mer's voice was not only present because Christine was her best friend, good enough to give a spare key of the house to, but also because she was married to Mer's favourite cousin Rehan, thus putting Mer in a proverbial pickle.

"How bad is it?" asked Mer, knowing that Rehan would never have thrown out his wife and child.

No response.

"Christine, what have you done?" Mer said it a little louder than she meant to.

Christine slumped into a chair and then spoke while looking away, "I slept with a client."

Mer waited for more.

"I was drunk and slept with a client." Christine said unhappily to herself.

None of this was comprehensible to Mer, so Christine added alarmed, "It wasn't now! It was five years ago, I was immature, and I got drunk and slept with a beautiful client. I never thought Rehan would find out and have felt deathly guilty ever since, but you know what he's like, intuitive, it's as if he saw the guilt in my eyes today and he just suddenly asked me, "Have you ever cheated on me?" Just out of the blue like that. I froze and that was it, he looked at me as though I'd shattered his world and … I know I have."

"But can't you explain-"

"Explain what? We were still married."

"I know, but that you made a mistake, that you were immature?"

"Mer, he looked at me, he looked at me not like he was angry or disgusted, no, I think that I could have worked with, Mer he looked at me as though I had, had torn his soul or something … and I have. So I ran away. I'm a horrible person … I'm so sorry," she blinked away some tears now.

Mer considered her, and knew that she was not going to ask her or her baby to leave. So she located some tissues and gave them too her. Mer could see that Christine had dragged a green velvet clad armchair into the kitchen and padded it out in thick cushions so that her baby could sleep through the drama.

The heavy drone of a passing bumble bee brought her back to her garden and it had come to Mer's attention that the new stranger was her neighbour. At that moment she considered what his impression would be of her; she had cast off her wedding ring almost immediately after her husband Zaf- as she called him, had walked out, probably expecting her to despair she thought and not rejoice as she did. She imagined that to her neighbour she would simply be a spoiled girl who lived next door no doubt, but how did he arrive here she thought, he couldn't have come from abroad, that was impossible, but his car, yes his raggedy little car had French plates, how strange.

*

After that day, Mer had decided to ignore the issue as she had been ignoring her own and was pleasantly rewarded by Christine taking charge of the household. Every day a nanny would arrive to take care of the baby when Christine went to work, the fridge was full of provisions and the kitchen was clean and tidy. She was grateful that Christine did not want to push wantonly on about the dissolution of Mer's own marriage or to discuss it to death; Mer knew that her friend could see that Mer had never behaved this way before and that whatever metamorphosis was perhaps occurring, it was best left undisturbed and not shaken silly by questions. It was thus a supportive presence, but there was also a gentle and silent push that Mer knew that Christine could just not help but emanate. Thus the resultant creativity class and who knew what else Christine would surreptitiously smuggle in to encroach on Mer's secluded and guarded psyche.

After a week, Christine had been working very hard, sometimes staying quite late at the office, she worked for an agent to the stars and helped manage not only their professional opportunities but also their day to day needs such as travel arrangements and accommodation. It used to sound very exciting to Mer, Mer suspected that Christine's next step would be to suggest that Mer visit the doctor and that perhaps she was suffering from depression and needed assistance. Mer, certainly had no intention of going to the doctor. What however did manifest instead was most unwelcome, for Christine instead suggested very lightly, "It would be so nice to have a dinner party in your lovely house, Mer …"

Mer froze where she'd sat in her living room to face the garden, she did not move an inch. Her back was to Christine who was standing up and looking upon an evening sky that in this summer languor graced the garden with long swathes of yellow and pink light, straining against the hours to hold onto the day. With such a dead and stony response, Christine had said nothing more on the matter until dinner, which had now become a much more formal affair as the two of them sat down in the kitchen at the wooden table, sometimes with a candle lit, all due to Christine of course, where she brought it up again.

"You see, I might have to do some entertaining for my work and because these are such high profile people they would love the privacy and seclusion they would find here," Christine softly chimed.

Mer looked away, a distant shift, like a roll within a far off wave informed her that she must have been somewhere near angry.

"Can you not take them out?" she asked weakly.

"With all the press and botheration, it would just be stressful for them." Christine had responded reasonably, still amiable.

"Christine ... Please."

"I'm sorry, I shouldn't have brought it up," Christine retreated.

Mer was so surprised at her withdrawal that she looked straight at her and saw that she was now eating her food meekly. Mer wondered if her own countenance had been so alarming that Christine had dared not push her. The idea was not brought up again and Mer was so relieved that she forgot about it.

Chapter 7

"Monsieur Armstrong, is the room to your satisfaction?" The hotel manager asked and looked at Peter Armstrong a tad nervous for the answer; Peter knew that look well, for billionaire clients must not be let down.

Peter surveyed the small meeting room set out with a silver tray of intricately constructed canapés and some whiskey and glasses. It was night, and outside the sounds of Paris did not intrude, but for a faint hum of the city; cars and bustling restaurants and cigarette smoke condensed into a blank quiet drone. Yes it looked normal, convivial, a small business meeting with drinks, all was at it should be. Peter nodded to the hotel manager who had to depart without his level of desired affirmation, and shuffled past the security men stationed outside the room.

Peter took a breath, he wanted this meeting.

Soon the door was opened again by his outside staff and two middle aged men in well-tailored suits entered. No one spoke until they were alone again.

"Peter," Michel Grimbaud, a man just as rich as he, shook his hand closely. They all spoke a tad quieter than was normal.

"Peter," Dominic Burgess, a man a little less rich, also shook his hand in the same way.

Peter ushered them to sit down, and proceeded to pour them each a tumbler of whiskey in crystal glasses that blinked light back from the chandeliers, which also glanced off the pale pink silk patterned wallpaper. "Thank you both for coming. Now stay calm, I am going to play you something," he added, and brought out his mobile phone.

The other men held on their glasses, unable now to lift them from the table.

"Your employee, Dora Belgrave, ever thought about how the press knows when you do something wrong! When you do bad things, like force through a flawed vaccination into the public health system, well she's your mole; she's the one who leaks things to the press."

The recording abruptly ends.

"How can you still have that!?" Michel whispered frightened.

"It's completely incriminating, I've destroyed mine!" added Dominic.

"I kept it so far because we are not done yet, and anyway it seems that my little flawed vaccination 'issue' never made it to the press -but your leaks both did. And so I called this meeting to see where we are, to see how far we have come and what we should do next. Don't worry I will delete it, maybe tonight. It was just a good thing to focus us I thought."

"Too much, in my opinion," said Michel, still gripping his glass and looking at Peter reprovingly.

"So, where are we then?" asked Dominic, in a voice that did not mean to be as fraught as it was. "How much more do you think they know, I mean they must know about us, because it was only us three that had these calls, all with a rogue employee each it seems. This man who called us, him or worse, who he works for, must know how we are linked."

"Alors, but it is no secret that we are friends, there've always been articles in those magazines about where we go out, or us together with our wives and families on 'oliday, it's been no secret, and maybe other people 'ave had these calls," protested Michel.

"Yes, but that must be it, even if others have had these calls," said Peter, "one fact, just one incriminating fact about one of us, would have led to the other two being sniffed at, no, I don't believe all three of us had a leak by coincidence."

"So what do you want to do now? I thought this was 'taken care of'," said Dominic, a little accusingly.

"Thank God you know someone like Maurice is all I can say," added Michel.

"Maurice knows our Minister friend and has been in touch with him over this matter, as you know as soon as this began I let the Minister know, as he has as much to lose as us. After the initial action, (the mention of which made Michel lower his head to stare at the table) we still had to track down who had made these calls to us, and we did, and for a time we asked politely in my opinion, for him to give us more information, but he disappeared or ran away, as you know, and we've had some relative calm for a while, there were no more calls made to us and we hoped he was just a fool who had stumbled into something, someone who maybe knew too much. We did always have to find our three employees' real motivation, or who they were working for, I, like you assumed it was a rival in business, but ... we have again found the young man who made those initial calls to us."

"What?!" Both the other men spluttered.

Peter held up a hand to quieten them. "Maurice is watching him. We will act when we know more, we just don't know who he is or what his motives are, he's English, and we have a tiny lead that the Minister and Maurice are working on to find who he is linked to, but considering how inanely simple Maurice found it to find him, as he told me, I'm confused as to what's going on, I would think it would take a lot of sophistication to be able to know our secrets, our private deals -it doesn't make sense."

"How was it too easy to find him?" asked Dominic, looking curious and worried.

"Well he just had all his calls redirected to a new number, but through a back door by using someone at the phone company itself -we too have people at that phone company, it didn't take Maurice long, he was confused by it, the old serpent, it seemed inane to him," answered Peter, pleased that Dominic at least was happy to discuss the grist and mill of the issue.

"So can't we just ... get rid of him ... like the others?" asked Michel, taking on blotches of colour, but still daring to ask this question, his head now back to staring at the deep brown polished wood of the table.

"Do you really think that's a good idea? In a way he is a living clue," answered Peter.

"Well I don't want to know his name, this 'as all gone far enough for me," retorted Michel, petulant now.

"I know, I didn't think you would. Don't worry, the Minister with his resources and with Maurice's help, this will all be sorted, it will go away," said Peter reassuringly, he was amazed at how convincing he sounded, almost fatherly. The other two were still powerful men, both almost as rich and shrewd as he, but perhaps had not yet had to fully feel the taint or price of their own crooked dealings until this episode. So they looked to him expectant and they were not relieved, but at least relieved of a portion of the burden, as with their simple regard, laid it more firmly upon Peter's head. Peter Considered Michel's weak nature in particular and put it down to the fact that he had simply inherited his father's munitions company, and had never had to personally claw his way to the top as Peter and Dominic had.

Dominic then gulped down his whiskey and looked at Peter, asking for his leave; Michel could still not manage to drink. Peter gave them a nod, "I think we are done here, I'll keep you informed."

The other men quickly left, both nodding their goodbyes, wanting to limit their eye contact with the man that had helped them in the end, to facilitate murder; their three respective whistle blowers had all been quickly despatched by Maurice they knew, but now with the re-emergence of the young man who had rung them in the first place, the problem, exasperatingly Hydra like -with a

43

new photo clue for the Minister and Maurice to follow, seemed to have sprouted another head.

Peter again sat alone now and noticed the canapés that lay exquisitely ready for them, decorated in oyster shells and colourful pink and green ensembles, and knew, that they were never to be consumed.

Chapter 8

"As I am sure you know, this department: the Department of International Collaboration, helps all government departments collaborate with their international equivalents in different countries, from everything from education to farming to defence. Your role is to analyse the trade agreements we make with others against our own trade goals, I know you know this Luc, but I want to explain why our department values its discretion so much, you can imagine in our correspondences with Whitehall, other departments, and then further internationally, at any moment, one thing said to the wrong person -it's a potential can of worms," Gemma finished.

Luc sat listening, looking professional in his crisp white shirt while his eyes gauged the essence of a red fabric folder placed in front of him. His cheeks had the faint kiss of apples however, as he only appeared calm, but was actually charged with a nervous thrill that made him sit upright, as electricity traversed rapidly from his abdomen to his throat.

Gemma stood by his desk, and continued to patiently explain the fundamental rules of discretion and secrecy to their new recruit and the procedure for how special documents entered and left the building. Luc tried hard to focus, but he was somewhat distracted by the changes that his life had undergone over the last three days, as the charmed weekend with his friends had suddenly overloaded his heart with joyful and wondrous things, which to him however felt stressful and strange. And so, his heart sat instead on a spotted toadstool in Wonderland, close to falling off, for it had itself generated too much excitement, thus now teetered on its own cliff edge of containment. The new home lavish and grand, the incredible gardens with mermaids, his old friends beautiful and gloriously alive again in his life and now these new offices, or rooms: he couldn't describe them, laid out as they were in thick burgundy carpeting and a hushed feeling, while cloaked with dove white walls, as though an exclusive expensive hotel. The big boss as Luc thought of him, was called Balthazar, he wasn't typically a minister in the normal sense as he couldn't be voted out, he was instead a 'Diplomatic Coordinator'. Most people in the public or even the press did not know about this division's existence or the part that it played in matters, although it was not a secret. The desks were old fashioned dark wood, scattered about the place, so that it looked much more like 1945 except for the high tech computers, poised sharply over each one.

Balthazar had not come out to meet Luc yet or perhaps Luc would be taken in to meet him, Luc hesitated to ask Gemma questions like that, everything was so out of the ordinary, he could tell that they had their own procedures; he was just surprised that he was a part of them now. It felt to him like too much bounty, very good in theory but in practice, unwieldy for one single human soul to tolerate. He wanted some fresh air but knew it would be much time before that was possible. Gemma worked with him patiently and he was grateful for it, yet even this fact piqued his curiosity as she looked so very much younger than he, although she wasn't. Her efficient short bob of blonde hair and sable sleek eyebrows sketched out firm lines over a pair of eyes however, that were wide and lively and did not suit the place; she would have looked better to him as a young barmaid, in a far off countryside pub, unfettered by the dark recesses and machinations of the powers that be.

As a first day it progressed as they usually did, in a flurry of new information, however straightforward, in the end difficult to fully assimilate, as even the layout of the building was new, never mind the intricacies of his post. Finally, near the end of the day Gemma came to him composedly and whispered, "Balthazar will see you now."

They only referred to him as Balthazar; Luc had not met him before even during the three interviews. His heart picked up pace but he knew that there was nothing to fear, it was just the method of his delivery, so quiet and hushed as

Gemma walked peacefully in front of him and soundless, as her dainty footsteps were muffled and eaten by the thick carpet.

She opened the office door for him and stood outside, issuing a small smile and nod to signal him in. Before he knew it a large man was striding towards him hand outstretched, bold and warm.

"Lucian, welcome! Sorry I couldn't see you earlier, this damned embargo feels like a never ending, unstopping emergency."

Balthazar was already vigorously shaking Luc's hand by the end of his sentence. Luc was very relieved, the warmth from his superior was another surprise and also yet unsettling as it was almost too familiar, but Luc still decided to welcome it. Furthermore, Gemma had continued to hold the frosted door open, only now did she gently close it. Once shut, the small words and murmurs from the larger rooms were shut out, there was only Balthazar here and he filled the room. He looked perhaps six foot two and was a touch overweight, had greying hair and a keen prominent Roman nose. He kept moving about the room, doing things, "Has Gemma shown you all the ropes?"

"Yes, she's very patient, sir."

"Oh ha ha, patient she is very true, do you like where you're living? Nice part of London you know."

"Oh yes, and I've lived in London before, in the Old Street area, during my Masters," replied Luc.

"Ah, so it's not all too unfamiliar. I'm glad m'boy, we are very pleased to have you on board." Balthazar took papers from one desk to another desk in a side area, on top of which was a tray in which a red sealed bag for documents lay full, the type Gemma had been trying to explain to him and on their way out gathered Luc, as there were no markings on the soft red coverings, it was a colour coded system

"Look at all these folders, one wrong move if I mix them up and it's a political trade wrangle at best, and I wouldn't dream what could be a worst case scenario. But don't you worry, that's not your concern. Now I'm telling you this straight, I don't mind what you do, if you want to bend the lunch hour in your favour occasionally or stay late, or start at the crack of dawn, I don't mind as long as you get the work done and show a bit of dedication, in my opinion, unlike so much of politics, what we do actually matters and we get thing done. Now, did I even say, pleasure to meet you at last, it's funny the interview system I know, but they do a lot of vetting for me."

"Yes, of course, sir."

"And please don't call me that, it's Balthazar, that's all." And with that he came and patted Luc once on the back.

All through this no one had sat down, Luc still stood where he had started in the room and began to feel now that his mind was chock full and needed a break, but as they were standing he did not know when he should leave, luckily Balthazar finally led him out and then gave him his own version of a tour. Then, back at his office Balthazar clapped him on the shoulder again and told him, "I hope you will be happy here," with touching sincerity.

On Luc's way out back past Gemma's desk which stood in a wide corridor that led to Balthazar's office, he saw her on the telephone, but a vein in her forehead had now appeared, marking out her tension in a lightning shaped fork, she gripped the receiver and bit her lip, so absorbed was she that she did not correct her demeanour until Luc was very close while walking past, as he rounded the corner away from her he heard her say, "Don't you think this would be better in person, not on the *telephone* … yes of course I understand the urgency," and then after a pause, in a strained whisper, "I've seen nothing, nothing at all!"

Even though Luc was now set free as the work day had ended, his final impression of the day yet was of Gemma's strained face and throbbing temple, and a red mouth twisted so that she could bite it.

Chapter 9

James quickly glanced at his appearance in the glass front of the giant newspaper office building; he had on a baseball cap and fake beard. Utterly ridiculous, he thought -but still necessary. He was ready for his task but his mind was hammering at him with more pressing problems and he tried to regulate his thoughts so that they should patiently wait, until this task was over. Yet as he put one foot in front of the other it was plain to him in a way that things become so without much thought, that he had been betrayed -there was no other explanation. So he took his place inside a large revolving door, in his left hand, a large manila envelope. He approached then the receptionist's station, there were two of them, sleek, preened young women, red lipsticked and efficient. One was on the phone, the other looked at him briefly then looked down and was still; he approached only her.

"Thank you," she said as she took the package from him, their hands briefly overlapping as they made the exchange and from which she did not withdraw from quickly.

James nodded once to her in thanks and turned around to leave. With luck, the vaccination scandal that Dora Belgrave had exposed, probably as her last act for the group, would reach the right journalist's desk by the end of the day thanks to his member: Penelope, on reception. Even if the journalist he intended it for didn't have at least 'two sources' or however many it was they needed to publish the story, the evidence was still damning, and worst case scenario, if they didn't publish it, he would have a member leak those papers onto the internet, uploaded from any foreign country, where things currently, were still harder to track.

Out once more on the street the thoughts struck like pistons at his mind and were relentless; as surely the unthinkable had happened. Dora Belgrave and two others were dead, all active members of his group. In all his time he couldn't imagine anyone wanting to betray them. For they had all grown up as family and friends, their organisation a secret between them, and never a cult whereby it was compulsory to participate. He had no one to ask for advice, his father and grandfather all dead, all gone, and what on earth was he going to do? He continued to walk along the bustling London street, the blessing or curse now of being so deeply secret and of having got away with it for so long was that they had never faced real danger before, not for his generation at least and now, three of his members dead, all had been his father's close friends: an uncanny sudden heart attack, a mysterious hit and run and a climbing accident -none of it rang true.

A siren could be heard growing louder; James looked up a tad from his reticent angle facing the pavement and could see two police cars coming at speed down the road towards him. His fake beard then felt enormously heavy, like a drawn on hairy target, it began to itch even more as he realised that he had begun to sweat underneath it. But, the police cars soon passed him, and the newspaper office as well. He took a breath, as he had forgotten to breathe. All they did and had done since 1945 was to find the truth and to help it to find the ears of the public. It was very simple, they sought to expose corruption amongst the powers that be, and they had had to be dextrous in finding methods to achieve this that did not lead back to them, to the source. The techniques they used had evolved with the times, but ironically for James he found with the massive advancement of technology, it became far easier to use old fashioned methods, such as the post; thus the Royal Mail often became the undoer of many a corrupt oligarch or government minister with their finger in the wrong pies.

As James strode on, still rattled by what was left of the echo of the sirens within him, he reassured himself of his history and his purpose, as though explaining it to a new member. He affirmed to himself that after the Second

World War wanting a better world as many did, his grandfather and a few of his close friends had decided to try to accomplish this and formed this group with no name, and three generations later, it had grown and flourished. These families had taken work in fields that potentially yielded much information about what people in power were up to. Even Anjelica, as a psychotherapist was not ashamed that her career also chose to serve their organisation first, so that she sought out the powerful in her campaign for clients. She was devoted to what they did not because she had been told to be, but because of the effects of what they achieved. James was just as dedicated, more so as it was his father's legacy and his father's before that, and yet today, the traitor now blighted much of what he had held dear, to taint its integrity; James tried to be calm in the aggressive sunlight upon him, the gravity of this was like a wicked ripple in time and space which must be righted if it were possible, it seemed at that moment, not.

Around the corner he now entered a huge and busy café which boasted long stretches of burnished copper upon its countertops, but he continued on, to the toilets at the back. Locking himself in a cubicle, he first ripped off his beard, but it did not give him relief, the red and now itching brand it left felt more like a staining mark. He changed his clothes and looked like himself again, and drew comfort from who he was to meet there.

He found a table and waited and ordered some tea, the waitress waited for more information, as the Italian cakes they specialised in were piled decorously high in the window and long indoor displays. James could not order cake, so he asked for the tea to be Earl Grey in order to placate her expectant look. He was to be joined by Anjelica, Mischa, and more importantly Michael; their man in Special Forces, the one who knew now what had happened to Dora, John and Elsa, and that they would now possibly need most. Yet, James sill felt grossly ill equipped to cope with this betrayal, which he was sure it was. How would his father or grandfather have managed it he considered? He froze again, knowing where his mind was taking him, to a dark alley, the places he was never supposed to go. Is it kill or be killed? Yet how simple it sounded, like sport, an alternative form of tennis. How was James supposed to kill anyone? It was unthinkable.

At that moment, Mischa arrived first, good, thought James, good, he would tell him alone.

Mischa sat down in front of him and instead of saying hello he asked, "All OK?" His chestnut mop, and wide soft grey-blue eyes drawing attention as they always did; for Mischa looked nothing short of an archangel to women, and he just could not manage to conceal it; his mixed Indian and English parentage not obviously visible, except perhaps that it was part of his allure, an ingredient in the mix that one could not place.

James sighed, and just came out with it quickly before anyone else arrived. "I think, we have a mole, those three deaths of our people don't sound right at all, and from the sound of it, the information that Michael's about to bring us will confirm it. He sounded angry on the phone, and I know he wasn't angry at me."

"Good God."

"I know. Mischa, I've told you first … What are we going to do?"

"Wait, wait, let's see what Michael actually says. If it is the worst, then …"

"-Then?" James looked at him firmly.

"Then, we deal with it. Has this, do you know if-"

"It hasn't happened before that I know of, my dad's dead, there are no archives, it may of course have happened before, but we're blind on this."

"What are our options?"

James did not like the question; it was too soon to face what his mind had been running from all day, so he did not answer.

"James?" Mischa frowned at him, still far from the sordid back alley that James mind hid from.

"Mischa, I'm so sorry ... sorry we ever dragged you into this."

James could not say it yet, so instead his mind focussed on Mischa, who would never have been a member if he hadn't stumbled into a room in James' house, aged sixteen and overheard a meeting between Edgar -James' father, James, and some other members. There was nothing to be done after that but to tell Mischa everything and hope that he had enough of a moral centre not to spill the beans. They were very lucky, Mischa had known James since they were young children and trusted him. Moreover it was a good age to have stumbled upon it; too young and the natural lack of discipline could easily have made a young boy blab, yet too old and it was possible to be too jaded and cynical to believe in such a cause; Mischa had been at the perfect tipping point between boy and man, to be transfixed.

"What the hell are you talking about? James, get to the point."

"Think, what the hell *can* we do?"

"What? What, no, what?"

Mischa finally understood.

"Look we don't even know what's really happened. Let's take a step back, let's wait for Michael," said Mischa.

James could see that Mischa's colour had drained as he looked expectantly at the door for Michael, instead, Anjelica walked through it and so both men looked at each other, "I'll tell her," said James in response.

Anjelica sat down, she loved this Italian patisserie place and James feared that he was about to ruin it for her. He proceeded to tell her just what he had told Mischa.

"But who would want to betray us, James? It seems fantastical; we're just not that sort of *organisation*," she said the last in a whisper.

"Jelly, I think it's true," James told her.

"So we have to find them, we can do that, if we can route out every bloody secret in the world, we can do this," she added.

"And then what?" James asked her, and Mischa closely watched their exchange.

"And then what? ... Oh, I see, that explains the *extra* tension between you two, not only the mole but what are we going to *do*."

"We may have to do something, awful," said James.

Anjelica, unlike Mischa had not turned pale or desired Michael's swift appearance, "Awful huh, oh God." She took a breath, but not a despairing one, and yet she too turned to face the doorway, waiting for Michael's news.

As they waited James realised that it may even be one of them, his sister or his childhood friend and right hand man, Mischa; but if it was, then they were already dead in the water.

Soon, Michael arrived, tanned, tall and muscular, with a head full of deep brown curls, the size and shape like those on old Greek statues. He had green eyes and a prominent brow, and his tan was very apparent under his short sleeved white cotton shirt.

"Hi Michael ... can we get down to business?" asked James, as Michael took his place at their table.

"James, Anjelica, Mischa," Michael nodded to all of them.

And they knew, they knew by his mild grimace, that things were worse than bad, for Michael, even though a soldier, a warrior to them with his job in Special Forces, was usually a very affable type, with a lilting Irish accent and a keen sense of humour, wiped away now as they held their breaths.

But at that moment tea for four arrived, in a modern white teapot and the waitress took her time and placed each cup, saucer and red napkin expertly before them. They were silent, wishing her only to leave, which finally, with a quick curious glance at their silence, she did.

And so Michael spoke, "James, my man, it's bloody awful. Dora was hit by a car, when she was still on the pavement, about to cross, not even on the road yet, the CCTV on that street in Paris was disabled, Elsa de Vere was only 47 you know, her 'sudden heart attack' may be more a death caused by 'toxins unknown', there were two versions of the pathology report, we found the original on the pathologist's home computer. And John, John McMahon, a climbing accident my arse, he may have been climbing, but his head had been bashed in, sorry, Anjelica," he said to her, even though she kept very still. "God help us, James, we're in trouble."

James put his hand over his chin as though to stroke the beard that was no longer there. "All three worked in Paris?" he finally said.

"Yes," answered Michael, looking firmly at James, ready for action.

"How do we find the culprit? Should we make a list of our members, I could look at each one and look at their motives psychologically?" said Anjelica.

James looked at her, the idea of such a list in solid form made him shiver in the sunlight, if it was ever found, it would be a disaster. Perhaps it was also too painful to look at his 'family' with tainted dark accusing eyes. They sustained each other in so many ways, locked as they were in a generational pact. And moreover now, come to think of it, letting their secret out would bring down three generations of the traitor's own family as well as everyone else's, this was strange, James heart quickened as he knew that the betrayer felt no love like this, even though they could not have been maltreated; like a Cinderella figure left alone in the cellar and unable to reach a fairy godmother as the secret could not be spilled. He felt instinctively that it was in a final rage that an opposite entity had been called forth, a demon rage he imagined, that was about to tear them all to pieces.

"James?" she asked him again.

"Yes … just thinking, no don't write it down, Jelly, I'll pay everyone I can on the mainland at least, a surprise visit, see if it rattles anyone." He would have to process each of his member's potential motives mentally, he would not write them down, for it would offend to look at the sordid ink on the page. "And you Michael and Mischa, look closer into what these three had in common,

55

including the stories they've leaked, this could be connected to some sort of retribution or sending us a message."

"James, what do you want to do once we find him?" asked Michael.

James again waited a touch before answering, "Let's see who it is first, to know about three of our members, not just one … it's got to be one of us I think. I just don't know, Michael, but we may, we may need your help."

Michael nodded affirmatively, but the others sat frozen. No one said anything. Then Anjelica tried to drink some tea, on lifting her cup, her hand shook, so she soon put it down with a clatter.

If Mischa, Anjelica and James could have fallen into an abyss beneath them it would have been at that moment, for it was then that they fully realised and had to come to terms with the bitter pill of their secret organisation, they had had a charmed life up until then, things had worked generally, apart from hiccups here and there, but now things had become far too sordidly real.

"OK. OK," James broke the silence and nodded to himself. "Look, we have to see who it is first, but if it's as bad as it could be then what happened to Elsa and Dora and John, all my dad's good friends, is what's going to happen to us … Got it? Good." He paused and then finally said, "Let's get out of here."

"Sorry, James, I know things are going to be hairy from now on, but … what about Luc? said Anjelica.

"Luc? … What?"

"We spend so much time with him, he may notice that something's not right, you and he, even with Mischa, you're all so close, too close," she added.

"Jelly, he's the least of our problems, don't worry about it," said James.

So soon they left, one by one, leaving James alone again, and he realised how much he contained; as there was no shelter for them, no police to run to, no sanctuary to hide in and no temple in which to confess; this matter had to be borne out for the moment on an internal stage and then resolved eventually, in secret.

As he started to consider everyone he'd ever known in search of this mole, he then thought of Luc again. He felt immediate relief that Luc did not have any knowledge of his organisation. He had no idea who James was in this respect and that the reason he was a genealogist was that it gave him an excuse to delve into people's affairs without suspicion, just like Anjelica. Looking at the cherry topped and thick colourful slabbed confections heading for people's plates, James took solace in Luc's innocence, as though it were now an untainted aspect of James' own life. He had never considered telling Luc, ever. It wasn't done. Knowing, bound you for life and it wasn't a fair or safe thing to do.

James put his hand in his hair, today a dark blonde that glittered sleekly, he knew that he would have to keep this from Luc and act far away from the truth, but it gave him comfort, like a saving grace; Luc would be saved. It had been hard to watch him over the last few years edge closer and closer to people and places that all wound back to James. A few years ago Luc was working at the European Parliament and James had flirted with the idea of inducting him, but he could not. It was a portion of James' own life that deserved to be left unfettered. For it was as if through osmosis that James was able to see their lives and childhoods through Luc's eyes, especially when he was with him, and Luc was gracefully unaware of the pressure that a secret could ring around one, even if it was a good secret. Luc saw their happy times and escapes and summer beach holidays as fitting memories of growing up as privileged young men, he did not have to carry so much knowledge of the past and of the underworld, that it came with you wherever you went, like an extra massive trunk, full of heavy muster. James feared what was to come over the next few weeks or months, and realised that it may be helpful for him to spend time with Luc, and not just for Luc's own sake (James could see that the loss of his mother Beatrice had left Luc on autopilot, tottering without comprehending, probably too busy to understand) but James needed to spend time with Luc for himself, to escape the certain drama of what he was about to do, uncovering a mole, and then … it was dark territory, back alley stuff and he felt revulsion to it. Being with Luc would be a solace, yes a definite necessity and coping stratagem, he thought like a general now and drew Luc into the plan in order to manage and surmount this monstrosity.

Chapter 10

It seemed at work that emergencies began and emergencies passed; currently Gemma was rushing from one room to another, at one point Luc was able to catch her eye as she waited impatiently by a printer nearby to deposit a vital sheaf, and she read him instantly.

"Some of the countries that we were supposed to sell our North Sea oil to right now are furious that we're keeping it for ourselves instead, and threatening all sorts against us, including trade tariffs, but other countries like China have waded in, calling us 'unscrupulous' and want to join in the 'punishment' of us for their own ends. We expected uproar from the countries we owe the oil to, but not the latter game going on," Gemma blinked alertly.

Luc still looked about her face for the type of tension that had caused her veins to protrude on that first day, and he did not see it, she was even modestly calm in the tempest, but more like the eye of the storm. She continued to then efficiently clarify, although Luc had guessed the next part.

"We're using the extra oil to power the country during the embargo, everything from sending barges up and down the country with locally grown produce to keeping the lights on, it's the Dunkirk spirit ... be it a bit underhand," she finished.

Luc nodded and she went back to staring fixedly at the printer's depositing tray, like an immovable midwife. He could feel the flurry about him as the situation took hold of the office, and so looking up from his monitor that contained nothing but facts about trade deals that were probably obsolete by now, he asked her, "Can I do something then, I mean, this sounds important, all hands on deck maybe?"

She considered him for a moment, and then shook her head, "It's OK, Luc, we've dealt with worse, it isn't as bad as it looks in terms of the things we sort out. But … if it does get worse, I'll get you on board." She smiled at him.

Luc nodded, and went back to his screen.

As the day progressed, the hornet's nest that was the morning calmed a great deal, and people were back at their desks, much less rattled. Luc looked about for Gemma to ask her if things had been sorted out, but she did not come his way again. The late afternoon contrast with the morning panic helped deepen his sense of familiarity with his office now and created an understanding of the place that humbled the beast somewhat, and also made him feel for it respect; it was indeed a most efficient tempest.

Yet, near the very end of the day a new sensation set in and he couldn't place it at first, it felt like a low level buzzing, a drone in the chest, he tried to dismiss it as fatigue or an overwhelmed sense of self; accepting a new life and circumstance all at once, but his chest felt heavy, his eyes wandered from burgundy carpet to blank cool walls, and he started listening to his own breathing, and the light tapping upon keyboards … and so, the drone grew worse and he went home eventually in a hurry, as if trying to outrun it, but it presciently kept his pace.

As he entered his building he saw on a noticeboard a slick and glossy poster advertising an art and creativity course, it started in one hour and Luc rushed upstairs and threw himself into the shower; his golden showerhead doused him vigorously, responding fittingly to his inner harassment. He changed so that he looked like a student again and made his way, to Regent's Park.

He had no idea how much it would cost, how much time it would take, or what it required, he didn't care, the little he knew was that he liked art and creativity.

Registration was reassuring, touching on old patterns and memories of university now pleasant and infused with nostalgia; such things as queuing and giving your name, while other people took charge, much like being part of a herded flock, in this case it was not clear where.

Soon, he was in an old fashioned classroom, even though he felt no mirth, a remote sensation of excitement threatened to break through his composure and self-generated bewilderment for being there. He had his own very old little wooden desk, luckily there was a stash of pens, pencils and paper on the teacher's desk, as Luc had brought nothing with him but his wallet. The day was nowhere near done as the sun in London in July did not fade away sometimes till past ten at night. The light lit up the creaky wooden floor and pale buttercup room lazily, and gave it warm tones of pink, golden stretches and orange glances; the strokes of another world, of hued possibilities. The shadows and highlights the late sun cast over the room and its occupants were thus rose, gilded and often grave, but at last Luc's tension vanished. The teacher had placed a half carved stone sculpture near the window, white blank canvases were stacked on the floor next to that and on his desk was a pile of used books, all of the same story but in different editions; the fonts on the latter changed dramatically from large and classical to mean and minimal in the sweep on an eye. Luc sat waiting in this new classroom while the evening light boasted so much day, as if trying to achieve more than its power, yet was weak in the way that the bright, bold, sure strokes of the noon day sun never would be; and so, as the light wound and stretched about the room to slacken shadows, and spread warm rouges, lilacs and peaches in nooks, corners and crevices where there would have been none seven hours ago, all waited in silence, and Luc was taken; the room had him, and woven a spell before the teacher had even spoken.

"We are here hopefully to go on a journey together. To explore literature and art and not only learn about the beauty of their construction, but of how they speak to us in so many ways, that we perhaps do not realise. We will explore how they make us feel, think, and perhaps even how they make us approach our own lives differently …"

Luc listened to his new teacher Mr Andrews every word intently; he had deep ginger hair that was most profoundly evident in his beard which was trimmed in the square style of the Middle Ages. His dress was casual, but from a bygone decade, in a white muslin shirt and pale cream trousers, made complete by an upper class accent, but his most commendable quality was that he was not bored; he'd begun his class with the fortitude of a sea captain or of a dedicated English teacher at school, determined to sail his children through their exams. Perhaps that was what he did in the day and so made no distinction; this evening class wasn't an annoyance or a burden to him, it was in some manner important. At one juncture, Luc turned his head to look at the rest of his class and all looked like Mr Andrews' props, with shadows and scarlets and greys lighting them up, cheeks self-rouging with the easy heat, they too seemed riveted.

They were to start with literature, the canvases would have to wait, Luc felt the faintest hint of disappointment and sadness, he did not want words he realised, he wanted the vivid medium of paint. Mr Andrews passed out copies of the novel, it was Tess of the D'Urbervilles, Luc's heart sank a little more. Turning around to observe Mr Andrews make his rounds, Luc received another surprise: in the far corner of the room, near the academic dust on the floor that seemed to accumulate in nearly every such institution and with the requisite tatty papers pinned to the wall, was the girl, the girl in the garden; Luc could not bring himself to call her his neighbour.

Once again her hair fell in dark and loose spirals about her neck and she looked pale compared to his last viewing. There were perhaps thirty students in all, so she had been easy to miss, tucked away as she was. Today she wore blue Capri pants and a stark white shirt as though directly out of the 1950's. Yet, her attention was not abstract, Luc could see that Mr Andrews had won her over too, her focus was upon him, even though she did not smile, she was present and not on the verge of grimacing as she had seemed the last time. Her toenails that peeped out through sandals were dark red in parts but also chipped in places, but she still carried it well he felt, as it made no difference to her poise.

She took the book, laid it in front of her and clasped her hands under her chin, her hair dangling while leaning upon her desk with her elbows, as Luc strained to watch her.

Mr Andrews was heading back to the front, now empty handed and asked, "Has anyone here read Tess before?"

A number of hands flew up, including hers; Luc raised his hand too but knew he could not remember much of it, apart from the fact that it was a tragedy of course.

"It would be wonderful if you can have read Tess by next week, please pick up a sheet from the stack on my desk letting you know the course structure, reading list and aims, and ... have a delightful weekend," Mr Andrews finished, and they were dismissed. As that evening was the introductory session and registration, it was not to last as long as in the weeks to come.

There were murmurs of approval in the class then scrapings of chairs and it was all over. Luc rose abruptly, trying to gather himself as the launch from the everyday to this classroom had been abrupt in itself, his cheeks and lips were swollen, thick with the heat of the room, which smelled of wood and books. He tucked his book and his programme under his arm and observed that the girl was rising too and placing her papers in her bag which she slung across her body like a ten year old. She had no jacket and her expression was composedly blank. But then, she sighed, a huge sigh, as if no one was looking. After her chest heaved, she looked at the floor for a few moments, she then straitened and made her way towards the door. Luc hastened to follow, knowing that they were going in the same direction, but forgot that he was still standing behind his desk with a chair yet close behind him —with his eyes on her departing back as he took a hasty step, with one enormous scraping crash, the table toppled onto its side and with it so did Luc, falling down hard as his ankle caught on a desk leg.

The resulting fracas had a stunned Mr Andrews rushing towards him and other classmates running to his side and the girl, already disappearing around the corner and slipping away; he prayed she hadn't seen who had fallen and grimaced. His ankle felt pulled and grazed, and other parts of him too were cut or bruised. After apologizing and posing very convincingly as 'well' for a few minutes, he decided to walk home slowly instead. In the cool breeze of evening, he realised that he could taste blood in his mouth, and put his hand to his lip, where yes he could feel it had split. He wondered then, why on hearing the commotion as she must have, had she not turned back to have a look, he would have. The answer he felt was in her expression and gaze; he still could not place it.

His ankle throbbed all the way home but did not make him seriously limp. The sun was truly glorious in its last throws; a breeze cooled his face and marked out his wounds, stinging the cuts all over him that he didn't know about yet.

In his flat, which had become stuffy through the day, he opened all the windows and washed his cuts, on his wrists, ankles, hands, ribcage, shoulder and forehead. He had a packet of plasters which he put on the worst affected areas, refusing definitively to put one upon his temple. He retrieved a slim bottle of beer from the fridge and sat down in front of the window looking onto the street. The accident had taken away any hunger for dinner, leaving a degree of trauma in its wake, he knew instinctively that he needed to sit still, but instead his mind focussed on the girl, the one who maybe lived beyond the wall, and why she didn't care enough to be caught by his accident, like everybody else had.

Chapter 11

Luc journeyed to work sore the next morning, it was Friday and he took with him his copy of his book; on his own borrowed copy he had a picture of Stonehenge by Turner, looking like it should perhaps in this case for a terrible dawn. The areas of discomfort all over his body conspired to create in him a general feeling of the worse for wear and by 10am he asked Gemma if she had any painkillers, which of course, she did. He professed a headache, Gemma handed over the pills efficiently, eyeing the graze on his forehead and blue ghost of a wound upon his lips, as if she knew that this was no 'headache' but had some other root. He felt well after that, pharmaceutically eased over and was able to settle, and there was calm in the office as the Chinese had backed down -after Britain threatened property bans in London for the Chinese and also Visa bans when travel would be allowed again; Britain could still show its teeth it seemed.

The recent emergency at work had been a good induction for him he felt, as now whenever Gemma started to run from room to room, her whispers urgent, he assumed that this is what they did. He watched important blue sealed folders enter the building with a hushed looking courier in a black suit and leave a vibrant looking red under the arm of Gemma, looking equally if not more important; Luc sometimes wondered if they were not secretly running the world.

Further, the droning sense of unease that had grown so difficult by Thursday had been greatly calmed after beginning his new creativity course and then the subsequent fall, which had taken his frayed nerves and shattered them further, perhaps having rendered them the largest favour of all: physical pain. The wounds took time to heal and Luc tended to them diligently, looking at them in the mirror; blue sometimes bloody, watching their progression.

In the shower after work that day, which he now enjoyed as the London summer had been uncannily prolonged; he too wondered the secret question that everyone supressed: where was the British grey weather? He liked the way that the bathroom was lit up in glittering white by the sunshine and that the showerhead gleamed and blinked gold in rounded curves when he caught sight of it. He put on a soft white shirt as he dressed to go to James' for dinner, it wasn't a formal affair of course but he still delved into the stash of colognes and scents that he'd brought with him from France, as well as so much else. He owned nine or ten different varieties that all ranged from sphere of influence: a couple of bottles in chic round-edged clear glass were used by his father and had made a good impression on Luc; they were no nonsense clear and full fragrances for men in citrus and musk. Another influence in an unimaginably green bottle was French and was the same brand as had been used by his maternal grandfather, the one who had been a spy, a good spy, smiled Luc, as he indulged in the fact; Luc's French Grandfather Jean, had spied so secretly and so well for the Allies that there was a room full of medals in Luc's still living grandmother's house in that small beach town. It was a legacy that Luc had taken very much to heart, especially as Jean had given Luc his own gold signet ring that boasted an asymmetric star, so that Luc wore it every day. The green bottled scent itself was a much bigger bolder scent than all his others, as perfumes in those days were quite obliged to be. Then, there was the also the fond bulk that Luc's mother Beatrice had given to him on various birthdays; they ranged in style from very modern and light to the old fashioned type again in fabulously shaped, green and deep blue coloured bottles.

Fragranced and clean, he took the tube to St. John's Wood, nestled in amongst hot and miserable commuters desperate to get off the tube and perhaps bathe as he had, and his journey would be short; so not long enough to tarnish his perfumed and cleansed sense of self.

But, very annoyingly, he'd forgotten something. He realised that he'd left Tess at his office, and so he made a quick decision to go and get the book there and then, rather than waste any of his weekend, his mood was relaxed enough yet, that he did not mind the detour.

Luc's office building was old and made of large well cut stone; it was of course not closed, yet very quiet, he knew that it stayed open all the time. He had no problems going back through the security gates with his pass; they were used to this he thought, people working all hours. There was no one about at all however; a sultry summer Friday evening in London had been enough to draw everyone out. After he quickly located his book upon his desk, he was about to leave when he heard voices, distant and muted though they were, he still felt submerged in an unusual level of silence for his workplace, and so he wanted to know the source of the sound. He closed his eyes briefly to listen, and was guided away from the main room, to the wide corridor that contained Gemma's station which would have been around the corner -but he did not go that far.

"I don't want to get him involved!"

"It won't be 'getting him involved', Gemma, it's his job, or could be part of it, it wouldn't be unusual, it's what some of our employees do."

Balthazar had answered Gemma -Luc was sure of the voices. His heart began a dance but he stayed put, listening, still around the corner.

"Yes but I don't want *Luc* doing this, it's not his job," she whispered now.

"It would be *valuable* to us," Balthazar explained, sounding like a patient father.

"I know what you're thinking, and exactly, no, this is not a good idea. It's like playing with fire, he shouldn't be put anywhere close, what if he gets too close or ... *sees*."

"Gemma, it won't do any harm, and in the long term ... it could be very useful indeed."

"I knew it. *Please*, you're not listening." Gemma seemed exasperated, but was not aggressive. "*Please* don't do this," she added, stressing the point as much as she could.

"I'm sorry, sweetheart, it will be a good thing, you'll see. I don't believe that Beatrice's boy would ever let us down."

Then there was silence between them, and Gemma sighed forcefully.

At this Luc felt that their conversation was heading for a close and so he darted back, thanking his stars for the thick breach of carpet that silenced his covert mad dash away. Hurrying down the stairs and out of the building he tried to take a gulp of air, which was far too hot and sultry and did not help him at all to breathe.

As he walked quickly to the nearest tube station, the pounding fear of being caught subsided and was replaced by immense confusion, he did not know what to make of what he had overheard at all, how on earth had Balthazar and maybe even Gemma too, known his mother?! Balthazar had referred to her by her first name, but Luc had never seen his boss before in his life. He tried to think again while on the tube; its rhythmic rolling more of a jostle and not a comfort as it usually was. What's more, he was so sure that Gemma liked him, he had been convinced of it. How had he failed her so completely in just five days? It didn't make sense and it rankled oddly, as though the conversation had not been about him at all, more about something that he should be kept away from.

With this last after turning it over in his head again and again, Luc had found that he had reached James house, and rang the bell.

"Hi, Luc, come to cook me dinner?" said James as he let in his friend. "And what happened to your face?"

"Hi. Oh yeah, I fell over yesterday, I'm OK, I've started a new evening class, anyway, I just went to work to pick up my book," Luc waved it in front of James, as he had had of course no bag to put it in, "and overheard something at work ..." Luc frowned.

"What happened? And what class?" said James as he ushered him to the soft off-white chairs near the large sliding doors of his kitchen; they looked out onto a parched lawn, with not a flower in sight.

"Just a literature class, fell over a desk -but the work thing, I dunno, can't explain, just thought my immediate superior, Gemma, liked me. I don't think she does now … don't know what happened."

"I'm sure she does, everybody likes you, Luc." James tried a cheeky smile.

Luc didn't want to go into the part about them mentioning his mother, and any more detail in fact, it was something that seemed ominous, and so he wanted to first tackle it alone.

"Anyway, it's nothing you can't fix. Come on, have a beer," said James as he went to retrieve a bottle from his fridge. "Mischa will be along later, and the kitchen is all yours," James said again with a grin.

But it worked.

"I'm not moving," said Luc, looking cheered up a fraction, "I work for the government and I've had a very hard week you know." And with that, Luc compartmentalised his problems and decided to call his father when he got home to ask if his mother ever knew a Balthazar, and told himself that he hadn't been fired (perhaps the worst being that he had been hired due to nepotism), and he could yet still prove himself to these people, if he wanted to, whoever they were.

After Mischa arrived, they ordered Chinese take away and all three men seemed very tired, and ate and chatted about the embargo, and the disease that had not hit the developed countries of the world yet.

Luc eventually went back home with his spirits a little lifted but exhausted, while the wounds and bruises all over him were behaving objectionably; he ached, and his cuts stung and smarted in the breeze.

Immediately after entering his flat he picked up the receiver and dialled for France.

"Hi, Dad. It's me, didn't wake you did I?"

"Not quiet, but nearly, what's up? Was going to call you tomorrow and ask you about your first week," said Luc's father, Vincent.

"It's been great, better than I imagined, can't wait for you to see the office, if they let me … Just a quick thing tonight though, I know you want to sleep, did mum ever have a friend name Balthazar? Last name. Or a Gemma Montague?"

"No Gemma, but hold on … Johnnie, yes Johnnie Balthazar. I never met him, Luc, but mum was round James' mum and dad's, Lulu and Edgar's so much, and I was always away for work that she did mention him, but, it was a long time ago, it would have been during lunches or picnics when I wasn't there. Why, son?"

"Dad, he's my boss."

"Oh," said Vincent in mild surprise, "but then, wouldn't you have met him before?"

"No, that's the thing, three interviews and two exams and I only met him when I started (!) You don't think, it was any, well, nepotism or anything do you? I mean, I really don't ever remember seeing him at James' parents' house."

"Well it would be a hell of a lot of people to persuade if that were the case then, with all those hurdles. Have some faith in yourself."

Luc sighed. "You're right. Thank you. Hope you get a good night's rest. Ring you on Sunday?"

"Yep, great, night son."

It was nice that they could have normal conversations now thought Luc and even able to mention his mother without breaking down. An achievement; and all within a year.

Luc felt a little less harassed by the ugly fruits of his eavesdropping now, it was just Gemma that he had to win over if not understand, but decided also to take some more painkillers before going to bed, to drown the protests from his wounded body.

On Saturday Luc immersed himself as much as he could with his assignment and read Tess in his garden. The searing sunshine seemed to cook his wounds and bruises; but he took it in, recharging himself like a battery able to cope with the heat like a true Mediterranean; overruling the cooler strains in his blood. Eventually though, his cheeks flushed and in turn blared out their own warnings against such emphatic solar exposure. But he didn't let her go, the lure of Tess, as it had been for teenage boys forced to read it in schools all over the world, she too was emphatic.

By Sunday late afternoon he had finished her and mourned her tragic end, even though he had always known of her fate, poor Tess; he had wanted to rescue her and then felt sorrow for such revered yet wasted beauty. It was at that time, when he was finally so lost in her that his wounds and grazes no longer smarted and that the baking sun had finished with him, that he became conscious of his surroundings again. With surprise, as if the last week had not happened at all, he saw the luxuriant English garden about him as if for the first time, and wondered in the deepest part of him, how he had found himself there. Until, he heard a woman's voice carrying over the fence.

He listened intently, yes, it sounded like the other woman, the one he'd met and helped on the door step with sharp black hair. She called, "Oh please come out, just for me, it's such a nice evening!" Her voice was gently pleading and mollifying as though with a sullen child, yet as it was company she was requesting it must have been from an adult.

Luc stayed very still. He wanted to find a way to take a look; he was centrally located in the garden and considered the option of venturing back to the elevation of the French Doors to find a view. In a few moments he sprightly tip toed back up to the entrance, up and into the mouth of the open glass doors and turned his head: he saw before him the scene of Christine sitting at a table and chairs which had been moved deeper in from the last time, wearing a ragged pair of denim shorts and a t-shirt while lounging languorously. Her hissing fizzy drink sat bulging with voluminous ice cubes, and she looked up squinting to meet the approach of the other girl, while Luc's own heart bulged. The other girl was holding the baby that he assumed was Christine's, and she was wearing loose flowing blue trousers that grew diaphanous in the breeze as she approached.

"Mer, this has got to stop." Christine admonished her and then retreated kindly, "at least improve, or make progress, you can't let this depression and unhappiness defeat you."

And then the girl spoke.

"Well, I am going to that silly class," she shrugged. "That's something. It's all I can do."

All her words, the entire delivery had arrived from a step removed, for Christine's reproach had not seemed to quite register for Mer; the response had been quiet and cursory. It seemed that Christine was now trying to restrain herself, not conveying all that was brewing or festering and instead took a sip of her effervescent drink. Yet, even though there was anger and frustration on Christine's part, it quickly ebbed into resignation. Mer, he imagined how it would be spelled in French: Mer, like the Sea. Now that he knew her name he chewed it in his mind, unable to find or fix it and she tossed her head back and held it there in an arc of choice, as if pleading for the sun's last rays to be bestowed upon her, it was a bewitching sight and more than he'd ever seen of her before. She did not care what Christine thought, nor more importantly Luc noticed, did she seem to need to.

Finally Christine proclaimed, "You will come out of this eventually, I know you can."

To which Mer snapped her head back to look at her and then unexpectedly for everyone, laughed. It was brief and surprised both of them, Mer then finished off by staring intently at a lilac rose bush.

Christine then looked at her tenderly and said, "My darling friend," and Mer nodded her thanks, with eyes still on the plant.

At that moment Luc's body rebelled; a headache flashed across his temple with his wound at its source, his stomach grumbled violently and he felt sick both with hunger and moreover thirst and so he finally went back inside, unable to stay and watch the ladies at their table.

Upstairs, he filled a jug with ice and water and continually refilled his glass; he had been inspired by Christine's vibrant beverage. He washed his faced that glowed ominously with the menacing sheen of an oncoming sunburn and thought about having some aloe vera in the house if London persisted in having a summer such as this; as from another continent. While he ate his dinner: some leftover pizza, a fried egg and a green salad he'd made for himself to try and cool down, the scene remained in his head, the women must be close, of that he was certain.

Then on finding that he had finished reading Tess and his homework, he considered Thursday and his evening class, he realised that it was a cause of actual happiness; he had not felt that emotion in a long time, it was an odd sensation, roving in his chest away from the darkness in a constant feathery swirl, off on its own dance.

*

It happened immediately on Monday. Luc had been told to come to Balthazar's office by a colleague but Balthazar wasn't there. Gemma sat on the corner of his desk instead and smiled at Luc as he came in, who shut the door behind him. He could not imagine his sensors to be so wrong to think that she didn't like him -it left him troubled again.

"Hi, Luc. All right weekend?"

"Good, thanks."

"Good. You've done well here, even in your first week, so Balthazar and I wondered if you would like to take on another role in the department, it isn't what you studied for, but it still carries a lot of responsibility."

"Yes, of course. What is it?" he said, but could only think of one question: how did you know my mother?

"Have you noticed that it is only me and two others, apart from Balthazar who take sealed document bags in and out of the office, well we would like you to join that pool of people."

"Oh, of course," said Luc, though his heart had sank a little bit, being a courier was surely nothing to get excited about, and he searched for something in her look, in her gaze that gave him the truth, a lead as to why if not her, then how did Balthazar know his mother so well, why did he respect her as he did? But they'd met, Luc's father had confirmed it, Luc reminded himself. If that wasn't enough, Luc needed to know even more, there was something he was being kept away from and in the same context the fact that he was Beatrice's son had seemed to sway Balthazar in his favour. But, he received no answers that day.

"Good," Gemma said looking genuinely pleased, confounding Luc even more, "I'll let you know when you've got your first run."

"Thank you," said Luc and nodded looking for her dismissal, so she nodded back.

He went back to his desk with a frown and looked at the odd red or blue folder at someone's desk with a new found curiosity.

*

Four days passed and Luc had spent them wondering at work when his time would come, when was he to bear an important folder? But Gemma passed him by at work, and did not approach him at all with that kind but serious face that he expected. Balthazar was barely in the office at all, so that Luc could not at least examine his face, for clues about old bonds. Knowing that he had few avenues for investigation; typing either of their names into a search engine would probably give him less than nothing with their level of security and clearance, and worse it may even alert someone, somewhere, that he was doing it in the first place. So Luc decided to be patient; as it was a mystery that had to be solved. Until then at least he was even able to muster a small murmur of cheer inside when 7.30 came about on Thursday evening, and all were seated for his evening class.

All was assembled as before, the exiting light of an unholy summer gilded the room and its objects into gorgeous newly painted relics, and recreated each person in woodland tones and ripened berry hues that were very much rich and borrowed. Luc was pleased that all was as it had been last week and that it had not been a fleeting experience. Then, his attention turned to his other preoccupation; he twisted his head to see her and there she was, Mer, in the same corner.

"Hello, all!" Mr Andrews called and straight to work, "I hope you enjoyed Tess, let's start with the overriding emotions that this work of art has brought up in us?" The class froze and then a few tentative hands flew up.

"Yes?"

"Powerlessness," said the girl, it was Mer, as clear as a bell and looking straight ahead, she then ducked back down as Mr Andrews turned to write the word on the board. Soon, it was filled with all else, all the 'beauty', 'pity', 'nature' and 'tragedy' that could be accommodated by a class of thirty, Luc said nothing; and strangely felt like an intruder.

After an hour and a half of intense discussion, Luc finally felt harrowed and hungry. He was tired not just from the evening but from all the expectation the last few days had kindled inside him. He had also been intrigued by Mer's reaction, she had been engaged far more than he had ever seen or felt and had almost vibrated with intent attention to the discussion, even taken notes. He panicked, was he supposed to be taking notes? Although Mer had not said any more, she had also been keen to listen to others, or nod and most of all to listen to Mr Andrews, quite rapt. Yet when class ended and the low screech and growl of the scraping of chairs took place she'd seemed shaken, as if she had taken a 'turn', as described in old books. She kept her head down and hugged her sling bag to herself, her hair flowed about, wisped and curled and her big eyes lost focus, as though at war with the passion she had just engaged with. This time, Luc wanted to depart when she did as he knew that they were heading in the same direction, perhaps he might be able to strike up a friendly conversation with her, with now home, abode and class in common.

He walked it transpired, a few feet behind her instead, Luc tried with all his might to make her engage or to slow down and look at him, but she strode alone, hugging her bag, determined to reach her home and nothing else. Finally, she was at her doorstep and reached inside her bag as Christine had done, but she found her key with ease. Luc crossed behind her and stood in front of his own door, at which moment while turning his own key, looked over to her as she turned hers; her door was much heavier and bigger than his and so took longer to manage. Luc then smiled at her conveying all that he could and she looked back, at first as though lost, unaware of what was being asked of her, and then ... she smiled briefly for him, before falling into the gulf of her open door and disappearing. It was something he felt, a small step.

Finally alone and his mind loose and tired, Luc noticed that his body had almost healed, only his ankle was still plum like and bruised, he considered that there was no sign yet that the embargo was about to end, or a feeling that the disease abroad was less of a threat, he tried not to think about all the media headlines that suggested in fact that his whole *world* was about to end; for hadn't he himself travelled to London, diplomatic papers in hand, as a foil to all this worry? There was hope, things had not completely collapsed yet, and he thought of his office and how they could seem to sort out so much disorder, and then grew troubled as he thought again of Balthazar and Gemma, and the secrets that lay there ... Thus, when he finally slept that night it was disturbed at first, and then with aplomb, as a surrender to complete physical and mental exhaustion; as if a stone cast over a cliff.

Chapter 12

Nothing too awful had happened yet. Not yet. Gemma considered this as she entered her home after a long day at work. What a hard week, she thought. Her ground floor flat had white, tall serene walls and high ceilings, and in her living room a giant mirror took pride of place, bordered ornately in thick patterned silver. She initially had never managed to have it hung when she moved here five years ago, and now liked it instead propped against the wall just as it was. After her week and the proximity she found herself in to Luc, she went to a cabinet in which there was a huge envelope stuffed with old assorted photos, all sizes and ranging from colourful, artistic or sepia to black and white, in this bundle she gently rifled, trying not to let her eyes linger in upon any one irrelevant scene, until she found the piece of frozen time that she sought. And there it was, unabashed, innocent of why she sought it out with such a critical eye and troubled heart.

The photo was in black and white; perhaps it was still fashionable to be so at the time, as colour was also available back then. There were four little children in the photo, all about the age of four and standing at the seaside; most of them unaware that the photo was being taken at all, as they were all immersed in their own world together: one blond haired little boy stared at his ice cream cone, another with light brown hair, looked foggily at the camera as though he was not sure what it was, a third chestnut haired little boy's face dimpled and smiled as though life was an amazing game, and lastly there was a small fair-haired girl, actually the only one to notice the camera; and she had smiled back at it as though to be photographed was a real treat. The girl was herself, the boys: James, Luc and Mischa respectively. It was the only time she had spent any of her childhood with them. It had been during one unusual summer when her parents had holidayed with all of theirs, now she wondered if it had been business, group activity business, that had made that happen, as it never happened again. Luc didn't remember her, she was sure that he wouldn't as he never had this photograph, for Gemma's mother had taken it. But Gemma, now without intention found herself looking at it fondly, and could hear the sea lapping loudly behind them as though they had never left, and the piercing gulls cries so very close, salt air, heat and tangled young tresses, and simple, untroubled joy -no, she could not bear to destroy this photograph, not one of the people in it was obviously discernible anyhow to a stranger, so, she looked for a place to hide it. As she stood in front of the giant mirror thinking, it was there that she caught her own blue eyes, and knew what to do. The mirror was old, and behind it at the bottom edge, some of the topmost brown paper backing was loose. So she gently pushed the photo in, where she could barely touch it again herself, and felt satisfied that that link had now been hidden, from the dreadful Minister and what he wanted from them. She felt sick, those three names, dead names that he wrote, that is maybe what he wants for them all she thought. And still she then reminded herself of her plan to wait and stay silent. If they had cameras in her house to see what she had just done she would know, her group had its own resources, and Michael did routine checks on such things for them. She reflected again upon Luc and the fact that she had known him once; looked into rock pools and played in the sand, and even taken his hand as they tried to walk into the waves together, a brief summer week, many, many, years ago and by the sea.

There was a heavy knock on the door. She froze. Another knock, and the seconds passed. What could she do, she had to answer it she told herself. As a stupefied thing she made her way to the door, but saw in her videophone picture, that there was no need to fear, but then she realised, oh but there was! What on earth was he doing here now? This was most out of character.

"Hello, Gemma."

"Hello, Sir John," she said to him; not venturing to say anything else until the door was firmly shut.

"It's funny that you call me that when we're alone and Balthazar at work, isn't it?"

"I knew you as Sir John for years before, and 'Balthazar' I had to learn, adjust to, anyway, it helps me not to blur the lines. Come and sit down," Gemma finished, gesturing at her ivory sofa, though she wished he had not come to her home, not now, if she was being watched, she could of course explain it away as office related, but it bothered her hugely nonetheless.

"Yes, I think I will," said the large man and as they both sat, he sighed and looked at her. "We've been breached Gemma. I'm sorry to have to come to the point so bluntly, but the three of ours who died -none were mishaps or accidents."

Gemma said nothing, carefully trying to weigh up her response while waiting for Sir John to tell her more.

"Dora, John, Elsa," he shook his head. "We don't know who it is yet, before you ask."

Gemma's giant mirror was before them on one side, reflecting the serene white and silver accented sitting room innocently, but mocked her secrecy with its recent hidden cargo. "What are we going to do?" she asked him, and not, if he was 'sure' about it, for of course it made sense, that Minister had to have found the truth from someone, and most likely it was one of her group.

"We hope that the embargo will not last too long, it's only been three weeks and the way the world is screaming global economic collapse, surely in can't last too long. So James will try and look for links between the three who died, to seek a common thread, he'll also visit everyone he can in person, a surprise visit shall we say, and see how they react."

"So you really believe one of us could do this, be this mole?" asked Gemma, her eyes a little wider.

"I don't know what to think, if somebody knows about us, an outsider, then it will get a lot worse very quickly, if it is one of us who leaked, which I cannot fathom why, then it's not only unusual, but we have to find them quickly and stem this tide," Sir John finished with a fierce look.

Gemma now realised fully her predicament, she wanted to tell Sir John about the Minister and her recruitment by him, but faltered, Sir John must trust her implicitly if he has told her cart blanche about the mole and not had her tested/questioned by James. What would he think now if she revealed the truth about what she knew? He would still trust her she felt, but James and moreover Mischa, may not, or become very suspicious that she had not reported to them immediately about this Minister. She was thinking very quickly and decided to try and get more proof, more ammunition about the Minister's culpability in order to clear herself fully, and then explain herself to James.

"What will you do with the mole, once you find him?" she asked, trying to be calm about her new resolution.

"It depends who it is I suppose, and why, for example if they were held to ransom etc. But if they've been paid off or done something really treacherous, then I'm afraid ... I think we will have to call in Michael."

Gemma went pale, she could not help it. Michael was of course Special Forces: guns, tactics and death. But then her former worry hit her again, "But are you sure it was safe for you to come here, you're so crucial to the organisation, maybe we should be more formal?"

"Oh yes, don't worry, Michael is outside."

Chapter 13

James awoke to a strange feeling, the curtains were drawn and his wooden bedframe and white bed covers looked serene and welcoming in the burgeoning morning light. He had been right he thought, spending time with Luc as he had on Friday night had proven a balm for all that was happening. James had already visited a few members in London, turning up at their homes unannounced, and having a light hearted chat with them, and informing them that there would be a review of all their work to date, not to evaluate them they were told, but in order to see if better lines of communication and links could be drawn between disparate members, to make them more efficient. It was of course a ruse, to make any would be mole panic, and hopefully try to cover their tracks or do something out of character. It was barely enough, but until Michael and Mischa finished their checks on links between Elsa, Dora and John -looking for a lead, there was little else he could do. He writhed with disloyalty with every thought and consideration of friend and comrade as betrayer, but he had to do this. He had to, or they would all die, and that spurred him on.

Once he had washed and dressed he considered some of the 'work' that he was supposed to be doing, it was true that he was a genealogist, at present he had a couple of clients and it did provide some income, but he was not sure how he would have coped if his father had not left him such a legacy. He did actually enjoy it, or maybe delving for the truth had become an instinct and he had even investigated Luc's history. He had never told Luc this, as Luc had never commissioned him and he didn't want to explain himself, as he often investigated anyone who was a close friend of group members, and also James had been genuinely curious about Luc's background.

It began with Luc's mother Beatrice who had been French, he remembered a long time ago when they were fifteen years old, a very conspiratorial yet proud Luc had told James all about his grandfather, Beatrice's father, who in short had been a spy for the Allies during the war. This was meat enough for anyone's imagination; but James knew that it had remained with Luc throughout his life and become a chord of resonance for him, a vital source of his sense of purpose; for Luc wanted the same sense of significance in his own life, forgetting the fear and danger and isolation that such a career could possibly truly contain. There are no real wars to fight anymore thought James sometimes in his low moods, in this apathetic materialistic world, but Luc, James felt, was still moved to fight for some sort of cause, it was in his blood he would have imagined, and it made him smile. James was weary even though he had just risen. It pained him even more that he knew what it would have meant to Luc if he had inducted him, it would have been the manifestation of a dream, yet, James consoled himself that at least he was not willing to risk the life of his best friend, as that is what it was coming down to currently. Also, the more deeply Luc wove himself into government, the more unstable the idea of revealing the truth to him became; loyalty could be swayed by ideology, passion, keen words and of course love, James knew that it was too late to risk it with Luc, as so much could have settled Luc's mind in favour of others over James by now, perhaps even loyalty to his work; it was too dangerous. If Luc had also stumbled in upon them at the age of sixteen as Mischa had, James would have succeeded, yes, of that he was sure; Luc would have sworn loyalty for his entire lifetime, it was the right age, the right tipping point between boy and man; between love and suspicion.

James had watched Luc's career intertwine itself around so much that would have been invaluable to them, Luc could have been an immense asset. The work he'd taken at the European parliament and now in the midst of the British governmental machine could yield such intense secrets, but James knew that at least on this occasion this was not necessary as they already had people in Luc's department. Yet, wouldn't Luc's loyalty have been superior he considered?

Wouldn't there have been an undertow to it, perhaps a strain of emotionality or even irrationality that would have bound Luc to James beyond the formal, or proper, it would have been loyalty above and beyond the call of duty or valour - the dangerous variety James supposed, that would cause either of them to risk their lives, the type of unbreakable bond that only a life-long friendship could provide. It was just as well he thought that Luc was not a member; it would have been too much to worry about Anjelica and Mischa *and* Luc - that would have been his whole world.

He headed for his desk hoping to stem his musings with mental absorption and immersion. The telephone rang out at that moment and startled him; the sound it made broke through the morning like a frightened cry, belting itself out, bleating from unknown origins and issuing fast into the peaceful bedroom.

"Hello?" said a voice, the fizzy line hinted at an overseas connection, James tracked the voice at a million miles per second in his brain; he definitely knew it and his heartbeat kept up with the mental momentum.

"Simon?! Simon is that you? -I hope you are just calling me about the weather," James added.

"I have no choice, I have no time!" Simon spoke hurriedly.

"Simon, don't!"

"Please don't put the phone down! Just listen, I will be as careful as I can, just listen."

The voice -Simon, sounded terrified yet subdued, James had to listen.

"I've done something-"

"-What have you done?" James broke in without thinking, alarmed.

"I've done what we, what '*we*' are not meant to … I've revealed some of us …"

James understood at once, and fought an obstruction in his throat. "How many?" he asked, although he knew the answer, he prayed the number was not higher.

"Three," Simon half whispered, and shame rose up like a sickly tide to taint the simple word, but both of them felt it.

Then a pause in which infinite accusations and howlings could not be uttered, obstructed both men, finally, in fury James choked out besides himself, "Why?!" He was too emotional to regret the question; but an almost palpable silence came back from the other side, vivid with the unsaid.

"You tell me why!" yelled James, but Simon was crying, it was not at all obvious, but James could tell.

"Do I have to say it?" Simon asked quietly.

But this completely threw James, he had not known what to expect as an excuse for this treachery, but it was dawning in him, how utterly stupid he had been.

"Are you trying to tell me, are you trying to say that this ... (he wanted to say murder) this, is because of her ...?"

A pause and then, "Yes," as if closing the doors on a tomb.

Both men hung on to their telephones, wanting to speak, yet stood stunted and gagged.

"But there's more," Simon added, worried again that James would put the receiver down.

But James was reeling, the locks on his inner vault blown open.

"Whatever has happened," James said through gritted teeth, poison infusing his saliva, "it was not worth what you have done!!"

"I know-"

"No you do not know!! You have destroyed everything, possibly for all of us, for what, for what!?" James spluttered.

"For love," Simon whispered but not cowed now, in the sliver of a whisper there was an attack. "But please, James, listen, there is more ..."

Silence.

And then finally, "I'm listening."

"I realised the horror of what I had done as soon as the first went down, I'm disgusting, I know, but James they want more, and I'm on the move. This could be it for me. I am where I was, I am embarrassed to ask … but, you are my only hope."

There was a long pause, too long for Simon, "James, are you there?!"

"I'm coming. Sit tight."

And the line went dead.

It was plain now that during a worldwide embargo on travel, James would have to get to Paris.

Chapter 14 Love

If James had to explain himself to a jury, or to his own members, he would put it thus, as a fairy tale, because that was exactly how it felt:

A long time ago, young James fell in love with a girl named Clara, she was a member, she still was in theory, although he had not heard from her in over two years. She was the grandchild of a founding member as he was, and he'd grown up seeing her pale face, heart shaped like Clara Bow's, she played to that as an adult by keeping short glossy black hair, although he thought that she was infinitely prettier than the actress. It had been heady in the first few years; they had been like lovers in the Resistance, driven by their ideals and bound by their secret world. But James became the leader after his father's death and had to tend to his flock night and day, it was no longer only James and Clara, it was James and all else she felt.

Tired of the resulting solitude, Clara eventually turned to another member for solace, who was young and enthusiastic and as devoted to the cause as James had been, before he had become so serious. Simon had advanced close to the inner sanctum: James, Angelica and Mischa, and grown comfortable with them. James had been travelling the globe consolidating bonds with members and rearranging lines of communication and diversion, as he did all the time. Slowly, Clara had realised that she had lost her lover somewhere in his fierce and determined progress. She'd tried to talk to James, but he promised to listen at another time. Finally, after three years of waiting for his attention, she considered her life and realised that under the stifling cloak of secrecy that they all lived, love had been the only recompense. So she stormed away, one wintry black night, screaming at James even though she was leaving him. He begged her not to, he wept openly and then could not face the truth of it for months; he believed she would come back.

Soon after her dramatic exit, Clara found Simon and took him quickly to bed, she had wanted to knock on Mischa's door, but knew that he would have thrown her out. Simon fell in love with her, as he was in love with the cause, he had been young when his beloved parents had told him everything, and he'd taken the cause to a joyous hopeful heart.

A year passed and James sent Clara love poems, gifts, and enormous bouquets of white roses. He learned about Simon almost immediately, it was his trade after all, but he was not deterred by it; James believed that Simon was a poor pawn in the game and James needed Clara too much to care besides.

After spending a year with Simon, Clara was summoned by James on business, for a report. James knew that he had no other means of holding her attention and was happy to abuse the rules. She came, haughty in stance, looking him straight in the eye, daring him to look back, which he did unflinchingly, and at that moment she felt an enormous undertow, it was unalterable; for she loved him besides her every effort. She said that she had nothing to report, but may have something brewing and would keep him posted. But, in the moment of the business-like discussion, she knew that she was his, and was deeply grateful that it had been decided for her: she was his, and would take him even if he were fat, thin, old, too busy, or unkind, luckily his only vice had been to be too busy. All of this was acceptable because she finally realised as they'd stared each other down, that he in turn, was hers.

She returned home full hearted and jubilant, she had given nothing away, although she had wanted to throw herself at James, to cover his face with kisses. She knew that she had to tell Simon first however, -poor Simon!

She sat Simon down and sank to her knees in front of him, he laughed and asked why she was on the floor and tried to join her there, but she pushed him back up, "I have to tell you something."

"Oh, Clara, you're so dramatic, what's this all about?" He was affable, joking, completely unaware.

"You will hate me." She looked at him unblinking.

"Don't be silly, there is nothing you could do that would make me hate you."

"Yes. There is."

Simon paused; as though a distant alarm was beginning to sound inside him, and she closed her eyes as if preparing for the guillotine.

"I am going back to James."

Simon stopped, frozen, the unexpected had stripped him of every defence, leaving him only a cursory figure in its wake.

"There is more," she added. But now rising and backing away, not wanting to goad him too far ... "I'm pregnant ... I think, just two weeks late, but I know my body ..."

He looked up at her incredulous.

"I am still going," she warned gently, yet now fearing his reaction. "Get away from us Simon, go on a long holiday, just forget we ever existed, I'm so, so sorr-"

And he exploded.

"Sorry!!! Sorry I'm having your child but I am leaving you anyway!? ... I was just a band aid ..." he muttered this last to himself.

At that she ran. They had lived in a cottage adorned by briar roses, now in winter, frosty and transformed into spiky black silhouettes. She ran from there, to the train, right to James' door upon which she banged frantically. He let her in and she clung on to him, still in tears.

He brought her inside and waited until she calmed down, making her sit, while he stood.

"Will you take me back?" she asked him openly, but it was like a challenge.

James laughed while turned away from her face and then said quietly, "Of course I will."

"No. Will you take me back no matter what I've done?"

James knew that it had to be severe, Clara never minced her words and he loved her for it, this would be very serious indeed, but his conclusion was the same.

"Yes."

"I'm pregnant."

James drifted to sit down on the sofa next to her and rubbed his hands over his face and then ran his fingers like spokes through his hair.

"Does he know?" he turned to ask her.

"Yes. I just told him."

"What just before ... just now?"

Clara had streaking tears; he knew that she wasn't heartless, in fact far from it.

"Yes."

"I presume you, we, are we keeping, are we ...?"

She nodded her head.

Surprising as it was, given the potentially dangerous world that James lived in daily, that this was a tolerable drama and he was then able to smile and reach out his hand to stroke her head.

Her face bloomed at his touch under the tears, she felt that she was the luckiest woman in the world and crawled into his arms as he consoled her.

Simon however did not know what had just happened to him. He became very drunk a few days later and called up to them in the snow, in the middle of the night. "Are you both cosy up there!!" he yelled while adding profanities into the empty night air.

James was soon at the front door and ushered him in. He sat him down and made him some coffee. It was remarkable that Simon still displayed loyalty to his leader and said nothing while James unilaterally decided that Simon would drink coffee. Simon took the coffee meekly as if seeking solace from a friend. Finally James spoke, "I'm desperately sorry. It *is* still your baby, you will have full rights, we would never deny you that. But if you wanted to go away, to get away from us-"

"That's what she said!"

"Sshhh. All right. Whatever is good for you. But Paris is available if you want it."

"You can't get rid of me that easily!" Simon shook his head, at a loss with events.

"We don't want to get rid of you Simon. You're still one of us after all."

"I have *nothing* now." He looked at James, as though it were actually a question.

"Yes you do. We're all in this for life; you will always be one of us."

Simon looked away, looking like he was beaten. Surely he had nothing.

That night James put him in a guest room and early in the morning Simon crept out, not wanting to face either of them.

The months progressed and Clara wrote Simon long letters of apology and asked him to be present at the birth; she was adamant not to take his fatherhood away. And by some trick, Simon was consoled, he had lost the love of his life but he was going to be a father, he told his parents who were alarmed by the circumstances but then also settled down to the joy of at least being grandparents, for was it not normal for children to have broken families and step parents in this day and age. And James was a very good stepfather to have, although they would never have openly said that to their son.

The lovers' love grew without time or effort, as though a magical garden; Clara understood James' responsibilities and knew that she actually had everything that he had to give. His ultimate acceptance of her had created for her a fecund reservoir in her heart. For James in actuality, the initial situation

91

had not been ideal, but as Clara was and always had been his sanctuary and he had fought so hard and relinquished all humility to win her back, he did not care that they were having Simon's child, it was just another idiosyncrasy of his life.

After six months, in which James had accompanied her when he could to her hospital appointments and she'd become quite large even for her term served, she had a violent and sudden miscarriage that to this day still could not be explained. It was horrible and bloody and the child had been large enough to be buried, which they did, all three of them. Clara however blamed herself. It was at the funeral, that James saw Simon looking at her, although there was shock and pity in his regard, there was also steel eyed blame. Clara was not slow at all and took the blame to heart instantly. She took it as deep as it would go, James, alarmed, could see where this was heading and after three weeks of her tears and mourning and feeling that she was being punished for what she had done to Simon, she left them both. She wrote them both a letter asking for space, and disappeared. James was devastated, he knew that what Clara believed could destroy her, but he let her go, knowing that as he had been complicit in hurting Simon, he could not help her. She had gone to New York and had barely spoken to him since. In James' estimation, knowing Clara's almost supernatural beliefs, she believed that the child had been lost because of their 'wrong doing', for hurting Simon so much, thus that neither she nor James deserved love, or to love each other. James had resolved to reason with her, but would give her time first; for she had after all lost her child.

Whether it had actually occurred just as this or so dramatically, had become completely irrelevant, for this was how it had been enigmatically staged within James' heart and now just as vividly spun into memory. It was a tale with a beginning, middle and an end, or so he had thought, but now it seemed far from conclusion, as a new gorgon had arisen and more destruction issued from this love affair, which he now had to face.

Chapter 15

For six months the dream was always the same, and now had become more frequent. Under harassed sheets, Simon remembered unwillingly as the dream flooded his inner eyes and mind, as though reminding him of a turning point, of a place and time at which he still could have done the right thing:

There he stood in a very starched white waiter's apron pouring coffee, eyeing the table centrepiece of purple flowers that were sat in an oasis, within which his mobile phone had itself set to record.

"You want me to supply free arms to any country you want to destabilise through civil war, uprisings or unrest?"

"That is precisely what we would like you to do, Monsieur Grimbaud," said the Minister.

"But what would be the reason for us, why?" Michel Grimbaud's grey suit had shadows and reflections upon it, as the hotel restaurant had its red damask blinds pulled down during the day, and so, the purple flowers instead softly punctuated the rouge dimness.

Simon knew that he was not conspicuous as he frequently passed this table, bearing in his hand a large teapot and looking efficient. He had made sure that the event catering company that he helped to run, often leant freelancers to hotels such as these, where so many 'meetings' took place.

"An exclusive contract with the British Government," answered the Minister, and Simon remembered the excited feeling inside him, as his own words sealed the Minister's fate.

The dream faded and her face appeared now, always her face, she never spoke; her silence not only tormenting him, but also admonishing him. Clara was the love of his life, and it was all such a joke. But why after such a triumphant gathering of information, did he turn, did he commit his treachery? He had felt jubilant as he'd taken off his apron that day, finishing quite more than a day's work as a waiter. Perhaps it was the bounty that he held, the recording of the Minister and Michel Grimbaud incriminating themselves, that led him to an unexpected sense of fury. For, he would be sending that bounty to James, and his blood began a slow simmer. It lasted the week, and in Simon's isolation from Clara and from James and Mischa and Anjelica –the friends he thought he had, he felt bitter, and more and more angry; he was the victim and now he had even been exiled. What justice was there in that? A month of the bitterness and hatred grew in him, and then he realised, that he would never be forgiven, or allowed to feel so valued within his secret group again. That this was it for him; he could leave and turn his back on it, and start with nothing, or …

He tried the bitterest Vodka he could find, and he kept with it all night, but there was no dulling his need for justice. James was too smug he thought, too successful, he needed to be brought down a peg, and in that prolonged isolation and then drunken fugue, Simon sought out and dialled the numbers of three Chief Executives in Paris, where three of his fellow members worked. He thought there would be chaos, some uproar and investigation to frighten James; he never imagined the quick and sharp claws of death to come down upon Dora, Elsa and John so fast.

And then they found him. Peter Armstrong himself paid him a visit at home, thanking him for his 'service' to him and his colleagues, and asking if he knew anymore? Peter was clever Simon realised, for he didn't ask Simon *how* he knew what he did, he wanted to milk the cow slowly. Simon asked if he could speak with Peter the next day, and came across as an innocent young man who had found something out, but said that he was very late for work and had to run presently. Run he did, and disappeared within the hour, sinking every moment, knowing the unholy mess that he had created.

Simon had not moved from his new single bed, as he'd moved from dream to waking and back again, the room was small, and had a forlorn hanging tapestry on one side, left over from a more positive tenant no doubt. As he drifted back to sleep, although it was daytime, his mobile phone rang, and in a split second he was sitting upright in bed, waking properly, very, very fast.

"Hello?" Simon answered tentatively

"Simon, it's me."

It was James.

Simon grew excited at once, perhaps freedom and a way out was possible.

"I need to know the names of the people you leaked to. I should have asked you the first time."

There was no safety in James' voice, no soothing tone, only firmness.

"Of course, and I should have given them to you earlier, but it was your home phone, so you know ... Yes, the names are: Peter Armstrong, Armstrong Inc. Michel Grimbaud, Grimbaud Industries, and Dominic Burgess of Axe and Shiffel. It was Peter himself that came to see me, he said it himself that his associates were Grimbaud and Burgess, who were so 'grateful' to me, and I've already told you about Grimbaud and the Minister. I'm beyond sorry, James. Beyond it, I never meant this."

"Keep the protocol," said James and nothing else, and then rung off.

So at least that was something, the 'Protocol' was a café that Simon had to go to at the same time every day; a known extraction point for him, if things should go wrong.

Chapter 16

The rain began mercilessly; it was Thursday evening in class, they would be discussing King Lear, and Luc was particularly looking forward to it as there was talk of acting out some of the scenes.

Mer had chosen her corner to place herself in as Luc tried to catch glimpses of her. That evening however, the weather had finally broken and a sudden chill wind streamed in through the gaping windows so that after a time, the nearest students got up and shut them. The sky turned white with an innocent yet mundane looking blanket of cloud and then as if involuntarily, turned grey, lilac and then a black violet. The classroom was now stripped of its usual gilded splendour but did not turn miserably into an adult version of the local comprehensive, but rose to the occasion of the oncoming storm so that the oddments and canvases strewn about took on the cast of a silhouette, constantly marked with crackling and slithering shadows as the clouds coalesced. The students turned grey and violet themselves, waiting for the inevitable rip and tear of the streaking white flash of lightening and a colossal rumble as if heaven itself was reproaching London town for it's over indulgence of summer. The students and teacher, lulled and cosseted by a summer season so enchanted, sat with hair on end in excitement as if they had never lived through a storm or knew of how it progressed.

Mr Andrews, finally after listening to the crashes of lightning and thunder for a few moments composed himself and returned to reading aloud the scene from King Lear that he was at, looking agitated but not worried about the synchronicity with which the text and reality were echoing each other. In King Lear the players lives were torn apart and the storm scene echoed it rather well, the atmospheric accompaniment that had descended to illuminate his class in violet and flashes of white, seemed to make Mr Andrews chuckle occasionally with pleasure. He could see the alarm and fascination on his student's faces and how they gripped the text books a little harder every time the sky was rent with sound.

Luc saw that Mer turned about each time the loud noises filled the soundless classroom except for the teacher's voice, and found other students doing the same, as if seeking support or affirmation that they were not about to be annihilated by nature, as children do, who cover their ears while their parents reassure them; the students looked to each other and some smiled or looked startled in return, being as supportive as they could. There was once a particularly loud crash that shook them to their boots, all stopped engaging and froze, Mer looked up from her text and saw Luc looking straight at her, concerned, in response she attempted a half smile and he smiled back. Mr Andrews soon drew his flock back in and his cadence and rhythmic delivery of each iambic pentameter and alliterated jewel of Shakespeare's prose gave them comfort in its certainty, as if this was exactly how King Lear was supposed to be experienced; at the edge of one's seat, pondering the nature of heaven, earth and existence.

When it ended all were exhausted the class had felt twice as long and the sky was thickest grey, sheeting down water in spasms and torrents. Not one of them had brought an umbrella and all were preparing themselves for a potential mad dash and a soaking. Mer was wearing an utterly now flimsy looking white cotton dress and open flat Greek sandals and her feet would soon be as if in a river. But Luc saw that she waited as the reluctant class exited, as if she was waiting for him to make this mad dash home with. And so it was true, Mer filed out of the room and Luc followed her. When they got to the precipice, the front doors of the college building, they stood for a moment and then waited for one to jump. It was her and Luc followed, both lightly running, but together, as if making sure no one slipped or was left behind. The rain was impenetrable and set up walls of water one after another to break through, they were sodden in ten seconds. They still had some way to go through the park when Mer slowed down, giving up on any attempt to stay dry, shivering she started to laugh. She laughed aloud and it was a though she was unable to contain it, and so stood still and bent over, when she was ready, she straitened and turned her face up to the sky and opened her mouth to let in the water and then shook her head and did not see how Luc regarded her then, with rapt fascination. They then strolled back, as wet as the rain itself but calm, even though trying not to shake. At their respective front doors Mer thanked him with a brisk wave and hurried inside into her home, not giving Luc a chance to speak. Luc in turn rushed upstairs to his flat, splattering the vermillion carpet in heavy dark drops; pleased with himself for no reason at all.

Chapter 17

Maurice looked at his gun, it was on the table by his side, and was not the only weapon he carried. The young man he was watching, did not go out very much - just to buy groceries, or essentials, and to a café in the afternoon. Maurice himself wondered how this young man had made the Minister so very upset, and Mr Armstrong too. And his methods, pah, pathetic, Maurice now even knew the full name and address of this friend at the telephone company who'd helped him to re-route his phone, though she had done a very good job, as he hadn't been able to hack into it yet, nor was he allowed to get too close to the young man to put a bug in it, he would deal with her later, first he was to just watch this man: Simon. And yet, even though Maurice was quite unimpressed with this current catch, it was still something, that Simon had someone at the phone company, and how could he have known, that so did Maurice; Maurice had someone in every phone company in France, and anywhere else he could squeeze in a contact, and if not that, then of course there are other ways of getting information ... But this man intrigued him, by his sheer lack of gravitas in his dealings perhaps.

This flat opposite Simon's that Maurice camped in, had bleak walls, all the better for Maurice to blend into them as he watched and watched, day after day, wondering what Mr Armstrong was waiting for. It was then that Maurice's phone rang.

"Allo, sir."

"Maurice, we've found her, the girl in the photograph, we know who she is, and we will proceed from here, and we also need to see if she only connects to this Simon, which I doubt ... because she works for the United Nations," the Minister finished.

"Yes, sir, I will keep the watch."

"Good, nothing else yet mind."

"Of course, no, sir, not yet."

"I'll be in touch very soon," the Minister rung off.

Intriguing again, thought Maurice who now watched Simon's windows with a new found respect and scrutiny, he narrowed his eyes, wanting to make sure that he was not being made a fool of by this young man who behaved so stupidly.

Chapter 18

In Christine's mind there were unfilled empty places, to which she was not accustomed. Her habit of continual movement, or seeming infinite dynamism had not been imposed upon her by the circumstance of a haphazard nurturing process, or the result of a manic response to a hidden hurt in the psyche. Christine enjoyed life, or had truly enjoyed life before her impulsive, overcharged joie de vivre had made her cross an essential line, to dash dangerously over the boundaries of her marriage. As Christine, though thoroughly modern, was one of a past generation, of those who were content to enjoy life without a secret undertow of guilt as anchorage.

It was for this reason, for it was as if she had been an innocent in her own unravelling, that her best friend Mer had taken her in. Christine did not mean any harm, Mer and most people felt that it was her appetite for immersion in all that glitters, her keenness to have and to have some more, that endeared her to so many, including Mer; even though it had resulted in her own undoing. Yet, even though Christine's marriage was in jeopardy and her gloomy heart sat now dormant, humbled, wistfully wishing her behaviour undone, she could not undo her own nature; that would have been akin to prising apart an oyster shell with one's bare hands. And so, even with this trial and its resultant wave of guilt that she frenetically, colourfully dammed up, hemmed in by so much activity that she stood giddy with it; she became enchanted by the Nash property, Mer's home. She gingerly walked in to the empty ballroom, her baby in her arms and threw her eyes over the black and white floor and saw it mirrored in a million opalescent flecks as the dormant, giant chandelier blinked at her. It was too lovely, and senselessly bleak for being empty. Instantly she felt irritated and brimmed with ideas that had neither head nor tail, nor detail yet, but bobbed joyfully in mental essence; filling her with a thrill so that her neurons flickered in excitement, knowing that they soon would have delft and precise content. She knew that her mind would shortly be unable to contain the effusive ideas and possibilities that this room alone instilled in her, her heartbeat quickened and thus, knowing that she would be in trouble if she had these thoughts too soon, she tried to force her body to exit the lavish room; but she did not leave.

It had been three or four weeks now that she had been living in Mer's house, Christine's husband was not speaking to her, he came almost every second evening to pick up his baby for a few hours whom Mer had to hand over at the door, he would not even enter the house. Christine wondered if she should be concerned that Mer had not been more vocal, perhaps demanding that Rehan stay and talk to Christine, but maybe that is what Christine had hoped that Mer would have done, perhaps would have done, if she hadn't recently thrown her own husband out.

It was true, that Christine had betrayed her wonderful husband. There was no excuse or reason for it and she wondered if 'thrill seeking' could encompass the answer. But what had she done (!) and moreover, would she do it again? The answer, perversely, would be a resounding, "yes", for it had been in fact a bewitching encounter, that young man's divine face and body had been too beautiful to belong on this earthly plane, and it still felt now as though it had been a haunting experience, although damning. And she knew yet, that it had been an opportunity that would never arise again; but how could she possibly explain that to her husband?

At three o' clock in the morning when she would awake with a start and a sharp intake of breath, she was overwhelmed with grief and remorse, stricken as such, by the lack of light in the dark room. What remedies could she provide she wondered, and an enormous sense of doom prevailed as a tomb door closed upon her heart as the answer: nothing, she knew. Yet she searched for a solution like a desperate mental dance that sent her to the past; where she could not undo it, and also did not regret it, to the present; where she had left her own home, to a terrifying future without her man, her own beautiful man. It had made her cry into the night, but she thought it was best to let him be, to let him calm down, if that were possible before she begged him, or did what she could for his forgiveness.

In the meantime, she worked hard and held her beautiful baby girl who had her father's huge eyes and downright feminine black lashes. Yet, baby Marina's irises were also a gem like green, the same colour as Christine's grandmother's and then her baby's head was crowned once again by her father's soot black hair. So Christine, full of her natural energies in these few weeks, had gone from room to room in that majestically empty house, passing Mer occasionally along the way, who like one of the decorative lamps or even the chandelier stared at her vacantly, and full of potential.

No, it was too valuable a space to waste. She would persist with Mer, although it was going to be challenging; Mer, she could tell was in no state to be pushed too far, it would have to be a slow and stealth like undertaking, an effect of surreptitiously breaking a dam. But then it came to her, as if whispered by an invisible force, like whiplash through the frontal lobe into a vision of her mind's eye. It could begin with a small meal, with the new neighbour and his friend she thought, she had seen them from the window sometimes. It was not a logical choice, not people they already knew, but she saw the picture: candlelight in the kitchen and a hot meal cooked by herself of course, with Mer seated, preened, dressed, and forced to attend. It would be the best start for her Christine imagined. With her plan firmly set in mind, she went about it cheerfully, knowing very well how Mer had reacted to Christine's first suggestion of any type of social entertainment at the property; it had gone down very badly indeed, Mer had frozen solid at the thought, eliciting a cryogenic response to any suggestion of socialisation and comfort as Christine saw it. No, she would make this as inescapable as the sudden vision in her mind, if Mer could forgive

Christine for betraying her favourite cousin, she would surely forgive her for this.

A wild electrical storm had begun, and held Christine's presence at the ballroom window. She looked down at her baby in her arms, and felt grateful that she had not wrecked at least this bond; this warm and soft, languid weight, still loved her back completely. She never knew that her love for her child would be so encompassing; or make her even more driven. The rain was quite torrential, and masked the windows in an engulfing wet drool, she wondered if Mer would be able to find a taxi home from her class in such a ferocious downpour, even though she would have to leave the shortcut though the park if she did so. Christine never imagined for an instant that Mer would walk -but there she was, utterly indecently translucent; her white cotton dress a draped oyster, moist and gleaming, an adornment upon her naked flesh. Christine saw that Mer must not have noticed her own state, as the extreme conditions outside did not allow time for self inspection, yet Mer was walking back as though there was no rainstorm at all, although she could hardly have been able to see through the sheeted torrents of heavenly descent. No, Mer walked untroubled, hair dark and dripping, as did the neighbour man next to her. Even though Mer looked beyond drowned and as though dragged up from the ocean, they both seemed calm yet still aiming assuredly for a drier destination. They appeared unfrightened of the cracks and purple-pink streaks of lightning splitting the sky, so vibrant and in violent tones that one could easily fear being struck down by the sound itself; the noise was all pervasive and Christine's pale stretched hands covered her baby's ears at each rent. Mer had not mentioned that she had spoken to, or knew the neighbour man. At this, Christine drew some delight, now a candle lit in her heart, the neurons came alive and her plan truly begun.

Chapter 19

"We don't have any couriers free right now, surely it can wait an hour," said Gemma abruptly, and put down the phone.

Luc was nearly at her desk but had not turned the corner yet; he slowed instead, and did a U-turn. She'd sounded annoyed under her professional manner; he decided that he could ask her his technical question later. His new plan had been to befriend her, even if it took a long time, for he couldn't befriend Balthazar so easily he thought, so that one day he could find out how they knew his mother; thus currently, he didn't want to ruffle her feathers any further.

He sat back down at his desk but before he knew it, muffled footsteps were thudding closer to him, he turned around and there she was, she had colour in her cheeks, and a look of anger that thank heavens was not directed at him; she took her expression out instead briefly upon the wall in front of them both, it looked back serenely, dove white, and so, as if it had absorbed her wrath, she turned to him and said with a glassy expression, "Luc, please come with me."

Luc followed, more curious than perplexed, what would she tell him now?

"It's time," she said. "Do you think you could pick up a Diplomatic Folder for me?"

"Sure, of course."

"Good."

And she proceeded to write down the address and whom he must pick it up from. Luc glanced at the name, and tried not to gulp.

"Right now, yes?" he asked.

"Yes, Luc, thank you so much, I would do it myself, but we have a joint video call with three heads of state that I have to be present at, just this minute."

Luc nodded, happy to be of any assistance to her, any at all.

On his way out, Luc realised that he had nothing to conceal the deep blue folder in that he was about to pick up, for its journey back; it was too important looking to carry in the hand, not unless one had a chauffeur driven car at work, as Gemma did. So he dashed to the communal kitchenette and dug out the best plastic carrier bag he could find; next time he would be more prepared and decided to buy a leather fold-over sling bag for the job.

He made his way to Mayfair, the address was strange: The Devonshire Club … it didn't sound like a government building.

On entering, Luc stated his purpose rather than his name.

"I'm here to pick up something from Minister Sebold … the Under-Secretary of Defence."

He was immediately led through various dark oak passages and green velvet curtained rooms. Finally, he was left in front of a door and the usher just departed, as if Luc knew what to do next. So he took a moment, there was nothing, silence, so he knocked on the door.

"Come in."

Luc turned the door handle.

"Ah. Hello. You have come from …?"

"From Gemma -I mean the Department of-"

"Yes, yes. Thank you. Here-" the Minister handed him a blue folder, not that thick, but just as important looking as Luc thought it would be.

Luc stood for a moment, not sure if he was supposed to sign anything.

"Is there anything else?"

Luc flushed, "Oh, no. Thank you." And he turned around to leave, glad he had the folded up plastic bag in his pocket.

After he exited the room, he heard something inside the Minister's room that he'd just left, like a door opening, and then footsteps inside, but right in front of Luc was another usher-like looking employee of the establishment, blocking his way with an enormous trolley covered over with a sheet, which through the gaps Luc could see was full of dirty plates. This lingering at the door had kept Luc's hand upon it a few seconds longer than normal so that it had not closed properly, and so had left open the sliver of a gap.

The usher-waiter with the trolley then spoke, "I'm so sorry, sir, I'll sort this out in a jiffy,"

He then bent down at his end, down to one corner of the trolley and started fiddling with one of the wheels, which was making odd clicking and sliding noises. So Luc stood waiting jammed up against the door and meanwhile took out his crumpled plastic bag and put the document folder inside. But then he heard something, the waiter was still almost kissing the carpet, very busy with the noisy broken wheel and seemed to look as though underneath the trolley.

"Have you spoken with Maurice?" said the Minister.

"Yes," said another man. (He must have been beyond another door inside the room, thought Luc).

"So you know that he's busy, tied up in Paris, can your men in New York do what I need? I hate this embargo, one has to constantly rely on new people, rather than use who we know."

"My people in New York will do exactly as we ask, sir, as *you* ask."

"All right, so Clara Elizabeth Day will be attending a Gala tonight in New York, you need to get her then, there will be lots of people and lots of exits."

"Yes, sir, and then …"

"And then you get what we need to know, beat it out of her if you have to … but keep her alive."

"Uh … She does work for the U.N., sir …"

"I don't care!" the Minister sounded enraged. Then he calmed down quickly. "Don't worry, whatever investigation there will be, I will give you every resource to tidy it up."

The waiter suddenly shifted his head and looked up at Luc from his strange angle below and grinned. It happened very quickly, and as the waiter stood up pleased with his repair job, Luc flattened himself against the door for him and the trolley to pass. Then, Luc almost ran to leave the building.

Outside, he thought fast, yes, he had an idea. Instead of taking just the tube where everyone could see what he was doing, he decided to take a bus part of the way, even if it took him out of the way. For he very much knew a Clara Elizabeth Day, who worked for the United Nations ...

On the bus, he made his way upstairs and to the back, he was very pleased that the raggedy plastic bag that the folder was in looked like it concealed things of very little importance and also, would partially conceal what he was up to. Seated and hunched over he tried to open the folder while still in the bag, slowly he slid up the few pages that were there. There, in black and white was a large photo of Clara -the love of James' life. So too all her work history, addresses in New York, in London, and phone numbers as well as medical records(!) travel history, income, the list went on. Finally as well, there was a note to Gemma, it said:

We've found the girl, you know what to do.

Luc was perplexed on so many levels that he had to force himself to calm down; the blood pounded in his ears so he tried to focus on the most pressing problem at hand. Then suddenly, as he looked out of the window as the bus passed a shop, he rushed to put the documents and folder back as they were, while at the same time getting up and pressing the bell a few times to stop the bus, and then hurried down the stairs. The bus came to a halt at the next stop, which was not too far from where he had to go. Soon, he had arrived at a downbeat looking mobile phone shop, the type that looked shabby and a bit suspicious for their very low prices.

He immediately asked the assistant for a Pay As You Go Sim card and handset, the very young man pointed to a few, trying to be helpful, Luc glanced at them at lightning speed, and chose something very low budget, with no extras like GPS, or even the internet. Pleased that the shop assistant did not try and engage him in discussion or try to show off more accomplished phones to him, Luc, with a newly assembled and ready phone in hand, rushed out onto the street, and found a grubby bench to sit upon. It faced the road and hundreds of noisy cars and vans passed him endlessly. He thought of what to write, slowing his breathing on purpose to help him think.

YOU MUST NOT GO TO THE GALA TONIGHT. Get out of New York, pack everything you need, DON'T go home again. Go somewhere where no one can find you. Write down this number, destroy your current phone, and store it in the new one you get. Do not use your name or credit cards for anything you buy. Disappear, please. Wherever you are, get out now. You are in grave danger. From someone who wishes you well: The one with Sandy Hair, not the Chestnut, and not the Blond.

This is what he wrote in a text message to Clara, and then after having memorised her mobile number on the bus, immediately sent it. He finally tried disoriented, to make his way back to work. Then his mind turned to, or rather turned on Gemma, so what did it mean: 'you know what to do'? He would watch her like a hawk from now on, all feeling of friendship with her dying a quick and violent death.

He reached his office building and pulled the folder out of its crumpled carcass of a bag; so he could look as Gemma did as she entered the building holding the folders.

No one looked at him, no one had guessed that he had broken every rule, his contract and probably the law, and as he made his way to her empty desk, he laid it there and wondered, what other secrets her station could possibly contain?

Through the rest of the day he kept feeling for his new phone in his suit jacket pocket, it had not hummed or rung or answered in any way. By 6pm he broke out in a sweat, and even said a prayer for Clara's safety, she would have got the message early in the morning her time, plenty of time to make plans and escape the Gala. So he went to the Men's toilets, and sent another message:

Please let me know if you are all right. And if you have succeeded?

Then made his way back to his desk. Nothing happened, no answer, so he got up abruptly and left for home.

He knew there would be no signal on the tube, so he eagerly took out his new extra phone as soon as he exited the Underground, but no, nothing. He began to panic now, so that he did not notice the front door before his own one open, or the fact that Christine had stepped out; she held three red ribbon tied scrolls in her hand, and as Luc stopped, she gave them to him.

"Please come and have dinner with us, next Saturday, and bring your two friends that I've seen you with sometimes," she said, smiling graciously.

Luc realised that his mouth was open, and then he managed somehow to respond, "Oh, thank you. Yes, yes of course, Thanks for these," he nodded, even smiled and waved them at her as he passed, his door key gripped now painfully in his other hand, as though getting home would solve everything; yet, it would give him privacy at least.

Upstairs at his flat the heat clawed and cloyed at him, and he stripped off his very good suit haphazardly, strewing the garments where they fell. Down to his underpants he grabbed a t-shirt, making a mess of the pile in the cupboard and put it on. Then he retrieved the new special phone, and placed it on the coffee table, and stared at it as if it was an object that could tell his fate. Suddenly, before his eyes it beeped loudly, that was all, but he fell upon it. A message read:

All right. Safe. Thank you.

Luc held the phone to his chest. He had done it, and he thanked the stars.

Chapter 20

It didn't take Clara long to throw everything she valued into a large suitcase, her precious books were in her Maida Vale flat in London anyway. She had already run to a shop and bought a new and cheap mobile phone, she'd called in to work and said she had a doctor's appointment, and had rented a car under a false name and had a standby false driving license. She was set to go, but the message- it hadn't been James' or Sir John's style at all, they surely would have signed their own names to it, but not if something had happened, and the mystery texter had not asked her for her new location to be, and moreover, her gut just knew he was to be trusted. But the final sign off, from the one with 'sandy hair', she was baffled. She just couldn't work it out, but felt that it was a man and not a woman.

She was ready at last, knowing that hopefully she was still safe here at present as it was the Gala that she had been warned off from going to, and so she rushed away from her apartment of two years, with even her black evening dress that she was due to wear tonight tucked away inside the suitcase; she was not going to leave that behind as she knew she most likely would never see this apartment again.

In truth, her life had never turned cloak and dagger like this before, but it was as though her instincts were ready for this, and so she drove, and drove on, to New England, and the remotest guest house she could find …

Chapter 21

Night was falling; James and Mischa were in Mischa's car, a sleek pale blue Mercedes, the headlights streaking the road as they coursed down a quiet motorway, on their way to the border, the docks: Dover.

James had not spoken yet, not with what he really had to say, he was waiting until they had left London far behind him, as though the countryside would manage better the horrible information that he had to share. Finally the time came, as they passed the darkened quiet fields of green and the sleeping trees.

"I had a call, Mischa."

"Oh, yeah?"

"From Simon, in Paris."

"OK ...?"

"Mischa," James sighed, he was glad he was not driving.

"What is it?" Mischa quickly glanced at his friend and then back at the almost empty stretch of road, as darkness grew heavier upon the fields around them.

"He said it was him."

"Him, what?"

"He said it was *him*," James muttered quietly.

"What?! ... So he phoned you and what, confessed?! ... But Simon? ..." Mischa made a face, "why would he?" Mischa now looked very confused.

"Because, of her."

Silence as Mischa computed, much faster than James had, what this meant. "He wants to destroy us all, because she, you ... broke his heart?"

"Apparently." James was pleased that Mischa was so quick on the uptake. "But he's sorry now, and they're after him, the people he ratted us out to, so he's in hiding and needs, can you believe it, my help."

"What will you do?"

"I have to get to Paris, and get him out. Hence this little field trip."

"And then?" Mischa quickly glanced at James again.

"And then I make him disappear."

"What?!"

"No, Mischa, no. Not that. New identity."

Both men said nothing, the dark fields and odd farmhouses flashed passed their vision constantly.

Mischa then sighed, "Will that be safe?"

"It has to be … what would you have me do?" James now looked at Mischa.

"Yes," Mischa looked ahead, "You're right, it has to be. Who else knows, just you? … This is a disaster."

"I'll tell Jelly and Sir John as soon as we get back," said James.

"Let's just focus on tonight," added Mischa, his knuckles firmly clenched on the steering wheel.

As James glanced at Mischa briefly, this man always by his side, he felt that it was another world that Mischa had stepped into at the age of 16, some strange world that locked him in as by the vines of an evil forest and bound him tight, everlastingly, with such secrets that he could never ever come back from them, not that he'd seemed to want to. And Mischa was himself a secret, as most people would never know the truth about him; that his mother was Indian and his father English and Anglo-Saxon; by the manner that Mischa appeared to others, there was no trace of the former. He had round soft grey-blue eyes, in a face that was as though the result of when a cherub grew up into an unmistakable angel, there was no other way to explain it, he had rich chestnut brown hair but when one knew of his lineage, only then could one see that his skin colour passed as English white, but was never quite pale enough. He knew fluent Gujarati and Hindi and no one could guess, so he liked to eavesdrop on the street, on the tube, when people never suspected that he was listening and moreover that he could understand. James could see that how Mischa looked had affected his life, it wasn't that he was just handsome, he had discerned that when Mischa had compared his fate to his darker skinned cousins, that judgemental or quietly racist people never made any assumptions that Mischa wasn't 'English' or that he may be Asian in part and so they gave him favour and took him wrongly to be 'on their side'. Mischa's parents were divorced and his mother lived well in her intellectual set, in a large house in Hampstead and his father had gone back to work in New York after the split, seeing Mischa when he could, encouraging him to go to Cambridge as his father had and his father before that; both of them never knowing of the secret that Mischa kept. And so it was another time when they had all lived before in Berkshire, before Mischa's sixteenth year, where in his friend's home Mischa finally learned of something that took his life tumultuously to where it was now. It was a dreamtime that past, for both of them James was sure, in which there where barbeques and trips to the beach in France to see Luc and his beautiful mother, who now, was also long gone.

Soon Dover approached and Mischa snaked the car slowly through the roads that lead to the ferry ports, James took out his camera and started to take pictures. Instead of lines of lorries waiting to leave they saw giant ships in port, dull and quiet, yet one of them had life, there were lights on, and much activity on the ground where there where white tents and people wearing white jackets and masks. Doctors, thought James, and lots of security too, there was a series of these white tents joined together by long stretches of tent corridor, James imagined, for swabbing and quarantine, that sort of thing. They lingered, the two of them, but thought against getting any closer, soon, James had gathered enough information, and they edged back and away, back to London.

After James had returned that night and called Sir John with the news about Simon, Anjelica standing by his side, he also explained his need to now get to Paris to him, knowing the difficulties at the ports. Sir John listened and informed him that the only way was through some sort of diplomatic channel, but that he would do his best, as James knew he would. Sir John had been his father's best friend.

The next day dawned on him like a burden, he had much to take care of, and yet he was to go to dinner at Luc's, so too Mischa and Anjelica. Should they all cancel he thought, but then, no, first of all, Luc was a great friend to all, secondly, if they were being watched, it would look well to have normal social engagements, and anyway brooding alone at home on a Saturday night would not transport him magically to Paris.

They arrived simultaneously, James, Anjelica and Mischa, all very much on time for Luc, perhaps not wanting to spend their Saturday night alone either. Anjelica had even bought Luc a small bunch of flowers, which she knew he would appreciate.

At the door outside his flat, after they had climbed the always dark staircase, Luc stood waiting, and was not as was usual rummaging in some recess, whilst leaving the door open for them.

He greeted them with a new energy, ushering them inside.

"Right, first thing, and I'm sorry about this, Jelly," said Luc and handed Mischa and James each a red ribbon tied scroll.

They were all still standing and began to unfurl the papers.

"It's an invitation?" James asked.

"Yes, I'm sorry, Jelly, they haven't asked you, because I think they haven't seen you around, but it's for dinner next Saturday next door, and I've sort of already said yes. Is that OK?"

Nobody spoke.

"Um, I guess so …" said James, a quick look exchanged between him and Mischa just before, to confirm that this was the best course of action.

"Good, great, make yourselves comfortable, James, can you just come and help me in the kitchen a sec," said Luc, while already heading off in its direction.

James thought that Luc was behaving quite out of character, the normal Luc would have spent a lot longer talking about those scroll invites.

In the kitchen, there was a fair amount of disorder, but a green salad had been made, some baguettes lay to one side, and some steaks wrapped in paper stood ready on the counter near the frying pan.

"How are you doing? Luc asked him.

"Fine, how are you? Work OK?"

"Yes all fine, just wondered, I know it's random, but I was just worried about you and never really hear you mention Clara at all, sorry if it's a hard subject, but I thought we should talk about it. Does she ever contact you?" Luc asked.

"… Not really, it's been two years she's been away, I know where she is, but that's it really. What's brought all this on?"

"Nothing, nothing, just you know, looking out for you, you haven't said anything about a love life, and you never told me the latest on her."

"No, I guess not."

"Can I ask, I mean, I saw her growing up, we all hung out, and you were obviously very close until quite recently, I know it's a weird question, well she was quite fiery, did she get into trouble ever?"

"Trouble?"

"I guess not, I was just curious about her character, to try and help figure this out with you," added Luc.

"Fiery yes, big emotions yes, but never she got into any trouble, not that I know of."

"OK, well I'm just philosophizing, you know me, sorry about that."

"It's quite all right," said James. This was too odd a question from Luc, especially in the times his group were in, *-but it's Luc*, said a voice in James head, and he did say weird things sometimes.

It was an odd dinner, on the one hand Luc was busy with his ingredients an entertaining presence as ever, although he too seemed weary today. James liked being here; Luc's home was always a neat version of a mess and bursting with curious items. James noticed the photograph of Beatrice alone without her husband Vincent, who James believed was still in their small beach front home in France. It was hell to lose one's mother James knew this, but Luc had been especially blessed with Beatrice, a friendly and warm human being with enough individuality to command respect from many sorts. James recalled one of Luc's stories whereby Beatrice and the family had been at Stonehenge during the summer Solstice many years ago; as the druids joined in a circle, Beatrice had approached them and asked if she could join too and she had been very welcome. This was part of a collective bric-a-brac of family tales that James had of the Avium family, and he missed her deeply too.

Luc had draped a deep orange throw over his miserable grey sofa and red ones over the smaller seats. Sitting there James felt comfortable, as if the colourful room's embrace was enough to shield him from who he really was. The others too sat easily about on the creaking squashy chairs, not knowing how relieved they would feel to be there. There was a strong and invasive aroma of frying steak now as they listened to Luc whirr about his little kitchen, occasionally there was also the sound of a plate crashing, this too was normal they thought. Anjelica was playing with some sort of rock that she had picked up from the coffee table, rolling it about in her palm, Mischa was doing nothing and just staring into space, after a few minutes he rose abruptly and went to the kitchen, offering to lend Luc a hand, then there was the sound of sweeping and crackling and tinkling glass as it was scraped along the floor. The men's voices were muted, coming up like warm and deep tones through the cooking sounds of frying and boiling and water gushing forth from the tap.

James began to feel a type of grief, for he was an imposter; never had he been of this world, not since he had known his family's secret and their cause and that had been also when he became sixteen. He wished he could wholly participate in what seemed like pedestrian concerns, such as how one's day had been at work, or the intrigue of one's love life, not however face such facts like they all possibly faced assassination. He shook his head, he must be fatigued and over dramatizing things, a small voice inside tried to state, that he was not.

In the midst of James' uncomfortable reverie Luc and Mischa suddenly emerged triumphant from the kitchen, bearing as many differently coloured plates as they could manage at once. There was the aromatic fried steak, buttered asparagus, roasted tomatoes, the salad now tossed with spiky vinaigrette, the few sticks of French bread and bottles of red wine. The smell of hot delicious food to an empty stomach dug into the pit of his, but James smiled.

After dinner they drank and sat about, and listened to the music that Luc played them, that had a range as eclectic as his acquisitive tastes. It was later on when Luc was in the kitchen with James and doing the washing up, that Luc said again, "Wouldn't it be good if Clara came back home, for your relationship I mean, is there no way she can come home?"

It was a bolt of a question, but James did not show his uneasiness, "I don't know … I guess working for the U.N. she maybe could come home, as they're transporting relief planes the news is saying, and also some important people and diplomats here and there, to sort the global mess out." James had answered with the truth, but now thought that Luc was telling him something; James knew Luc too well and conniving wasn't his game.

"So, you think she should come home?" James asked him with a smile, "for me."

"It would be nice I think, the world's pretty screwed up right now, this embargo and what next, what if God forbid the U.S.A has a breach with the disease, better if she's here, no? So her work could let her come ..."

"Yeah it would be better, you're right," said James, his mind computing fast. As they both made their way back to the living room, James concluded that Luc must be aware of some plans at work, and became worried, for wouldn't Gemma and Sir John have informed James if there was any trouble set for New York? The ideas didn't leave James' mind alone, but one thing was also certain: Clara was now also incessantly in his head again.

After he left Luc's that night, it was hard to sleep for James, although if he could, he would not sleep again for a very long time. An hour after retiring, he woke pierced by a vision, alone in the dark wrapped in his crushed and unhappy sheets, his heart flickered briefly with the image of Clara, but she looked on at him as though through an impenetrable veil; and it took some deep breaths before he could fall asleep again.

Chapter 22

Luc was apprehensive as he entered the Devonshire Club once more, this time he was more practiced at reception, with new smart fold-over bag ready, but he hoped the pickup would be quick, he knew this Minister was a corrupt man, and also that their latest prey, Clara, should have escaped them. Luc broke into a sweat as he approached the door to the Minister's room, but how could they find out that it had been Luc who saved her? He hoped not, and anyway what choice had he had?

He knocked on the door, despite every nerve in his body wanting to turn around and walk away. It's all right he told himself, there is still some law left in this country ...

"Come in."

Luc entered, trying to look as green as he had the first time -but it didn't work.

"Ah, Mr Avium ... Come in. Please sit down."

Luc did as he asked and sat down in the chair across the desk from him, wondering how the Minister now knew so well his last name.

"Ah, you new recruits, you'd be surprised how many of you go down the same route." He then opened a laptop, turned it to face Luc, and pressed a button for it to play a video.

It seemed to be a replay of some grainy CCTV, and there was Luc at the back of a bus, looking at a government classified file. Of course, London buses often had cameras now, but he never thought they would have tracked him down this fast; they must truly have been sore about Clara's disappearance. The film continued and showed him leaving the bus, but then there was no more, thank God, no more of what he did next. There were often cameras on the street, mounted high upon building corners, but sometimes they malfunctioned, Luc with every fibre was banking upon this.

"Why did you suddenly get off the bus?"

Luc thanked his stars again -they didn't know.

"I realised that I was going in the wrong direction, I wanted to get off and walk to the tube."

"I see. You realise how much trouble you are in?"

"Yes, sir." (But hopefully not as much as Luc imagined).

"I do understand," the Minister drawled, "it's just too tempting sometimes, these folders, but you have signed all sorts of Official Secrets Acts you know."

"I know, sir, you're right it was stupid curiosity, a really foolish mistake."

"A mistake that will cost you your job, and any job you ever wanted again in government."

Luc said nothing.

"However ... I can see that you're very new, and these things do happen, so I have an idea ... maybe you can help me ... and this can all go away."

"Sir?"

"I want you to keep your eyes and ears open at your office, there is a subversive group that I believe has penetrated that office, I can't tell you what they do, but just keep a look out for any funny information, you know? Things that don't fit. Specifically I want you to keep an eye on your boss. Come come, don't look so shocked, it's a great deal I'm giving you, better than well, treason ... I've left your new job still intact for you and that's something."

Luc was numb. "... Thank you, sir, yes ... I'll do my best."

"Good," the Minister said, very pleased with himself, and at last he allowed Luc to leave, with of course another document folder to take with him. "I trust of course, that we will not have the same problem again," he said as he handed it over.

Luc shook his head.

He could not believe that he had got away with it, somewhat, however, now it seemed he was on this man's radar, and he realised was being blackmailed by him by his possession of that incriminating CCTV video. At least he didn't know that Luc had saved Clara. So was Clara part of this so called 'subversive' group Luc wondered? But then he considered the Minister's methods: violence, potential murder and now blackmail, and so was not sure if Clara was at fault at all.

On deciding that he was in a fair amount of trouble, and so too Clara, Luc came up with a new plan, one even less graceful, but hopefully successful. He did not stray on his way back to his office, he came back diligently, in and through past the security gates, and then before heading upstairs, a quick left turn, to a set of Gentleman's toilets.

No one blinked an eye at this. He locked himself inside the cubicle, and looked about one last time for any cameras. He took the papers out of the document bag, and once again his mouth fell open. For there inside, was a large picture of Simon Hughes, who Luc knew to be an ex-lover of Clara's. The typed note this time said:

Another route of investigation: Simon Hughes.

Also here is the number of my Associate, if you should ever need any assistance in your investigations, his name is Maurice.

Luc looked at the mobile number given for this man, and noticed that it had a French pre- code. Luc took out his phone and stored the number, he gave it the name: A, for Associate.

Now convinced and perplexed that Simon was in trouble as well as Clara, he considered what to do. It was interesting that no other details had been given for Simon as there had been for Clara, just a name and a photo. He couldn't think at that moment, but he thought it best to leave the cubicle and head upstairs.

There at her desk was Gemma, and she looked at him a little longer than he expected as she took the file from him.

"All, all right?" she asked him then.

"Oh yes, fine." What could he say, he wanted to ask her so many questions, but he was in enough trouble already, and she seemed to work for this Minister, so Luc smiled instead, a smile so warm as to make her forget where he had just been, that they both knew was a strange location if nothing else, and what Luc could possibly, really know about it.

Chapter 23

Why is dawn so cold in England? No matter what the season it feels the same; as if the breaking of day has its own stasis in time, and feels cold because it is not used to life yet, as it stands between now and the past. In those few displaced moments, all of time and its possibilities can be felt and yet, also as a beginning like all others; it beckons. If you were outside amongst only leaf dense trees, green grasses and cold air as James was, it could even feel as though it was ancient Britain upon whom dawn was breaking; as nature braced Herself, ready to begin in bleak pale white skies and quiet chills, yet self-assured, creating the feeling of a pagan past; so much quieter and devoid of machines and yet bristling alive, with true power, potential and life.

From a distance a hulking figure walked closer but in a steady manner. As he came even closer, James sat down on a dewy bench and waited.

"Good morning, James."

"Good morning, Sir John."

"Well, what can I do for you lad?" he asked kindly.

"I know you know that I need to get to Paris and soon, but there's something else."

"Oh yes?"

"I want Clara home."

"James, you know we can't let our personal feelings intrude on things …"

"I know that, Sir John, something strange happened the other night, you know about Luc and how close we are, we had an odd conversation, and I know him too well. He intimated that Clara should come home, that the world was not a safe place at the moment. Did he stumble upon something at work? Something he's not allowed to tell me, that you of course can?"

Sir John looked confused. "M'boy, the only thing that Luc would be allowed to see would be trade reports and analyses, I honestly don't understand."

"Well, I suppose he did say that he wanted her to be back in London to help what's left of my relationship with her …"

"So, then maybe you're being a bit-"

"Paranoid. Yes, I of course considered it, but also that he was right, especially with our breach. I want her home, Sir John, look at this way, I won't be able to think as clearly if she weren't."

Sir John considered him, and then nodded. "I'll get her back, I'll find a way."

"Thank you, thanks for understanding. I didn't want to do this over the phone, it sounds, you can see … selfish."

"James, say no more, I do understand, I've been married for 35 years, and I've *wanted* to be."

"Thank you," said James again while looking straight ahead. "She won't like it you know, she'll be furious."

"Would it stop your decision?"

"No."

With that Sir John was about to leave when James said, "Oh one last thing, once again as I requested since you told me he got the position, please keep Luc away from things that could connect with us, I know you disagree, that you think he would be a good asset, a good support for me even if not in the group, but I want you to keep him away."

"Very well, but, I may have acted against your wishes slightly, I've given him permission to be an official courier, I thought it could help us generally in some way, I'm sorry, but I still think he could be helpful."

"Luc is not to be 'used' in any capacity, please understand me, Sir John."

"I do understand, but I think in your youth that you do not, that we need to create resources were we can-"

"Our friendship is not a resource."

"No, that is too crude, but I saw you as boys, as Mischa is to you, so is Luc. I *know* this, I cannot unknow it. I'm sorry old boy that I made him a courier and I'll try and keep him away from our side of things."

"Thank you … I do understand, you know, what you're trying to say about Luc, I've thought of it myself so many times. But he's an adult now; he wouldn't take to our world."

"You sure? You never know."

"Maybe, I don't want him to have too."

"That, I understand too well. Well then. Take care m'boy." Sir John rose and then nodded to James as he set off, back towards his humming Daimler that was ready for him in the cold early morning light, quietly alive in the distance.

As James rose to leave in the other direction, he digested what he had just set in motion: Clara's return. Oh dear, she would kill him, but he would enjoy even that. If her fury was all that he had of her, then he would happily take it, and his heart leapt to his mouth in pure excitement. As he walked through the park, morning was shaking off dawn's dubious stake in current reality, now everything was firmly present, and the colours brightened; it was summer after all.

Chapter 24

Luc had spent a tense few days, every day he wondered what the Minister actually wanted from him, and if he would be grabbed off the street, abducted and then meet Clara's planned fate. Nothing as such had happened, and he drew strength from this, but he knew he had much to solve, it was only a matter of time before the Minister would do something else, or ask for more, of that Luc was certain. So now he not only needed to know how Balthazar and Gemma knew his mother, but also what kind of trouble Clara and Simon where actually in, and moreover if Gemma was indeed in league with that evil Minister. Luc laughed openly at his desk at the incredulity of his position, he'd only been in this new job a short while, and look at the mess. He went back to looking at his monitor as some colleagues had glanced his way as he laughed. Instinctively he felt in his side jacket pocket for the extra phone, he did this many times a day and also peeked at it; to see if Clara had left another message, the phone had become his talisman of sorts, as though his way of keeping her alive. No, he didn't want to just sit here, and his plan to make good friends with Gemma seemed more appealing than ever, so he rose, a report he'd completed in hand, and then he also grabbed his latest homework from his class: a copy of Chéri by Collette.

As he ventured nearer Gemma's desk he felt that the office always had an energy of its own; no matter how Luc was feeling before work, once he entered, the place was like a functioning fog, an enclosed world. The soft white pristine walls exhibited not only dim and grey shadows but also possessed an echo of the deep flesh colours of the carpet, its burgundy flashed palely all about them; Luc liked it, but it was also unsettling.

There she was. She had her head down, staring intently at the document that she was reading. But when Luc's padded footsteps although soft alerted her of someone's presence, she looked up, eyes wide, "Luc?"

"Oh sorry, didn't mean to startle you." He looked at her but with concern, for she was white as a sheet and her voice shook ever so slightly. And then she smiled warmly at him, warmer than she ever had, it was very maternal, he was glad to smile back. Yet, simultaneously as she did so her hand he noticed fanned out gently but completely on top of the document before her, to try to cover it. Although she held his gaze, Luc did not make the situation worse by looking at the desk, he obliged instead and kept his eyes with her ragged ones as she gracefully slipped from behind her desk to stand in front of it, closer to him. "Is that for me?" she asked, one arm outstretched.

"Yes, it certainly is." He handed her his report.

And to his surprise she then asked, "Are you well? ... I hope you're settling in well, I see the books on your desks sometimes, is it for recreation, or are you studying?"

Luc flushed. "Yes, I'm on a course, an evening course, he held up his copy of Chéri, oh look I'm really sorry about leaving the books on my desk-"

"No, God no, it's not a problem. It's lovely. I was just curious; I think most of the young women in the office are, really."

"Well, I just like to have the books handy to read when I can, like at lunch, you know. Have you read it?"

"Don't worry, Luc, I have yet to catch you 'reading on the job', and yes, I have read it. So beautiful and sad." And she smiled again.

Yet her face yet looked stricken still behind the friendly veneer; he wished he could console her for whatever had made her sad, but it was too soon, such intimacy would take time yet to build. He had nothing to do now but leave, his own eyes burning to look down at her desk, at what she had hidden from him.

Instead, as he padded away he added, joking quietly, "I'm going to hide the books."

"Don't you dare, the ladies will be devastated," she quipped back and turned to return, to the furtive item on her desk.

It was more than a touch paper that had been lit. For what could be contained on a piece of paper that could shake Gemma into a stricken self? He stopped walking and looked about him, the quiet whirr of machines and gentle hubbub of voices was just the same, the room contained him, but he began to realise that he did not contain the room very well; it encapsulated but did not allow any mastery, possession or authority.

Back at his desk again he began to think methodically about how he would go about finding the truth, without: a)losing his job, or b)committing any form of treason and going to prison, and c)alerting the Minister any further of his activity. He was not going to burgle Gemma or Balthazar's filing cabinet (not yet, perhaps he thought uneasily), thus left was continuing to look inside the document bags he couriered for information, and then only surreptitious chance; if Gemma read frightening documents at her own desk, then that was his best opportunity. So the most he could attempt in his mission in the office was some very quick leaning over a desk, still, he thought, it was better than nothing. He looked at his copy of Chéri, and did not put it away in the drawer.

In his mind he saw it again, the image of her stretched hand fanned out like steely knives flat upon the document, it was a desperate act, and foolish, he wore glasses; he couldn't have read it from that distance at all.

Such thoughts stayed with him all through the day even when he had arrived home, where he went to his window and looked down upon the street; as usual there was nobody there, an empty summer. He wondered what his neighbours were doing, and then remembered that he had dinner with them on the coming Saturday; he had agreed without thinking, mostly to get rid of Christine at the time, and so he thought of Mer, and then her downcast face came to him, and he couldn't imagine her enjoying an indulgent meal.

With a jolt, he grabbed his keys and headed downstairs towards the garden, he was fatigued, just fed up of the extreme stress of the last few days, he took of course the Clara-phone with him as well as his own, and his copy of his book. He liked the swooping dark bannistered stairs and seeming absence of neighbours. He reached the French doors and looked in his well-practised manner to his right, to see if any of them were there.

They were not in the garden; Luc went off anyway to find a seat. He chose an old cast iron chair, definitely made for a lady and sat and massaged his temple by his favourite water feature; where small statues of forlorn mermaids looked about in constant distress or confirmed ecstasy. Little fish swam about, underneath the sound of water trickling into itself. Even in such a mystery as he knew he was in the midst of at work, he still strangely now thought of her, Mer, as if she had slipped into his mind through a back door while he'd been so anxious; even though they'd never spoken, the idea of her was like a relief, a place where not Clara nor Simon or the Minister or Gemma could touch, or sully.

Chapter 25

"Hello, Larry?"

"Clara, where the hell have you been? What's happened to your phone?!"

"I'm sending in a doctor's note, Larry, I'm so sorry, but I'm too sick to work, they're running tests, it might be Mono (she thought glandular fever in her head) And don't worry they don't think it's *that* disease."

"No, of course, thank God," said Larry, Clara's boss. "But it's not that, I've had a call from London, they need your help, some advice with your area: Post Disaster Coordination, it's the Department of International Cooperation."

"Aha," said Clara, now frowning. "What do they want exactly?"

"Well, they want you there sunshine, getting you on a plane and everything, I know you're special missy, but so do they, and they've politely requested your help ... I don't want to turn down the British government ... but if you're sick-"

"I'll call you back Larry." Clara hung up on her boss abruptly. She then looked at this second mobile phone that she had just bought for today to call into work; the New England trees rustled with a strong ocean breeze beyond her window.

Her fingers then dialled for London.

"Hello?"

"Sir John, I'm sorry if I wasn't supposed to call you, but what's going on?"

"What? Clara? Is that you?"

"Yes, Sir John."

"Where are you?" he asked firmly.

"I'm ..." she hesitated. "Sir John, did you call my office?"

"Yes I did, child, we need you back, urgently."

"So did you send me that message? Was it you?"

"What message? Clara, you're alarming me what's happened?"

"And why do you want me back, is this one of James' ideas?"

Sir John was very firm now, "It is not. We have a situation. Get home, and where are you?"

"I'm in New England."

"Good, get on this plane-" He proceeded to give her an address of a private airfield and departure time; it was in five hours' time. "I will call your work and say it's all been sorted out."

"Thank you, Sir John."

"Oh and, Clara, don't go home, go to this address ..." He rattled of a different address that was also in London.

And ominously with that, she knew was heading home of sorts and yet still unclear about the mystery man who had no doubt now, saved her.

*

There were a few official looking people on the UN plane with her, one or two she could recognise from afar, they were not to land on the mainland, but the Isle of Wight, for disease control reasons. Clara was not looking forward to what she would find there, so she tried instead to sleep, incarcerated as she was by her flying metal airship she could do nothing else; but she kept her new phone with her, with her saviour's number the only one stored.

Soon enough they landed, and it was worse than she expected, white tents, swabs, blood tests, hair samples, men and women in masks and white coats; she felt like a leper. But didn't take it too personally, it was tiresome but necessary, she supposed. Finally, an hour later it was all over, they were using state of the art equipment she could see. And she was then unceremoniously allowed to make her own way. The ruffled passengers now shared taxis to the nearest train station.

Finally, on the train that rattled all the way to London, she began to think of James, and the fact that she was now in his orbit, and he in hers. It made her excited, and thus then angry, this better not be one of James' scams to get her home and closer to him, for if it was, she would kill him.

Chapter 26

Christine as usual had been completely right, annoyingly so, about the creativity course. Mer however also knew that it had become a new found distraction from her problems and personal life, and so she had thrown herself into it, with abandon; her booklist brimming with ticks upon things that she had read for it or bought. It was very pleasurable to study in this way, with no sense of pressure or possible censure from any quarter. She had also begun to marginally participate in the class discussions, but still held back, from lack of will or more importantly an unwillingness to make links and bonds with the others.

She knew that one of her classmates was her neighbour; thankfully he didn't sit very near her in the classroom so she didn't have to make conversation with him. Then she thought herself absurd, as he was a very appealing man and that surely he should move her in some way. But then, the truth seized her: she was still married and out there, somewhere, was her husband.

She did not want him. This was now certain, but at last she knew even if it would be demanding, that she had to see a lawyer, that it may be time to rent the split apart. It was alarming however, she had not discussed this with her mother or father and they did not know that there was such a serious problem, away as they had been since the spring, not able to bear witness to the pot that had boiled over by early summer, when he'd walked out. Once again, absurd. How had she let things slip so far into chaos?

Holding her copy of Chéri in one hand as she sat on the chaise longue, her legs bare again for the heat, she realised that not only was she looking forward to going to her class tonight but that she relished being free and able to talk to whomever she wanted. It was at that moment that Christine came in and if she had had time, Mer would have realised that an ambush was coming. Christine of course was far too quick and spilled her story with too much voracity for Mer to be able to maintain any defence.

"Hello, love." said Christine and Mer lowered her book, yet Christine was marching closer and closer, so that Mer had no time to answer.

"I've done something." The words bolted from Christine's mouth.

Mer became still, her eyes fixed, ready.

"What's happened?" Mer asked, a modicum of fright flickered on her face and she hoped that it had nothing to do with her husband and family, or anything for that matter.

"Look, I couldn't help it, but I think it will be good: I've invited the neighbours to dinner."

Mer was blank.

"For this Saturday; I'll do all the cooking, don't worry you don't have to do anything."

Mer had no words.

Then, Mer grew quietly furious, but Christine continued.

"It's just dinner, with some beautiful looking people. It is a gift, from me to you. Enough, now. You kicked your husband out, or he left whatever, good for you! You haven't told your parents, you will. You don't have a career or a life left, you will. You're a young, beautiful woman, with her own giant house and everything to live for and a warm and wonderful personality underneath this (she gesticulated over Mer's person). I know you don't want to know, you want to wallow, you want to destroy yourself. I know. It's such a waste that is all, and it's becoming an indulgent one!"

Mer's mouth was slightly open.

"All right? Good." And Christine flounced off.

In a few moments' time Mer registered what had just happened, and still had no words.

Chapter 27

"So far I've done some research on the girl," said James. "It seems that a Mehreen Jani is the named owner for that whole house next to Luc's, it had been a gift from her father, you know. She did a Bachelors in the History of Art at Edinburgh and a further Masters in the same at Oxford, then she worked at a Notting Hill art gallery over the last few years, until about six months ago."

"Why did she leave?" asked Mischa, as once again he was at the wheel of his car, driving them east, to more dilapidated parts of London.

"I don't know, but I can't find her working anywhere."

"Right," said Mischa, frowning.

"I tried to get as much as I could on her background, but it's a lot harder to get at family trees of people from foreign countries, records aren't kept as diligently as they've been in Europe for the last thousand or so years. But still, because of the British presence in India, some things have been noted really well- especially when natives and British officers had had any forceful impact upon one another."

Mischa glanced at James, intrigued.

"… It was all because of the house; it made it easier for me. Such a property … these houses are still mostly inhabited by the extremely wealthy or aristocrats, they'd originally been built on the orders of the Prince Regent for the consorts of the incumbent George the IV, you know. I found that the girl's house had not been purchased by her father at all, but 'claimed'. Even in my line of work, I was intrigued. Before it had been owned by Mehreen's father, who owns many other properties in London I might add, it had been in the family of a Lord Cavendish since it had been built. It took some delving, but I found amazingly that Mehreen Jani's father had 'claimed' his house with a letter from the late Lord Cavendish and the deeds themselves, that he'd brought over from India. However the house, had been initially left to *his* mother, Mehreen's grandmother, Leila.

"I didn't know what to think, but it's a bloody huge gift, I don't know … my imagination, I even thought either Leila maybe saved Lord Cavendish's life or something, or more … that they were lovers. The deed was uncontested, as this particular Lord Cavendish didn't have any immediate family to fight for the house, and after being empty for so many years, having been maintained by the keepers of the late Lord's estate, it had been impossible to contest. Did you know that the law firm still exists today, that had been informed by Lord Cavendish himself, that he'd gifted over those deeds."

Mischa raised his eyebrows.

"And the only time that the house had been used in the last century after Lord Cavendish's death, was by the British Army during World War II; it had been requisitioned as a place to use for meetings and also for looking after top officials from other countries."

"It must have seen a share of entertaining during the war years then," said Mischa, "parameters permitting. What a story, James, I wonder if it's all really true? It's harmless enough, but it's like some sort of an Anglo-Indian fairy tale."

"I know, it has a charm to it, of course we can't ask her about it, but who knows, maybe something will come up on Saturday so we can."

"We're still going?"

"Yes, we've got to look normal, and until I can get to Simon, we've got to keep occupied. OK so, Christine Bates' history on the other hand has been much easier to get. She and Mehreen have been friends from secondary school but are also related now, as Christine now surfaced as a 'Mrs' Jani. I found Christine's husband at a very different address."

James sighed, this was pleasant digging compared to the sad sordid secrets that he had to uncover and leak to the world; things that caused wars, moreover things that could have prevented wars or famine and death.

"Christine comes from humbler roots, her mother was a school teacher and her father a concert violinist, but they're both retired now and live in Yorkshire. She works in the entertainment industry looking after the needs of very famous people. She's recently had a baby ..." and James was still not sure why she was living in that house, maybe the husband was away and she was just visiting, but he was sure he would understand it on Saturday.

"Oh, one more thing ... Mehreen Jani's name came up as 'married', but that's not the impression I get from Luc, he says it's just the two women and the baby there, and he's always spoken as though she was single, there is also no change anywhere from her maiden name."

"Right," said Mischa as they began to slow, pulling up into a gravelly driveway, of what looked like a cross between an old barn shed and an office building.

They waited in the car both men, and soon crunching footsteps could be heard approaching, James wound his window down, and a slim man in his twenties and wearing a flat cap approached, he wasn't all that tall, but had the type of blue eyes that had a cheeky glint in them.

"Evening, Marty," said James,

"Evening, Gents." Marty handed James a fat and large manila envelope, James handed him a smaller yet fat envelope in return. "Thank you very much, sir." And Marty tipped his hat, and made his way back through the gravelly path, his footsteps receding with a pronounced crunch.

James then opened the package; in it was a new passport for Simon, and everything he could need from National Insurance number, to medical history, to school reports. With it in hand, James was now ready.

Mischa started the engine and began to pull away when James said, "She's coming back, Mischa, I got Sir John to order her back."

Mischa did not say anything; he knew when James was talking about Clara. "Kicking and screaming?" he then asked.

139

James nodded, knowing that they were forcing her back, perhaps like an Aphrodite that had never wanted to surface from the waves, which is why the sea had foamed and boiled as she'd arisen; actually a furious goddess.

Chapter 28

Mer was acutely unhappy as she dressed. Her frame sagged as she tried to hold herself up, she was not sure why she was attempting this, perhaps it was her upbringing, but that boy in class was soon going to be her guest, so she felt she ought to start being more polite to him. It began in the bathroom as she looked into the mirror, her black hair hung spiralled about her face limp and loose, she sighed, yet reached for her over-stuffed box of tricks. Make up could fashion so many dispositions and glamours, if only men knew she thought, that that damson flush, or exuberant rosy lipped coquette, the dark flash of the eyes, could be as simple as astute powder and paint, to animate an inanimate, create a living doll. It could be real of course, the inner magic could simultaneously shine forth, but not tonight; Mer worked as a solemnly as an artist and soon joy and vivacity bloomed, but only upon her face.

It became trickier when she was trying to choose what to wear; her usual understated style had been an unconscious choice and agreeably safe, but now she doubted herself and wondered what she was supposed to look like? A flash of panic seized her and she wished Christine was about to give some instruction. Mer considered telephoning Christine as she was still at work, but then thought that that would give Christine far too much satisfaction. No, this would be a solo mission, Mer cringed. Her face looked pretty and if she tried to smile she looked flushed and joyful, yet at present she appeared as a doll with no soul. Try harder, she thought and pulled out a white cotton dress, a red summer cardigan and high heeled sandals. The fire engine red colour touched her as dissonant, as though to upset her blood, but she threw it about her shoulders nonetheless. She looked at her left hand, utterly naked and childlike without her wedding or engagement rings which she had cast off so quickly, thrillingly, as soon as her husband had left. She was happy with that bare uncluttered hand, intensely pleased that it was free and unadorned. In pursuing her divorce, she'd find a final recognised cleaving she thought gratified, even if no one knew about that yet.

On her way out she passed the baby with her nanny playing together safely, which made her consider the relativity of her trifles; she wondered what her cousin, Rehan thought of her for harbouring his adulterous wife -so much to confront, but first this irritation of a dinner party, she could feel the now warm dusty powders occluding her face; she needed every ounce of strength.

It was balmy as she walked on empty paving; luckily her neighbour/guest was nowhere in sight, perhaps already there. There were a few odd people on the streets but London was still wonderfully empty as everyone, although not on holiday abroad, had gone to the coast or countryside this year; business was still in a way, booming for Britain and at least there was a silver lining to this embargo she thought, but when would it end she wondered? She had followed the progress of Britain's coping strategy, of using barges to move produce and using North Sea oil for fuel for this embargo crisis. But now, blackouts were soon to be introduced to ration the power, and also there were threats of coming shortages, giving rise to the likely possibility of rationing being imposed. Other countries however had severe fuel shortages, or droughts or medical emergencies and no one could help them, but not Britannia; at present, she was making do. Mer mused however that she did now miss her mother in New York; and how she had grown content with lying to her parents, still thinking that Zaf still lived with her and that all was well. After the initial lie she had avoided speaking to her mother very much, her parents had assumed that she was still in a honeymoon phase and did not want to be disturbed, she presumed and hoped.

The classroom hummed with voices, many students had made friends and were conversing before the teacher arrived, she felt like a complete fool on entering looking as she did, but it all occurred so fast: *he* inevitably turned to look at her as she stood in the door frame and so she responded with a small wave and smile, so quick as though a physical reflex and then rushed to her seat. But the neighbour boy yet still regarded her, please stop, she thought, she had little left. She looked up from her seat and he nodded hello again with a smile, she gave a little smile back and with thanks to all the angels in heaven, Mr Andrews walked in at that moment and all faced front. Her heart was rapid.

As the lesson progressed the sun was delicate, summery yet sophisticated as it dappled them warmly; the old wooden chairs and tables grew rose coloured, then fawn and ochre as the colours changed. Sometimes, when a student's stationery caught the light it glowed a blanched white, otherworldly, yet not remotely eerie as it was a cast of summer and it engendered trust. They sat lulled by the room furnished as usual in hues of ripened berries and woodlands, so that no one could possibly fear it, only yearn to be part of it; this rich solar creation that they bore witness to, was no siren song.

Yet the boy seemed distracted, he kept turning slightly to look at her throughout the whole lesson, although not trying to get her attention. She wondered what it was he was looking at? Hopefully her makeup had not had a mishap. He then once surreptitiously looked at his phone held under the desk; Mer didn't think she'd noticed him doing that before, no he had seemed a good student.

Finally the lesson on Chéri, ended; they had talked about so much beauty that it took a few moments to disengage. Then, it felt tricky; Mer braced herself but was prepared. The class shuffled and rose, chairs scraping noisily and he came easily to her as she slung her bag over her shoulder.

"Hello there," said Luc, his voice was pleasant, masculine yet with a gentler touch, she did not realise at that point that it had to it, the most tiny and remote French inflection.

"Hello," she said demurely, and put on her smile.

"My name's Mer." She surprised herself. "I believe my, my housemate Christine has invited you and your friends to dinner on Saturday, you're my neighbour I know. I'm sorry I didn't tell you my name the other day, it was just raining so much ..."

"My name's Luc, really pleased to meet you."

He had a warm gate thought Mer, there is nothing to fear here, she decided quickly and soon she proceeded out of the class with him and felt much relieved; she could talk to people it seemed, without the world coming to an end, it had been a pleasant turn of events.

"I don't know what Christine's cooking," she told him as they walked the thankfully shortish walk through the park, in which there were long silent stretches but no feelings of awkwardness.

"Shall we bring anything?"

"Oh no, not at all, I'm sure Christine's completely organised."

"Have you lived there long?"

"Not that long," she answered vaguely. "But how do you like it?"

"When I first came here, to be honest I was really shocked, it's really grand, and your friend Christine told me to look at the gardens, she was right, unbelievable, it's great to be posted here."

Mer wanted to ask him what sort of 'posting' he had and where had he come in from, but they had reached her front door.

"I'm going to ask you about that on Saturday night." She stood facing him, lifted up by the heels while her red cardigan was more than alive in the mellow sunlight. As they parted, she was much relieved although highly surprised if not impressed with herself; he was warm and friendly and she was glad that he was coming to dinner she decided, then there was a tinge of excitement and anxiety, laced as it was with that most heady youthful elixir: hope; something she had not felt since she had been seventeen years of age.

Chapter 29

Gemma felt a knot in her stomach, but she took a step forward nonetheless, one after another down the oak panelled walls, green velvet curtains at junctures that she had begun to loathe, and soon she was before him, with of course -nothing to offer.

"… So, nothing. Is that what you're saying?"

"Minister, I've honestly heard nothing at all."

"But we gave you two new avenues of inquiry, this Clara woman, and Simon Hughes, really? Nothing at all?!"

"If my superior is involved in something unsavoury then he is very discreet about it."

"I'm going to ask you something, would anyone be able to look inside the document folders that I send to you?"

"Anyone?"

"Anyone apart from you, like your superior?"

"Um yes, yes he would, if he chose to, but things stay on my desk." Gemma hesitated to continue, thinking that with every word she was trapping either herself or maybe someone else.

"Well, I'm going to tell you. We've had an incident. The woman Clara, we had an operation to pick her up, but she disappeared that very day. Not a coincidence I'm sure, so bloody well keep the documents I send you hidden!"

"Yes, sir, of course, sir."

"Now go, I'm sure you've got the world to save."

Gemma exited quickly, her mind reeling again. She had to speak to Sir John urgently, thinking that she would tell him the whole truth now, but she would go home first. She needed to feel safe, even if it was to be an illusion.

Finally back in her white and silver living room, Gemma glanced at the enormous, wonderfully intrusive mirror as though wishing it could answer her questions. She had been informed now that Simon was the mole, she was most unimpressed with him of course, so in theory she could go right to James and tell him the truth, but the fact that the Minister had found Simon, and Clara (!) meant they could be closing in, even if it was slowly and she thought that if she contacted James or even Sir John, that they would act or change the status quo, and so, it would only lead the Minister to James sooner. No, this Jeanie stays in its bottle, 'till she could do more, or knew more about the Minister and his motivation, so she closed her eyes and tried to breathe.

Then, there was loud and quick knock on the door. Gemma waited, wondering if she hadn't been imagining things in her anxious state. Again, now the knocks were louder. Gemma glanced at the grainy picture in the entry-phone and then lashed with her hand at the door handle as though to tear it open.

"Get inside!" Was all she said to her visitor, it was all that was safe.

Once inside, the visitor spoke, "Oh, Gemma! They've sent me to you! I'm so sorry, didn't you know?"

"It's not that. No I didn't know, but it's not that ... Welcome home, Clara, I'm sorry about that. I'm just really security conscious now ... now that we've had a breach."

"We've what?!"

"You don't know? I thought James would have told *you*."

"Not at all, I knew something was up because I've been ordered home, well sort of, ordered to what turns out to be your address. What breach? Tell me?!"

Gemma was still recovering from the fact that she had the most dangerous person she could (in the position that Gemma was in) now staying with her. How was she going to keep her hidden? Had Clara been followed or even seen coming here?

"... Clara ... I'm going to let James fill you in. It's the best way I think."

146

"Why can't you tell me?"

"There's detail ... which will better come from him, please trust me. Also, (Gemma was thinking fast) because of our situation, and my position in the government, can you do something for me? Something just between us?"

"Of course, Gemma."

"After you go and see James, don't leave this house again."

Both women paused.

"Just trust me, I mean you were called home after all. I am very high up Clara, do you see what I'm saying, what I'm trying to do?"

"Yes ... I think so. I know it's to protect me. Thank you; I'll do what you say."

"You could just phone James you know?"

Clara sighed. "Now what would be the fun in that? Sounds like, I really need to hear it from him, what's happened."

Gemma nodded, knowing she had indeed achieved the best case scenario without telling Clara that she had been recruited by the Minister, and indeed if Clara had been followed, or if they knew where she was, the game would have been up quite a few minutes ago.

But then there was another knock at the door. Both women stayed completely still. When Gemma did glance at the entry-phone, she could have groaned with the dangerous absurdity of it.

"Sir John?" she said as she opened to door to him, after having made sure that Clara could not be seen through the open door.

"Gemma, my dear, you had me worried, been trying to call you all afternoon, your phone's off," he said striding in, and then on seeing Clara standing in front of the mirror, "ah, I see you now know why I was calling. Sorry for the short notice, Gemma."

"It's quite all right. No problem. Though I wonder, would it be better to hide out of London for Clara, or somewhere unknown?"

"Better right under everyone's nose I thought, better to keep an eye on each other. Also, I'm on my way to see James, something's happened, just in the last hour, you've been out of the office so you don't know, there's been a joint decision amongst many countries this morning- there's going to be a mass evacuation of major Cities: London, (he then looked at Gemma with an undertone) Paris, Berlin, New York, anyone who can basically afford it, for cleaning, so that after it's done, travel can begin again and the embargo be given the boot.

"Oh … I see," said Gemma.

"This information is not remotely public yet, all right, Clara, especially you -you can't tell anyone."

"No, I'm sure she won't, she's only going to see James herself for the, latest information, I felt it was better … more informative."

"Oh yes. I agree," said Sir John.

Clara looked at both of them with a high level of astuteness, on seeing this look, Sir John said, "settle in a bit first my dear, wait a couple of days, he's a little busy, and I have to see him myself today as you can see."

"Of course, Sir John, so neither you, or James sent me a message?" said Clara.

"What message? The one I left at your office to come home?" said Sir John.

"Um, oh yes, all right, so that was you. Thank you," answered Clara.

"Well …" he looked at Clara for a moment wanting to ask more questions, but instead he said, "goodbye ladies, keep yourselves safe." And left them soon after.

Gemma looked at Clara's one big suitcase that reflected back at them through the mirror and knew that her whole life must have been packed into it. "Come on, I'll show you to your room, and make a shopping list, I'll get everything you like."

Chapter 30

It wasn't that Clara liked to keep secrets; she didn't like them in fact. The biggest secret she kept, her allegiance and membership to the group, was enough for many lifetimes. Now in her new cream clad bedroom, marooned in Gemma's flat, she thought about the fact that she had concealed vital information from Sir John, well really; from James. Unwilling to sit alone in the bedroom and consider this, she went instead to her en-suite bath, it too was set out in ivory, with modern glass shields and metal bars to hold the towels, it looked very much like an expensive hotel's bathroom, and Clara mused that Gemma was even organised down to this degree; she wondered then, what would it be that ever made the girl crack?

Clara slipped off her clothes like an old skin, and maybe another life, as she wondered if she would ever resume it exactly as it had been in New York. She did not fear it, this change, instead then grew anxious that she was actually a little pleased; happy to be in the same city as her James. And then she looked at herself in the round mirror above the sink, as though with just one look with those huge almost black irises, she withered love and quietened passion itself. She had no right to love him; destruction had been its issue, and she did not deserve any more love ... not yet. Her hair felt lank, the general feel of the jet plane clung to her body in its staleness. So she glanced at the side of the bath and there true to form was some bath foam by Floris: a make used by their grandmothers, but even now still available in Piccadilly. She ran the taps, and they filled the bath with voluptuous hot water that rose now in frothed peaks from its scented additions. Clara was tall, and as she glanced at her navel and belly that was flat, she had then an unwanted glimpse of the past where it had swelled with her baby; she looked away, and let the hammering hot water take her thoughts elsewhere.

For it was her secret text message sender's style that had made her keep it a secret from Sir John and James; if she had told them, they would hunt him down, and this saviour did not want to be found. He *was* her saviour after all, and she owed him that much: to respect his wishes. It was his last words, how he'd described and tried to identify himself to her that twisted itself around her thoughts, and she wanted to work it out by herself, not have him tracked down by James. As she slipped into the bath, the heat and gentle pressure of the water enveloped her, she even ducked her chin under the water line as if trying to hide her thoughts there. She would find this helper on her own she decided, and with that took her head down once to submerge herself completely for a second. Newly arisen, crowned with suds, she blinked and smiled; she knew it was the right thing to do.

Chapter 31

It was Saturday; there was so much to be done. Mer watched Christine storm about her kitchen, she had already transformed the dining table, setting it with a continuous decadent line of heavy silver candlesticks, and chosen a theme of red napkins in neat rolls upon plain white plates, and then long, pure white candles to grace the tall silver receptacles with. The table was large and glistening dark, big enough to accommodate plates of food and adornment both at once. Lastly, she'd placed a bouquet of flowers into an old enormous blue vase at its centre, choosing white lilies and had commented, "They're a funeral gift in France you know, but their perfume's so heady … it doesn't matter."

The kitchen, although was still one could say organised, felt a touch frantic as well. Christine had made tiny chickens, stuffed with sour cherries, garlic, herbs and rice, served with a hot pepper relish and Georgian bread that contained melting white cheese. For her starter she had created a crab and crustacean cocktail on top of bitter rocket leaves, and for dessert; a choice of dark chocolate torte that she had commissioned from a friend or a Pavlova with passion fruit and peaches. The wine had been duly delivered by the same wine shop that catered many of the events for her work. Christine seemed content; most things were done, or could be reheated near the time, and Mer knew that she would have to hold the fort when Christine was in the kitchen and she worried a little, but it was all too late now.

"I'm wearing a simple black dress by the way, not entirely glamorous I know, it's the same one I can also wear to work," said Christine as she bustled about. "It's the sleeveless one; I think I look incredibly pale in it, well, compared to you."

"You're silly, you'll look lovely, pale is nice too." Mer considered her own skin tone which could range from almond to pale olive to café au lait;

something she had always been aware of growing up in Britain, and not always comfortably. Christine would think that she herself looked neon-white thought Mer, how silly, Mer knew that Christine would look lovely; what was it about fair people and not finding their own paleness desirable?

Mer had no idea what she was wearing; instead, she hovered about the kitchen looking guilty as Christine chopped and stirred, but Christine had reassured her, "I'm fine, I'm fine," more than once.

And so, finally, she was finished and Christine raced upstairs to wash her face and hands and to change into the black dress, even if it did make her look stark, as Mer also went to face her closet dubiously.

While these intense preparations had been occurring, Luc had been assembling himself. He'd started early because he knew that it took him time, however he was nearly ready as he approached his aftershaves and colognes in still, but glinting jewel coloured bottles, some had pungent dark liqueurs inside that had yet, not repelled a woman to date. He chose a bottle that was clear and bright, it's label in the bold black and white lettering style of the 1950's, it's scent mild, suffuse with lemon and lush grasses and it came out as a puff of mist. He was wearing a white shirt and jeans, it was a relief to be doing something in the normal world he thought at last, but sadly it made him uneasy; normality had lost its pleasures …

His obnoxious buzzer sounded, wrenching him from his expectant state for an instant; it still annoyed him very much that this should be his buzzer, in such a house. James and Mischa were going to meet him here first; perhaps they were apprehensive too, as they all really didn't know the neighbours.

They arrived in jeans as well, yet looked smart; Mischa wore a pale blue shirt that offset his face very well. Luc observed in Mischa his father's soft blue eyes, knowing that it was never apparent that he was Indian, except that when he let you in, he had his mother's easy warmth and friendliness and not an ounce of cold reserve anywhere; the latter Luc felt, was an Anglo-Saxon trait. Thus Luc set his own mother's Gallic roots apart, along with the rumours of Tunisian blood as well somewhere in the family to embroider his idea of himself as a warm and friendly soul. Luc's father Vincent was English, which meant of course in actuality that he had Irish and Dutch blood too. He would ask James to do his lineage he thought. Yet the name, Avium, his last name, surely that sounded like Latin and Ancient Rome had been such a mix of many things and peoples, he wondered if James was able to reach so far back?

James was wearing a black long sleeved top that too set off his hair and face and they were ready; although they didn't move. They dithered and lingered, Mischa and James spoke quietly in the corner and Luc went to look out of the window as if he expected other guests to be arriving at the ladies' door. The sky was still bright with day but wore it now as a sigh, as evening lurked and came on in strange streaks of yellow and pink near the horizon; being summer in London, sunset was still a long distance off. It was approaching 7pm so they shuffled out and even glanced in the mirror near the front door before they left; as Lucian's door closed behind them, he felt that they could not go back in there, that moment had passed and now they were launching into something else, even though the vermillion carpet greeted them baldly as ever, they were on their way, that is all that he knew.

The immersion into the summer evening was brief but balmy, as they walked towards Mer's door they were immediately impressed by its formidable size and height; it stood before them black and overlarge, finished by a huge silver knocker shaped into a wreath of leaves and flowers. A light breeze ruffled hair that had been carefully made, whispering that true evening and twilight should have been there, but was not. None had wanted to be impressed by the formidable door, they had all passed it many times, but this was different; at that moment this door strangely, was there for them, and it stood before them, quietly beckoning.

Lucian walked forward, his hand raised up to reach the knocker and grabbing it firmly, he then rapped it three times, preferring it to the bell. He felt nervous and strangely excited.

They waited, and then there were clicking noises before the enormous door fell open slowly, gracefully, without creak or heave. And there stood Christine, she smiled as she let them in, a lady in black, her dress baring her back and arms, and she did look nice thought Luc. The entrance hall was as he remembered but warmer, more fulsome, improved as if a curse of sparseness had been lifted, and then the pearly beige floor winked at him, it had been washed and scrubbed anew it seemed. The Art Nouveau lamps were lit now and became glowing statues; green-gold florally adorned nouvelle women who took now pride of place. He turned to see James and Mischa's faces, no, they had not expected this, but apart from benign surprise there was something else in their expression, Luc could not discern what it was, but they both shared it.

She guided them through a small part of the long corridor that in the end would have led them to the kitchen he could see, but turned left before they reached so far. It was a sitting room that backed on to the garden on one side, they had French doors in common, and on the other side of the room, the street side, was a long oval, almost black dining table, decorated as if for a State occasion, some of which Luc had actually attended. Yet before he could grasp it fully, he stopped, as there she was, being introduced by Christine to all of them, his heart beat a little harder and he tried to focus on what Christine was saying, it was important he realised; from it he understood her name again, 'Mer', definitively so, and the fact that this enormous house was hers. It didn't fit, this diminutive girl wearing cornflower blue, living in this house; it was not so much the size of it, it was that to him young women never lived in places of such magnitude alone, not in stories or the movies, and never in reality. Christine *did* live with her and so too Christine's baby, but where were the men or other people or family in general?

Mer's skin looked burnished to him, apricot mixed with almond and olive hues, her dress was girlish cap sleeved and low necked, yet she still looked very, very untouched by any form of sexuality; she had wide, big brown shiny eyes that sometimes were embarrassed when Christine introduced her, so she hid her face subtly with a downward twist of her neck, to draw forth her curls as a screen.

James and Mischa seemed guarded to Luc for the first half an hour, Mischa could especially not let go. Luc thought that both men had been taken aback. The enormous house and its décor, the elegant woman who played the host and the quiet one who owned everything, the table laid as if for a cult or king, the sheer unfinished empty grandeur of the place and the fact that they all hardly knew each other …

"I haven't entertained in so long that I've gone a little mad, with the scrolls and the dining table, please humour me, I couldn't help it," said Christine.

She then handed them each red wine, in glasses that had been blown so large that surely the glass could not maintain such curvature. And led them to sit down, the chairs were very old fashioned and upholstered in velvet, yet one in plum, one in emerald green, one in burgundy and so on.

Suddenly, James asked Mer, "So, did you decorate this place yourself or …?"

And she spoke.

"Oh," Mer said shaking her head. "No, I, well I've only been here for under a year, and so much of this," she gestured around her, "was already here, I like it though." She frowned and continued, "I usually love to decorate, but this house, *this* house ... has its own tastes," and she shrugged.

All three of the gentlemen had listened to Mer completely, as if they knew that she had not been so animated in under a year.

155

"Yes, I can see it would be hard to fit in furniture from more modern decades," said Luc, with that imperceptible French inflection of his that made his voice not at all accented, but very different from everyone else's.

Mer nodded and smiled.

Soon, the blue sky outside became heavily streaked by pink, apricot and gold, which in turn gave the room blushing hues and new shadows in the corners, so that Christine rose and put on some lamps. Mischa, meanwhile who had said very little and smiled politely instead, relaxed his frame a touch and settled back into his burgundy armchair as he cradled his huge glass of red wine in his hands.

James too had begun to respond now in earnest. And even though they all knew that Christine had a baby, no one politely asked about the father, and ignored a small baby monitor on a side table. Luc caught Christine looking at Mischa when he had smiled; this was completely normal as he was just too handsome.

Christine asked Mischa what he did for a living, after explaining her profession to him in Artist Management. He replied in a voice as attractive as his face.

"I'm an Academic, and I also sometimes teach English literature at Cambridge," he said, tantalisingly self-assured.

"Oh, what sort of writers do you like? Or admire?" asked Christine

"Old dead ones," said Mischa, and then smiled at her.

"You know that Mer goes to an evening class on Thursdays, I think they're doing a lot of literature at the moment, oh and so is Luc of course," replied Christine.

"Yes we are, we did Tess of the D'Urbervilles By Thomas Hardy, and we did King Lear," said Mer nodding, demure, but not shy anymore.

"Yes, which did you like better?" Luc asked Mer directly. This subtly startled her a little bit and she cast her eyes down to think, hair quivering at the ready.

"Well they're both so sad, Tess, was beautiful and tragic, but King Lear, well that was so deep, so many layers, it troubles the mind it's profound ... I think none -I'm tired just thinking about them," she answered.

And they all laughed. It was the wine that had loosened their tongues and gated minds, so that as the evening progressed, they found each other funny and endearing; such charms may not have worked on any random or sober passer-by.

The most laughs arose when James informed them that he was a genealogist, not from the women, but from the men. Mer and Christine were trying to be polite and genuinely thought that it was an interesting career but it was also James himself who thought that it was amusing. Christine, who had been refilling everybody's glass so swiftly that they hadn't noticed, had just opened the third bottle.

"But that *is* fascinating. Why are you both laughing so much?!" Christine asked Luc and Mischa.

Mer ignoring them all, then asked James, "Have you done any interesting people?"

"Oh, he has, but he won't talk about it, thinks he's a priest or something, thinks he has to be confidential," said Luc.

"Yes I have, but people have asked me to be discreet, I don't think I would get more work if I didn't keep my reputation," said James.

Suddenly Christine ran off, as a keen savoury smell wafted into the room.

Looking about Luc asked, "Can we help her?" In a house like this, there would have been servants he thought and he realised that Christine was managing by herself.

Mer looked a little perplexed and then stood up. "No. Oh no no, I'll just see if she's all right," and left the room as well.

The men were left sitting on the sofas.

"What do you think then?" asked Luc.

"They're very nice," said James.

At that moment something shook, buzzed and beeped in Luc's pocket, it took him completely by surprise as he had forgotten about all the shadows he'd been trying to chase over the last two weeks. Knowing he could not take out this extra, odd looking low-tech phone in front of his best friends without questions, he excused himself, and went to find the bathroom.

He progressed down the corridor nearer the kitchen, where he caught sight of what was going on there. Mer tentatively stood in the kitchen where Christine whirred on like a machine. Steaming dishes piled high were ready on one side as she retrieved burnished Poussins from the oven; nothing looked too precise or perfect, but it's sheer quantity and redolent splendour was desirable.

"I was going to offer to help … what you really need is a trolley though," Mer stated, and Luc thought of butlers and maids, he was sure that that was what they would have used to despatch the hot food to the table in one go.

"Ha! I found one!" Christine gestured to the right of the kitchen. She then pulled forward a rickety wooden thing with dusty wheels that had two levels to pile plates of food onto. On inspection from his position down the corridor, Luc hoped that the trolley would not collapse on its way to the dining table.

"Where exactly did you find it?" Mer asked curiously.

"In the corner, inside the pantry, underneath an old sheet."

"What I don't know about my own house," said Mer, shaking her head.

As the women busied themselves, Luc took the moment to check his message, it said:

Home now, and safe. Thank you.

Luc thought for a moment about what Clara could mean by 'home' so he asked her:

Home, meaning?

And she replied:

London, England.

Luc had many thoughts at once, one of them being that she had managed to get on a plane during an embargo, (but when he'd quizzed James he had told Luc, that could be possible for UN staff) as well as the fact that she was safe, and lastly that she was still communicating with him. She must have worked out who he was he thought, and felt pleased with himself for getting something right, although, London was where the Minister also lived. So he wrote:

I still recommend that you stay inside, if you know what I mean.

And she replied:

I know, and I am. Thank you again.

Relieved Luc then realised that the dishes had been loaded and that the two women together were ready to push the trolley; Christine steering in front and Mer pushing behind. Luc before rushing back to the living room saw that they were laughing and were trying to compose themselves, before they too reached the living room.

Back at his seat and ready, Luc watched Christine enter and announce: "Gentlemen, please come and take your seats for dinner."

She giggled on the way out, once again faced with her locomotive apparatus. The guests walked over to the table where the plates had been laid and took their seats. Luc thought that he might look pale, he certainly felt it. Slowly, creaking, the women brought in the food trolley; it was a sight to behold: one pushing, one pulling, but trying so much to look serene. The three men were looking either at the trolley which was in a woeful state, or at each other and biting their lips.

"Do you need any help with that?" asked Mischa.

"Oh no, we're just fine." Christine replied; head still down to mark their path.

As the wheel caught again and they juddered to a halt for the third time while making their way precariously over the floor and various carpets, James and Mischa were quite engrossed with the sight, but for Luc, even after the shock of the text message, the finest sight was Mer; innocently pushing along, her whole top half jangling every time the wheel caught, but she persisted, and looked down with a graceful smile and then gave an even stronger shove, and so it seemed that she was enjoying herself, but it was as though it were an unexplored feeling.

The sun finally began to set on them, leaving them an exotic array of streaking dark oranges, diminutive purples and blue shadows. The tall lamps came alive with more vigour as the day began to fade; in this room they were of an older style than in the entrance hall, capped with draped and pleated shades upon them, but where one was a dusty orange another was a foggy plum and so on, thus as the day exited, the room glowed in balls of colour shaded light.

After Christine and Mer had filled the table with the dishes of food they ushered everyone to help themselves and so they did, offering fare to each other and to the women as well. Christine had seated them all on one end of the enormous dining table so that it felt like a stolen corner; a fragment of a banquet to be enjoyed by all of them, especially by Mer, thought Luc; who looked as if she didn't own this house and all its glass and silverware. The food was flavoursome, and as the men complimented her upon it, Christine informed them that, "I had a green eyed grandmother who could cook, maybe I got it from her."

At one point Mer and Christine started discussing if one of them should go and check on the baby, so Luc chose his moment to speak to James, it didn't matter that Mischa was there.

"So, what ever happened to that Simon then? I know there was all that stuff when he got in the way of you and Clara, but you were friends once, do you see him anymore? Is he still around?"

James said nothing for a moment. "No, we didn't keep in touch after the whole thing, it was ugly you know ... Why do you ask, Luc?"

"Just popped into my mind you know, I'm back here and because I was away and missed so much, I feel like there are so many loose ends. Does he still live here?"

"Um no ... I think he moved ..."

"Where to?"

"To Paris," said Mischa, while glancing at James.

"Oh, OK. I guess they have an embargo too, by the way, how long do you think it will go on,?"

Mischa then helped himself to spicy relish and said, "Everyone's taking their holidays on the British coast this summer you know, as we're all stuck, so I guess it's been good for someone, but I don't know how much longer it will go on."

James then added his perspective on how the economy would recover, and Luc was glad that he had managed to change the subject.

Finally everyone had filled their plates more than once and Mer was cutting her meat with a knife and fork quite intent and engrossed and quiet. But Luc was watching her, nothing else, just looking at her, lost in something and unaware of his food, his friends, or for the moment himself for that matter. He realised the extent of his wholehearted desire for Mer, and it had probably been in his regard just then, by which anyone would have been accidentally anointed if they had seen it; as being witness to it was like an inadvertent baptism, into something ardent, sacred and private.

It was remarkable that an evening of five people who did not know one another very well at all could succeed, indeed did succeed thought Mer. Much was due to their personalities but without the significant setting nothing would have gone off so well, she knew. If it were not such a sultry summer night in London and they had not had so much red wine coursing through their veins, it may have been a trial.

She thought that Luc was attractive but in a very different manner to James: Luc was a little bit shorter than James, though not short, broader and carried a warmer gate. James looked like a classically beautiful lean and tall Englishman with a dark blonde mop to boot, but there was something distant yet in this, as though he were a living statue. Luc, instead was earthy, approachable and yet James had been so polite to her, she then blushed, luckily no one mentioned it. Christine then excused herself to see her baby again, and Mer's stomach tightened, knowing that she was alone and had to hold the evening together; but she tried to set sail steadily, mast aloft high and then threw all caution to the winds as she began to speak. She was very afraid that someone would ask her about how she owned the house. They were delicious though, these men, she felt a dim chuckle inside, their cheeks were red and hued from heat and alcohol and perhaps, pleasure, although she was not sure. She knew that drink alone could make anyone happy, for a little while at least. Christine had opened the windows about the room at the front and the back by the garden, there was a great stretch between, and the breeze was rich, redolent with the earthy dregs of a heat drenched day yet cool with the oncoming traverses of the night. It stroked their cheeks, bound gently about their bodies; such a welcome visitor.

Mer proceeded instead to ask questions, "So, Luc, what may I ask do you do?"

"Oh, I work for a government department, I'm an analyst," he said, his cheeks like deep red apples, and that night to Mer he looked anything but the sort, if someone had put a guitar in his hand and placed him on a beach it would have been more appropriate, she remembered him properly now from the day he had moved in and that over filled car; and she'd liked him even then she remembered.

"Very hush-hush?" Mer asked him.

Luc sighed, "Not for me, but I'm sure it is." And he smiled at her; the lamplight lighting up sparks and flecks in his hazel eyes.

Mischa, she felt had been the most reserved at the beginning of the evening, such a shame as his face was too beautiful, that kind yet masculine face had an ethereal quality, but his demeanour kept one from staring; although one could not help but steal glances. He had relatively released his grip on himself by the time he had reached the table however, but Mer could see, as the wine pulsed in her blood and infused and altered her senses: that he did not trust her, he did not trust Christine and he did not trust this night. Such a contradiction to his visage, but Mer feared that she was getting quite intoxicated now and resolved instead to drink some water and eat the last few bites upon her plate. At that moment Christine dashed in, looking refreshed and cheerful and started to clear plates onto the top of the trolley. She then produced a small stack of dessert plates and brought up like a magician: the chocolate torte and a cream towered Pavlova that she had burrowed into the base of the trolley.

They were all so tipsy by then that they broke out into a spontaneous applause and Christine assured them, "I am incapable of producing such things, I had my friend make them." Her arms shone as pale white marble as she ably despatched the plates and served. Mer felt cheerful; what a guileful surprise that was, another magician's trick, she was not sure if it was how she wanted to feel, but the drink allowed it a stay, be it brief.

It was soon however after dinner that her guests left, for how much could strangers truly talk about? Although it had gone so well, the night was finally over and that was also a relief. The men left in a little procession with much thanks at the door and two hot kisses for the women on each cheek from every one of them. The door then closed with a deep resonance behind the men, blocking out all sound so that the women would not be able to hear them speak in the street, or listen to what they might say about them.

Chapter 32

Monday morning was like no other thought Luc; everything had become absurd, as though his life had turned a corner into a parallel universe.

"London in short is to be evacuated for two weeks, and it will be in two weeks' time," said Gemma. "Mass cleaning will take place, and the Army will be in charge. An information document with all the details is on each of your desks including which camp you can be bussed to unless you make your own private arrangements, extra details about when, how, which bus etc. etc. are all there, so please don't worry, from what I have seen it's very well organised. Other big cities (that can afford it) around the world will be doing the same, like New York and Berlin, and hospitals here will be evacuated immediately to other ones in the home counties to help get people settled."

Luc sat down and began to look at his information booklet, in it he read about the proposed efficient cleaning of all sewers, the underground, the streets and gutters etc. There were also it stated, no exceptions to this evacuation of inner London, and Luc wondered how the Army would manage to move thousands of people out.

"This news is to be launched on all television stations in one hour and please don't look at me like that, we didn't know about it till very suddenly, the heads of state suddenly decided. There is to be no negotiation and no choice, I might add. It's serious, so make your plans everyone." Gemma finished and the whole office stared at her for a moment, then started to shuffle papers, or rather pretended to start work when really their minds were focussed on where, when and how they should each go.

Luc was not pleased, he was just fed up of feeling like a pawn rather than a participant, at least he had not been sent or rather summoned by that Minister again, things had been quiet in that area, and Luc felt worried that he had lulled himself into a false sense of security. He knew that that Minister would call on him again, and for that he had to be ready. He then wondered if perhaps Gemma and Balthazar would be staying in London, they surely would he thought. His department always flew about as if it ran everything. His frustration mounted, and then Gemma strode past him, her hair in a flurry, righteousness in every stride, and so struck alight as though a match in Luc's mind -which became an idea: he would wait for her to finish her work today, and then see what she did and where she went after that. Luc knew it was risky, if she saw him he could always explain that he was on his way to visit a friend, but it was all he had, and new events kept falling in front of him and unravelling before he had any grasp of them, so that he had the feeling that he was running out of time, for his sake and for Clara's, he had to know more.

And so, he waited patiently at his desk, following Gemma with his eyes whenever she walked through the room, in case she had her expensive leather satchel with her and looked like she was leaving. It was a tense day, and of course he got little done, but he was in his heightened state, able to listen to the conversations of all around him, they ranged from:

"I'm going to my mother's, maybe they'll let me leave a few days early if I take my work with me? I want to beat the traffic."

And:

"Yes, I heard that the traffic's going to be murder, I mean it's definitely going to be isn't it? Someone was saying that the motorways out are going to be sluggish from today on ..."

Luc had no thoughts yet about where he would go if forced out of London, his only thoughts upon his current task.

Finally at close to 7.30pm, when many had already left, she passed him, handbag and satchel in hand, so too a bag of groceries probably bought at lunch time. Luc rose, checked his pockets for his wallet and both his phones, and began his journey, his heart was not dancing, it was pounding.

This may be pointless, she may just be going home he thought to himself, and the groceries very much suggested that, but he didn't care, maybe he would then still find out where she lived, and have one more place to look in to, to search if need be. He knew that she did not take a private car home, thus she would be on public transport, a tube he hoped rather than a bus, where he could hide himself better amongst the throngs of people.

He came out on to the street, he had given her a one minute lead, and yes, there she was heading in the direction of the tube station. And so he followed her, it was not that difficult, as long as he kept his head down while at the same time constantly looked to see what she was doing. Finally, her tube journey ended and he found some air again, and a much clearer eye-line for her, she had come out not that far, at South Kensington.

Luc was cautious now, this may be where she lived and there were less people to hide behind, he was glad that she was quite tall, and that her blonde hair today was like a beacon; that beckoned him on. She turned down a residential street, and Luc slowed his pace, but then as she had her back to him and seemed to be opening her handbag, Luc sped up, he needed to see the exact address.

But Gemma did not need her keys, for while even as she held her door key in her hand ready to use, the door opened, and Luc could not believe what he saw there-

Even after the door had closed behind Gemma, Luc still stared at the spot, stunned and also, very confused. So he tried to re-establish what he had just seen; it was not something to be wrong about.

Yes, that had been Clara, the shock of black hair, large eyes, and she had been smiling. Not only that, but Clara was too hard to mistake for anyone else; her beauty was hypnotic, it was a magnetism above all else and still confused, his mind suddenly went on a tangent thinking that if Mischa and Clara ever had children, then they would look like demi-Gods. Luc needed to snap out of it, but the blood rushed to his face, all he wanted to do was to march to the door and bang on it -he knew Clara, he had seen her often at summers or Easter holidays in his early teens when she would be found at James' house, he was furious, more out of frustration than anything else, but he tried to count to ten and dull the impulse, he had to wait. Clara and Gemma were mixed up in real trouble, the last thing he wanted to do was to make things worse, especially if he was not sure if the Minister was perhaps even somewhat right (never mind his methods) in his pursuit of Clara. So he did a very forced about-turn and marched himself back to the tube station, thinking how that young girl he knew, with black soft hair, could possibly have done anything wrong ... it felt like he knew her, and not in the sense of knowing someone well, but that, as they had all easily sat around together while so young and tender, often speaking little, that he knew of her essence, of the core of who she was –and even now he could not feel that that essence could be bad. The fact remained however, that where Clara considered to be 'safe' and 'home' was at the home of someone he thought wanted to do her harm. And James knew nothing, not even that she was back! Luc continued to frown, feeling somehow betrayed, although no one had done anything of the kind.

On the tube again, people's conversations washed over him, though nothing could blot out the awakening sight he had just seen, but people were making audible and resolute plans like he'd heard at the office:

"I'm leaving as soon as I can, better to get settled, you know" and, "I just can't believe it, wish I could afford a nice hotel, but they're all heaving!"

And so it went on, finally distracting Luc away from the one and only vision searing his mind: Clara's face at the door. Then, finally, he considered as he lifted his head to notice the other tube travellers, engrossed and perplexed by the coming evacuation as they were, that perhaps because London had been through the Blitz, it was as though the echo of the wartime spirit was still resonant there and so, like a latent memory, seemed now reactivated; as he could see that people were still moved by this Blitz type spirit and were mentally prepared to leave; trusting their ushers: the government, the Army, the disease, and were content for themselves to behave appropriately and so to leave diligently. And even as he exited the tube and walked on, an eerie excitement filled the streets; quietly expectant, as if droning spitfires were expected overhead.

But Luc was still frowning as he approached his building, where once outside he rubbed his face. It was then that the silver wreath of flowers at Mer's door caught his eye, and with a tired and numbed brain, he approached it and then struck again the knocker three times.

Luc waited, not knowing whom to expect. Finally, the heavy door waned into the house; too slow to reveal the object of desire immediately and released on its hinges unhurried.

And there she stood as plain as day, looking a little worried to see who it could be and then surprised to see Luc, as if it took a moment for her to recognise and place him. Finally, she spoke, "Hello, Luc. How are you?" She asked it as though he had indeed come to visit her and yet he had, he did not want to be alone, and James and Mischa were unapproachable now, as he had too much to conceal from them. Mer stood there still, too surprised to know what to do next.

"Hello, Mer … Did you hear the news?" he said with fervour.

"About the evacuation ... Yes …" And she seemed sombre at the thought.

Suddenly emboldened by this he asked her, "What will you do?"

"I don't know," she said, and shook her head, then she looked at him and asked, "do you want to come in?" She was graceful all the while, if not also perturbed by the idea of the evacuation. So in they went, and she took him down the corridor, to the kitchen.

"Would you like something to drink?" she asked him pleasantly, "and oh, please sit down."

Relieved to do so, Luc took a chair and sat down in Mer's usual place at the big wooden Kitchen table.

"Yes, thank you, what are you having? Or … anything," he said.

"Hmmm, it's still hot." She opened the fridge door and looked inside, as though she had no idea what was really in there. She found some elderflower cordial and triumphantly pulled it out. "How about this?"

Luc nodded.

She proceeded to fill glasses with cordial, ice and lemonade, "I invented this drink myself, a long time ago," she told him and finally she placed a glass down in front of him: her offering, then seated herself opposite with her own.

"I hope you weren't busy?" asked Luc, his eyebrows raised in question, he realised then that he was seated at the edge of his chair, as if ready to fly off, and then Clara's face appeared in his mind again, but he forced himself to sit back, and listen to his Mer, there was nothing else he could do right now he told himself.

"No, no I wasn't, actually I was reading for class. Do we still have class this week, do you think?"

"Honestly, I don't know, people have already started leaving …"

"I'll phone the college tomorrow, to check," she stated, and they both took a sip.

"Mmm this is delicious, thank you."

She nodded her thanks and seemed utterly different now to Luc, like a bud that had shifted its first few curved in petals, ready to arc one day.

"Will you leave? I mean, I know we have to -when will you leave? Will you stay in the camps?" Luc asked her.

"I have no idea," she looked uncomfortable. "I haven't thought about that. Yes, I know it's on the news, and we'll get the letters soon from the council apparently, but it's like, well it's like it's happening somewhere else, to someone else … does that sound strange?"

"I know exactly what you mean," said Luc, although, he could not fully fathom or understand the disengaged fog that Mer had created for herself.

"What will you do?" she asked him and he too had no answer, the concept of 'will' seemed pointless, as they had no choice. He ran his hand through his hair in a characteristic gesture and for the first time seemed distracted, but she brought him back.

"Let's stay!" she joked, and he was so surprised that he laughed.

He looked at her, she had on a lime green soft cotton t-shirt and a pair of ragged shorts. Her skin was light brown and even paler in places; he made a note to ask her later where she was from, although he meant her family, as *she* could only ever be from London. He admired again that her dark brown and black hair fell in unhurried curls about her neck, her bare limbs were so comfortable in her own kitchen, and Luc doubted that she would have left the house like this. The heat though, even in the cool of the tile floored kitchen had made her mouth quite unnaturally red, probably a warning sign that things were not quite right, but it looked like the colour of mashed strawberries and she tellingly held the ice filled glass to her cheek and then her temples, black lashes closing briefly each time. Once again in any other country it seemed, it should have been sunset, but the light in the kitchen was wild, blazing, yet so past its peak, and still not soon to rest. A very old fashioned brown rimmed clock on the side stone wall showed that it was 8.30pm and Luc realised that he was quite hungry when he briefly glanced at it.

"Would you like to have some dinner?" Mer suddenly blurted out. "I mean … are you hungry? Or do you have to rush off?"

"Um no, but are you, I mean do you have plans? I didn't mean to …"

"No, no haven't planned anything."

"All right then. Shall I help you?" he asked, at this she looked momentarily blank.

"I think I will need more than your help," she then confessed with a half-smile, I can't really cook all that well."

"Of course." He was so relieved to be doing something mundane and yet with *this* girl, and he soon brushed away feeling awkward.

He followed her lead and she opened the fridge, as if the vault of a safe, unsure of its contents. He peered behind her, wondering what she would find there.

"We could make pasta?" he offered. "That's easy."

"Yes, good idea." And she then produced various packets for him to choose from.

Realising soon that Mer was very grateful and probably couldn't even boil an egg, he grew in confidence and opened the fridge door for himself and soon various cabinets too, taking out what he needed, each time asking if it was all right for him to use such and such.

Luc had decided to make tagliatelle with a fresh tomato sauce. It was very simple, as he didn't want to demand too much. He became busy putting a large pan of water on to boil and she asked if she could help, so he set her onto the tomatoes and let her cut them into quarters, he noticed that the knife she was using was razor sharp but she continued in hard concentration, as the fresh cut juices swam about her palms.

"How many should I cut?" Her hair fell about her face as she was bending her head forward, not having thought about pinning it back first and now had hands too red and sticky to manage it, yet, it was not like Luc to mind some disarray. "We should make some for Christine too," she said, although a thought and not a command.

After some time, where much effort had gone into sourcing and tracing what they needed in the kitchen, everything was either boiling or simmering and Luc spoke, "I'm really sorry, I didn't mean to come over and make you do all of this." He then sighed, actually exhausted he realised. He looked at his suit jacket hung about the chair, and thought about looking at his Clara-phone again, as though she would leave him another clue, but, then turned away from it, trying to block it from his mind, as the chase was futile tonight.

And Mer laughed, her hair bobbed and her small hands now washed clean and hastily dried, stirred the boiling pasta. "But *you're* doing it all! I should apologise to *you*, you're my guest. Also, no one's ever given me a cooking lesson and today I learned so much. I'm grateful Mr Luc- what's your last name?"

"Avium. We think it's Latin. What about you, what does your name mean?"

"Actually," and she looked down as she spoke "My full name is Mehreen, it means the Moon or, of the Sun, or grace and kindness, or even something to do with Mithra ... there's some discrepancy."

"Wow, what language is that?" Answers at last, he thought.

"Urdu, or Hindi, not sure, one or both of those."

"So your parents are from there?"

"Yes roundabouts, my parents are Indian, but my mother is Parsi, do you, I don't suppose you know what that is?"

"Yes I do actually, they are Zoroastrians from Iran that came and settled in India a few hundred years ago, and they are very fair skinned generally," he reeled off.

"Well done," she raised her eyebrows. "You're the first non-Indian I have not had to explain that to." And she smiled at the boiling pot.

He wondered then if she ever broke out, yelled, tore at something like a wild and wilful thing. She tasted his sauce however, to which he had added a great deal of garlic, a dash of sugar and finally a knob of salty butter to finish and then, as though seized with some of the vigour he wondered if she ever possessed, she said, "Mmm, this is delicious."

"You're surprised?" he laughed.

"Honestly, yes. Sorry. Well done. Christine will love this."

Luc hoped that Christine would be working late.

He placed the pasta on the table now dressed in a shiny gleaming red sauce, made suddenly bright as Mer put on the lights; giving up on a waning sun, although it had far from set. A massive block of rustic Parmesan sat beside the plate and Luc thought it too presumptuous to ask for some wine, but Mer quickly produced a bottle of red. Mer was going to go off somewhere to look for those wide tall glasses as they had used before, but Luc suggested using small water glasses instead, like they used in France at home, and she was intrigued, as he knew that she would be.

They were very hungry by this point, and ate dinner in silence for the first three minutes.

"This is wonderful," she said again, mouth half full, her plate red and messy against the vivid backdrop of the green t-shirt.

"Thank you." He looked at her and gave her his warmest smile, he could not imagine where he would have ended up this evening after this last attempt to find some answers, but now sore of heart, he was pleased instead to be here. In truth, there should have been some French bread as well and it would have felt truly authentic to Luc, like a meal at home.

Finally, fed, sated and emboldened by her praise he picked up his glass to toast, but she raised hers and spoke first, "To my Chef."

To which Luc bowed to her at his chair and they drank. It was the finalé, and then a door closed from far down the corridor and Christine could be seen stalking towards the kitchen, as she spotted the male figure with her back to her, she slowed, and then gained pace, as though she knew who it was.

They fed Christine, Mer singing Luc's praises and gave her wine, the baby was with her father tonight, but as soon as that was done as well as a discussion on how Christine would have to go and stay at her mother's in the north for the evacuation, Luc left.

Chapter 33

They did have a class that week but it would be the last class until after the evacuation was over. For this last week they had been asked to read 'The Great Gatsby'; it seemed fitting for the end of an era.

Mer was already seated in class as Luc arrived, and wore a little white dress cut in the style of the 1950's that flared out at the waist. It was sleeveless and completely exposed the bare skin of her arms which caught Luc as demurely seductive. She wore her heeled sandals, but only some sheer lip gloss with then, blackest mascara. She seemed distracted by her book and even though her head was bowed to look at it as he entered, she stirred slightly as Luc went to sit down, some colour in her cheeks. Finally she looked up and Luc glanced over at that moment and waved. She waved back, in a friendly way.

Knowing that she was Indian now, Luc looked at her quizzically; she still looked like a hybrid to him, as though Italian or Greek mixed with Indian, or some other delicious concoction. He wanted to see her again, but he felt he had been too forward, stressed as he had been he had acted on impulse and now did not know how to approach her, for how many times could he arrive uninvited?

That day all the class had attended; they knew it would be the last until after the evacuation and all that that entailed. Yet no one was sure what that *would* entail and as they sat firm, book or pencil in hand listening to Mr Andrews' every word or gazing out of the bright windows, silent yet still they were very much where they wanted to be, for none wanted to leave, none wanted to go. It was Mr Andrews' passion for literature and involving teaching methods that were unusual and had easily stemmed the typical potential for boredom; for as he loved and believed in literature as a thing of awe, so too did they.

Luc glanced at Mer often, he sometimes caught her eye and she smiled back. But then as the class wore on Luc started staring at the dappled shadows on the walls that were pink and bruised plum as the sun wound its path through evening, and he became still eyed like a languid statue, yet exuded heat, as though rendered immovable by his hidden furnace, and then of course it happened. The Clara-phone, now set to only vibrate, clearly made its presence felt in his pocket. Luc's heart leapt to his mouth. Luckily the halfway point mini break was moments away; So Luc heard the words but could not listen to Mr Andrews anymore even though the others were generally rapt. And yet, there was a level of distraction in the class that was an underlying force, for at the back of everyone's minds, were plans and planning, a humming subconscious: how to leave? When to get out? What to pack? ... It was hard to be there Luc could see, although they all wanted to be; their loyalty eroded by impermanence. None of it made sense however, as they were all coming back.

Luc held his phone through his pocket, as though trying to appease it and asking it to wait. Finally, Mr Andrews declared a break, and a hum of movement began. Luc took out the phone.

I need to know who you are.

Said the message, from Clara. Nothing else. Luc thought quickly, and grew annoyed. This was definitely a bad idea, never mind if he was not sure if Clara, Gemma or Balthazar even could deserve his help, if nothing else if he revealed to Clara that it was him, Luc, who'd helped her, he worried that it would bring everything a step closer to James, as they were all so connected, Clara might tell James, or want to speak to him about it, or ask James questions about Luc and his position, (especially if she was on the wrong side) and this would inexorably draw his friend James into the circumference of this mess. No. Luc was resolute, under no circumstances, not until he knew more. So engrossed in his thoughts had Luc been that he didn't notice that all were settling again, or that Mer had been looking at him.

Finally, when the class did end, Mer rose from her chair among the throng and Luc joined her to walk home.

"Nice class?" Luc asked her.

"Very nice," she said sadly, "I don't want it to be disrupted like this."

"No, but it should be all right once we come back, don't you think?"

Mer looked at him with a sort of gloom, "Have you decided? Will you be leaving? When will you go?" She looked into his face for an answer.

"I haven't thought about it enough, but now, well yes maybe James will go to his old family home in Berkshire, maybe I'll go there with him. But what about you, any thoughts yet?"

"You know," she bent her head conspiratorially as they walked, "honestly between you and me," and she then lowered her voice, "I am *really* thinking of stocking up and hiding at home."

So she was serious; the demure, quietly spoken girl wanted to break the rules and hide from the British Army and from the government. Luc began to laugh, from the sheer audacity of it. And then as they rounded upon their home, there was another surprise: James was standing outside Luc's front door.

"James? How you doing? All OK?" Luc asked as they both came over to him.

"Hello, Mer, how are you?" James asked Mer instead.

"Very well, thank you," she said.

"Just came to drop in see how you are, hope it's OK?" James said to Luc.

"I have a very busy schedule, you should have made an appointment, and anyway, Mer and I are making plans to break the law."

"-What?"

"Well Mer is anyway, can you believe, she's thinking of staying and hiding at home during the evacuation."

"Really?" said James, drawn in and lowering his voice. "You're going to do that?"

Mer became uncertain, as though her plan had seemed innocent enough but then said, "Yes," defiantly. "What harm will I do? I'll just hide."

Luc looked at James, both were a bit surprised. "It's not a bad idea, what do you think?" said Luc.

"I think she would get away with it, you on the other hand would be tracked down by your office."

It was a genial comment, but ultimately a slip. Luc had not consciously registered that James had referred to his office as though he knew it well and its workings and its power; so it nagged Luc as a thought with no words or clear form, as just numb nudge, from of all things, the truth.

"Yes that's a point," said Luc, "we've been told to leave and I work for a government department, so it really would be very naughty if I stayed."

"But if you hid?" Mer asked.

"I don't know … maybe it's possible." Luc began to consider it, pursing his lips and nodding.

"Please start packing, seriously. He's coming with me." said James.

"I am?" Luc asked.

With that, soon Mer bid them goodnight and James came upstairs with Luc, where Luc gave him a drink and watched him massage his temple and run his hands through his hair, on occasion.

"So," Luc asked, "all OK otherwise, love life?"

"Jesus, you're like a mother hen. I have currently got no love life."

"Hmmm, I see. All right, just wondered." And Luc thought better to ask him if Clara had now contacted him at all.

"What about you?" asked James, with every intonation of mock suspicion possible.

"What do you mean?"

"*Mer.*"

"Oh, oh *that*. You noticed. Well, there's nothing to be said ... She doesn't give anything though, do you know what I mean? I mean, not like that, she's kind and nice, we had dinner, but, I can't explain ..."

"You like her a lot."

"Yeah," Luc sighed.

"Give it some time, I think she needs time," said James.

Luc nodded, and rested on his sofa thoughtfully, and then thought of Clara waiting for a response from him, which would not come, while James stayed there and was often quiet, 'till midnight.

Chapter 34

As Luc rose the next day, he immediately looked at his Clara-phone, as though waiting for more communication and also, as he knew that she would not be satisfied with his silence. He had first met Clara properly at the age of twelve, although he imagined that he may have even seen her aged eight, but was not sure. Her parents had a holiday house nearby theirs and so it was often in the holidays that he used to see her, but it was James that she used to steal off with; off to the woods, or to the banks of a stream … why would she possibly remember Luc at all?

It was so tempting to communicate with her, to tell her that it had been him, to claim that glory; but it defied all logic, and it wasn't safe he reminded himself. He was tempted also, knowing that Gemma would go to work, to go and bang on the door where he knew that Clara was staying, but that would be foolish too, the very thing required of him now was patience; he knew somehow, as things were playing out before his eyes, that his moment would come.

Instead he dutifully went to the office; Balthazar rushed out soon after and left, and Gemma stayed glued to her desk, and her phone rang continuously as though a hotline to the one in charge; which in some ways it was. His colleagues were focused, the lost and confused of four days ago already had plans for where to go and when for this evacuation. But Luc's focus was upon his superiors, and the red and blue folders that tantalisingly came and went. He had blissfully not been sent to see that Minister again, but then again felt an urgency in his chest to find out more; so that he had some ammunition for when that time came, for it would, he was sure. He considered now following Balthazar, and laughed inside at himself; the man travelled at all times in a chauffeur driven car, and probably had who knows what kind of security measures in place. No, he would have to befriend him as he was trying to do with Gemma, to which the evacuation had proved a real spanner in the works; occupying and engrossing both of them in turn.

The day ended with Balthazar storming back in, his face barely acknowledging his staff or where he was, Luc watched as he marched what Luc thought was to his office, but instead as Luc rose to follow, he saw that Balthazar stopped at Gemma's desk, secluded as it was in her large corridor, and just looked at her, she rose as though levitated by his gaze out of her chair, and then followed him into his office, where the frosted door then blocked out all sound, and left Luc with only their shadows, that were gesticulating.

It strongly gave Luc the feeling, that whatever it was, they may be in it together. He wanted to wait, and watch to see if anything happened next, but it was well past the time to go home, so Luc had to leave, eyeing the office door for as long as he could.

The new feeling in the air caused by a looming evacuation was now prevalent: at the office and on the tube, on the streets; as if everybody was waiting for something: a climax, or an answer. He showered as he did after work as it was still hot, but nowadays often with his eyes shut; as though trying to cleanse away the dark place of intrigue that his work had become. He put on a white t-shirt and navy shorts, and went down to go and sit in his garden for a while, to catch the last of the birds singing and the sunshine; his simple distracting pleasure. As he approached the French doors he looked by habit to his right and saw Mer in her garden, curled up in a chair with arms crossed against her chest. He had never seen her like this before, usually her calm placid mask was neither happy nor sad, it was just evocative of some distant form of distress, too veiled to grasp, but today she was downright miserable. She held a tissue in one hand, and then she took a very deep breath. She was in pale, soft blue shorts and a white peasant top, that would have blossomed about her frame in billows had she not been so tightly wound up about herself. He waited: for movement, or Christine, or a baby crying -nothing came; there was however a breeze, that lifted some of her hair, now a mop from her face and she bound her arms tighter about her, it was a fresher breeze, yet still full of the scent of hot grass and flowers.

In that moment, he did an about turn and headed back towards his own building's front door. As he stepped outside for the first time, apart from the day of the storm, since he had come to London that summer, had it become cloudy, a dull white, yet it was still clammy and the breeze picked up again, insistent. He took the few steps to her door and rang the bell.

Soon, she peaked around her cumbersome door, as it opened by her own hand; she obviously wasn't expecting anyone.

"Oh, Luc. Hello ... Is everything all right?"

"Oh, um yes, I was just, well ... I just wanted to say hello. I know you maybe have plans ..."

She was nodding, although her look at first was far away. "Why not. Of course ... please come in."

She led him down the corridor to the kitchen, not considering the television or garden or any other potential activity. Suddenly, she began, "I mean it you know, I'm staying, they can do what they like. How can they spot or track every one of us." She didn't require an answer.

In the few days or weeks that Luc had had with Mer, he marvelled at her defiance, and then grew perturbed by its innocence.

"I'm sorry I've led you here," she said as she realised that they were in the kitchen again. "What would you like to do?"

"Um ... we could look at your garden, to see if it is like mine?"

As she led him again, she managed to give him a smile, her mascara was slightly smudged, like a hint of gothic about her eyes, she took him back to the living room, where she opened her French doors, they were not locked, and led him down three steps.

Her garden was glorious, much like his, but wilder and also emptier in parts, with a few stretches of plain grass where the green metal table and chairs had been placed, and where she must have been crying just now, before the dense alcoves began; but these were of a more generous size and widely spaced out than his, and so created deeper areas of foliage that were hidden in each section, where light could not easily penetrate or illuminate; a secret garden indeed.

As she took him down to where the alcoves of flora and fauna began: there were hanging boughs and occasional statues, lost maidens, or fulfilled ones looking suredly upon all they surveyed, "Do you like it?" he turned to ask her, stopping their stride.

"You know, I do, I love it. It was a gift from my father you know, this house." She was not ashamed, or boastful, it was just a statement that she made.

"So, tell me about yourself?" she asked him finally as they strolled. Her questioning him now gave her surer form, but like that of a bitter metal.

"What would you like to know?" he asked her earnestly.

"Everything. From the beginning as well." She looked at him unflinchingly.

"Are you sure? This will be very boring ..." he smiled.

"All right, so your parents, do they live here?"

Oh dear, she had struck the wound far too soon, but Luc decided to overcome it quickly. "Well my father is from here, actually they both lived as James' parents' neighbours a long time ago, and my mother was French from a small town in south-west France, she, she passed away last year," he said with much grace and also as quickly as he could.

"I am so sorry." Some colour grew about her cheeks. "Any brothers, sisters?"

"No it's just me," he said, but smiled to reassure her that this was no bad thing.

But her cheeks were of a darker hue now; he could see that she wanted to undo any pain she may have caused him.

"So, I suppose James and Mischa and you are very close? You all look it. It's good to have friends like that."

"Yes, it is, and you and Christine, you seem like that?"

"Yes," she nodded. "We are, but she's also my relation now, she married my cousin, things are a little rough for them, so she's here with me ... I mean of course she *is* my friend, but family now too, it's not somehow the same ... friends can be a sacred thing I think."

He listened to her, not wanting to interrupt.

She fired again, "So tell me about your work, are you allowed to speak about it, I mean to say, are you really an analyst, are you not a spy?" she smiled.

Luc felt then a dark and crimson tide flood his heart, his work ... "I wish I was." Luc smiled, "My grandfather was a spy though, on the good side, he worked with the Allies, he was my mother's father, my granny -his wife, is still alive, she still lives in their same town by the beach. And there is a room there just in memory of him, with his picture and medals on show."

"Gosh."

"Yes and this ring," he showed her the little finger on his left hand, upon which was a gold signet ring, that in one corner had the small indent of an asymmetric star. "This was his, he gave it to me."

"What a lovely thing to remember him by."

"I myself, write reports about trade and UK government business deals, though I think what everyone else does in the department is actually very important, they're always rushing about ..." he shrugged, hoping that his remark had seemed casual enough.

"Do you like it?" she asked him, point blank.

Luc blinked. "I like where I am, the job has good prospects, so I hope to progress in it ... I would have preferred my grandfather's work though ..." he said as it made her eyes shimmer and widen a little bit.

"Yes, it does sound very exciting."

"Do you work, Mer?" He was direct back, finally.

"I do … I did, at an Art Gallery, I helped procure. I have a History of Art degree." She was stating things but seemed unsure. "But I gave it up … for a little while … I'm taking some time out."

Luc sensed deep water; it seemed that tonight's confessional had been designed for him alone and he realised that he was also being swept away by her many questions, as though it was a revelation, everything must come out, or like a forthright Cinderella at the ball before midnight, forcing out a confession before the bell tolled. He wondered how far this confession would extend to herself, but he did not ask her anything more yet.

They then talked about where he had learned to cook, it was his grandmother who had taught him, the one who lived by the sea in France, both his parents had worked, so it had come as a necessity sometimes, and with that as fluidly they decided to order pizza for dinner, and Luc stared up at the cloud thickening sky feeling some reprieve whilst being with Mer in her garden; as though hidden from the whole world.

When their food arrived they sat and took their hot thick slices hungrily, and Luc poured wine which was ruby red into the same small tumblers she produced now. Luc saw that Mer could be seen to be enjoying herself, and yet with a kind of brutal intensity, a punishing kind of joy.

The evening was not as bright and attractive as they had been in the last few weeks; the clouds had come over in a sulk and had also trapped in the heat stubbornly. The wine however was oblivious to its setting and worked its charms as well as it could, although Mer had not had very much of it, she seemed calm and steady as she asked, "Do you have a partner?" but her gaze flickered as though she knew she was on hazardous ground now, for many reasons, as it verged on impertinence or overfamiliarity, if nothing else.

Luc looked at her earnestly, not embarrassed by the question in the least. He had grown up around women, his aunts and his mother and the manner in which they discussed all the unflinching grist and nuance of everything.

"No, I don't," he answered simply.

"Was there someone?"

Luc felt again a thrill, as she pushed him.

Luc nodded, "Yes there was, her name was Stephanie, it lasted six years ..." and for the first time faltered.

"I'm sorry," she said politely.

"It's all right, it was a long time ago, after my mother, it really doesn't matter."

In all, Luc had responded to her inquisition without an ounce of retaliation, defensiveness or malice; but how he sorely wanted to ask her the same questions.

The clouds had thickened into a blanket of viscose white. "Shall we go inside?" she said. He agreed although it bothered him, feeling it would not be the same inside and unexposed.

They carried their debris with them, the pizza box and wine, and he followed her as she led him to the kitchen, it must be her favourite room he thought, funny, as she couldn't cook.

"Is Christine working late tonight?" he asked her as he took his normal seat in the kitchen.

"Yes, but it is a party connected with work, the baby's with her father."

Luc then grew brave, the lights lit in the kitchen were a warm yellow, showing that Mer's lips were swollen, probably from the wine and her hair was blown about into an unruly mess, sensing this she pulled her hair together with one hand, trying to force it into shape. So he asked her, "What about you, Mer? Was there someone like that for you?"

"Actually ... I don't think I have ever had *that* experience."

186

"Really?"

"No, not in the way I think you mean."

Luc had no idea how close to the edge they were, to the truth, or that she was skirting around a blade and still enjoying it. So she quizzed him further on whether he believed if there can only be one great love in a lifetime. His answer was philosophical at first, factoring in degrees and types of love and then finally, it distilled itself down to a simple, "Yes." In the following pause she then asked him, "Would you like a different drink? I keep giving you red wine, but we have everything-"

"It's fine, I like wine, it's the French in me, I'm used to it, I mean, I enjoy it."

It had been a strange evening, like going to a Victorian funfair and visiting the cruel and strange sights, like mysterious tarot readers and bearded ladies and distorted mirrors. Exhausting too; Luc left after ten at night, savouring the night air for a few moments before returning to his own front door, and yet it had still been a balm to everything else, and he felt relieved that the Clara-phone had not sounded again that day. As he walked up his vermillion carpet, he knew Mer had been naughty if not mischievous in some way by her questions and also that he had indulged her, and that moreover he would continue to do so, for a time at least.

Chapter 35

Deep in slumber, it wasn't an exact sound or noisy disturbance that woke Clara; instead she woke with a dry mouth in the dark and had no idea what time it was. Then she heard it, it was not as though anything was moving about, but one can tell when there is life about, especially at night.

So she rose, all the time her ears cocked, and opened her bedroom door slowly, all was dark, but she could hear the sound clearer now, someone was breathing, and then to her relief there was then a sigh. So Clara made her way to the living room, and there in the dark was Gemma, sitting cross legged upon the floor, in front of her now darkened, dormant mirror; and in the mute glow of a far off street light that still remained, Clara could make out the streaks of tears upon her face.

"Gemma?"

"Oh, I'm so sorry, I didn't mean to wake you!"

"Don't be silly." And Clara came and sat down next to her. "Will someone please tell me something about what's going on? Then I might be of some help, at least to you tonight."

Gemma started to cry again, "Clara, I can tell you this much, three of our members are dead. Elsa, Dora, John McMahon. All Gone. Michael's checked - they were murdered. Oh God, Clara, we're in *so* much trouble."

"Jesus, why couldn't any of you have told me this?!"

"It's complicated," Gemma said through her tears.

"OK, OK, I'm dreading this but I have to get out and see James ASAP, but first, Gemma ... I realise ... I need to see Sir John, it's urgent now."

"You want him to come, now?"

"No, it won't be long 'till the morning. But can he come then?"

Gemma nodded. Clara then leaned over and put her arm around her shoulder, and Gemma continued to cry; and Clara started to fathom slowly, a little of Gemma's terror.

*

The morning was well past dawn, when Clara back in her bedroom but now fully dressed, heard the doorbell. She rushed at its sound.

"Sir John!" she said, "Thank you so much for coming."

"What is it, sweetheart?" He strode into Gemma's living room, as Gemma made sure the door was firmly closed behind him.

"Sir John, I didn't tell you everything, probably because no one had told me *anything*. But Gemma told me about our three in France. I'm so sorry. And ... I've been an idiot ... I just wanted to say that I received a message: to go into hiding in New York, it said that I was in grave danger and not to attend a Gala I was due at that night. And he never asked for my new address, and seemed very concerned about me."

"Oh my God. So that's what you did? That's why you weren't in the office?"

"Yes. I ran away. I thought it must have been you or James, but now, in hindsight ..."

"Show me the message!"

"I can't. I destroyed it, because I destroyed my old phone like he told me to ... I honestly thought it was you."

"Well ... at least you're all right. I'll get on to James immediately, I wish you hadn't destroyed it. But I understand. Was that it, child?"

"Yes, Sir John, thank you so much for coming, I'm so sorry."

"It's all right." And with that he quickly left, a look of determination on his face.

Clara sighed, she had done what she could, Sir John and James did need to know that this had happened, but she would still try and find her saviour first on her own. For this was no foe, she was certain. *Then why did you tell them?* A voice asked her, and she replied: just in case it helped them in any way, if there was a puzzle to be solved, if it was a missing piece … And soon, she would see James, and he of course, may read her secrets by just looking at her face.

Chapter 36

James had been asked by Sir John for an urgent meeting and so had chosen the old Tate or the Tate Britain as it was now called although it was like a giant ancient Roman palace, its size alone perfect for disappearing into. James sat near Sargent's 'Carnation, Lily, Lily Rose', and had a sketch pad in hand.

Sir John arrived, Roman nose now posing a strong tan, his whole face glowed in fact, but he always wore a good suit and would have been very prominent had the museum's dimensions not been so vast, like a lost palace of Atlantis. He sat down next to James.

"Sir John," said James in greeting.

"James."

"I wish I could have seen you again before the official announcement of this evacuation, but there was no way to get away. It's not a bad idea, trade is at a halt and you know that as soon as the cleaning is over the travel embargo ends on all countries that have been so 'cleaned'."

"Paris?"

"Yes, exactly, I hope Simon will be all right."

"He'll have to manage, I'm sure he will."

"This isn't why I called you, James."

James looked at him. Sir John was seldom this reticent. "What is it?"

"Clara spoke to me, we have a new situation. Apparently someone sent her a text message while she was in New York, telling her that she was in grave danger and to go into hiding. And, not to attend a certain Gala. Was it you?"

"What? No ... Show it to me!"

"I can't, she said she destroyed it on that person's advice."

As Sir John filled in James on every detail of what Clara had told him, James felt the room start to swim, and some sort of thudding had begun behind his ears.

"We need to find this person," said James finally, with a glint of steel in his voice.

"I know, but they did help her, remember that she said, and she thinks it is a He, that he never wanted to know *where* she was hiding. That's something."

"Or something very clever. Why the hell didn't she tell you immediately?!"

"She didn't know anything, she still barely knows anything, James, about what's happened, and … why, we want you to tell her, we can't have her running off again, it's too dangerous."

"Sir John, I was the reason that she ran off in the first place."

"I know, but she knows that three are dead, and now with the severity of the message she received, she'll listen."

"She won't."

"Listen to me, you will *have* to manage this, James, from the sound of it her life was at stake, I think she has understood that now. She *cannot* run off."

James massaged his forehead, then ran his hand through his hair. "She's still at Gemma's?"

"Yes, see, she's staying put. Though she is determined to go and see you, and we won't be able to stop her unless we tell her everything -things only *you* can tell her."

"OK, call her up, stall her for as long as you can, tell her I'm busy, away, whatever, I'll find a way to come to her, I could go to Gemma's immediately, but I'm worried about Clara's reaction, as soon as she knows about Simon, I don't know what she'll do, so buy me some time. It's just a few days until the evacuation, and that will buy us even more time with her."

"All right m'boy."

"And Luc? He's been asking me some oddly searching questions, about Clara and Simon."

"I honestly feel his role at the office is to a minimum, he just does his reports, he's nowhere near us; Clara and Simon is what he knows of *you* ..."

"All right ..."

"James?"

"Yes?"

"This *will* be sorted, I'm working on you getting to Paris, the best bet is to go with someone like me who has diplomatic clearance, but it will be driving. You would still have to hide in the car during the check points though."

James nodded.

"How long can he wait, in Paris I mean?" the great man asked.

"Honestly I don't know his status. But no one has been ... has gone down since the three, apart from this Clara complication." James frowned. "He's hiding I'm sure. I want to have our people in France check up on him, but it's just too dangerous to be anywhere near him for any of them, I'll call him before I leave just to check, I'm keeping communication to a minimum right now."

Sir John nodded, his face had lost its usual jovial aspect, he patted James on the shoulder and then made his way out of the white cavernous palace of the museum, into a side street and his waiting Daimler, sleekly humming in the street.

James watched him stride off. A dull thudding began again in his ears, but instead he wondered when he would be able to reach Paris now, he was sure that Simon was still alive as they wanted more information from him, that was the point, he would be useless to them dead. Had Simon led them to everything? Their whole organisation and set up, which as yet had no name; never before had they been so vulnerable. So many governments were in the pockets of big business, which in turn often had links to much shadier sorts, and so the three who'd been killed would have found it easy to draw an executioner to themselves. James heart began to race again, he wished he could just reverse time and for this whole sorry affair to crawl back into itself, it was as though he was now instead watching the knife go in, and was powerless to stop it. But he would try, he would reach Paris, retrieve Simon and make him disappear with a new identity, this was his plan, a little unstable as it left Simon free, but it was his final decision. He would not have him killed. He could not; it would make him the same man as all those that he fought against, and so, redundant in his quest. The thudding became insistent now, and yet he still forced his mind away from it …

Instead he thought about the fact that it was Friday, and just over one week before the exodus from London, he wondered if he would be able to reach Paris before or after that event. It was a strange occurrence no doubt this evacuation and he felt now a little unconvinced about it, surely they could do all the cleaning that they wanted at night or in the early hours? But such musings had not worked, not at all, and a deep red colour began to flood his face.

They tried to kill her.

His heart pounded, his breathing became shallow, someone had saved Clara, but surely she'd been exposed, and he realised at that moment, alone, seated in front of the glorious painting, truly, finally, what things had come to now. So he took out his phone and dialled the man he had just so recently said goodbye to, and gave an order; one that he knew would never leave him whole again.

Chapter 37

It had taken Michael six hours to get here; the waves of the marina where he stood tall and strong, lapped and slapped at the brick walls that shaped it. Dusk had fallen in the south of France, sleek white boats and yachts bobbed before him; but he knew which one he was headed for. With a crown of darkening curls he looked at his watch, which could stand the watery depths and all manner of shocks and knocks; for he had to be timely. He then looked down at his ankle where a knife lay strapped up inside and concealed beneath his trousers, so too, bound to him were two syringes -that he should not knock about, and finally, under his shirt, strapped behind his back, one gun and then on the other side, another. He looked about him, every muscle and sinew alert, there was no one there, so he sat down at the water's edge, and dipped his feet into the Mediterranean blue depths, and soon, slipped so effortlessly into her embrace, that it was as though his robust and sturdy form had been nothing but an apparition, now moving quickly under the sea, and making its way through the waters, to bring about nothing, but an end.

Chapter 38

Murder, murder, murder! The black murmurs were inside, but James let it go on; he would not stop this.

He had returned home in a daze. In his bedroom he sat on the edge of the bed and felt a new kind of nothing, which was actually a hushed violence inside.

Would it be hours or days he thought, wondering how long an assassination would take. He imagined that he should know, given the amount of assassination plots that his group had exposed or foiled.

He kept thinking of his sister and of Mischa and of course Clara, in order to convince himself that he was protecting them and all of the others. And would they judge him for this? Perhaps yes, or worse perhaps not, and James thought of Mischa and wondered if he would ever have turned out like this, with such a soldier's steady heart, if he hadn't known James. But James wanted to wait first, until it was over, not because of cowardice but because he did not want to hear any dissent, or anything to unnerve him or to shake him off this course. He would wait. But how would he know? His targets were three high profile men, yet only in the world of business and finance, seemingly only socially connected, although he knew that they were linked in orchestrating the killing of their employees; namely James' members. Perhaps it would be mentioned in the secondary news, the lesser news that was tucked away under blazing headlines, the latter that were currently so busy screaming about the end of civilisation as we knew it if the embargo did not end. The disease itself had quite truthfully run rampant in cities that were filthy, such as those that still had slums, the cleaning offered a ray of hope it seemed, to make the world a normal place again, or back to how it had been at least. He would have to read the small stories, looking for the names of three very big men, who in lesser times of upheaval would have been on everyone's lips.

He scoured the Internet and kept on the television flicking between news channels. Hours passed, but he had to know.

James knew that all three would have to be dealt with simultaneously in order not to be able to alert each other. A name then finally appeared: 'Michel Grimbaud has died of a suspected heart attack at his office.' The room began to spin, James reached out blindly to try and find the sofa's edge which he unsteadily sat down upon, he did not know how he felt, he felt an alien numbness, it was a sensation like no other, but unmistakable: he had just killed a man. Murder, murder, murder … dangerous ideas were trying to intrude; for had this man's wife loved him and were there distraught children left behind? But James quickly banished them all, his breathing shallow, he sat with his arms limp by his side and so then the bile rose, and suddenly he dashed in an ungainly manner to the nearby kitchen sink, where he vomited violently.

Once purged but still numb, he cleaned his mess up in a trance and created for himself a simple balm: a large glass of water bulging with ice that he held to his temple, and then went back again to the computer screen to scour the news. The television repeated and looped its news stories, at present a journalist was showcasing rows and rows of tents in Buckinghamshire, one of the evacuation shelters, his point however was that most of these would probably be empty, as it was generally only the very wealthy who lived in central London and they would either be going to country hotels or staying with friends in the countryside, or renting, or even very quickly buying country properties for the purpose by laying down quick solid cash; they too it seemed, were not convinced that things would be the same after the evacuation was over and preferred to purchase something lavish yet concrete to stay in, as many of them could not fly away home to wherever they really lived, like the far off sands of Arabia.

They were all dead he was sure, all three of them, but it was simply that Grimbaud had been found first. The others had to be found, so he waited. He rubbed his eyes in front of the screen, waiting for the second name to appear. Then it happened; 'Dominic Burgess reported dead at home, cause unknown.' That wasn't good, 'cause unknown', that could mean an autopsy and an inquest and who knew what else, yet still, James knew that even if all such investigations did occur, the death perhaps could even be seen as suspicious for decades, but no one would be able to get to the bottom of it. From his own experience of trying to expose the truth about the so called natural deaths of prominent people that had been very much assassinations, he knew about how these things worked and how easy it was to get away with them.

It was a morbid exercise, but James never considered calling off the watch; if even one of them was still alive, knowing what had happened to the other two; they would surely know what was going on and orchestrate a return strike.

At last, on a remote Reuters news feed page there was a single sentence: 'Peter Armstrong has been reported dead in a boating accident, in the French Riviera.' That's why it took time he thought, the news had had to reach back to the shore, although it was already a suspicious incident he considered, annoyed, as the boat would not have been going anywhere being just moored there, but it was better than another 'heart attack' he felt.

It was done, and yet he felt broken spirited, soon too, he would have to witness his little sister apprehend him for the first time as a murderer, so be it, but he needed her and Mischa and he consoled himself now by the honour of his choices.

He realised that he was utterly exhausted, the battle somewhat won, his hands bloody and as he laid down to rest, his broken thoughts instead turned to Clara, and the kind and loving things she used to whisper to him before they slept; her memory gave rest to his ragged emotions, and put them under a necessary paralysis, lest he let them loose.

Yet, while trying to surrender to sleep even under an emotional blockade, the thoughts crept in like spiders, but they were not what he'd expected. It had been so easy you see, he'd never realised that he had this much power, one word to Sir John and three people were dead and Michael had been their instrument, his thoughts flowed soon dreamlike, and he thought of Archangel Michael with his sword ... and then James did finally succumb to sleep; because despite his struggle with himself over what he'd done, he was still yet relieved, and the next day he would confess.

Chapter 39

The next morning James had woken in his bed and for a full minute he had been calm because he had forgotten; as the amnesia lifted, it then came back to him, he felt at first horror but also then shamelessly, relief. As soon as he was able he then summoned Mischa and Anjelica to his house. They came immediately and he suggested that they set off for the park; it was not lost on either that such a suggestion sounded ominous.

As they sat down upon the grass, James spoke, "I have taken action." He paused; he had no idea how to phrase it.

"What's happened, James?" Anjelica asked.

"I rang Simon."

Both of his audience raised their eyebrows.

"Simon has had help from Louise in making his lines of communication safe," James replied simply.

So they waited now for more.

"The first time I heard from Simon, I was furious and also really alarmed that he was talking to me on an unsecure line, we try to keep our phones at home safe, but you know … so I didn't ask him, was not able to ask him, about the nitty gritty. But the second time, I did."

James paused again, not intending the dramatic effect that he was creating; it was essentially just to keep himself and his words stable. "We've lost three people, thankfully no more since then, all three worked for completely different companies, I … I asked for the names of the people that had Simon betrayed us to."

He took a breath, they waited. "The names were: Michel Grimbaud, Dominic Burgess and Peter Armstrong. Yesterday, I learned that Clara may have narrowly escaped something terrible … so I phoned Sir John."

James paused again. Mischa who was sitting cross legged, turned to look James in the face. James said nothing but matched his gaze -yet with blue eyes of fixed and vacant glass, and a jaw set in stone. Mischa blinked, and then slowly grew stone white, closing his eyes briefly before looking away; he had understood long before Anjelica. She, looked from her brother to Mischa to her brother again, James tried to keep his face neutral, the distance in his eyes continued, for a far off bondage held him to, as upon a meat hook, kept him at bay, as some savage gravity of conscience threatened to devour his soul if he ventured too near himself; so he hovered juxtaposed between this world and what awaited him inside, and thus, a glazed look was all he could manage.

Anjelica waited mouth slightly open, for either to speak.

"So, then what? Are we going to do something?" she asked both of them finally.

James looked at Mischa, for the first time, asking for help.

"Jelly," said Mischa looking at her square in the face and now white as a sheet. "They're dead," he told her quietly.

"What do you mean they're dead? What happened?" she asked blindly.

It was exasperating, why was she being so purposefully stupid?

Mischa tried again. "That's what calling Sir John with the names meant," he said, very patiently.

"So we ... we ..." she trailed off, but James was so relieved that she had said 'we' and not that accusatory *you*.

Anjelica became mute, her eyes focussed on something beyond them.

"It was Michael," James spoke to Mischa and Mischa nodded back.

She asked then finally, "So they are just gone ... It's over?"

"Yes, it might be over now," said James, "but we don't know who they told, or if they just used their own thugs to do their work. But if they're connected with someone above them or any government, -then others know, though I do think if it was the latter a little more would have been done to us by now. I take some comfort from that."

"So you think these three men must have just gone through their connections with the underworld to attack us?" asked Anjelica.

"There's a problem with that," Mischa spoke again, and with some authority. "The deaths of our people were made very skilfully to look like accidents, underworld offensives can be more aggressive and cack handed, though not always, but by and large they skip finesse, it's government agencies that can really do death with grace."

"It's true …" said Anjelica.

"Well if that is true, we've still sent a message and if we can get to Simon, we can stem this tide," stated James.

"You think we can stop this?" Mischa asked him.

"Yes, I do."

"… What do you mean 'get to Simon'?" Anjelica asked quietly.

James laughed hollowly, it was brief but genuine. "Jelly," he said gently, "I only need to get Simon back home, I am still planning on helping him find a new identity."

James saw something flicker in Mischa's eye that knew that that wasn't the answer, but he fell short of any retort, probably considering as James was, that they were all murderers now, would they now start murdering their friends?

But Anjelica was undeterred, "Is that safe?" she had the gall to ask.

"What else can we do Jelly?" said James.

"What would dad have done, about Simon, I mean?" she asked her brother.

"I think … he would have done the same thing," answered James.

"But making someone disappear in those days was easier wasn't it, less technology," said Mischa.

"I know, I know this, and so it will have to be an intense effort to keep Simon safe and a secret. That is my plan," said James.

Mischa rubbed his eyes thinking. "All right, if we not only keep Simon a secret and also surveille him without his knowledge, this could work -I don't trust him anymore."

"I'm sorry to bring this up, but that's all very well, but what if they, they kidnap him or something, people will reveal anything under torture, it doesn't take much …" said Anjelica.

James looked at her. *"What would you have me do, Jelly?"* he asked, looking at her again.

Mischa looked at her too, waiting for an answer.

She shook her head. "There isn't an answer is there," she whispered.

No one had an answer to Anjelica's last, but something yet had cleared, for it was as though the blood on James' hands had been shared, communed, and so created in them a new courageous resolve; potently forged through a bloody solidarity.

Chapter 40

There was screaming in Mer's living room. At least Christine and Rehan had been polite enough to close the door thought Mer, but their voices harangued each other in a loud verbal storm. Mer had retreated to the kitchen and tried to occupy herself with tidying up the breakfast litter musing on how she had not told Christine about Luc's visit the night before. Christine had returned in the early hours of Saturday morning and Mer had been in no mood to gossip about herself. Christine and the baby were due to leave on Thursday night, or would that change now that husband and wife sounded close to killing each other. It was at that moment that the phone rang and she picked it up imagining it to be her mother from New York, worrying.

"Hello?" she said.

There was a pause.

"Hello?" she asked again, thinking that perhaps there was a delay on an international line.

"Mer?"

"… Zafar?" Her mouth stayed open after its utterance.

"Have you been well, all um … all right?"

"Yes, all fine," she tried not to be too abrupt.

"Where are you staying for the evacuation? I'm staying with Raoul, you know Raoul, do you remember the address? Let me give it to you …"

"Of course," Mer then took a pen and paper and dutifully wrote down where her husband would be staying. "I'll be staying with Christine at her parents' in Yorkshire. I'll have my phone; I don't have the address right now." It did not bother Mer in the least that this was a blatant lie.

"So, please take care of yourself … I'll be in touch," her husband said sincerely.

She ended the call with a polite goodbye and then while standing there decided that she would start divorce proceedings as soon as the evacuation was over, her husband it was obvious though, seemed to think that they were just having minor difficulties.

Baby Marina had been left on a green velvet chair in the entrance hall, and in her confusion and loneliness had begun to cry. Mer got to her just as the living room door opened, and Mer saw Christine's face: red eyed, pale and also furious, on seeing that the child was with Mer, Christine turned back to the waiting tempest and once again closed the door behind her.

Mer took the baby into the garden, where she sat down and observed that the child was happy to soon fall asleep in her arms, a soft bundle, a small vestige of aliveness held at her breast. She thought of last night and how she had shared her table with Luc and how she had been in such a brittle and fierce mood, prodding and poking him for answers in response to which he had been always been generous; although that Circe like strength had ebbed now especially since her unwanted phone call. She wondered what Luc was doing today; perhaps he would come and see her again before he left. That was a pertinent point, she had to leave too. She considered if she should stay in one of the Army supplied tents, it sounded amusing, but not something she actually considered; she imagined a nice country house hotel by the coast in Cornwall, she was faced with the choice of the latter, or to stay with Christine's parents, and that had to be avoided. The hotels would all be bursting, fully booked she told herself. Then she thought how nice it would be to go away with Luc, to stay with his enclave of friends, she wished that she could do that, it felt truly free. She needed a solid plan; it was a burden to have to think. She decided to telephone the hotels on the Cornish coast, to have a stab at her vision, it was worth it to try and to get a solitary train there on her own. Then, a crash was heard in the distance, and Mer considered what item in the living room one of them had thrown; it was no matter, she did not feel attached to any of her clutter.

After retrieving her lap top and mobile, strangely Mer found herself in luck; a modern spa hotel enticingly named, 'The Scarlet' had caught her imagination and had a final room to spare, everywhere else had been booked up with a burgeoning waiting list. She planned to leave on the Friday, the day after Christine and so bought her train ticket in readiness. She was pleased and hoped Christine would be too with her neatly made plans. Though it then occurred to her as she booked her return train journey that not only she, but that *everything,* would return, including her parents and maybe even Zafar; perhaps then, even another type of life. People had been postponing their lives until after the evacuation was over, when the embargo would also eventually end, and so, she knew that her solitude was about to be fully and abruptly ended too, she tried to gather in herself some sort of system of defence, but instead her breathing became shallow.

*

That night, Christine had settled on the sofa, nestled cat like and was watching the television, in deep retreat after the morning's domestic mauling, that had led her tattered marriage nowhere. Mer sat with her distracted; she had told Christine about the Cornwall trip to which she had responded positively, but soon, Mer could not watch television any further so she went up to the second floor and into the empty chequered floored ballroom, from there she looked out of the window, there was barely a car to be heard from afar or anyone on the street; she was finally lonely she realised, she had not been lonely in all her period of solitude since her husband had left, and she wished that the embargo would not end, even though she knew that that was extremely selfish.

Suddenly, she dashed to her bedroom and checked her face in the mirror, hurriedly applied an apricot blusher onto her cheeks and brushed her hair quickly, harshly, smeared clear gloss on her lips with her fingers and raced down the stairs whilst calling out to Christine, "Just going out!"

She was out of the huge door before Christine could ask anything of her at all, but Mer was in a hurry and she urgently pressed the buzzer for the flat that said no. 6, praying that Christine would not open the front door after her, to ask where she was going.

Chapter 41

Please don't ignore me, this is urgent, I need to know who you are.

Luc looked at his special phone and sighed. At that same moment, his buzzer sounded and he jumped. He was determined to ignore these messages from Clara if he could, as long as she wasn't being specific, he highly suspected her plain curiosity at the root of this; revelations right now would do no good.

"Hello?"

"Luc, it's me, Mer. Can I come up?"

"Oh, of course."

And the electricity could be felt jangling through Luc's building's shabby front door as it released its clasps to let her in. It was poorly lit and the red carpet had large swathes of blackness to navigate through, while she only had an old wooden bannister to hold on to, to make her way upstairs.

"Do you know where to come to?" Luc called in the dark.

"No, I don't," she called back.

"I'm so sorry, they really must get more lighting in here, follow my voice and I'm coming to the top of the stairs to find you."

As she reached the summit of the staircase and stood at the first floor landing, Luc didn't want to alarm her with his footsteps coming towards her as he knew she couldn't see, or when the dim light bulb would soon highlight his sandy untidy head. "I'm coming towards you, stay still."

"Hello, Luc, are you busy? You must be going out, I just thought I'd say hello ..."

"No, no please come in." He then ushered and led her to his home.

She did not protest. His door was ajar and he led her in past the bathroom, where there was the scent of heady men's cologne.

"Really? Am I not disturbing you, you must be busy?" she asked.

"No, no, I've spent the whole day out, was just watching television, London's half empty now anyway."

"Yes, it's true; I can't even hear any cars."

"And, as well as the hospital patients they've created a special area for tourists to go to that were stranded here before the embargo began, with entertainment put on for them and everything, so they would have left as well today too."

"I didn't know that, is it a secret government thing? Is that why *you* know?" She smiled at him.

"No, it was on the news just now." He smiled back, "I don't think they tell me anything at work. Come and sit down," he said, and hoped that his Clara-phone would stay silent for the night. He led her to the sofas covered in vibrant throws to conceal their dullness.

His flat was warm he thought then, her house was much cooler, too vast to trap in the heat like this. She was wearing her navy blue dress that he had seen before. She sat down, legs bare and wearing flip flops.

"How are you?" she asked.

"OK, I suppose, I think I am like you, not happy to leave either. Are you still sticking to your plan to hide?"

"Unfortunately no, I'm going to Cornwall, to stay at a spa hotel," she added quickly.

"That sounds very nice."

"Yes, I hope it will be. What about you, special government tent?" Her hair bobbed with her humour.

"Well we *are* being given the option of a special coach, but it's not a formal thing, just turn up for it if you wish, so maybe yes, we might have reserved tents, but … they haven't mentioned that, so I don't know. Cornwall sounds fun?"

"Yes ... Shall we ask questions again today?" she suggested playfully.

"If you like." Yet Luc was wary, it had been uncomfortable the last time. "Though, are you sure? I might ask you questions too this time," he said.

"All right, maybe it's a bad idea," but she smiled.

"Would you like some wine?" Luc changed the subject, she nodded and he reappeared with a bottle and two small glasses that were more suited to containing a small amount of juice.

"Where is Christine tonight?"

"At home," replied Mer, whom he saw had for the first time, a small and naughty grin.

"I'm glad you came all the same," he said, though so politely that she started to blush and so, looked down at the carpet and pretended to ease the creases at the hem of her dress. She sipped her wine and he sat down to face her with his.

"Is there anything you would like to do?" he asked.

"You know, I would love to see what your garden is like."

"Absolutely," he said and took up the wine bottle, which he put in the crook of his arm and held his glass carefully with the same hand. Mer picked up her own and followed him out; he seized his keys swiftly with his free hand, and did not bother to lock the door as they left.

They made their way down in the dark; it was lighter in fact outside, as twilight stretched itself into a pale blue balm of an evening. They could see this through the French doors which he had led her to in the gloom, the garden was still awake; lit up in low key lighting, dotted about for just such evening strolls.

His garden had much more foliage per square foot, trying to please as it was so many residents, it was there to provide a service, not like Mer's garden; that seemed to serve itself, and had thrived well before Mer had arrived. He led her on through each secluded alcove and water feature, "What beautiful statues ...

mermaids and nymphs …" she said. Finally, he led her to his favourite part: an alcove where very little could be heard from the rest of the city.

She sat down on a green rickety chair and sipped her wine. "This garden is better than mine."

"It is not. Yours is just more open, it's different, but it has its own charm."

"Thank you. I like this though, all these different looking sections …"

"Yes it took some time to choose my favourite place," he said, nodding at the foliage around him trying at that moment to appreciate the mermaids peeping from under the waterlines, eyes in deep shadow from the absent sun. There was an enormous tree that framed their alcove to one side and in the evening air it cast it's woody scent. As usual none of Luc's neighbours had chosen to make use of the garden again, maybe they had already left he thought. As they sat together no one spoke very much for a few minutes, instead they saw that they had placed themselves around a commanding water feature, about which a few mermaid statues poked their heads and tails above the water line. A small watery cascade bubbled playfully onto one side mimicking a spring, it was a sight that fixed them and Mer especially stared into the pool's jade and shady depths. It was not a sunken pond but a mass contained in high sided stone, purposefully rim lipped and round edged, grand even on this small scale, yet the water was a murky green as from a forest and it was thick with creatures as fecund muck is wont to be, more evident from the greenflies and other winged insect sprites that alighted and as quickly disappeared. Their oval emerald bath for stone mermaids although grand and defended in high sided walls, still looked like an unwitting outlet for a babbling brook; it's green swirling murk reassuringly containing much life. And still no one spoke.

"I can see why you like it," she said finally, but did not know of their shared pleasure at being so comfortably hidden in there, inside so much beauty.

After a time of this not uncomfortable silence as they sipped and admired the plants, and Luc could feel at least a small distance from the message he'd just received –he dared to say then, "It's your turn you know."

"My turn?"

"For the interrogation." He smiled.

"Yes ... it probably is ... but I'm not going to help you, and you'll have to be specific, to ask specific questions." She bowed her head at this last, shrouding her face with her dark curls.

Realising that she had made general conversation into a challenge, Luc sensed even more that Mer did not want to talk about herself, so he treaded carefully, as he would have done with no one else.

"Where did you grow up? Do you have family here? Did your father really give you the house?"

"Here, in London. I'm an only child, like you, and my parents do usually live here, but they're stuck in New York. And yes he gave me the house," she answered quite simply. It did not occur to Luc to ask her why.

"Do you miss working?"

"Yes, yes very much."

Luc could see in her guarded eyes that she also saw his frustration, that there was an essence, a central core that he was nowhere near, like being lost in a repeating maze.

"That's it?" she asked, almost teasing him.

"No." He smiled and was goaded, his face started to flush. "Do you like living here, Mer?"

"Yes I do, very much."

"Can I ask you, without being rude, why you are having this time off from working?"

She sighed. "I needed a break from everything and everyone for a while, I suppose."

"Did somebody die?"

"No, no one died." She looked at him innocently.

"Were you depressed?" he asked outright.

"Yes, I was."

"But, you're not anymore?"

"No, not anymore." And she smiled at him.

Luc had had enough, so he ceased his grilling. There was enough in his life that put pressure on his mind.

She finished what was left in her glass that he had on occasion refilled without her noticing, he watched her tasting the last of the dark acrid liquid about her lips.

"I saw you move in, you know."

"You did?"

"Yes, you were unloading your car for a long time."

"It's always like that. You could have said hello?"

"I suppose I could have …"

"Tell me about your work?" She had turned the tables on him; it was supposed to be his turn. "Is it fun, dangerous, boring?"

"Ah well now, you know I'm not allowed to speak about my work," he smiled.

"Is this what you've always wanted to do?"

"Well you know I really wanted to be a spy," Luc tried ironically to change the subject.

"Well I might too if my grandfather spied for the allies, it's so inspiring …"

"So basically, I suppose I just wanted to do something that made a difference," he shrugged.

"What a legacy … when I did Art History I loved learning about the time and the context that the art was made in, it has such a major effect, because I think that we're the product of our time *and* the past …"

"Oh, I agree, you know I think we have some Tunisian blood, somewhere, and the Avium name must be Roman, so that's so rich in influence itself. I want to ask James to do my family tree."

"Yes, that it would be fascinating. You see James a lot don't you?"

"Yes, I suppose." But Luc did not want to talk about James, as his thoughts again began to sag with Ministers and Gemma and Clara … "What about you? All those influences from India and then Iran on the Parsi side? Don't you want to know? … I'd love to know." He leaned forward to refill her empty glass and then shook the bottle, now empty. "Shall I go and get some more?" he asked her.

She pushed back her curls from her face and looked at him; it was unnerving, he never knew what was coming next.

"Do you mind awfully, if I call it a night?"

"Not at all," he said politely but was disappointed, and he realised that for the first time, that he had left the Clara-phone in his flat.

"I'm so sorry, I think I just suddenly feel very tired," she said rising and closing her eyes briefly.

"But, you're here till Friday?" he asked.

"Yes, like you."

"I will say hello before you go," he said with a smile and led her back.

They walked back up the dark corridor feeling the rustling carpet under their feet, until his building's front door let in some murky light, he came out with her, the air was not fresh or cooling, it was close, stifling and lank about their bodies; the heat weighed heavy upon it, as though the night air could not let go the day's soaring temperature; there had been no release.

"Good night, Luc, thank you so much, and for the wine."

"Good night, Mer." He smiled at her.

Then she grimaced.

"What happened?"

"I didn't bring my keys!" she exclaimed, although she kept her voice down. "I'm going to have to ring the doorbell." She sagged now.

Luc was perplexed as to why this would be an issue, he could see that lights were on and was sure that Christine would still be awake, but Mer turned to him and spoke, "I don't want her to know …" she whispered.

He felt a thrill, a quiver at the thorax.

"OK," he whispered back and ducked into his own door holding it slightly ajar so she could that see he was still watching, to make sure that she reached inside safely. She had surprised him again; she wanted to hide him from Christine; it hinted at the clandestine, and he felt that sharp thrill once again.

He saw her steady herself ever so slightly, drawing in a breath of warm air, the drink had slowed her, and then she rang her own doorbell. When her door opened and he could not see anything within her house, Mer looked straight ahead and not once back at him, not even with a surreptitious goodbye glance as she stepped inside; and so disappeared, having said to him not a word.

Chapter 42

A rose had shrivelled, unable to bear the summer heat any longer, and was like a faded ember of itself; its coarse and unyielding leaves the colour of dried blood. In Mer's hand it looked frail, and like a betrayal; for this is what summer could also do. As she gazed at its withered petals she thought of Luc and she began to squeeze, why had she gone to his house last night? She should not have. The rough petals now fell about her hand and brushed her forearm as the breeze took them here and there, and she closed her eyes, but it was no good, she thought of his face, and his gait, and then looked at her hand, strewn as it was in a blotch of burgundy and amber. It was before breakfast as she sat in her garden, when a purer type of quiet could be found, she turned away from the desecrated flower and let her mind wander instead … she had flashbacks often, but usually at the tail end of a dream. They always began with intricate sprawls of henna, a thousand patterns and designs imprinted upon her hands, arms and feet; like dark pungent lace. Over her head a red net fabric, adorned with crystals and flowers, soon to be lifted after the words of prayer bonded her to her husband; as she had been in no mood to be wholly demure and moreover, had not been expected to be. She had sat in heavily embroidered red and pink silk brocade, in a traditional dress called a Garara, something resembling a full skirt, actually a set of wide trousers. She'd glittered and shimmered in textured layers of adornment which left no part of her unembellished, as her henna patterned hands and feet also bore their own vivid designs. She looked at her husband to be through the encompassing red net, her face underneath, hot and listening to the holy man speak as though in tongues, some of which she understood and much she did not; she knew only of when to say, 'yes'.

The scene then shifted to another episode of her multi occasioned wedding: to when she had worn a white sari with a golden weave for her mother's sake and tradition, a thick gold border had weighed heavily upon one shoulder; again, she'd faced everyone glowing from weeks of facials and a sense of excitement that she could not find the root to, as she was finally there, the 'Bride', her destination had been that moment; and she had nothing to hold onto but those fine fabrics and her garb and flowers. The latter were plentiful, everywhere in throngs about her, white, lilac and pink, hung in baskets, garlanded about pillars and adorning the tables of the ballroom at the Dorchester. Such heaving flora, finally thrown as petals over her head when she approached the awaiting white Rolls Royce to say goodbye to her parents in ceremonial custom, she'd cried tears with full force, even though she was to move less than a mile away to her new house -with which, she had no idea or clue, how far she would truly fall in love.

With the trace of such a memory like the ghost of a communion wafer in the mouth, she got up quickly and shook away the last of the rose from her hand. Marching to the kitchen, she then announced, "I am getting a divorce."

Christine, who was preparing the breakfast table, just looked at her, the baby in her own chair continued to suck on a torn piece of toast.

Last night, that surreptitious Saturday night, Mer had returned from Luc's and Christine had let her in and hovered expectantly by the door waiting for her to explain where she had been, but Mer had just said, "Good night," and proceeded up to bed, Christine had not pursued it, choosing instead to raise her eyebrows to herself, as Mer had walked determinedly as a stranger, up the unlit stairs to her own bedroom.

Christine now tilted her head. "A divorce isn't cheap you know." She said this gently, although Mer felt the hint of a provocation.

"We were only married for six months, surely that counts, wouldn't it help?"

Christine pursed her lips slightly.

Mer then considered that she had enough savings to be able to live without working for perhaps five years, but if she had to pay for a divorce, that could cut into it, of course, she could sell the house and never have to work again, but she had no intention of doing that, it was her home and she felt safe in it; it's empty grandeur was all that contained her at her worst and she wouldn't leave it. "The house is all in my name though ..." she added, thinking aloud.

Christine looked puzzled.

"In case Zafar thinks he's entitled to any part of it."

Christine still as yet had said nothing, this was, both knew, completely out of character. Then, finally she spoke, her gaze unflinching, "Why?" she asked.

Mer shook her head, as though willing the question away.

"*Why* do you want this, Mer?" she persisted.

"It's too hard to explain ..."

"Try."

"It was ..." she cringed, "... his scent."

"What?" Christine looked even more confused.

"Oh, no! Of course he was very clean, lovely aftershave, he took great care in is appearance, you know that."

"Then, what?" asked Christine.

"You know how we all have a natural scent, a sort of essence, not a bad one just the scent of Christine or the scent of Mer?"

"Yes ...?"

"Well early on in the relationship, I knew it bothered me, but I chose to ignore it, it was all right, I tried to like his aftershave, the smell of the shower gel, soap etc. but when we got married ..." She paused and looked at Christine, who understood after a millisecond.

"I realised that it grated on me, the essence of him, it mingled, it overpowered his aftershave, it was everywhere ... You see, we fought every day, we didn't agree about anything, we had different tastes and I *resisted* him, I didn't want to give in, it's as though I didn't want to get along, I couldn't bear his natural sort of essence on top of that ...

"It's *all* my fault. Completely. It's not that he expected me to agree with everything he wanted and everything he said, but he didn't expect me to resist *everything* he wanted and everything he said. I didn't want to give anything; I just wanted him to go away."

"So, you didn't love him?"

"... No." Mer hung her head.

"But, you *married* him?"

"I know ... I thought I loved him, he was kind and sweet, but the arguing, it was impossible. Does it make any sense? He wasn't bad in any way, he did nothing wrong. He was just him, and I didn't want him."

Christine nodded somewhat. "But you seem angry at him as well?"

"... He didn't understand why I would want to keep the red chaise longue that came with the house in the ballroom, *why* I like it. He didn't try to understand and that makes me upset! Even though I know that he's a good person. And then I realised that I liked living in a way that I chose ... I don't miss Zaf you know, not one ounce since he left, it couldn't have been love, you see?"

"... So, you're going to get a divorce, get a job, and live here?"

"Yes." Mer answered feeling nervous yet excited at the same time.

"And if Luc didn't live next door and have interesting, gorgeous friends -it wouldn't be half as much fun."

Mer coloured. "You're right. It wouldn't. But I'm still going to do it," she answered back, her hair bobbing with the effort of tackling Christine's onslaught.

The baby, still stuck in her special feeding chair grew restless, fed up of being held captive and shuffled, trying to find a way out.

Christine nodded a little to her friend, before lifting Marina from her bondage, leaving Mer disturbed as Christine had not stood her ground as she usually did. Christine instead left the kitchen with her child; leaving Mer alone to consider her own thoughts.

Nervous yet resolute, Mer then decided not to bother Luc again that weekend, possibly put off by Christine's insinuations. In the end she sat in the garden and read and was restless for a great part, looking about as Luc may be in his garden too.

The next day, on Monday evening she waited by her window for Luc to come home but as the minutes ticked past seven, he still did not come and she turned away from it, trying not to look anymore, for she was feeling as though she was in a new and as yet unsung chapter of her life; and so, unleashed. But yet, she could not help herself , thus another hour passed and Luc had still not come home … instead, she saw Christine approaching the front door and went downstairs to greet her, to have dinner together; for who knew she thought, if that arrangement would soon change as well.

Chapter 43

The week began with a sense of the unreal as Luc went to work on Monday morning; there were only half as many people on the tube and on the streets even less, the cafes and newsagents were still open; although in a mournful quiet state, their clientele absconded.

Everyone was present at work however, no special dispensations had been afforded, he wanted to ask Gemma if she would be staying while they all left, and he thought that before the incident with Clara he would dared not have been so personal.

Then, little to his knowledge he did not hear Gemma approach as she marched to land suddenly before his eyes.

"Hello, Gemma, all set for the evacuation?" he asked her, and gave her a smile.

"What? Oh, yes all ready."

"Staying somewhere nice?"

"I wish. Luc … I'm so sorry, everyone is swamped," she lowered her voice, "can you do a pick up for me? Same place as before."

Luc felt the chair beneath him dissolve a touch, form and gravity nothing compared to a wave of foreboding, and yet still, a chance to inch towards the truth. "Of course, right now?"

"Right now," she whispered and nodded.

She looked pale he thought, her concerned and caring demeanour, utterly convincing. He gathered his things, and made his way; back to Mayfair.

It was still bright, it was as though a foreign Sun had been lent to them for the duration of this embargo, he tried to run over in his mind all the things that could possibly happen now: hopefully he would simply pick up a file, or he would (most likely) also be asked questions about Balthazar, to which he had no answers. Lastly, there could be a surprise request or favour asked of him -Luc had always feared and suspected from the beginning, this last.

With such musings, it was with a jolt that he soon found himself already there, and walking down the green and oak corridor, soon to be found knocking upon the Minister's door.

"Come in," said the Minister, so innocuously.

Luc walked inside, and did his best to look, low level, unknowing.

"Ah, Mr Avium, have a seat. Enjoying the new job? Well, I'll get straight to business, here is your package," he pushed over a diplomatic blue folder, "and have you got anything for me I wonder?"

"For you?"

"I think you know what I mean, your office, your boss, anything you've noticed, anything at all?"

"Honestly, I haven't. He's either out of the office in meetings a lot, because of the embargo, or spends the whole day in his room, door closed."

"Tut tut, Mr Avium, I was hoping for more ..."

"I did my best, sir."

"I think if he is out so much, then you can jolly well have a little search of his desk. What do you say? Eh? Sound OK to you?"

Luc was speechless.

"I'll get caught," Luc managed finally.

"Well, sunny, I suggest that you don't! Either way you don't have a choice, it's your decision." The Minister then smiled.

For the first time in that Minister's office did Luc colour, but it was a flush of nothing but anger. "All right," he said, and grabbed the folder as he exited.

Luc took his usual route back, and then on entering his placid yet elegant looking office building, turned towards the men's toilets, and locked himself in a cubicle as before.

There, he prized open the latest catch, and saw before him only one letter, it said:

Action to be taken during Evacuation: AFFIRMATIVE. More to come.

Luc searched the folder for anything more, any other scrap of information, but that was it.

As he reached upstairs and his own office, he noticed a sparseness, and so he asked Dorothy, a co-worker, where everyone was.

"There's a massive meeting at Whitehall, seniors, aides, and Army chiefs, everyone has to go, just not us analysts, and I'm glad." She smiled and then looked back down at her typing.

"How long ago did they leave?"

"Oh, about ten minutes."

"Thanks, Dorothy." Luc knew, possessed as he was with a blue folder in hand, that no one at all would blink at him heading towards Gemma's desk with it. For, he had decided, not to search Balthazar's desk -but hers instead.

She wasn't there of course. He walked closer; turning around to look as though he were looking for her, or rather to see if anyone else was present, then he turned back and let his eyes quickly scan her desk for any papers on display. Her desk in fact was neatly stacked and ordered as if she had already left, which wasn't the case and a half drunk mug of tea stood in a discreet corner demonstrating otherwise.

Luc walked around to her side of the desk, behind which was the corridor wall, and felt every ounce of her cool aura, territory and presence. After placing the diplomatic folder at the centre of her desk, he then grabbed a pen and piece of paper, posing to write her a note, and as he leaned over the desk, he quietly opened her first desk drawer. There, he was greeted by a small exquisite looking box of chocolates; the sweet, thick, smell was unmistakable, and truly incongruous. Then he opened the next drawer, in which were many plastic files and in the third and last, some pens gathering dust. His heart was now racing and his hand shook. So he went back to the first drawer and opened it to be greeted by the sweet cloying scent again. He then turned to the second drawer and let his fingers fan down the stack of clear plastic files and random papers, as if hoping to make contact with the right one in that way. There was nothing, and he had been there for far too long, so he went back to the small smart box of chocolates and opened it, grazing the prettily sculpted contents with his fingers as they melted soon to the touch. Feeling annoyed, as there was nothing there, except that he now had chocolate upon his fingers, he tried to put the box back and he heard a small feathery rattle. Quickly, he lifted the single tray of sweet morsels and there underneath, saw a folded square of white paper. He was faced with a quick choice to take the entire thing and run, or to try and open it there in order not to be faced with having to replace it later: he chose the latter. Hoping that it did not contain illicit narcotics as that was not the sort of secret that he was after, he looked up to check if anyone was there and then very quickly unfolded it, and took out his mobile from his front pocket. It was a single simply typed page and he quickly took a picture of it, then folded it up as best he could and replaced it, seized the note he'd been pretending to write, and left.

He sat back down at his desk, heart racing dangerously; perfumed with anxiety, guilt and dark chocolate. He didn't dare yet to look at his phone and waited for a few moments; as though everyone could return precisely at that moment.

Yet, all was still empty and quiet, and slowly, Luc took out his phone and brought up the picture that he had just taken. At first he did not understand it, then, he could see that it was a list of addresses. His eyes scanned the list, it was probably a staff address list, he groaned inside, but then, hidden in that way?

No, surely not. He read each address, there were ten of them, something kept making his eyes scroll over the list and then, he kept reading a single address over and over again: 64 Elysium Avenue NW8, London. It wasn't his address, it was James'.

Chapter 44

Luc stood outside James' house and stared at it, as though he had never seen it before; it was a large and beautiful house, quite individual looking, with a touch of Victorian Gothic, as were so many in St. John's Wood. There was a tall hedge that secluded the ground floor windows as the deep blue front door stood quietly before him. The windows were dark, no one seemed to be in, but Luc still touched his finger to the doorbell. Earlier, on that Monday afternoon, five days before the planned departure, his wait to leave the office had been unbearable. He had tapped away at his keyboard for as long as he could at his desk, unable to concentrate and nervous that Gemma should approach him; for they'd all come back late in the day, looking harried and stressed. Finally, at 7pm he'd escaped; bag clutched in one hand, not heading home, but to an address on a list

He waited, and to his surprise the door soon opened. James was just as surprised to see him.

"Hi, Luc ... Everything OK? ..."

Luc nodded. "Hi, James, can I come in?"

"Course."

"Sorry to come unannounced," said Luc, stepping over the threshold.

"Don't be silly, what can I get you?" James asked as he walked over to the kitchen where in one corner, off-white sofas were assembled invitingly by sliding glass doors; they looked blankly into a sparse garden.

"Anything, whatever you're having."

James took out two bottles of beer and handed one to Luc, ushering him to sit down by the doors.

"You know, Mischa and Jelly have already gone; left early, beat the rush."

"To Berkshire?"

"Yup, and settling in fine, she says it's weird, like being in quarantine, which I suppose it is, Friday OK to leave for you? After work?"

"Yes, sure, and you, how are you doing?"

James did not have time to answer.

At that moment the doorbell rang again and James was so surprised by it that at first didn't get up, and just listened to its sound instead. "No idea who that could be," he said to Luc puzzled and then shuffled off to answer the door.

Luc waited on the sofa, started to chew his left thumbnail and stared out at the back garden, which was quite unkempt. But instead of it being a delivery man at the door or someone who could be ushered away, he heard footsteps approaching him, loud compared to James', a staccato stamp like the most definite tread of high heels.

"Hello, Luc," said a voice standing in the kitchen doorway, a silhouette of a woman in shadow, Luc rose a little in his chair too see more clearly -but he knew that voice.

Luc immediately got up.

"Hello, Clara … how are you?" It was all Luc could think to say.

"Am all right, and you? Happy to be back?"

"Well, Luc's got a fancy job now, Clara, he works for Her Majesty's government," said James.

Not one ounce of it, not even a trace, there was no recognition in her face, she hadn't understood that it had been him who'd texted her, thought Luc, and yet he continued to seek the flash of the iris, and comprehension.

"Oh, well, we're all such bloody do-gooders," she said.

"Clara," James admonished her.

"I'm sorry, Luc. That was rude, I'm happy for you, honestly I am." And she came and kissed him on the cheek. Her lips burned upon him, while she smelled of gardenias. And yet still, she saw nothing, knew nothing thought Luc, *she still did not know that it had been Luc who'd saved her.* And now Luc knew that he had to leave, the trace of her lips on his cheek like a burning echo, or reminder, so he asked, "Are you back too?"

"I don't know, Luc," she said. She was wearing a chic black dress as well as glossy black heels as he'd expected, and her shiny dark hair curled about her chin.

"I've got to go; it'd be nice to catch up though?" Luc suggested.

She smiled and nodded, not a flicker he thought, and he went himself to kiss her on the cheeks goodbye; as if by sheer proximity he would then be able to glean the truth, or transmit to her his real role.

Soon, as the front door closed behind him, he could only guess what could happen between them next; theirs was a difficult love, but then, would that be all they would discuss? His heart was now full of suspicion, so he didn't leave immediately; he stood outside the house and looked about, but there was nobody there, barely a car on the road. The evening settled well upon London, and the house was so quiet, finally, Luc shook his head and headed back home, plotting and planning how to tell his friend, about what he had found.

Chapter 45

It had not gone well, not initially at least. James could see that Clara was very angry but didn't want to show it, indifference was a far more sophisticated form of rejection so she wavered somewhere between the two.

After Luc departed, they were left still standing and facing each other.

"Would you like some tea?" asked James, abandoning his beer.

"Tea would be fine."

James made himself busy in the kitchen and Clara sat down upon the sofa by the clear doors, but said nothing.

Finally, James approached with two cups of tea with matching saucers and placed them upon the glass coffee table before them, he glimpsed then a glint in her eye as her head turned to face him in the dim half-light that his kitchen now provided.

"Why am I here, James? What the hell is going on?"

"Clara, I'm going to tell you everything, you know I will, I would never drag you back here, back near me … if it wasn't important … Can we just have some tea for a few minutes though?"

"OK," she nodded, looking somewhat more understanding than before. "But can I ask you something else then? Or maybe it's connected and the same thing, but why have you been keeping a check on me at work?"

James looked confused.

"Someone requested my file a few weeks ago, from another agency; my boss thought I was after a transfer."

James became more alert, "Clara, it wasn't me. And I don't like the sound of it at all. Do you know exactly who requested it?"

"Well no, I assumed it was you, and bloody ignored it. I can ask my boss."

"No don't … we don't want to show that we know."

"Jesus, James. I found Gemma crying one night … Three dead!" she whispered.

"Really, Gemma?"

"Yeah, you know that OCD miss perfect was never fully her."

He nodded, then after they had sipped their tea, he gestured towards the garden; she understood, put down her cup and followed him outside.

Gradually he explained, standing on the lawn, some way from the house. "You know now that the three deaths amongst us were not accidents ..."

As he continued, she began to gaze at him like when she was eighteen years old: interested, earnest, and blazing. Her cheeks flushed while she looked him square in the face; he was not looking forward to the next portion, so he rushed it along and it came out in a stream.

"You know that we have a mole."

She nodded.

"The deaths were suspicious and Michael confirmed this, but then I received a phone call from … Simon." At that point he looked down at the grass to continue, "Clara, Simon had rung to confess to me, and no, I don't understand it either." As he spoke on, without her noticing, he gently placed his hand loosely about her upper arm. She stood there transfixed before him, or, like a rabbit in the headlights.

"I still don't understand? ... What on earth?"

"Clara, he was hurt, that's all it was, he didn't just lose you and his child, he thought he'd lost all of us, and his place in it. He went a little crazy I think alone in Paris, and he wanted to hurt me, that was all … and now, well he's in hiding, the people he leaked about us to, want more, and now I hear about not only your file being requested but that text message(!) you received. What the hell, Clara, this is serious; you should have told me, or at least Sir John!"

"But I thought it was you! One of you. I didn't know about all this. And anyway sounds like that message saved me in some way, from what you're saying. It sounds like a good person, doesn't it?"

"Clara, do you know who it was? Are you keeping even more from me?" James' face was nearer hers.

"I don't know who it is; I get the seriousness of it now though, OK."

He looked at her then and her eyes were dispossessed as though somewhere calculating, realising that it was *her*, of course, that it was all her fault.

"I should have done more, Clara, this is my fault as leader, I should have taken better care of him."

But Clara wasn't fooled at all, nor was she interested. As he predicted, she tried to escape and realising that he had her in his grip, yanked her arm away with a force which must have hurt her, but James held on, though yet was concerned for the condition of her arm.

"Listen to me! ... Listen to me." James insisted and she stood still but looked back at him, defiant. "This is not your fault!" he said, but he was not convincing enough.

She struggled again, still mute with shock, understanding that Simon's life was in great danger and moreover that the safety of everyone, the entire group was in jeopardy because of her, it was not completely true, but it was the version that she was taking in James was sure.

"He is responsible for his own actions!" James insisted.

She had angry tears streaming down her face but still uttered no words or sound.

"Clara, listen!" James yelled now, "It is NOT what you or I would have done no matter how horribly we were ever treated! This was his own choice!" And James finally realised the impact of what he had just said, to himself. This stopped her at last from such a damaging train of thought; he finally had made her see.

Slowly, she sank down, and he let her go as she sat down cross legged upon the grass, probably ruining her dress and shoes. He also sat down in front of her as she rubbed her face and looked like a ghoul, her eyeliner smudged.

"What are we going to do, James?!" she finally asked him despairingly.

James was relieved, that she was still there and listening.

"I have to get to Paris, and get him out."

"But the embargo?"

"Well *you're* here ..."

"Yes, but-"

"The only way to go is with a diplomatic vehicle, Sir John is trying to find one, we can't make this look like it was our idea, can't raise any flags."

"And then what?"

"Well and then ... I bring him back." James sighed. "He will have to disappear. Stop the work, become a normal person, change his name ..."

"Would that be enough?" Her voice was distant.

"I hope so, it has too. Would *you* trust him again?" he asked her honestly.

"What about the people who know, that he leaked to, or rather know something, if they *really* knew we'd all be in trouble by now, there's some comfort in that," she responded.

James faltered, oh dear God he thought, he may lose her forever now, but he chose to tell her; the truth was concrete, she would find out eventually and if he kept it from her, their bond would never be unsullied again.

"Clara, I have had to take some very difficult decisions, Simon has helped provide information, he's so sorry, Clara, we hope we know how far the secret could have spilled out." Faltering now he asked her, "What would you have done if you were in my position as leader?"

"All roads lead to Rome ... to James, then to all of us ..." she said thinking. She looked down at the grass solemnly, and then she looked up at him with alarming quickness and said, "What have you done, James?"

James was startled, it had taken her far less time to reach that dark back alley than it had him, it showed on his face and he was wide eyed looking at her, but this did not distract her.

"What have you done?!" she said.

He did not look away.

"Michael …" he answered.

"Oh my God."

"Clara, it's for all of us, if they've found you, they've found me."

"Who knows?" she asked without hesitation.

"Anjelica, Mischa and Sir John, everyone else has been told to stop working."

"So we are on lock down?"

"Yes, until everything is sorted out with Simon, unless something is earth shattering."

She nodded to herself, and he was so thankful, that she had not spat at him, or disowned him, that she was still present. Although yet, she looked removed as though on leave from herself, her colour quite absent.

Finally after a silence as she was lost as to what to say and James waited for her to speak she said, "Will you tell me when you go, to Paris?"

He looked at her and then replied, "I'll try."

Then she got up, pushed her hair away from her face and made her way jaggedly back into his house, her heels uncomfortable with the lawn, her clothes strewn with dry grasses and creased carelessly, he followed behind.

Inside, he asked as she retrieved her bag to leave, "Where will you go?"

She looked at him blankly.

"I mean for the evacuation."

"Oh, Sussex."

He knew what that meant; she had an aunt who lived on the Sussex coast.

"I'll drop you back; don't leave Gemma's house again. I'll get you an escort to Sussex, and a team to keep watch there as well."

She nodded, and seemed very far from the brazen woman who had earlier entered his house.

Chapter 46

The next day, Luc went back to James' house again after work. He rang the doorbell but no one answered. He stayed there and rang it intermittently for fifteen minutes. Still nothing. Then he phoned James, his phone was off and it went straight to voicemail. But Luc left a message; something innocuous, that just sounded like he wanted to see James.

That night, Luc had still had no reply or response, and near midnight thought of going back to the house again, but then he received a message from James:

So sorry, been out all day. Will let you know as soon as free.

Luc was relieved to hear from him; but still not satisfied. The next day having not had a message from James all day, he went back to the house yet again, still nothing. So Luc decided to try and call once more, this time the phone rang, yet long enough to finally go to voicemail, and Luc did not leave a message, for he did not want to say the wrong thing.

On Thursday, Luc tried to ring James before he set off for his house after work, but again could not get through. So he sent a message instead, asking if the drive out of London was still on for Friday, to this he got a reply:

Definitely. See you at 8pm on Friday. Don't pack as much as usual.

Luc drew comfort from the idea of the safety and privacy of an enclosed car ride where he could finally talk to his friend, he then began to feel a little unwell, but felt a night's proper rest would fix it.

Luc's anticipation grew as he sat at this desk on Friday afternoon; people were neatly ordering their desks, knowing that they would not see them again for over two weeks; they had been given leave to go home at 5pm. As he waited for the hours to pass he began to feel weighted in the chest, as though constricted. And by 5pm he felt awful, he made it home, looked at his packed bag and then began to search for some painkillers for now a pounding head, sore throat, and aching chest, plus the oncoming kiss from a wave of fever. At that moment while he rummaged, his phone rang.

"James?"

"Hi, Luc, I was just calling you- God you sound awful!"

"I feel awful … I think I have the flu … I don't want to infect all of you …"

"Don't be ridiculous."

"No, James, don't worry there is a special transport out on Sunday night for us, so I might be a bit better by then, I'll take that and then well-" Luc cringed, he desperately needed to talk to James, he admonished himself for being so considerate, but even as he spoke, he was finding it a little hard to breathe.

"I can wait 'till Sunday. That's no problem," said James.

"Oh, that's great, thanks, James." He could wait two more days, thought Luc. "So, we'll keep in touch?"

"Yes definitely, I am *not* leaving you here alone. See you soon," James added and then rung off.

Luc put down his phone, and then broke out into a sweat, still short of breath, he knew he had no medicine, so made a decision to go and get some while he still had strength -if the chemist was still open! As he grabbed his keys, he shivered, and then it hit him, his symptoms had progressed very rapidly through the afternoon, and now thunderstruck, he stayed rooted to the spot for a whole minute. What if he had the contagion? -The disease that the whole embargo had been about. Luc's heart started a rampage, so he stood still trying to think: everything from the fact that going out for medicine might infect others, to should his colleagues at work be told immediately as they'd had contact with him? But then, he came to a more useful conclusion: the first symptom of the disease, officially called: NA17a1995, was a dry flaky rash upon the chest that quickly turned green with infection. Luc ran to the bathroom and ripped off his shirt. His chest had no rash, and was not green. But he waited, as if it would occur before his eyes. Still, of course, nothing. Then, after putting back on his shirt, he went to his lap top and looked up the emergency procedures for NA17a1995 and its symptoms: first the rash, the green chest, then coughing, fever, coughing up blood, blood in the urine, convulsions, then death, all within days. As Luc had no medicine he made himself some hot water with honey and lemon, and sipped as he occasionally went to the mirror to check his chest while he waited. He wanted to be sure before he alerted any authorities, for; it did very much feel like the flu.

After an hour, and yet a still clear chest, Luc crawled to his bed, his body swaying as his flesh had grown sweaty and moist, a burgeoning heat grew in him that had not yet begun yet to work its fury. As he settled down, he pulled the duvet on, then off, then half on, as his body lost its thermal navigations of itself, finally he settled on a half huddle with it. He considered that it might be better to make camp in front of the television, so he could watch the mad journalists swinging from helicopters trying to get a glimpse of the soon to be exclusion zone that was central London -before the Army helicopters ushered them out of the sky at gunpoint, as they were threatening to do. At that moment, his obnoxious buzzer sounded, which in his condition startled him. He made his way slowly to the intercom, which of course for him had no picture. "Hello?" he asked.

"Luc, it's me, can I come up?"

His finger hovered over the release button for the downstairs front door, and he said, "Mer, I think I'm ill, I don't want to give it to you."

"Luc … I just want to say bye, I won't come too close."

Luc peeked down at his chest, still nothing, and the rash would have appeared in the first hour of illness apparently. He was sure that he had begun to feel ill at least 24 hours ago. He pressed the button; he could hear the high pitched quiet scream of electronics as the mechanism functioned; perhaps Mer at least could get him some flu remedies before she left.

He stood at his front door holding it ajar and waited, trying not to look as if he were holding on to it, as he burned.

Mer was coming up the stairs and approaching his landing with the buoyant air of a traveller, ready to set sail or in her case wave people off from the train, she bobbed almost, although the landing was dark as usual, so that he could not fully apprehend her cheery gait, only guess at it from the feint outlines and rhythm of her approach. Of course as she came closer this all changed, and her face grew concerned as she slowed to look at him, a metre away from his door.

"Luc?"

Luc nodded, not trying to reply, but in fact trying to buy time, and he then indicated that he wanted to reply with his hand held up, as suddenly, he bounded ungainly in his feverish haze, his body panicking, as tried to reach the bathroom in time, where he then retched violently.

The release had been necessary as he felt well purged, but not better. He waited for more, and the non-negotiable urgent demands of extreme nausea to pass. He was far too ill to be embarrassed, finally he realised dimly that the bathroom door was still half open and there she stood, sidling in as he flushed and used his hands against the walls to guide himself to the sink where he then washed out his mouth. She held a glass of water and was looking around for something. She handed him the glass, which he sank with against a wall, sat down upon the bathroom floor and sipped, while she grabbed a hand towel wet it under the faucet, sat down next to him and wiped his brow.

"You should have told me you were this ill," she said gently.

"I didn't know I was *this* ill," he said feebly, but still incredulous at how unwell he was.

"You're burning up and soaked through, you need to change your shirt and wear something comfortable."

"OK," he breathed, trying to gather strength.

Slowly he stood up and she supported him as they walked to his bedroom.

"Oh, Mer, I don't want to make you ill!" he attempted.

"If you tell me where your clothes are, maybe I can get them for you?" she replied instead.

Luc sat on the edge of his bed and pointed to an open wardrobe, with some t-shirts folded on the bottom shelf. She took her hand to feel down the edge of the pile until she found what she was looking for and pulled out a very soft, old grey faded top. She approached him, he looked at her willing his arms to move and take his work shirt off, but it was taking some time. Before he knew it, she was unbuttoning his white shirt, one by one, she had slim fingers; a rustle of fabric is all that could be heard between them. Bit by bit his chest became exposed as the shirt ebbed away, she eased it over his shoulders and pulled it down over his clammy arms, he tried to help her and wriggled his arms so that the cuffs didn't catch, until she took the shirt away and placed it upon a chair by the wall; his skin shivered waiting for her to remedy the situation. But this was the difficult part, he was ready and he had been preparing himself, but it would take a great deal to lift his hands over his head to put the T- shirt on, yet she went away leaving him shivering further and came back with another towel, which had been dowsed with very hot water and she started wiping his torso with it, first his neck, downward firm strokes, then his back, all the way down, then his front, at which moment they both hesitated, but she plunged to the base of his abdomen and then wiped his arms including his hands up to his fingertips.

"I have to do this," she said, "you're soaked through with perspiration; it will only make things worse if you lie down like this. I learned this from my mother, I was ill like this once and it was the same thing, sweating buckets, shaking, she did this for me."

"… She sounds nice."

"Yes, she is."

Mer proceeded to help him put on the t-shirt and he did feel cleaner and fresher, yet he longed to lie down, but it wasn't over. She had found, gasp, a clean pair of boxer shorts and demanded that he remove his smart but drenched work trousers and underwear and put them on, on this occasion she left the room and did not help. He obliged slightly revived by her efforts and also by the most delicious prospect of being allowed to lie down soon afterwards.

"Are you still feeling like being sick?" she asked as she came back.

"No." He shook his head feebly, eyes half closed.

"Because we can go to a hospital if you want to, though if you have been sick and don't feel nauseous anymore, just have a fever and an achy body then it is … probably just the flu."

"No, no hospital. They will be closed anyway, but no ... the flu … must be."

"Sounds like you *do* want to go, we can go to a hospital out of the central zone, it's not a problem."

"I think, I'll be all right."

"OK, Luc."

And he laid down, not asking her for a thing, took some paracetamol that she had found for him in her purse and some water, which he could see she had brought a clear jug of and a glass and had placed them on his bedside; Luc then closed his eyes and fell into a deep hatred of the flu. His body shook on occasion, He was freezing then sweating profusely, every part of him ached and he simply wanted it to end, but it would not and he had no idea from whence it had come; but it had him.

*

The next morning he woke, sour tongued and chest aching; he needed water urgently and reached out to his bedside, where there was water but in a different jug. There were also pills to numb and bottles of cough syrup, honey lozenges, Vicks vapour rub, Tiger Balm and Echinacea; but it was not his bedside, or his room.

He tried to sit up but it had been a misguided idea, instead he settled for a remote crown lift, to try to scan his whereabouts: it was a large room with a wooden floor, there wasn't anything else there except a Victorian side table, an empty wooden desk against the far wall, fitted wardrobes and pale green, thick brocade curtains to his right, set against clean magnolia walls that stretched from a high ceiling to floor, they were drawn so he began to doubt the hour; it could be any time; the sun may have ended its London campaign and Luc could not tell. He could feel his wrist bare and lacking the load of his wrist watch, as he turned his hand in askance he then turned his head and there it was laid out for him at his bedside, it read 10.30 -am? -it had to be. He reached finally for the ready glass of water, with an inkling of where he might be, but still yet unsure.

The drink was good at first, cool salve, but the effort it took to sit up was not a pleasant surprise, he could feel the fever beginning to start its rage inside him, the first shivers ran over him and emitted warning signs as his sallow cheeks grew flaming red and his skin bloomed with heat, like being caressed inside by a wicked fire. He wanted to call out to his new unknown host, to find out where on earth he was, he looked again to his bedside at his mobile phones that had been also dutifully laid beside him, there was no landline however. Yet whom should he call? It would be a strange phone call: Hello, am I in your house? So he waited instead, drifting in and out of waking and dreaming and burning; letting the fever consume him.

Eventually, after perhaps what was not a very long time he could hear something, a distant clinking of crockery, as though on a tray, he did not know how he'd guessed the part of the tray, but he knew it was the case, that sound amid now footsteps, grew louder, the clinking was still gentle yet, as though the objects were shivering themselves at the prospect of meeting him. The sound halted, Luc was now sure who would open the door -but it was not who he thought it would be.

Mer stood, as pale in the shadows as she could become, with limp hair and wearing a green t-shirt. He could smell strongly what she had borne to him, and his stomach turned about with nausea, although he knew that he hungered as well. He was sure in his strange perhaps deluded retrospect, that it would be Balthazar that would have come through the door, or his wife Elizabeth. He still had no memory of how he'd reached here, thus from the décor and the memory loss he had considered that only Balthazar with his resources could have managed such a feat.

Mer brought the tray to his side on the enormous double bed where he was marooned, and placed it next to him, pressing it over the thick white embossed bedspread. She then sat down by his side and waited for him to eat. He didn't move.

"Hello," he said feebly.

She knew as much of him by now to see that there was humour in his voice and a question too, although he didn't have any strength to say any more.

"Hello, Luc. Yes, I moved you," she answered.

Luc looked confused.

"No, I didn't carry you, we walked here, to my house, I may have half dragged you though."

Luc still looked confused and managed to raise his eyebrows, questioning.

"Look, I wasn't going to leave you like that and it was a lot easier for me to help if you were here you see. If you don't get better by the last transport tomorrow, then we will have to stay here and I think that that will be easier in my house, don't you think?" she said simply.

After a pause Luc said, "I see," croaking mildly, then nodded, and even in his state he was bemused. Then he looked confused again. "But I don't remember …?"

"You don't remember coming here? Not even a bit?"

Luc shook his head a fraction.

"Your fever is monstrous! Please have some of this."

He looked down at a sturdy white bowl, full of a clear golden liquid.

"Of course, I didn't make it, it's Knorr Chicken noodle soup -it's very good though," she insisted, "it helps."

Luc keenly wanted to laugh; he thought that she may know that as she held back a smile herself, one corner of her mouth tugging upwards, she ended up chewing on that side of her lip. Finally, after not laughing she said, "Please try and have a bit, my mother always forces me when I'm ill, though she of course knows how to make real soup."

And so he tried, for her more than for himself. He knew that it was going to be an effort of will. The fever was only at its preliminary stages in its cycle, he was only hot and sticky, not at the stage yet where he would freeze and shake yet while burning as he had experienced for the first time last night. The hot liquid had a salty tang, he truly did not want to eat but she was right, he needed to nourish himself. Next to the hot wafting bowl was a side plate with a piece of bread with butter on it. There was no way that he could attempt that he thought; luckily she was not pushing the bread upon him as yet. After a few mouthfuls he fell back exhausted onto pillows, that she had propped up arms outstretched behind him and so she tried, "Do you think you could have a bite of bread?"

It was her manner, so very polite and gentle as well. It felt impossible however. "Mer, I just can't."

"Just a bite."

Gentle, but firm he thought.

"OK." He leant forward and sank his teeth into the bread, it was a foreign object, quickly to be masticated and pushed down into him. He put the remainder down, but she was satisfied. With marginal new strength, his brain cells awoke briefly.

"But you're still here! ...Your holiday?" He tried to exclaim but his voice did not carry very far.

"It's OK, honestly I don't mind."

"No, no, you should go, there must be another train?"

"There is, today, but I'm not going to leave you like this."

"Please don't miss your holiday, your spa and seaside," he pleaded.

She shook her head and he gave up, he had nothing left to fight with, he could feel guilty when he was better he thought. She moved the tray to the floor and came nearer his side.

"Time for pills?" she asked. "I think so," she said to herself nodding her head.

She held out two fat, white round pills to Luc, which he took, and then gave him some water. He did not bother to ask what they were, he did not care; he was dreading the chills and shaking, a taste of last night that was possibly approaching.

Then she said, "Luc, I had to stay, all the hospitals are closed and if you travelled now you could become really really sick, honestly in my position, what would you have done?"

He half smiled a thank you, his eyes glistening slick, the irises lank without light. He settled down, she helped deconstruct his pillow backrest and left him to rest, as he awaited the onslaught.

The pills eased the pain in his chest and tried to marshal the fever, as though keeping the flames low enough for a simmer and not to boil over. He had no idea how long had passed, he had slept, the pills had worked well to let him lose himself, to calm down, he tried to see his watch in the gloomy light, all the numbers seemed the same but alien, like half hidden gold hieroglyphs in bedside shadow. He was cold, oh no and knew that he must be very hot indeed, for his body began to tremble, to shake -impossible, and perspire, it went on and on, an exercise from hell, until his stomach muscles and back ached from it. He heard quick footsteps and some sort of exclamation. Speedily something hot and wet was being passed over his face and arms and over his torso, he was then dried and clothed again, that was all he knew.

Later still he awoke and it was dark, there was not a sound, he couldn't believe that it was night; it made him depressed at the thought. The fever had subsided, he felt cool but weak, the last few hours had thrashed him from within. He needed to go to the bathroom and drank some water first too. He had no idea where the bathroom was, but there was a white door on wall at the other side of the bed, so he tried it.

What a house this must be he thought as he found his en-suite, inside, he looked in the mirror under the bathroom light, he was now wearing a red t-shirt, she must have made him change again, probably during the scrub-down he thought; this is not how he had imagined her taking his clothes off, that was certain. Worse still was his face, his eyes had the dull and tainted look of a sick man, some honey brown stubble was emerging and his fine hair was plainly amok. He quickly splattered some water over his face at the sink; it stung him cold, his body's sensors irrational, haywire. He smoothed down his hair with the water and wished he could clean his teeth, of course, there by the sink was a new toothbrush in its packet and some toothpaste and even some mouthwash. The girl was quite diligent he thought and now felt not only lucky but truly guilty. She must have brought over his clothes as well, to keep being able to change him as she did. For all her gentleness and kindness, that last was quite bold he thought.

On his way back from the bathroom, he managed to reach the curtains, they weighed heavy in his hands as he tried to pull them back to see, it was actually only early evening, not yet night. Then he walked like a weak old man back to the bed and laid down in a collapse, he wished he could call her, but she came soon enough, perhaps from hearing his footsteps or the running water.

"Hello? How are you feeling?" she came in asking. Boldly again she came very close to him and put her hand on his forehead, Luc laughed and she pulled back.

"Sorry, you're usually half unconscious when I do that."

"It's OK." He smiled. "What's the verdict?"

"Well, your fever has gone down I think."

She was blushing however; he could tell even in the shadows, her face had its own cool heat. He longed for the curtains to be opened fully but he would do it himself, he had already ruined her holiday, he would not treat her like a maid.

"Do you think you can eat something?"

This again he thought, negotiations.

"I suppose I will have to?"

"If you can."

Polite as always he observed. He must be better he felt, his brain cells were far more active and he was finding things amusing. The idea of food yet, made him very unhappy however.

"What would you like?"

He sighed. "I don't think I could manage much you know."

She looked at him steadily. "Toast and butter, then soup?"

He nodded, he was resigned and didn't want to be impolite.

She quickly left, on her mission.

He was now faced with his own task, he placed one leg gingerly upon the cool wooden floor and then the other, the worst was to come, his stomach muscles were in pain from any effort after the shaking, so he clenched them in order to try to stand up. It was a feat and the room swayed as he became vertical, he was a bobbing ship, each step towards the window was unclear and unsteady and the room became a lie as it's so called sturdy mass let him drift forward. He thus reached as though through a dream to the window, how had he become this weak? Resting at the wall before his undertaking, he took some breaths and then pulled heavy green fabric to one side and draped it over a gold hook, he repeated this with the other half of the curtain and could now see the deserted street below him, not a soul in sight; like the first day that he had arrived here, but it was later in the day now, much, much later.

He was still perched at the window ledge when she returned; it was good that London was deserted as he faced it in his boxer shorts, the window ledge low enough to expose him in this high ceilinged room. She brought the same tray, more soup and more bread, but stopped at the doorway. "Are you all right?"

"Yes, just wanted to open the curtains," he said, still facing the street.

"You should have asked me."

She seemed genuinely cross. She placed the tray on the bed and rushed over to him, she held his arm and back, he did not realise that he had been holding so tightly onto the ledge, and led him back, the ground still greeted him as a sponge; she alone seemed firm upon it.

"Thank you," he panted as he sat on the bed.

"Silly you, you know."

"Yes, probably."

She went around and brought the tray of food to his bedside. He did try to eat and found that he could manage more than before; he must be on the mend he thought, as it felt as though somewhere inside him he was starving. Yet, after a half consumption of the meal he heaved with nausea and quickly pushed the tray aside, Mer guessing at his state and quickly moved the tray to the floor into the corner of the room. He took some breaths to calm his stomach and Mer went over to the window to open it wider. He was glad of that; the air touched his clammy face.

"I know you still feel dreadful, but I think you're getting better you know."

He nodded. "Yes I think so, though," he laughed "you wouldn't think it to look at me."

"Yes, it's the sense of humour, definitely better I'd say."

He tried to smirk, but it got as far as a hint of a smile then lay back down again.

"Is there any way I can call you, I mean, am I on a distant floor?"

"You're next door to my bedroom."

"Oh."

"You can call me, but I don't think you can call out yet, can you?"

"No, not yet."

"Don't worry, I'm about."

He was content with that; he was still dreading the night. Illness had turned him into a child he thought. He looked also at his phone; he wanted to check in on James.

"What did you do today?" He asked in his new weaker voice. "Apart from make packet soup of course."

She laughed. "Trust me, be very very glad I didn't try to make real soup."

He nodded seriously, then still looked at her for an answer.

"Today, I watched the news … we should get you a television in here thinking of that, and I spoke to Christine," said Mer her face calm.

In actuality, Christine had yelled at Mer on the telephone for not leaving London.

"Was she angry?"

"Well, yes, I didn't know you knew her so well."

He shrugged, in his new minimalist style.

"I also made plans; I went to the supermarket and tried not to look conspicuous as I bought as much as I could, to last two weeks. Today was their last day, they closed at six." She looked both nervous and amused at this.

"You stocked up?" Luc tried to raise his body in some alarm, but failed physically, his heart thumped away rampant like an erratic clock.

"Mer, there is a transport tomorrow for official people, I'm allowed to go on that, I can leave tomorrow, and also James has stayed back to pick me up tomorrow as well -you can come with us."

"I don't think they'll be too pleased if I try to get on a government transport and, I wouldn't want to impose on James like that, I mean I don't know him so well, and does he even have room? And you Luc, you can barely stand. But I'm happy to stay by myself, really."

"I don't want you to stay by yourself, no way. Please come with us? We'll make room," he pleaded.

She shook her head.

"Mer, you're right really, I can barely stand and I shouldn't go on a long car drive, but staying, I don't know, we could be in trouble ..." But then he thought about the last document he had intercepted, and of what 'action' that was going to be taken during the evacuation ...

"I know, but honestly if we just stay indoors where's the harm? We're not hurting anybody," she said.

Luc thought as fast as he could, he could go with James and give everyone the flu, but at least be able to talk to him; or ... he could stay, and try to discern what 'action' the Minister hoped to undertake during the evacuation.

"Though, I suppose you will have to really hide; it's one thing for me to break the rules, but for you with your position ..." added Mer.

But Luc had made a decision, and not only was it truly foolish for him to travel, but also that the most destructive force in the equation seemed to be the Minister, and so, it would be better to focus on what he was up to, though it was a huge wrench, for he had to help James as well. "This is going to be interesting," he said finally more to himself, and they discussed leaving no more.

Luc settled down on his pillow again, Mer left the room but said that she would be back soon. It *did* matter, he thought, he knew. He hadn't been in his new prestigious job for very long and now he was about to break the rules in perhaps a very grand way -but perhaps illness would be an acceptable excuse, but when the Army was involved, he couldn't tell how strict they would be; this was even for him, potentially a bridge too far, although he knew that he was still going to do it. He weighed up the possible repercussions and everything depended on being caught, he must not be caught, that was all.

Mer returned with a smile and a small television set that she balanced with some difficulty between strained arms.

"Let me help you!" he said in some alarm looking at her and tried to get out of his bed.

"Please don't, it's done, look-"

It was true, she had placed the television upon a far off table in the corner of the room and set about plugging in the wires, he hadn't even made it off the bed in time to help her. It was unfair on her he thought, they really hadn't known each other for long enough for such kind treatment as this and yet he knew, that sometimes people were just thrown together.

"I have to make this up to you, you know," he said.

"Just get better." She looked at him hair everywhere while bent over and plugging things in.

"Here." She walked over to him and gave him the remote controls. "They only have the BBC News on, I think they're operating from a field somewhere, the rest of the TV stations aren't functioning and yes the channels from abroad are, but for some technical reason, or general transmission reasons we can't have those either."

"News will do."

So they watched the News, which consisted principally of journalists in helicopters swooping over the camps, or articles about the food being served or type of entertainment on offer there. However their central message was that there weren't very many people in the camps as so few people actually lived in central London and the very rich that did were all in hotels or private homes in the country. It was true, many camps were half empty or less, Luc worried again, wondering if he would be missed. Occasionally one of the News helicopters would hover excitedly over outer London, trying to catch sight of what was happening in the centre; one such incident brought on a heavy reaction thought Luc, as Armed Forces helicopters were sent to ward off the television station's small and paltry one, from then on the military patrolled the perimeter zone from the air, he and Mer could hear them on rotation and all they did was to remind Luc that he was, possibly, in trouble. After the initial few hours of listening to the helicopters' hacking drones, pertinent as there were with no other sounds to diminish them, he then became a little acclimatised and they also soon lessened in frequency; the airborne reporters had been well and truly frightened off.

That night, after Luc had dozed off again for a while, Mer tried to give him more of her staple: soup with bread; this time a ready-made variety fresh from the chilled section, 'Summer Vegetable' it was called she told him, it made him laugh, he wanted to be able to go to the kitchen and to cook them something decent, or to go to James'(!) but Luc dared not even go and visit his own home now, he may steal there very late at night when he was better to find more clothes he considered, but he was in hiding now, truly.

The list then again invaded his mind and once more Luc felt impotent, he considered just phoning James about it, but knew enough that speaking on the telephone about such matters would not be wise. He was sure that James would contact him tomorrow to ask his plans, what would he say?

She gave him some more round white pills although he could have taken them himself, he could see his house keys also glinting on his bedside table, mocking his limited freedom. At that moment, while she stood at his bedside they suddenly experienced their first blackout, which startled them both. The lamps blinked and then all light and power left the house, as though it's spirit disappeared. It took a few moments before they realised what was happening, even though blackouts had been forewarned some weeks ago. Mer then travelled alone in the dark, guided by holding on to the walls, to her bedroom where she had fat candles and matches in her bedside drawer, stashed ready since the first day of the announcement. She returned as an apparition, holding in one hand a lit white candle and in the other a bundle for Luc to keep for his own.

She placed the candle on his bedside, first forcing its wax to drip down to the surface of the table to affix itself there. Now she sat with him as Luc sent a message to James, casually asking James how his day had been, to which he was grateful that he received a prompt reply: James said that he was just tying up some loose ends, and then soon, Luc unwillingly drifted off, with nothing but that small flame flickering about the room.

The next day he awoke with a very dry throat, the fever had come back in the night and he had shaken as before, but she had not come to help him, perhaps she was embarrassed now or, as the blackout had continued for hours she had not wanted to make any unnecessary journeys. He drank some water and looked at his phone, no call from James yet. He tried to rise and could manage to sit up although his head pounded with a headache, for some reason he had expected his illness to be over. He needed to bathe so he made his way to his bathroom, again the floor felt like a cavernous sponge and the room wavered about him, as though it wasn't sure if it should enter his consciousness. Luc prayed that he wouldn't faint and his breathing became heavier as he tried to remain steady. He stole into the bathroom, leaving his dirty clothes in a pile on the ground. There were towels handy, as he expected that by now she would have left for him and some shower gel as well, except that the products were girlish and feminine; she had obviously not been completely prepared for this. He didn't care as he switched the water on, he let it become very hot, stepping in to the steaming gush his skin reacted as though it did not know where it was or what was being done to it; the hot water felt like a white shiver and not a stream of heat; at least he would be clean he consoled himself. He kept it as quick as he could and soon smelled of nectarines and strawberries and watermelon, and he laughed as he dried himself; each motion was a slower labour than he could have imagined in his well state.

As though having achieved a great feat he re-entered the bedroom with a thick white towel wrapped about his waist and at that moment he froze, as did she, standing on the other side of the bed; as if they were two people caught in a summer frieze in the middle of a bedroom. It was a standoff, but they didn't know why, a tiny fraction of time in which none could move. She broke first, turning away, apologising, but she did not leave the room as he put on clean clothes, another t-shirt with boxers. As soon as he was dressed she rushed over and helped him back to the bed, it was true that he was shaking now from the effort.

"You should have called me," she said, gently admonishing him, but he couldn't resist it.

"Why, would you have bathed me?"

"No," she blushed fast, "but I could have been near in case you slipped, or fainted …"

"I knew you would find me eventually."

"Hmm." She seemed torn between embarrassment and laughter.

Once he was back in bed, she went off to make him food no doubt, he wondered what ready concoction it would be this time, and his telephone rang.

"Hello," Luc panted.

"Are you all right?" James asked, alarmed.

"No, not really, it's a fever and everything else."

"Are you OK to travel?"

"Um, well, I'm not at home …"

"What, where are you?"

"Next door."

"I see …"

"She's been looking after me," explained Luc.

"Are you too ill to travel?"

"… I think so. Is that all right? To go without me?"

"Luc, I don't care how ill you are, both of you need to get out!"

"James, when it started it was so bad that I thought it was the *Disease*."

"So, what are you saying? Luc, the Army are evicting people, there are helicopters, armed helicopters chasing News people in the sky. It looks serious."

"I know. I know." Luc stressed again. "But she's not budging and I'm not leaving her here alone, she would be stranded because of me, yes, I said staying at yours for her would be fine for you."

James sighed. "OK … Just keep your head down though; you don't exactly work for the local supermarket."

"I know, you're telling me. Are you leaving now?"

"Should be," said James.

"Do you want to come and say hello, or bye?"

"I would, but then, can't really afford to get ill right now, sorry, Luc."

"No I completely understand." But Luc was disheartened, on the one hand if Luc had told James right then about the list at least they had known each other for over three decades, their link in the world well established, it was quite another to be discussing possible names on hidden lists, from *Mer's* home, even if on personal mobiles.

"Have a nice time," Luc wished his friend.

"You too," said James.

As they ended the call Luc felt cut off, the last boat was about to sail, the last chance. He could hear then distant clinking and smelled the tangy fragrance again, of hot salty soup.

She came into the room, today she was wearing a red t-shirt that he had seen before and some light pink shorts, it must still be sweltering outside he thought. As she bore him the tray he sat up to receive it, today she placed it in his lap but still then sat on the edge of the bed next to him.

"Mer, James is still leaving today; do you want to go with him, with us? He's happy to have you."

"Are you going?" she asked.

"Only if you are."

"Are you well enough?"

Luc didn't answer, he felt after the last phone call, that if he kept in touch with James, and made sure that James was safe and all right, then he could manage to postpone his vital discussion with him, and instead try and focus on the Minister's plans within London, if anything seemed out of place with James at any point, then Luc would take the risk and reveal his knowledge about the list on the telephone.

"Well ... that is that ... don't you think?" she said, trying to sound fair.

Luc nodded, his mind made up and by now was anyway exhausted, suddenly, he only wanted to sleep, he couldn't remember if he had taken his wonderful white pills but he must have, the room swam a little before him and his hot eyes closed.

The day then passed as the previous one, with waking, soup and more rest. That night, she did come and he shook violently, sweating while his body was in a burning fury. She wiped his body, his face and arms, making him change again. This time Luc managed to speak as she did this, through his chattering teeth and quaking body, "W w we m must stop meeting like this." He tried to

255

joke as she wiped his chest with a wet hot towel, but could say no more. She did not reply but only looked at him concerned. That was all that he could remember of that night, apart from uncomfortable dreams that he awoke from with burning eyes and skin that tingled. That night mattered to him, it was a threshold; for the next day they would be fugitives.

Chapter 47

The following day Luc awoke to a sudden small sound, it was a text message from Clara, and even though there were no nasty raps at the door from armed guards waiting to take them away, this was not a pleasant surprise.

I want to keep you SAFE. Please let me know who you are? You have been a true friend.

What an earth did she mean keep him 'safe'?! It would do no good to reveal himself to her, not yet anyway, too much was unknown.

Monday passed as the weekend had and his new day's routine now included a very exhausting shower which he would attempt when he woke up; it made his room smell of soft fruits, or like a fancy woman's boudoir. Mer, he noticed had no telephone calls; perhaps they thought that she was at her spa in Cornwall, although Christine knew the truth. He wondered how Mer had spent her days while he slept.

That morning she greeted him cheerily, she seemed excited as if they were two naughty school children, and he greeted her with an equal smile which vanished as he coughed. She was becoming bolder he thought, on this occasion she sat on the side of the bed and took his temperature, which wasn't too high she was pleased to see, he remembered last night, she had been there as he'd shaken uncontrollably, shivering as though casting off his flesh and leaving behind a skeleton of ice, though he'd also burned and burned, straight from his core. She had been there in the dark, never switching on the light, she managed very well without it, she had by now run her hands over all of his upper torso, be it with a towel and he had never ever touched her, except for a polite kiss on the cheek when he had been well.

"Your hair looks nice today," she said to him.

"It's sticking up in all directions, isn't it?"

She nodded, laughing with no sound.

"I did brush it after my shower, you know."

"Yes, how was your shower today? Did you manage?"

"Didn't pass out, if that's what you mean."

"Dizziness?"

He shrugged.

"I'm sorry I don't have any manly scented products, you haven't complained yet, but I'm sure you've noticed … the room smells lovely."

Luc had not seen her be this cheerful before and with humour enough to tease him as well. She was busy opening the window although she only peeked out cautiously initially, as he would have. She wore a dress today, powder blue cotton and was barefoot, her arms shone in the sun as her back arched to push the window up open and wide; the window was as old as the house and functioned gracefully despite its years. Luc was pleased that she was not unwell because of him, perhaps not yet if it was incubating … he prayed not. After she'd neatened and prepared the room and let the air in, she approached him, this time holding his hair brush, he had no idea where she could have got it from, however she must have planned this he thought. She held it out to him, but he did not take it.

"Be my guest," he said to her.

She pursed her lips, but took the challenge and reached forward to brush his sandy brown hair, she was careful to keep her bust and torso at bay, to Luc's disappointment, she was not an obvious tease, she was not a tease in any way, yet she did torment him then, he wondered if he would shake again that night; it was as close as they ever came.

"Do I look serious now?" He asked with that slight French inflection.

"Yes. Yes you do … sorry, not sure how to brush boys' hair."

"It's all right; it will be wild again as soon as I hit the pillow."

She sighed. "Yes, I know."

"Mer, what are you up to when I am incapacitated, I mean, asleep?"

"Well, at first not much, I watched the news a lot, and kept my ear out for you, but now I've been reading, from the booklist Mr Andrews gave us, I even have some paints, thought maybe I would do some of that you know." She stopped and then chewed her thumb and forefinger.

Luc did not say anything, she was still sitting on his side of the bed a hairbrush in one hand, her loose curls hung about her head as she looked down slightly, then she looked back at him.

"How do you feel today? Ready to walk about yet?" she asked.

Luc sighed, "I would love to be able to get up. Nearly threw up in the shower though."

"Maybe tomorrow," she concluded.

He nodded, he wanted to thank her, to cook and feed her, to pour her wine and to thank her properly; she was laundering his dirty clothes now, he had many reparations to make he felt and then wondered again why she lived in such a big house, alone. He knew now that she had been alone until Christine had come to stay, in which he had played his part and then he felt very unwell suddenly, and reached to his bedside for his pills. She helped him and gave him water and he sank down, soon on fire. But even knowing what was to come, he attempted his task first and tried to text James, to ask if he was enjoying Berkshire, to which reassuringly Luc got a prompt reply that he was. It was only morning; Luc felt he was becoming worse. He was dismayed at this turn of events, within a few minutes his fever had flared up wildly and every fingertip burned and then oh no, he began to feel cold, his muscles were still sore and in pain from all the shaking he had done since Friday, never finding a chance to recover, but now it was daylight, the curtains were open and warm air had flooded the room from the open window. He could see her face clearly, as she of course would be able to see him. He fought the fever, he fought the spasms that were about to overcome him, for the first time he was embarrassed for her to see him like this; the night had been such a helpful refuge, it had been well enough to shiver in the night, in the dark shadows, but not now and not like this. But she was ready; he could see that soon she had a special bowl, full of hot water and a dash of her nectarine flavoured shower gel and two sets of hand towels, one for wet, one for drying.

Luc soon surrendered and his body began to crash against itself, he was furious with it but then there were no thoughts, only the acute cold, while his eyes streamed with heat. He was not sweating as yet, so she put a wet towel over his face and wiped it, as she did this he grabbed her other hand and held it to his chest, attempting to keep himself steady, to little avail. It was intriguing that there were no thoughts in his mind, only the pain in his sides, his pectoral muscles and his back muscles; all sore, demanding to seize again and again. He did not let go of her hand, so she stayed close, he grew more clammy and realised that he was perspiring heavily and so soon, she began. She released his hand and wet a towel in the sweet smelling hot water, to place it upon his face, wiping it like a child's and then laid the towel at the base of his stomach, just above his boxer shorts Luc noticed remotely despite his delirium, she pushed his t-shirt up and wiped swiftly, diligently, she then rolled him onto his side and did the same for his back. Knowing the routine, Luc assisted as much as he could as she changed his shirt, although his body rocked in daylight, he was truly ashamed that she should see him like this, but something new happened: the tremors stopped, typically they lasted longer, or at least they felt endless. He could see her clearly, sitting at his side and he was curled up around his torso, his body a ball of pain. His breathing slowed and he looked up from his downcast lashes, perhaps his body was winning, the virus had lost a battle at least, and she was regarding him, not his face, but his chest and abdomen.

His new fresh clothing had rolled upwards and was held gathered under his clenched arm to reveal his body. He watched her, as she stared at him; she did not know that he was looking at her, as his stomach moved in and out with each breath, less ragged now. She reached forward and Luc quickly closed his eyes, she tugged at the ends of the t-shirt to release his iron grip and pulled it down over his exposed stomach; for the first time he felt her fingers, as they glanced over his abdomen, they too felt like flickers of ice.

He opened his eyes and she was looking at his face.

"Thank you," he whispered and she surprised him again, as she reached forward to stroke his forehead and cheek. She was very concerned about him, it was plain to see. Her hand was cool, as she moved it down his face, she felt his lips which were still too hot to the touch, he wanted to kiss her hand, but did not dare, and then, she left him; the release of sleep came soon after.

When Luc awoke, there had been made some additions to the room; a green velvet armchair had been placed by the window, but facing him, and there were a few books on the floor as well.

She came in with his tray, it must be lunch time, at least for him he thought, feeling that all time had been lost. He was able to sit up and he asked her, "Do your family know, Mer?"

She looked up at him bewildered.

"About you staying here, not being in Cornwall?"

"Oh … that. Well they don't know yet, my parents have wished me a good holiday, I thought I would tell them in a few days when they can see it's all right to stay here. They're still in New York, so I don't want to worry them."

"Did you think I meant about harbouring a man in one of your bedrooms? No, I didn't think you would tell them that." He smirked.

"How do you know that my parents aren't liberal enough to be all right with that?" She looked at him squarely.

"Are they?" he asked, half seriously.

"Well, I don't know anymore, I haven't really tried their patience, who knows, maybe they don't care about these things anymore."

Luc frowned confused, for if her parents were conservative even in small matters, how had she been able to live by herself in such a big house? "Did you all used to live together in this house?" he asked her casually.

"Oh no, this is my house, they have their own flat in St. John's Wood."

"It doesn't make sense you know, you living in this big house alone, when your parents are from an Indian type background, girls like you would either be living with them, or have your own flat, but not a whole huge house ..."

"You like this house, don't you?" she said smiling.

He was caught off guard with the question. "Yes ... it's very nice."

Then she looked at him, "You're quite observant too, usually I'd be annoyed that you're being stereotypical, but you were fair, yes some girls like me from my background do live on their own like Anglo-Saxon girls, but not in palaces such as these." She gestured about, smiling wider.

"So then, how did this happen? Is it because other family members live here sometimes?"

"Not really, my father gave me a house, I accepted." She nodded at the last words.

Rubbish, Luc wanted to say, he didn't believe it. He would try again at another time he thought, but then couldn't wait, "Will you tell me, one day?" He asked her in a very different manner, as if from one who actually knew the truth; and so, he had her.

She looked at him unable to know which tack to take, although she was composed, her cheeks grew redder than a blush. "Maybe I will," she said with equal tone and he left it at that, she sat down next to him and his tray as he tried to eat.

He wanted to ask her more, but dared not, he didn't want to upset his host and he knew that he was very close to doing so. He drifted off soon after eating a very small amount and did not sweat and shake through the afternoon, while Mer took up her place at the armchair like a sentinel and read her book.

That night as Luc slept his body attempted to recover, his muscles still ached and his whole body felt as though it had been in an accident, but he had a dream. In this dream he was running through dark streets with cobbled stones, he ran and ran and as in dreams, it all felt utterly real. He was terrified that 'They' would find him, he did not know who 'They' were, but it wasn't good, clearly. It was a sunless place, the night was pitch black and old fashioned Victorian street lamps lit his way; it may have been a bygone Whitechapel or a setting for Jekyll and Hyde. He was finally in an alley and at a dead end, he could feel 'Them' approaching and he began to scream, he didn't know who could help him, but he was desperate and screamed with all his might, but his scream was too visceral, he could feel it tearing at his throat, everything he had ever wanted to say was contained in that scream, tears ran down his face with its ferocity and he choked as he woke up, Mer's face inches from his. He was sitting upright and had arms outstretched which she had clamped hold of on either side of him, he was panting and his eyes as hers, were wide open.

"Luc! Luc! You're dreaming, wake up, wake up!" she said.

He was awake, but realised that he had been shouting and from their position, possibly grappling with her.

"You were having a nightmare, it's all right it was just a dream, it's all right," she said firmly.

He collapsed back onto his pillow, trying to shake off the terror of the dream, after a few moments he looked at her, "I'm so sorry, was I shouting?"

"Screaming actually … are you all right?" she asked gently.

"I think so." Although he did not feel all right, his heart still pitter pattered, it was as though this was just another chapter in his dream and 'They' were still close.

"Can we put the lamp on?" he asked.

"Of course."

And she lit up the room; it was a mellow buttery light, thankfully not a searing white cold one as in the dream and she was wearing silk pyjamas; blue again, it must be her favourite colour he thought. He was relieved that the light was on; some dreams do not leave even when bidden.

He closed his eyes and again he felt her hand on his face, stroking his hair and his cheek.

Then she held his hand which was burning hot, he did not remember falling asleep again, or of putting the lamp off, but he woke the next morning and the room looked peaceful as daylight tried to creep in about the curtains.

How did he get here? He thought as he dozed mellow in the morning light, how had life changed so much since France … this new place, from his flat, to his workplace, to Mer's enormous home, how does anyone get anywhere? He realised that he hadn't spoken to his father in some days; Luc thought of him alone now in their French beach town. It had been easier for Luc to leave there although it had been unbearable at the time, but Vincent was the reverse, he would not leave and their home was exactly as Beatrice had left it; she had had many, many ornaments in her home and there they remained, quiet, untouched. Luc did not know where his father would go now; it was not something they discussed yet.

Luc shook his head, which ached and clanged as a rusty bell and tried too to shake off thoughts and memories of his mother. He attempted to sit up which was easier than he'd expected, drank some water and felt a ripple of pain through his muscles from movement in general. As he padded off for the shower the floor felt less spongy and the room coalesced into a more tangible reality; perhaps he was better. He went to the bathroom mirror to see: he had lost so much weight, in just days his cheeks had become hollow, as he could only manage soup or a little bread or rice that Mer was trying her best to supply him, but his eyes looked marginally brighter. Yes, and he was standing without feeling too exhausted, the next test would be the water: the hot shower pounded him, but it soothed his muscles as wafts of nectarine scented steam surrounded him. He took a deep breath away from the shower's stream, it hurt of course, but he could do it, no nausea or shaking. As he finished and dried himself he was pleased although yet tired now after the scrubbing, ready to lie down.

She was standing in his room of course when he was fully dressed and had finished doing his hair in the mirror, he did it for her; he knew it would be undone soon enough. It was beginning to feel as though they lived together; but both were still formal, knowing that they barely knew each other. She helped him walk back to his bed and as he sat down he could not restrain a quick but mighty wince.

"What hurts?!" she asked in alarm.

"Nothing, it's just from the shivering at night, muscles hurt from that, that's all."

"I can imagine."

Luc ran his hand over his face and hair, he looked fed up.

She sat down next to him and gave him a smile. He smiled back. Then she rose and left the room, probably to get him more food.

The days were passing so far from how he'd imagined, he was supposed to be in Berkshire with James, and getting to the bottom of why his name was on that list, but instead, he ate, slept and let chemicals flood his bloodstream in order to cope. After lunch and during his afternoon nap he thought he'd heard a phone ringing in the distance, at that same moment he heard his Clara-phone beep. He reached for it, but then to his horror felt the beginning of the fire again, his breathing quickened and then he was soon freezing; a cold sweat that began to such an effect that it was as though his body was rejecting all fluid, thankfully these sweats were not odorous, only producing eucalyptus tinged clamminess from the products that he rubbed upon his chest. He was galled again that this was happening in the daytime, when she might *see* him; he preferred it at night, in the darkness. Perhaps she was on the telephone, he briefly glimpsed at Clara's message:

Please contact me again. This is important, I am trying to help you, please understand.

And now he was shaking violently, freezing, burning, sweating, he cast the message out of his mind as nothing new, though he knew he would have to address the issue of Clara's persistence as soon as he was able. Mer came finally and ran to his bedside, Luc was in agony, his muscles could not take any more convulsing and his face became a repeating wince every time he shuddered. She rushed for her kit, for her bowl of hot water that looked like an offering and first removed his drenched t-shirt before she started, when he was in this state, she lost all of her deference and instead charged ahead. He lay flat, although curled his arms in and across his chest like an Egyptian mummy as he shook and she wiped him with her hot scented water, his torso showed some ribs, but was not so starved as to look unpleasant; he was even now still sun-kissed from France, where he had sat shirtless in front of the waves, lost in grief. After her ritual and when she'd clothed him, she walked over to the other side of the room and then, crawled onto the giant bed. She lay down behind him on her side as if replicating him, his back faced hers and she put her arms around him as he still seized. His strength was no match for her and he feared that he would hurt her as he shook, but they found a rhythm by which her arms over his were not harmed, her body was flush with his and she kissed him on his shoulder while he rocked, to try to soothe him, however for the first time Luc wanted to cry in fury, he tried not to and passed his tears off as watering streaming eyes, which they were.

Slowly, the shaking passed and he was completely exhausted, but she did not let go, she lay there one arm over his chest, the other over his right shoulder upon the bed so that her hands met over his body. Occasionally she broke from this and stroked his hair, Luc tried to breath freely, he was still very hot from the fever which had never left and she instinctively felt this and moved away, but did not leave the bed, he turned to lie on his back and closed his eyes.

Just before he was blissfully able to sleep he saw her lying there, far off on the other side of the grand bed, a statue apart from the rising chest, with eyes fixed on the ceiling; and at the back of his addled mind he wondered why she was still there.

Hours past, or was it minutes and Luc woke up reaching instinctively for his water glass, but there was something else in the room, a warmth, another something. He turned his face about and there she was, almost in the same position as before, asleep on the other side of the bed, it had been warm enough to not need a cover and a yawning stretching light streamed in from the half open curtains that marked the late afternoon. Her hair was swept across her face and her chest rose and fell with no care or concern for where she was. He liked that she slept as though lost, his sleeping beauty, he didn't want to move in case he woke her, so he watched motionless for a while and then took his water.

He was surprised that she had held him like that while he shook, she, who had always so carefully kept distance between them. She was a puzzle he thought. She slept on, as if it were her who was exhausted, even though by now Luc had moved about, been to the bathroom and back and shuffled upon the bed. He was clammy but felt more energetic, she slept on undisturbed. He had put the television on at a low volume before she woke, at first not sure of where she was and then lifted her head as though to wake herself up quickly, knowing very well indeed where she was; her eyes grappled to focus, they looked at him blinking beams of will.

"How are you?" he asked her.

"Sorry, I didn't mean to fall asleep …"

"Nothing to be sorry about." He smiled.

She moved her body which was still heavy and sat up, at that moment, she felt her right hand, that was closest to Luc give way, he had taken it.

"Thank you," he said earnestly, holding her hand.

She looked back at him and tried to push back her hair from her face, having just woken from wanton sleep, and smiled. He still did not let go, so she lay back down again. As she lay down, she was able to claim her hand back with a gentle fluid movement; she asked him then, "How are you?"

"Honestly, I don't know, but I feel better right now."

"Hospital?"

"I know what you mean," he sighed, "but don't you think it's just a fever?"

"Actually, I do, because remember I said I've had something like this, that's why I'm not rushing you to the nearest Army barracks to ask them to help. I had this once, and my mother knew what to do about all the shakes and cold sweats, so that's what I'm doing ..."

"... And, so well."

She left soon to prepare them both some food which they ate together on the bed and then settled down on her side again. They watched the news and then she brought her book and read it also upon the bed while Luc dozed, medicated. That night was the first in which he slept without incident, and he awoke to find her still there, she had also retrieved her own white duvet, leaving him his own. How did he get here? Luc wondered again, the curtains were closed but sunlight still trickled in around its edges and how long would London's deviant summer continue?

He sent another text message to James, who in essence replied that he was well again, and that they, him, Mischa and Jelly, had had a picnic today; Luc consoled himself by the fact that at least he had not made them all ill and ruined their break. After that he picked up his Clara-phone and looked at her last message. He doubted she would quit, and he had to come up with something that would sate or stall her, but she was not at that stage yet. In his depleted state his mind drew a blank as to how to do this without giving in to her demands, but today at least his head did not swim upon waking, he only felt as though run over and broken by a truck, his muscles recovering, smarted from his movements, nor did he feel hot, or have any fever for that matter. He went over to take his shower and the room presented itself as a solid sensation, rather than a waking dream, the impression of the water was hot, although it made him feel delicate, as a worn away athlete or battered warrior. When finished he emerged towel around his waist, torso damp and she slept on, so he stripped off completely, selecting clothes from the washed pile that she had left for him now on a chair by the wall. He dressed slowly and sighed from the effort but then he noticed that she was watching him, her head was tucked in near the covers but her eyes were definitely open and she did not feign sleep either when he looked back at her; he wondered how much she had seen?

"Good morning," she said, rubbing her face.

"Good morning, how are you?"

"How am I? How are *you*?" she asked.

"Not bad I think, but then I thought that yesterday…"

At that, she left, and took her covers with her, walking sleepily and saying that she would be back.

Luc was able to sit up on his bed he reached for the remote control, he had no full idea what had been happening in the world even his immediate world of London town; if there had been helicopters overhead he had either been too delirious to notice or had become immune to the sound.

The television flickered into life from a blank profoundly dull black screen. There were more shots of the camps, people sitting in tents, what people were eating, queues and most importantly two journalists arrested and in jail for trying to break through the blockade and sneak into London. Luc's heart did a belly flop then hammered erratically: they were in deep, deep trouble. He could understand people receiving a severe verbal warning and being escorted out of the restricted area, but arrested? He wondered if it was legal, apparently so. He sank deep into his pillow as if trying to hide and peeked up fearfully at the window, craving to look outside now. So he put down the remote, his hand by then had become fashioned into a claw around it and crept there, which wasn't easy as it meant tensing his abused muscles. A loose feline prowl with a stoop was all that he could manage, his body hurt immensely. He did not open the curtains but peeked out from one side, nothing, there was no one there but unexpectedly, at odds with what he was looking for, he saw that the day was beautiful; there were two pigeons looking at him from the tree in front of the house, they stared very aware of him, then as Luc looked past them and the empty abandoned road, the entirety of Regents Park unfolded, with no visitors, tourists or families to litter it, green and sprawled as yet released glory, back into its wilderness; it was quite content with itself, to the naked eye looking exactly as it had before all of this began.

Luc closed his eyes to try and listen and a very distant drone, a hushed racket had its own sound frequency in the air, so the patrols continued. He sighed and sloped off back to his bed. She came back with toast and juice for him.

"Have you seen the news?" he asked her too keenly.

"No, what happened?" She turned around to face the television that was still on at a low volume and there was the headline, emblazoned across the screen: 'Two journalists arrested over London trespassing.'

She looked at him, not certain of his measure of agitation.

"It looks like they are taking it very seriously," he said to her, asking her to understand.

"I can see, don't worry ... we'll stay hidden."

He wasn't soothed, but he was now determined to stay concealed.

Later that day Luc woke with a start, having fallen asleep after his toast without realising it, disorientated once again. The television was still on at a very low volume but he did not register yet what was happening. Slowly, wakefulness came in waves to him, his mind engaged and he lifted the clammy covers off to feel some air on his body, instinctively he looked to the other side of the bed, she was not there.

He thought of her, at first fondly and with gratitude for how she had nursed him over the last few days and then, he could not place it, but an emotion rose in him, close to agitation and he wanted to shake her, his waking sleeping beauty, as if to get through, to awaken her, to break her seal and destroy the stillness that she herself generated; like an invisible shield, a fortress cage of the psyche that kept her at bay, of which she herself was guilty of. He was irritated although he knew he had no means to chide her by, or of any right to either.

Finally after these musings something new caught his eye: 'Journalists released- Arrests deemed illegal' and moreover, 'Many people found still hiding in their homes in central London'. His eyes popped. Obviously some journalists had made it past the barricades which stretched with barbed wire across the frontiers of Central London and it's inner suburbs, probably easy to surpass if someone were to skip through deserted back gardens, which is exactly what had occurred, not only that, but they had brought their cameras with them and found a few people still here, where they shouldn't be, just like Mer and Luc. Faced with this the government had started to issue new guidelines: anyone still left inside the exclusion zone was to telephone a certain number and to register that they were still there and furthermore were then advised to stay inside their homes for the duration. Luc was surprised; he thought at least that they would be escorted out after 'registering' instead, the government was offering these people help, for if anyone ran out of supplies such as food for the duration they were to ask for assistance. How strange thought Luc, things were no longer so draconian and he felt relieved, although there was no possibility that he was going to put himself on this so called 'register'.

At that moment Mer came in.

"Have you seen this?" he asked her excitedly, pointing to the screen.

"Yes, I have, it's good isn't it?"

She looked well he thought, she must have had this illness before, she had no trace of it thankfully, he tried not to smile at her lime green t-shirt, her loose curls looked washed and fresh as did her face, she had soft lounging shorts on in a pale grey and had grown comfortable around him he thought, at least in terms of dress. Her legs were pale brown, almond and pale in crevices, glancing the light off her shin bones and there was a dimple or two on her thigh, that she did not shrink from showing, she was slim, yet still soft in places. That lime green shade was a colour from childhood, utterly vibrant and yet still upon her fallen under a cloak, to look as near demure as it could.

"Feel like walking?" She asked him nurse to patient.

"What?" He had adjusted to his new quite limited lifestyle, where would she want him to walk to?

"Time to move about a little bit you think?"

He smiled at her sheepishly. "How much moving?"

"Well, what do think you can manage?"

"Kitchen?" Luc said, although looking at her to see if it was a good idea.

"All right, let's give it a go then." And she waited expectantly.

Luc sighed and began to shuffle of his clammy refuge of fabric and down. "You know I am not dressed for public outings."

"It's only me." She was smiling and began rummaging in his bag of things by the bathroom door; she dragged out a faded blue grey dressing gown and slippers.

"I see you have been planning this," he said looking at her, smirk at hand.

"From day one."

She brought the items over to him as he sat on the side of the bed with his feet ready on the bare floor, she dressed each foot and then she helped him to put on the gown, Luc caught her scent as she ventured near, also of soft fruits, as she must have caught his; he was sure by now that he only smelled of nectarines.

"Ready?" she asked him.

"Ready," he nodded.

She stood up and waited while he rose slowly, she placed her arm to link warmly with his and led him for the first time in days, out of the bedroom door. It was hard to believe, when he came to the landing that the rest of the majestic house existed, he would so like to very much explore it when he was better. At present she led him like an old man, step by slipper padded step to the staircase, the landing was dark in the day without the lights on, and he could see the winding broad swooping stairs that awaited him.

As they descended by each step, his muscles smarted from the action, so she leaned in to support his back with her arm and had her side pressed to his, his breathing was laboured but he looked straight ahead and Mer did not ask if he wanted to go back, as though knowing that it was not what he wanted to do.

Luc focused on each stair and in truth longed to sit down, but he wanted to continue as well, he liked Mer's large yet rustic kitchen, he could sit down there he reasoned with himself as he could feel his stomach muscles begin a quiver and a shudder.

Finally they reached the bottom of Mer's elegant swoop of stairs. She let him stand at the base for a minute, before proceeding carefully down the corridor to their destination. She was ready for him; he could see a green velvet armchair in the kitchen waiting for his arrival.

"Nearly there," she said, but looked worried; he could see that she now regretted this idea of hers.

"Yes, nearly there." And he smiled at her.

They reached the kitchen and Luc creaked himself into the armchair, his muscles shuddering.

She went to the kettle and set it to boil, making him some tea without asking and she looked unhappy.

"I know you think I'm not well, but I am, I'm all right, Mer."

"Really?" she asked, she looked very concerned now, the invisible veil had fallen away and her eyes shimmered luminously, swept over with possible tears. "I feel awful ... I hope this doesn't bring on your fever again, I don't think you're ready for this, I was just following what my mother did with me, I'm so sorry."

Luc thought that Mer looked truly unhappy, and was sure that this situation did not warrant so much remorse. "Mer, I'm fine, I'm at my destination and it's so good to be somewhere else, actually I keep thinking, I really want to explore this house when I'm fully better, if that is all right with you?"

She nodded, but she had tears ready in her eyes, one blink and they would fall so she wiped them away with the back of her hand which made her look even worse; her eyes had betrayed her and Luc felt in her a waiting rupture, a ready threat of release and he took a deep full breath, even though his chest seared with pain, but yet as if breathing freely at last.

"Come here," he then said to her.

She moved close to him and stood by his chair as he instructed, not meeting his eyes. He reached out one of his hands and clasped it around her upper arm, and then he dragged her down in a fluid motion. She found herself in a warm engulf, perched on his lap, but unable to settle there. So Luc put both his arms around her and slowly she gave up, turning her face away ironically to hide it from him, close to his chest, which grew wet. She cried quietly, at no moment yet did he ask her what the matter was, he did not interrupt.

Finally, she gathered herself and placed her chin upon his shoulder, wiping her eyes with a hand that she looped over his clasp about her. She could not speak yet and took in uneven breaths, trying to calm herself.

"What a pair we are," Luc said, trying to laugh but wincing as his muscles shuddered beneath her and so she laughed a little too.

"Yes." She nodded and she did not let go of him yet, he was warm and solid and still beneath her.

"I'm sorry, Luc. I don't know what happened."

"You're exhausted from taking care of me." He tried to laugh again and grimaced instead.

"No, no, not at all … no," she protested. "You've been a pleasure ..." and more quietly "… are a pleasure."

Luc did nothing and neither did she, no one moved.

Finally she sighed and tried to stand up, her cool cheek brushed past his hot one as she disentangled herself from him. Standing up beside him she put her hand on his forehead and then on his cheek -clinically now, although he looked her straight in the eye as she effectively held his face, and then she withdrew, cast her face away and turned to the sink.

"I think you should stay here a while, have your tea and read a magazine or something before we try going back," she said, fiddling with some washed crockery.

"But you'll have to entertain me, there's no television here."

She laughed and it cracked the melancholy, splitting it apart, relief.

"Even better, I could watch you cook, I could instruct you from the chair," he added.

"Ha, the results would be the same, get better if nothing else but to eat a decent meal again."

So she did as he said and tried to cook pasta sauce, she chopped an onion as he verbally guided and it was still butchered by her whatever he tried or said, although he noticed that she had improved perhaps without realising, as she paid attention to the red sauce when it bubbled away, knowing that she mustn't let it stick or burn.

He enjoyed watching her like this, she was busy enough not to feel self-conscious while he had an excuse to regard her with her back turned, making sure that she did not burn down the kitchen. The combination of the surprisingly exhausting trip down the stairs and Mer's emotional turn had in truth left Luc feeling quite shaken, he had no desire to move and try and climb back to his bedroom yet and worried as he could feel his appetite crawling away from him, like a sick animal.

She was so engrossed with what she was doing, novice that she was, that she had not turned around and fully comprehended how pale Luc now looked, his breathing ever so slightly laboured under the waves of heat that flashed about his temples and skin, though departing quickly, but leaving a sinister sensation, like a kiss on the forehead from a mafia don, '*later*' they whispered to him as the shivers departed.

Finally she was finished and laid before Luc the simplest home cooked pasta sauce with linguine, he did not feel like eating anymore, although a faint hint of appetite did plead and gnaw at him in a distant recess of the abdomen. So he still attempted it. "Well done, Mer."

She beamed a big smile; even her widest smile was like a full moon, glorious, enchanting, but ephemeral in its glory.

"Thank you," she said pleased with herself.

Luc was making a gargantuan effort and ate what he could. He needed to collapse, it was his only wish. As soon as they'd finished he did not wait for her to clear up and requested that they try going back.

They were ready for the expedition in the kitchen doorway and when he was upright and leaning on her, she finally noticed that he was quite the worse for wear, and frowned to herself and held the sturdiest arm around him that she could; finding his body solid and heavy to manage as they effectively tottered.

As they made their way she glanced at him when she could to see his condition, he was very pale, a kiss of moonlight under his skin.

"It won't be long 'till we're there," she told him.

He nodded in response not wanting to speak while trying to breathe and walk at once.

The stairs were another matter. Each step was a labour, he leaned on her heavily and she could barely support his weight. When they reached the first floor landing, they had an interval, Luc clung to the landing banister and Mer clung on to him. He was as white as a sheet. They hobbled excitedly through the final stretch and when Luc reached his bed he was feeling too awful to be elated, yet he was. He sat down and then immediately rose again, much faster than Mer thought he was capable of and raced to the bathroom clutching his stomach involuntarily as the muscles screamed in pain from the exertion, he promptly then vomited in the loo. Mer stood at the bathroom doorway and watched him, her food promptly rejected. Luc knelt by the toilet, arms clutched either side of the seat and heaved, until there was no more, he had tears streaming down his face but did not move until he could feel that the wrathful tide had ebbed, he first wiped away his streaking eyes with the back of his hand before Mer could see, and then with the other pressed the flush.

He pulled himself into standing position and turned to face the sink and mirror, which he did not bother to look into. He splashed what felt like Siberian ice cold water onto his face and then rinsed with mouthwash and then finally brushed his teeth, all the while she stood at the doorway as if waiting for him. Once finished he turned to face her and she reached out a hand, that he took. She led him to his bed, never before had a bed been such a solace. He curled onto his side underneath the covers and could see that she was filling his glass with water from the jug, although spent; he could smell now that even his sheets were perfumed with the scent of nectarines. There was little light in the room, just a mellow glow from his bedside lamp, the rest was dark and blue black, the curtains that billowed meekly from the night breeze, revealed total darkness outside and a quiet that Luc had never heard before in London. No helicopters that night, just the breeze and Mer, rustling through the room, her bare arms and legs in lovely hues from the lamplight, her body carved out by this mellow glow and bruise hued shadows that enveloped the room beyond. She sat on the side of the bed in between him and the bedside, she put her hand on his forehead and pushed his hair back, her fingers cool prongs. Luc was beyond her, in his own place of respite, he felt her about him, but could not engage; he trusted her enough now not to mind this. He had his eyes closed, but he knew that she knew, that he was awake.

He felt her then get up to leave, she did leave the room, but soon a large amount of rustling could be heard as she re-entered, he felt the weight shift on the bed, then heard footsteps coming closer to him, he could feel her near as the lamp went out and the darkness soothed him more than he could imagine. The light footsteps continued, but for only a very short while and then he wanted to open his eyes in surprise but could not, as the bed moved and shifted, she must have climbed in at the other side and yes, brought her own quilt. Although Luc was aching for sleep, curled as he was into himself, his mind circled around this fact, too tired to examine it.

That night of no sound, no helicopters, of course no traffic and no human voices, they could have been in the countryside; beyond the road outside that ringed around the massive park, the creatures, trees and flora had also been abandoned in Regents Park and left undisturbed, waiting and wondering. If Mer and Luc had been still awake they would have experienced a blackout then, and so, even the house grew still, all its power gone. Luc slept very deeply, soothed by the night air breeze, his fever did not return, although it felt as though he wanted to sleep forever. Mer slept too not far from him, he did not know it but when she had first laid down, as his back was to her, she had watched him for a long time, before closing her eyes.

As a new day fell upon them once more Luc turned to see if she was still there, in case it had been a dream, but she was there, asleep, her hair again half cast across one side of her face. He lay back on his pillow; truly it had been an awful night. She stirred now and opened her eyes in one fluid motion like a doll to look at him.

"Good morning," he said to her.

She was not awake enough to answer so smiled on her side as she faced him, blurry with sleep. She then closed her eyes again and Luc let her rest. He wanted to move her hair back away from her face, those loose curled strands, as she did to him often and without his permission. He turned his body so that it faced hers and then reached out his hand, he touched her face as he tried to sweep back her hair that draped over one cheek, and she seemed to freeze where she lay, she opened her eyes and looked at him, too still to be pleased with him, but he did not take his hand back immediately, he only retrieved it after a few moments had passed, wondering why she would not accept what she readily gave to him.

*

Two more days passed, and Mer did not leave Luc's bed, yet nor did she behave as they were nothing but civil bedfellows, unless he shook with fever, at which time she cast off her deference, and now those dramatic fevers had ebbed away. So too, had the ferocity of the Army, as they were reporting on the television how things were for the people (like them) who had stayed behind and phone calls were being broadcast between journalists and the people still there, hiding; they spoke of how they went on walks unhindered and about how they were coping and so on. Some even drove about. Luc was engaged, as though transfused with new blood, and a plan in him immediately ignited. Even at his worst, he had sometimes texted James twice a day, all was well in Berkshire it seemed, and at that moment, as if on cue, his Clara-phone beeped, angrily if it could, felt Luc.

You MUST contact me, it's for your own safety. If you do not, I have no choice but to hand this phone in, please understand.

And so now it really began, thought Luc, this is exactly the sort of thing he had been expecting from Clara. At least he felt well he thought, even if his body was demolished. So he replied to Clara, with the truest request:

Just give me some time, please, if you can.

It was ironically the most honest thing he could say to her. He waited, she did not answer, probably thinking, he thought. It was a good sign; if she actually had to hand his phone number in to whomever, she would have immediately replied with a deadline. Luc remembered Clara as wilful, her messages had been so personal, and emotional almost, that he did wonder if it was only her own desires that made her want to know who he was. Then he reminded himself of what he'd saved her from, and knew that there were still very dark forces at least around her, that had to be circumvented.

It was Saturday, and Mer today had not been in his bed upon waking. The light was dimmed considerably compared to the last few days and the gloom now an unusual sight during London's strange heatwave. His throat felt dry and he was troubled by the silence in the room, possibly in the house; it had weight. He tried to sit up, his muscles protested; still he could hear nothing at all. Without thinking he realised that he was getting out of bed, slowly pushing the sheets away across his torso which even though was a mild agony, he could now bear well, as he had become used to it. The wooden floor still had the warmth of many days embedded into it and he crept slowly out of his bedroom, walking with his usual hobble to avoid using too many of his stomach muscles. As he reached the doorway he was drawn not to the stairs but to another side of the landing; Mer's bedroom. There was still no sound of life as he neared her room, which he had never seen before, the door was open and he shuffled closer, willing himself to be very quiet, he had on a pair of woolly socks to complete the usual attire of soft t-shirt and boxer shorts which gave him added stealth.

In Mer's doorway he stood, and there he found her, sprawled in the middle of her bed, her hair across her face, her black t-shirt raised to expose her stomach and wearing those same soft grey shorts. He looked at her and then at her room: it was almost as Spartan as his was, the bed was large but curled about in gold metal work and on one side was a dressing table quite laden with perfumes and other bottles of things. A lonely high backed chair sat vacant adjacent to it and that was it, he could see that she had her own bathroom too that led off from the back of the room and that the lamps by her bedsides were at least something to notice; much like the full sized women who stood arch backed at the entrance of the house, Mer had lamps again in the size and shape of real women; now offering up balls of light in only one hand as the rest of their bodies and clothes twirled and twisted about a central pillar. They had a form of regal satisfaction, like the female effigies that graced great ships, here in pinks, peaches and gold, and yet; they were quite diminished in this empty room. Mer stirred a little; there were no clocks for Luc to look at to check where they were in the day, although his stomach was rumbling.

He didn't want to wake her, so he left her there and made his way back to his own room next door, happily letting himself slide a little upon his socks. He went to peak out of the side of the curtains, it was grey, but not the usual English greyness that he and Mer had grown up with, it was the ashen beginning of the blacks and purples which heralded an ominous storm, and as he gazed he saw the first maiden drops of rain begin to fall and splatter; at that moment as the rain began in earnest, he very much wanted Mer to wake up. There was once again nobody outside, no cars or Army trucks either and

Regent's Park itself across the road, a green and unentered mass, could perhaps already be wild with neglect he imagined. As he turned away from the window, it occurred to him that he was not feeling weak and did not have great need to return to his bed, so he ventured back to the hallway and inevitably back to stand in Mer's doorway. As he'd made his way shuffling and sliding in his thick socks, he heard the rain intensify wildly from the window, which he hadn't shut. It was uncontrollable rain already, pounding the streets in a cascade, a stored up torrent to pour forth in answer to all the endless heat. She had not moved or stirred and now her dark and shadowy room pulsated to the sound and rhythm of the rain as the shadows of it danced; but she slept on untouched. Finally, Luc hesitated before deciding to leave, at which moment there was an almighty light that flashed about her bedroom, as if splitting it open in electric white and then the heavens bellowed a crack of thunder that shook Luc, so that he held on to the door frame and when he looked back, Mer was sitting bolt upright, breathing hard and looking terrified.

"Mer, Mer, it's all right, it's just a thunder storm!"

She looked at him still very frightened, her mind absent due to her aborted sleep.

"Mer, it's me, it's Luc, it's just a storm!" he insisted

She wiped her hair away from her eyes and nodded; he made his way over to her and sat on the side of her bed. He put his arm around her and another crack of lightning lit up their electrified faces and an even louder violent din from above made them want to cower. She rubbed her face and listened also to the rain coming down in sheets. As she nestled into his side, she was still so sleepy and they sat there in the dark while the worst of it occurred, none of them dared to move or to switch on a light. After some time, they heard the thunder moving off to terrorise another part of the city, Mer sighed and Luc removed his arm. He still sat there as she shuffled off the side of the bed and then walked by him to her wardrobe, she pulled out an over large red cashmere wrap for herself and a blue soft blanket that she gave to him. He put it about himself and said, "Mer, will you come out for a drive with me? Apparently everyone who's here is doing it. And yes, I'm OK, I swear, just a bit creaky."

She looked at him, and saw in his eyes a determination.

"… All right," she said uncertainly.

"Good, get dressed, I'll make us some toast." And he went off, leaving Mer still standing there.

Mer had a quick hot shower, and after a while Luc was padding about her room, and called through the bathroom door, "We're having breakfast at yours today, I'm sitting on your bed with the toast."

At which moment she was getting out of the bathtub, and drying herself, she still had one leg perched upon the bath edge and as she had turned to listen to him, looked like another one of the Art Nouveau lamps that adorned the house. As she came out, a towel wrapped around her, Luc was dressed and ready: he had on a pair of blue jeans, a beige t-shirt and a pale green cotton pullover. She held her wrapped towel firmly, and then glanced at the window; the storm had passed, and a bright sun was acting as if nothing had happened, never mind the soggy dregs in the streets. Luc saw that she then chose a summer dress to wear, and took her clothes with her back inside the bathroom as he ate his toast.

Finally, Luc let Mer eat two slices of toast. And then said, "let's go."

"Are you sure?"

"Yes." He said no more than that. So they reached the front door and prepared themselves, keeping their keys and telephones ready and with them, Mer also kept some little white pills in her bag, just in case. The old and heavy well-made door beckoned itself open, letting in the light and also the quiet; for there was no sound but their own.

Chapter 48

James was still in London. He had been given false hope that there would be a last minute diplomatic mission to Paris, which Sir John would be going on himself; it was cancelled at the eleventh hour as it was thought best to happen after the evacuation. Thus, he had spent the last few days before the evacuation waiting in Dover, to no avail. Restless now, he tried to do some exercise in his living room, he dared not go for a run outside, although he longed to. On the final Sunday, he had decided to stay in London, in case there was still any hint of a diplomatic transport to Paris, as Sir John said there might have been; the French wanted to talk trade urgently with them after the economic urgency of the embargo. And yet, knowing she was now in his radius, most of all James wanted to see Clara, to grasp the back of her head with his hands and bring his fingertips up through her hair, and to kiss her mouth ...

During the evacuation, James had spent every evening since seeing her like this: looking out onto his parched lawn, especially as London had emptied itself and he was faced with days of an unknown quiet, and it had become a habit, this, waiting for Paris, at least no one else had been threatened or died since he last spoke to Clara, who was under a heavy watch, and yet, he had received a very odd call from Luc today, saying to: "Look after each other", James began to suspect strongly that Luc knew a little more than he should, but James could only deal with that after the evacuation ended, he thought.

Tonight in his solitude, he had been sitting by the sliding doors to the garden in almost darkness, he had on one distant lamp in the kitchen but it did not fill the room, his posture was posed for sleep with legs dragged out on the ground before him; he missed his friends and Luc but he liked London to be so peaceful like this, not a car nor a siren broke into the warm night air and what an uncannily hot and unusual summer it had been.

His eyelids were drooping to a close, when he opened them again to half look at the dark garden by his side, black far past evening and unyielding, devoid of the solar glory of the day, his eyelids returned to their place of repose and then his home telephone rang out like an electric scream; it woke him up so abruptly that he answered it within a split second although his body was jangled -he had made sure it had been by his side as well as a packed bag, ready to go.

"Hello?"

"GET OUT NOW! RUN! GET OUT NOW!!!"

At that moment the glass door to the garden was smashed in above his head, sending the noise of shattering glass though the house like a warning shriek, but he'd stood up in time to avoid a skull full of shards. Grabbing his wallet and mobile in one hand that were also on the little table next to him, he ran without thinking, he ran for his front door yet he was sure that surely there'd be more of them coming from that direction too. He was right, but they had already passed through there and had fanned out into the adjoining rooms; leaving the front door unobscured and blissfully wide open. He knew his house better than they did; and the time it took him to shoot down the corridor from his kitchen to the front door, was a fraction shorter than the time it took them to double back from where they were, to head to the commotion and noise in the kitchen. James then ran to the side of his house where he kept of all things, his bicycle.

Shoving the mobile and wallet in either pocket, he took the bicycle out as quietly and speedily as he could, and pedalled for his life; if he weren't completely deranged with fear he would have seen the comedy of his getaway. He knew that taking the car would have meant making enough noise for them to know where he was and to follow him, he could see that they had come in cars, obviously very stealthy ones; he had decided to take the bike as his road was quickly bisected by another that he planned to turn into after five seconds of riding, otherwise he knew 'they', whoever they were, when they rushed out, would quickly see him. He turned his corner and could hear shouts and car doors banging. The good thing about an empty London was that there were so many places to hide; and so, everywhere became a hiding place. He quickly turned into the side of someone else's house, most likely long gone, it was dark and silent and he stayed there listening. If they had not seen the bicycle, then they would not understand how he had gone so far in so little time and thus would be searching in the wrong place; if they had seen it he reasoned, well they would have reached him by now. He waited, concealing himself as much as possible behind wheelie bins and junk; whoever they were, they had not considered upon every house in London being a potential hiding place. James heard cars driving off and then driving back again, this went on for ten minutes; maybe they had finally realised that he literally could be anywhere. James looked at his watch and decided to give it at least twenty minutes of silence before he moved, he knew he should wait longer but he was rattled and wanted to get away, a cool breeze brushed past his face, a wisp of cold interspersed the sultry air.

His allotted time passed, he chose to set off, he blinked and could feel something itchy on the side of his left temple, but he had no time for that now. His limbs were stiff even though it was not cold, and in the time he had been stationary he'd had time to think about where to go; he could not visit any of his known friends' addresses, not one, and definitely not Sir John's, it had been a woman's voice on the phone, he knew who it was. Yes, he had decided where to go; it was not that far away at all.

James pulled up slowly to his safe house and dismounted, wanting to walk the rest of the way to the door. He had not been followed nor heard any rumble of a vehicle, he planned to have a look, surveying the building to see if it was safe and then he saw it, a light on at the first floor and before he suspected the worst, he saw the outline of a woman lingering behind the curtains, and so, he began to bang on the front door frantically and ring the doorbell at the same time; he could feel something at the side of his head, his left temple, but he did not stop and banged with his fists.

Chapter 49

Luc seated Mer in his car and switched on the engine, its roar tore into the daylight, but he didn't care. He was glad that she didn't ask him any questions yet, and he drove on, to Mayfair. He did not think about what he could achieve by such a mission, but he attempted it nonetheless.

As he approached the Mayfair club that always filled him with dread, he saw with pleasure that its windows were dead and lifeless. As he pulled up he nervously glanced at Mer, knowing that he was placing her in trouble potentially, if not danger.

"Mer, I have to do something, can you wait in the car?"

"I can, but what if I get caught, or questioned?"

Luc sighed, knowing that in all scenarios of being caught it would look better if they were together, like two lovers out for an adventure. He glanced back at the building, there was no one there.

"Please, I have an important errand; I'll be as quick as I can."

She nodded.

Luc got out and walked the little distance to the front doors, he tried the handle, and then rang the doorbell. Nothing. He looked around, knowing that there were CCTV cameras here, though he suspected such things were switched off, so he went around and to the back of the building, to where the giant bins were kept, there didn't seem to be any cameras here, so he tried an unassuming looking back door. Locked of course, but quite flimsily, he took a nearby loose brick and hit the handle hard twice, he had to inhale and steady himself at the second blow.

Luc considered that they may have a silent burglar alarm, but there weren't any police here anymore, so no one to man the patrol for such things; Luc was sure that this evacuation was so unusual that everyone had left London, with total faith in the Army.

Luc pushed open the back door, and waited. No live alarm screamed back at him.

Then he ran through a corridor, past some back rooms and kitchens until he found some stairs, it was a bit of a maze, but sure enough and soon, Luc found the familiar dark oak panelling and deep green velvet upholstery of the entrance hall, and followed his route, to the Minister's rooms.

There, he found again the door locked and deciding against kicking it open in his current health, he looked about for something to help. He found a nearby chair set by a wall and unceremoniously lifted it up and bashed it against the handle; the oak split, spitting the odd splinter where the handle was once firmly set, breaking apart enough for the door to swing open.

Once inside he began to hunt, for clues, for papers, for anything that could help. He first attacked the desk, more locked drawers. He looked about for where the keys could be kept, feeling sinkingly foolish; of course they were locked. He had looked everywhere he could, even ran his hands under the base of the chairs, and could feel every second ticking past. Realising then, that he might have achieved nothing here except arousing even more suspicion by the state of the door, he turned with balled fists, and kicked in fury a small dark wooden ornamental looking chest. After a loud 'crack' it fell ungracefully upon itself and spilled its contents.

Luc crouched down to take a look, and realised amazed, that it was maybe a case of hiding things in plain sight. For upon the floor was a paper file, and as he turned a manila hued cover, he came upon his own face, in a large photograph. There followed a brief history of Luc's work and education, and nothing out of the ordinary, like a C.V. But there was also another piece of paper and this was a list:

Dora Belgrave: Eliminated.

John McMahon: Eliminated.

Elsa de Vere: Eliminated.

James Mackay-

Anjelica Mackay-

Mischa Brearley-Jones -

Sir John Balthazar-

Clara Day- Whereabouts unknown.

Simon Hughes- Under surveillance.

Louise Sands- Possible secondary importance.

There were a few other names on the list that Luc did not recognise, otherwise the box was empty. He took a photo of each page of the documents with his phone.

He then hastily began to try and put everything back as he found it and even tried to wipe down everything he had touched with a dish cloth he had brought with him, stolen from the kitchen, remembering to do the back door when he left.

Once the room looked as it had before, apart from the broken door handle, and the papers all replaced, Luc ran, back to the back alley, and then to his car. As he did up his seat belt, he listened for anything, such as sirens or approaching cars … but nothing came.

As they drove away, Mer asked, "All done? All ok?"

Luc felt the incongruity of her cheery gait. "All done," he said and tried to smile. "Can you just put up with me a little bit more, just another errand or two?"

"Of course," she said, her hair bobbing, enjoying the drive he could see.

Luc headed north, to St. John's wood, still there were no other cars, and the traffic lights were switched off; this gave Luc faith that CCTV cameras would have been seen as superfluous too.

As he slowed into James' street, he looked about, he had no intention to park, and as he passed James' house he slowed further, trying to see if anyone was watching it. He could not feel any life, so after a few seconds, he drove on, he sorely wanted to then drive to South Kensington, to Gemma's house, but that was perhaps too dangerous, Clara's messages alone rattling his brain. He thought that perhaps the hiatus in London had interfered with the Minister's operation, whatever it was, as James seemed to be all right, but Luc's breath quickened as he thought of the piece of paper he had just seen, with the term 'Eliminated' occasionally plastered. No -he would phone James NOW.

So he dialled James and James answered; but as though no urgency or cloud of death hung over him at all.

"How's things? All ok?" asked Luc

"Yeah, absolutely, how about you? You sound much better."

"Yeah I am, I *really* need to see you, James …" Luc left a good pause, hoping that James would, perhaps could, understand at least the urgency without him saying it.

"Oh, sure, but we're both stuck …"

"I know …" Luc left another huge pause. "Will you *look after each other* until then?"

"… Absolutely …"

(Luc could feel at least that James had grasped that Luc was speaking differently.)

After the call ended like this, Luc shut his eyes momentarily, the frustration was maddening, but James sounded well, and under no threat; James' voice always soothed Luc nowadays. Then he looked at Mer, who looked serenely unaware.

"All of the traffic lights are off, (let alone the CCTV, he thought), they've only left the street lamps running at night, maybe to help carry out whatever cleaning they're doing ..."

"Yes, it's like it's all ours ..." she said.

"Come on, now I'm going to treat you to something nice."

He owed her that much, and knew he would otherwise go insane with worry about James, and Mischa and even Jelly!! Who were on that list, it was sinking in at last, and he had a wild impulse to break the barricades and drive to Berkshire there and then, but then, Luc knew that his presence alone would certainly not protect James, no, he needed a way to safely communicate with James; he needed a plan. He tried to temporarily shake off the worry as he took Mer on a drive, and they pulled up through the Mall slowly, it's wine red tarmac made them feel small and yet important at once, and there it was, Buckingham Palace, it's flags fluttering, signalling many things, although Mer said that she could not remember which standard or flag positioning meant that the Queen was at home or not; perhaps she too like them had stayed. They drove then slowly, both hearts a quiver, realising the potential gravity of where they were, dimly expecting police cars to swarm around them. But it was over soon, only the pigeons had watched them as they pulled up to the palace gates and lingered observing, they did not get out of the car; both wanted to soon be away from there.

They went back over the Mall to Trafalgar Square and to Luc and Mer's surprise, the fountains were still functioning, considering that the traffic lights were all switched off this seemed very strange indeed, perhaps a ridiculous oversight. Luc parked and they got out of the car. He took her to the giant lion statues that girded Nelson's base, and then, began to try and climb one. "Come on, Mer, let's just not think about anything!" he said, wanting to forget himself; now wishing he had never come to London.

Mer, easily joined Luc in his feeling of bizarre abandon, and as she climbed, in order to mount the lion she had had to hitch up her summer dress and almost ripped it in doing so. She then bruised her inner thigh by having to sit upon the lion's back too abruptly, but did not mention it to Luc. She sat right behind him, unable to move for her own dress had forced her into a fixed position; she had had to put her arms around his waist for support and was jammed close to the warmth from his torso under his clothes. There, she was also trapped with his scent; she remembered immediately that it was this same scent that had caused her to stare at the ceiling as she'd laid in his bed, after having held him during his shakes, her mouth open and herself, unable to move. The sunshine above came down upon them and her face was at the back of his neck, there was nothing to do for her but to inhale, as she still could not move. When Luc eventually clambered off the lion she said to him while still astride it, "Luc, I can't move. You'll have to help me, it's my dress ..."

He immediately obliged and came to try and help to pull her off, after some delicate attempts, he ventured a more brutish approach, which resulted briefly in her dress rising far too high; but he did not react to this, being too much of a gentleman to do so.

Strangely Mer was not embarrassed either for they had shared so much, even a bed in some sense as well, so she let him hold her hand as she limped a little to the car, one inner thigh had that dull ache that she knew tomorrow or the day after would become a blooming bruise, but she did not care about that. He sat her down inside the car until she said, "I'm all right, but I wish there was a café we could go to." But they drove home of course, and she glanced at him to see his pallor, which seemed infused with a new kind of vigour.

Mer set about to the kitchen and asked him how he was feeling, he knew what she meant and said that he did not feel tired or feverish, that he was well, though none were completely sure.

She decided to make them lunch, but it was soon obvious that she had no idea what she was doing, this had the desired effect and he took over her attempts to slice an onion, he asked what she was intending to create, she had no idea in truth, so smiled instead in response.

He made her a simple cheese omelette, and seemed to concentrate quite hard.

"I'm glad that refrigerated eggs can last two weeks but on inspection … the rest of the provisions … But you've got a lot of frozen food which's survived the occasional thaw and refrosting from the blackouts ..." he said.

They ate heartily, greedily, like hungry children, this was a very late lunch and neither had done so much or wandered so far in a long time. As though ignoring their troubles they sat back on their chairs, sated, then they decided to go upstairs; none wanted to tidy up.

In Luc's bedroom he went to lie down on his side of the bed and Mer sat down in her chair noticing that he looked a little paler now, then he sat up again and looked too full of energy and on edge. He put the television on and they saw that they were showing a documentary about how and what had been cleaned in London: displaying the roads and the tubes lines and sewage areas and all other places where filth could accumulate, they presented the workers performing the tasks and then the two of them both considered how they had seen nothing and no one on that day. Finally Luc said, "It must have all happened in the first week, while I was bedridden."

"Yes, it's true that's when we had the helicopters and they were angrier about trespassers." Seated upon her deep green velvet chair, Mer looked down at her aching thigh and then said, "I'm going to go and change."

In her bathroom, she took off all her clothes to survey the damage, something deep, dark and red flowered about her inner thigh and she knew that it was of the sort of slow growing mark that would reach dark purple; she did not bruise very easily but when the injury was robust enough the results were distinct. She had already had a shower that day, so she washed her face to refresh herself; Luc was so used to seeing her without make up that she did not wear it at home anymore, although she felt that she looked ill without it. She came out of her bathroom naked, looking apprehensively at the bedroom door which was open, she decided upon black soft muslin trousers which billowed gently in a Turkish style and came in at the ankle, like a dark genie. She wore atop of it that same green t-shirt that Luc had been used to seeing her in and in her state of fatigue and an aching thigh she wanted to be comfortable above all else.

She came back to Luc's room to see that he had switched off the television and instead had sat in her velvet chair and was looking morose; the afternoon had a stretched light that was pulled about the room, not as stark bright or potent as it had been in the morning, on seeing her, he calmly said, "You look lovely."

"Thank you." She was caught off guard by this and thought to herself that she had not dressed for him. So she gazed at him, she had grown used to him she realised, and felt warmth in her heart for the sense of trust and safety that she felt, and she smiled at him with these thoughts -but it had been a mistake. Something in his face changed; his hazel eyes held her face and locked on with an expression that she had seen before -not upon Luc and not upon her husband's face either, but in films; she recognised that look, and began to step backwards ever so slightly.

"Where are you going?" he asked her, and so; she was immediately no longer able to step away.

He stood up and she looked to her side and at the floor, fiercely probing her mind, searching for a retort, but what she did then utter made it worse, and she realised her mistake even as the words were spoken; as if a genesis in sound, as her own voice unwittingly gave birth to the moments that followed.

"I hurt myself …" she said, hoping that that would take them somewhere else.

"What happened, where did you get hurt?"

He was of course genuinely concerned, but now she faced her problem.

"On my thigh … the lion."

"Where? ... Let me see!"

It was just inevitable that he should ask her that last.

"No, it's all right," she said more faintly than she intended, where was her voice?

"Show me."

So, reluctantly, she lifted her leg and placed it knee bent upon the end of the bed, undid the string that pulled the gathers of the trouser in at the right ankle and lifted her trouser, up higher and higher to reveal her inner thigh; her bruise was truly magnificent, it blossomed wine red, pink, maroon and the faintest blush of purple was coming on as she knew that it would, it spread across and about her leg like a giant tattoo, a salute to their day.

He reached out a hand gingerly to touch her embellishment. "This is horrible," he whispered.

"It's all right, it'll be all right," she answered, trying herself not to whisper.

But he did not take away his hand at her words, if she were herself she would have been changing the subject and leaving the room graciously, as she had always done while he was ill, but she did not move and spent the moment perplexed as to why not. He had spread his fingers as if to grace the length and breadth of the wound, tracing its parameters, she wanted to shiver, but was still immobile. She wanted to pull away, yet she watched his face instead; that look that fixed upon her injury.

She was as unyielding as a statue, so he took his other hand and placed it gently behind her head, waking her a touch, and so she took her leg down from the bed to stand in front of him, wanting to shake, certainly from internal struggle more than anything else. He moved closer to her, too close, undaunted by her stillness at last, but then, only put his cheek upon her own and did nothing else whilst keeping his hand in her hair. He let the moments pass, she did not move and so he did a simple thing: he kissed the side of her cheek; he must have been able to hear her heart hammering like his, but for different reasons she thought. He kissed her cheek gently again, now a little closer to her mouth and there was nothing she could do for herself, so she turned her face to face his and pressed her creased brow upon his temple, then her arms rose majestically as she placed her own hands behind his head and let her fingers meld into his soft hair, she finally then pressed her unsure mouth onto his cheek. It was not a kiss but it was enough, so he took her head in both of his hands and without any hesitation, planted a small kiss upon her lips, that was all, and waited, until finally she kissed him back with enough force to break open any seal; she had lost this battle.

They didn't speak very much throughout the affair, and now undressed and unravelled, she mused on the part that she'd wanted most; his weight and limbs all about her and to be so close to his scent laced with nectarines; surrounded at last by this, she had no desire to speak at all. But, this was not how she had wanted it to be with Luc, not that she had ever let her mind wander so far, she couldn't stop herself now and she knew that she could be destroying every chance with him -after he found out as he would, that she was a liar.

She slept or dozed, hiding herself from her own conscience, she'd lost track of time, but it was dusk which could mean nine or ten o' clock in the summer here. Luc was fast asleep, still not perhaps at full strength she was sure. She smiled once at the sight of him and then tried to slip away from under the sheets without waking him. She carefully put her clothes back on, finding them at the foot of the bed and then descended downstairs to make them both some supper. She had the idea of making them Club Sandwiches, such that she had feasted upon during childhood summer holidays in a private country club in Bombay; an easy memory of air conditioned pavilions surrounded by palm trees and Indian heat. She soon realised yet, facing the diminishing contents of the fridge that cold meats and fresh things were as such gone, it was Saturday and they needed to survive for over a week, until everyone would come back. She did have many things frozen, but most fruit and vegetables were finished, they had only cheese, butter, eggs; but she did have tins of tuna, she vacillated over what to do, she knew her culinary limits but she did not want to be defeated, not tonight, so she made him as lavish a tuna sandwich as she could muster. She added spiky mustard and a pinch of cayenne to the mayonnaise and placed inside, a sliced up pickled cucumber to create a bite as well, to this she adjuncted a side dish of black olives from a jar and finally placed everything upon a wooden tray leftover from the unknown history of the house. She added two short empty glasses that she would fill with red wine from a bottle that she had laid alongside the plate and a smooth, sleek, flat slab of dark chocolate that concealed orange peel pieces within. Finally, looking at her offering she considered that perhaps she wasn't as lacking as she imagined after all and headed upstairs with it, towards him.

He had his eyes half open when she returned and smiled at her sleepily in the half lit room, from the light of the landing where she stood she felt a flutter; for, for the first time ever with him she was nervous. But he sat up, pleased to see her, so she placed the laden tray on the bed and put on the lamp opposite to where he lay, it made the room glow in mellow light; Luc's hair looked completely wild and out of control and it made her giggle, as though guessing this he started to run his hand over it to try to bring it down.

"Dinner?" she asked him.

"Hmmm, what's on offer?" He asked with the faintest hint of genuine concern, which offended her briefly.

"Have a look," she told him.

He nodded taking the challenge, openly observing the fare that was far above her calibre of reheated soup and buttered toast.

Whilst they ate and Mer felt more at ease, as this was what she was used to, dining with him from a tray upon his bed, she was uncertain as to how to approach the very recent memory of what she'd done, she had dammed her mind against any true recollection of it, yet it gave her a sharp thrill every time the recent images refused to be subdued.

She poured out the deep red wine into the little glasses that she had learned to drink from, from him, and she did not hesitate to imbibe; the alcohol immediately sent itself like a hot streak into her blood and she was so glad that it could help her to relinquish her anxious grip of that moment, as though a medicine. While they sipped, they discussed trivialities such as if Luc would be well enough to go back to work by the appropriate Monday, most definitely, was the answer, they did not discuss where he would be living, it was not relevant to the evening, she did not like the mention of that Monday and so drank a little more.

After they were finished, Mer tried to take the tray away but he put his hand upon her fingers that gripped the tray handle, and as though he possessed a current, made her quickly release it. He pulled her deftly towards him; unbothered by the messy refuse as the lights flickered and died to herald another blackout. As he pulled her in, Mer surrendered to her own intoxication, she flowed as though a dam burst as she finally let herself go; and so she became an embodied pulsing thing, able to feel a magnified thrill made permissible by the red wine, that had metamorphosed her into a driven creature bent on damnation, who wanted only him. And so, Mer took leave of herself; she had a churning Neptunian sea within her, an unalterable otherworldly oceanic depth that she wanted them both to be swallowed by; for her to take him in, for him to take of her, there was nothing now to stop her from curling her body around him with eyes divinely closed after so much internal damning and restraint, and she did so without any other desire but to drown with him, or be dashed to the rocks.

It must have been a period later while Luc had fallen asleep again and the power resumed, that she had risen in the dark to acquire some pyjamas. She'd considered sleeping naked, but tonight there was the faintest chill in the air, Luc had not stirred at all as she'd come back in her new attire to climb back in with him. She had chosen something special to wear that had been kept aside for her wedding trousseau; the pyjamas were pure silk and emerald green, with a dragon stretched across her back whose tail arched in a wave, to the base of her spine; but the dragon was a discreet embossed jade upon the emerald, and could only be caught sight of in a certain light. Luc slept on oblivious, completely naked; a heavy presence by her side.

Settled down she began to eventually think about what she had done; she considered if Luc would forgive her, moreover if he would understand. Why hadn't she just told him that she was married? She squirmed, it was never appropriate she thought. These ideas swirled, she considered telling him in the morning, but felt pain in her heart at the thought; he would run, she was sure, and the charm would end. She wanted a solution, to try to make him understand, but could not think of one. Also, perhaps it was not a substantial enough affair to rock the boat, perhaps she should just enjoy what she could of him and it wasn't worth any revelations or dramas. In this final thought Mer realised something horrible, in that she wanted him to be substantial, she wanted him to stay and that moreover she wanted him, *all* of him. Oh God, how had she reached here? She must have been blind she concluded, with eyes wide in the dark room. It was no use, so she put on her lamp and rose to approach the window, the ongoing silence in London, at first such an enchanting idea had now at last grown a tiring presence and weighed upon her to oppress her; she did not know what she wanted in its place, but she finally wanted the silence to end. Luc stirred a little and looked at her through still sleep ridden eyes, soon he rubbed his face in an attempt to wake up and she said nothing, she did not know what to say to him now, she wanted to approach him, to curl up around him and be tranquil in that bed, but could not go near … facing him she gripped the window ledge with her arms behind her -but a voice in her mind said that tonight was not the night for revelations. So she let go of the claws that her hands had become behind her back, and began to walk towards him, when, she heard a noise … At first she was so removed from any other idea than that of being with Luc, that she had no idea what the noise could mean or of where it was coming from, Luc too, had lifted his head to listen, unable to place such a sound. They both waited for the next instalment, as if sure that there would be one.

As they were motionless in a half glow from the lamp, sure enough the sound that had come into that room began again, and was that of simple thumping, probably at the front door, which was strange as there was also a doorbell, soon enough, that too was being pressed and pressed continually and hard, if that were possible. In a flash Luc jumped up to find his underwear and clothes, Mer tried to leave the room to go and answer, but Luc called out, "Don't go down without me!"

So she hovered at the doorframe waiting for him, she was not as alarmed as he was; observing Luc, perhaps she should have been. They did not speak to each other as they shuffled quickly down the flight of stairs, that great black door that muffled the sound of the outside world gave no glimpse as to whom was so frantic behind it. The doorbell was incessant, she tried to undo the latch and open the door, but Luc put his hand over hers, ushering her to move aside, so he himself could face whoever it was first, but she would not move away and so they stood jammed against each other as the door opened heavily in upon itself, revealing to the outside Luc and Mer, so close, as to be almost clutching each other; the sight in front of them however kept them in such a position, for longer than they intended. The night air was still sweet as only summer air could be, but with that kiss of ice in its midst, that had made Mer want to be clothed earlier, in deep green and silk.

It was dark but the street lamp behind the figure cast enough light to let them know who it was, but they both could not believe it, as half the face was covered in blood, which had begun its descent from his temple and flourished around the flaxen hair, making it dirty, dark, sticky and wet; vividly anointing a whole side of his face and casting those blue eyes to peer out of a streaked and bloody façade. What made it even stranger was that his knuckles were white and clutched upon a bicycle by his side. As those two or three seconds passed, the visitor made his own decision as he was faced with frozen hosts and turned to lift up the bicycle and quickly came past them and inside with it, shutting the door behind him. He placed it against a wall. Now Mer was running towards him with one arm outstretched to his head, Luc however still looked on in shock, with his mouth open. It was Mer that spoke first, rapid now, as James' insistent fists had been at her door. But she did not ask the obvious question first; instead she was distracted by his wound. "James, your head! Does it hurt? Did you fall!?"

"James, what happened?!!" asked Luc, very soon after, his own face burning.

James had no idea about the state of his head; he only knew that one side of it felt very hot and sticky, so he stared at Mer confused. Then he made his way to the foot of the stairs and sat down upon it, he tried to put his head in his hands, and as he began to do so, a searing pain flashed across his temple and his head began to throb; which it probably had been doing all along. During this action he let out an involuntary gasp, and could feel Mer and Luc in motion about him.

"Luc, please could you go and find the medical box from the kitchen, and get a bowel of hot water and some soft cloths!" she said.

Together, they washed and dabbed at James' cheek and face, Luc was the one that approached the actual wound on the side of his head, he examined it and mumbled something (to Mer) about how he thought it would be all right, that it had bled a lot, but it was just a gash, be it a nasty one. Mer gave Luc some antiseptic spray, which Luc took to apply without giving any warning, and so James gasped again as it stung. All three of them suspected that James probably needed stiches, but there was nowhere to go for that, so they said nothing. Mer provided instead some surgical tape and they could see that she was attempting to apply small strips across the wound to hold it together, like material staples. James did not say a word throughout this. Mer took a final wet cloth to wash James' hands that he'd given to her without reservation, she wiped off the blood and the dirt and they shook a little while suspended in the air, waiting for her delft glances.

Finally, after James had been washed and bandaged while sitting on the stairs, with a pile of blood-stained cloths by a bowl of red tainted water, he was able to gauge more of his circumstances, and Mer gave him some painkillers to swallow while Luc had asked him now four times: "James, what happened!?"

And it was during this onslaught of kindness that rained down upon him at the foot of those majestic stairs, when James recovered himself somewhat (he took comfort from Luc's conviction that his head wound was not too grave) - then felt truly grateful to them both. His head ached in a rhythmic way echoing his own pulse, as it had now been stabilised by their ministrations. And so, it was in this place, in her home, that James made a decision that perhaps in hindsight he realised he need not have; he could in the end have lied, but it would not have done at that moment to lie and betray the very people who had openly witnessed and washed away his spilt blood, he could not do it. So he looked at Luc directly.

Luc looked back at him also squarely, and then asked him again, "James, what happened?!"

"I think I need to sit down properly."

Both of the others immediately took each one of James' arms to help him to stand, and then the three of them walked slowly over to the living room.

They placed him upon a plum coloured sofa and propped cushions around him, then went to find seats themselves on other soft chairs on either side of him; they could not now sit together, so close. Mer had lit a tall brass and green domed lamp, but not the main lights, so the room was softly lit as they waited for James to speak, as if waiting to be told a story.

James imagined that the painkillers had started to take some affect, not that they could stifle the enormous roar of pain that was now just a heavy constant thud in his head, but enough to make it more bearable. The room drifted ever so slightly as the medicine reacted in his blood and James blinked to focus again; his perceptions softened by his recent trauma and the chemical attempts to numb the pain.

"I was attacked …" he began and saw shock on Mer's face, but only grim expectation on Luc's.

"I was attacked," he continued, "but that's not the whole story or even the beginning of the story …" Alarm grew inside James's heart, he was breaking every rule, stop, go back, he told himself, but it was too late, as if his tongue had taken its own wayward decision and he could not curtail it. What was he doing? He was insane, he chided himself, but he had to tell them, they had to know, because at that moment, James feared for his life, and as he had now burdened these two by running to them, they should not only deserve to know the truth, but also, if James were to die, be vital in spreading the word -so that the chaos could at least be contained and others could run or escape. Hindsight was of no use in the moment, an unhelpful hindrance to the immense in that case palpable, power of the present. So James went on; more afraid now of what he was doing but, as he was sure he faced his death, it had to be done. "Luc, you have to forgive me …"

Luc said nothing, his face very still.

"You *must* forgive me; everything I've done is to protect you …"

But Mer interrupted, "What are you talking about, James? What's happened?!"

At this, Luc held up a hand to gently silence her, showing clearly that both men were fixed upon each other.

"A long time ago …" James said almost to himself, "this started a long time ago. My father, his father, after World War II began something. In short, I, we, are the descendants of that ... this thing that we do. You have to understand that after the War there was a great need to make things better, make a better world, what happened was that someone, my grandfather, wanted an alternative to all the lies we are told all the time by those in power, so he and a few friends established a way to accomplish this, they chose to covertly find means to reveal the truth about many things: like shady business deals masked as 'public policy', or assassination attempts, or new infrastructure forced upon the public because a deal had been struck with the manufacturers, rather than there being any real need for it, even faulty vaccinations being passed through … it was all as some sort of counterbalance to help the people.

"All those friends had families and children, and somehow organically, the secret survived and those children took up the same mantle, my father gave this body of people form and direction, a code even of who to tell, or rather not to tell, as to betray our secret would be to bring everyone down with them. And lastly, there was also the ability to opt out, not to practise as it were, so no one felt doomed or pressured. I, simply am now the leader of this group, with my father and grandfather gone. We don't have a name or anything like that and all would be fine, whether you agree with what we do or not -and trust me, when you see the hideous truths that we do reveal, that keeps those in power somewhat accountable, you would be on our side. But … something terrible's happened, one of us, one of us has betrayed us, and now we, I, am in trouble. I was still here at home, and some people attacked me, and I ran. I don't know who they were. I came here tonight hoping to just rest here and not to trouble either of you …"

But Luc asked a very different question, "Who knows about this, apart from us now of course, who's part of this?"

James didn't like this question, so he went on, with some dread. "Luc, we were *not* allowed to tell anyone, please understand that it would be a life sentence…" he stressed.

"*Who* knows, James?" Luc was quiet and like ice, and Mer's face was upon his with a look of surprise.

James hung his head and sighed, "Anjelica of course," he said, looking up at Luc to see him absorb it as a blow that he was expecting, but then Luc looked ominously expectant, still looking at James.

"And, Mischa," added James.

Luc nodded, now an ugly and grim expression on his face.

"I know, I know," James put his hand out and made a gesture to try to placate, "Luc, please hear me out." His head swayed with the effort.

So Luc sat and waited, hurt visible in his eyes. Mer instead looked incredulous.

"Mischa is an anomaly," said James, "he walked in on us discussing it, me and dad, and we had to induct him, or create a massive security risk-"

"You didn't trust me," Luc then stated plainly, visibly upset and now looked at the floor.

James then tried in vain to make him understand and finally, as when a kettle reaches its boil Luc spoke again.

"All these years, all these years you kept this from me, and don't say you had to because Mischa Knows!" Luc then stood up to go on "... You carried my mother's coffin for Christ sakes, you both did! Even Jelly knows! And now you're in trouble and I don't mean the type you think that you're in, but it may be the same thing, I don't know. But I did some digging at the office and found your address on a list. I didn't know what it meant and was going to tell you, but then the evacuation happened so I wanted to tell you in person and not on the telephone. I was going to tell you, I was loyal to *you*. Not, to her Majesty's government first!"

James looked at Luc calmly, Mer did not, as she didn't know Luc so well as to realise that the worst of it, verbally at least, was over.

"I know you're disgusted with me. I expected you to be if you ever found out. But I need your help," replied James, plainly.

Luc turned his back upon him and faced the curtains.

"Do you know what the list means, do you have it?"

Luc sighed and then turned around, "I have a photo of it on my phone. But there's more, a lot more, there is another list ... it's a long story."

James raised his eyebrows and then frowned quickly, as it ached.

"Yes, well maybe you're not the only spy around or whatever you are," added Luc.

James thought Luc wanted to laugh at his own joke, but he'd said these words angrily, petulantly.

Finally, Luc spoke, quietly practical again, "Do you think they know about this place, were you followed here?"

"I don't think so; they never counted on the bike, or the fact that the whole of central London, every street and house has become a hiding place."

Luc nodded, thinking, and then said, "Perhaps you'd better ask Mer if you can stay here, it's her house after all ..."

And so the bandaged man turned to her, "Of course … Mer, I know this is a terrible thing to ask, but please can I stay here, until … until I can manage a safe way out?"

Although she did not show it, Mer was in a high state of surprise ever since she had heard the banging at the door, and James had now asked her in his most plush and polished manner for refuge; visually, he still looked beautiful to her, be it a little broken. Yet no, she thought, no! But was she going to throw him out to face, well according to him, his death (?!) Could she do that? The waves of thought moved quickly, and were touched by the fact that James had a dark allure, that yet, also made her nervous.

As she replied, her rapid heart fought with her conscience. "You can stay here, James." She nodded to him, but the underlying emotion she felt as she spoke however, took against her, as though moved by the deep internal sliding of a tectonic shelf, for, what had she done?! But she dared not reprove herself.

After a pause, where Luc sat in a visibly mixed state of shock, anger and hurt, James on the other hand seemed calmer and relatively relieved. So Mer went off thus to prepare a room for James, she'd decided as she took her leave of the friends to keep James on the same floor as them, even though it would be more private for them to have him on the floor above. Yet any distance made her nervous, she knew that they were all on new ground now, and she felt suddenly dizzy at the foot of the grand staircase where James had sat caked in blood, as if she took on a residual echo, a vibration from what had been his fate, she held on to the bannister to steady herself; perhaps the ark of truth was finally docking within her and it was so, that this harbour could only be turbulent.

On the way up the stairs Mer then became very conscious of her attire, of her loose bosom underneath the vibrant, dark green silk not covered up by a dressing gown, she wondered if James thought that perhaps she always dressed like this at night, and not perhaps that she had dressed like this, for her lover.

Up on the landing, she decided to put James at the end of the corridor furthest away from them, it would be embarrassing enough when he realised what was going on if he hadn't already, which perhaps he would have if not so preoccupied. Mer shook her head to herself, one thing was assured, she was glad that Christine was not there and that the decision had been hers alone. She had no choice, Mer always concluded every time she worried about what she was getting herself into, as she put sheets upon a never before slept in bed; no matter how much she wanted Luc's approval, she would not send James out into the night. She could claim innocence she resolved, she had no real links to James and was just doing a favour for a friend, that friend being Luc; but another voice inside niggled and made it very clear that this was all about Luc and that she was not calling the police or the Army or whoever was in charge now and throwing James to the dogs, precisely, because James was like a brother to Luc. This last was too much an examination of her own character and she did not like what she was seeing, so she resolved to herself that very few people would have ever been put into this quandary and many would have abandoned ship immediately and saved themselves, but the question was: if it were not for her feelings for Luc, what would she have done? And then she felt better, the truth was concrete she thought, Mer took in Christine after she'd broken her own favourite cousin's heart, and she took in Luc knowing that he, they, could be in trouble because of where he worked, yet wasn't this different? She had no bond with James, but, if he led such a committed group indeed, that revealed corruption … then was she not doing the right thing?

She wondered then if she were now in an alternate universe, but she stayed anchored on the spot, knowing in her stomach that she was in the midst of something complex and compelling and that there would be no exit, not at least until she had more facts. And she could still not believe that both Luc and James were so calm about the so called 'dangerous' mess that they were in, and that James' tale had been accepted so wholly; it was as though her own ship reached the shore of this reality far more slowly and so she hovered near the bay, afraid to find land.

When Luc had first looked into James eyes tonight, he'd seen something in the blue, a freezing, as though there had been terror, but now there was something else, something abandoned, beyond, which those eyes could not contain; and so, Luc, despite his suspicions, felt a wave of pity for his friend, whatever it was, a hot perhaps irrational surge of loyalty could not help but purge Luc's blood of doubts about James

Downstairs, after Mer had left them, there was silence between the men. Then Luc spoke, "Are Balthazar and Gemma with your group too? How did they know Beatrice? … Was she a member?"

"Both Gemma and Sir John are in my group. But why… how do you know?" James tried to frown again.

Then Luc tried to explain his knowledge from the beginning, from his first evening when he overheard his mother's name on his boss' lips.

"I'd just forgotten my book at the office you know. It was completely bizarre hearing Balthazar mention mum. I phoned dad later that night, he said that she had known a 'Johnnie' Balthazar. It's too weird. Is that why he hired me, like a favour to you?"

"No. Absolutely not, Luc. No way. In fact I was getting jittery about how close you were getting."

"Well, we wouldn't want that."

"Luc, *please* … Look what happened to me tonight, this is not what I want for you …"

Luc nodded eventually, and then grew annoyed again, "Yeah, but it's OK for Mischa?"

James sighed.

"I could have always helped you, you know that," Luc added.

"I know. I'm sorry."

Strangely, the apology -falling short of many years of deceit, still placated Luc, who grew a little softer; the blood had seeped through James' white bandages, and there blossomed in wine dark blooms of trauma, still yet stemmed.

"I was given an assignment, to be a diplomatic courier."

"That's not in your job description."

"Oh, I know. You don't look happy about it?"

"I had asked Sir John to keep you away from anything or anyway that lead you closer to the hard stuff. Sorry again," James added quickly.

"Well now, from what I overheard that first night, Gemma didn't want me involved and Balthazar did, it must have been for this courier job. I just thought at the time that Gemma really hated me, but she's so nice, it didn't make sense at all."

"No, she was probably taking her orders from me really seriously."

"But, it didn't sound like that; honestly she was really pleading with Balthazar."

James paused for a moment, as though deciding what to say, "I'll find out a lot more when I can speak to both of them."

"Anyway so, here I was confused as to what I'd done to Gemma for her to dislike me, and also wanting to find out how the hell they knew mum. Was … was my mum involved with this, James?"

"Luc, no … no, not at all. She was such a sunny soul … Sir John was at our place a lot, and so was she, leisure and business sometimes overlapped, and they were both at our dinners and picnics and stuff. He must remember her from that, you too I imagine. Yeah … he knew you."

"Oh my God."

"But, it's no big deal, just one of those coincidences."

"OK, so I was finally sent to pick something up. And now it gets really weird. Before I go on, James, is Clara a member?"

What colour left in James' face soon drained, and his gory bandage crowned him more starkly. He tried to speak, but no words came out.

So Luc went on, "I went to this strange place, not a government office at all, a private club in Mayfair, just men you know. But I had to pick up something from Minister Sebold-"

"The Under-Secretary of Defence?"

"Yes. It was no big deal at first, I took the folder and left, but the door to his room or office didn't close properly, and I got stuck in front of a faulty food trolley. That's where I overheard some stuff. It's going to sound crazy, but maybe not … This Minister sounds like a bad type. Do you know about him?"

"I may know some things, but I'm sorry, I still want to protect you from them."

"All right, well, he was talking to someone else, I don't know who, and they were plotting to kidnap, a Clara Elizabeth Day who worked at the United Nations in New York, and … beat the crap out of her if she didn't cooperate."

James mouth opened slightly.

"I didn't know what to do, so on the bus back to work, I looked inside the file-"

"Jesus, Luc!"

"I found all Clara's details in there! Her photo, her work history, old addresses and current, numbers, even medical history! James, I was supposed to deliver that file to Gemma ... and I did."

James face began to colour again.

"But before that, I went and bought a Pay As You Go phone, and sent her a text to escape. I didn't tell her it was me. I didn't know if she was bad or good, but I knew that you were connected to her, ha, I wanted to try and keep you away from it!"

After a pause James said, "She did escape. Thank you, Luc."

"So she *is* with you, but I guess we need to ask, is Gemma?"

James put his hand on his mouth, "I didn't want to say this earlier, but it was Gemma's voice, on the phone, I mean before they broke in, a split second before, my phone rang and it was her, telling me to get out."

"So, she's your mole ...?"

"But, no ... I know who my mole is ... and Gemma helped me escape, it doesn't make sense."

From James' confused yet closed face Luc decided not to ask at that moment, who his mole was.

"... So then I was relieved that she was all right, I kept in touch and kept asking Clara at intervals if all was OK."

"You did what? You kept in touch?"

"Yes, why?"

James shook his head, "She told me she destroyed the phone when I demanded to know the number.

"Well she wants very much to know who I am, to 'protect' me she says now, and she's getting insistent."

Understanding now dawned on James' face. "She thinks you're her saviour and didn't want me hunting you down ... I think it's better for now if you don't tell her it's you. Not until we sort this mess out. Clara was staying with Gemma when she got back to London; I want to contain all information I can, if you know what I mean, I urgently need to alert Mischa about all of this, it's maddening! I don't even know if everyone else is all right! Mischa could at least protect the rest of us! …"

"We'll find a way, James, calm yourself if you can … but, should Clara be staying with Gemma if you suspect her?"

"I know, but if that Minister knows about Clara and me and Mischa, then I think Gemma seems to me the only one he doesn't suspect, it would be hiding under his nose… unless as you say Gemma's turned, but go on …"

"All right … well after that … I was sent back to the Mayfair club for another pick up. Well, the Minister's plans couldn't have gone well because I'd made Clara run, so, they played me a recording of me looking at the diplomatic file on the bus. He then blackmailed me to snoop at the office for anything unusual, and to target Balthazar especially, or else."

"What did you do? James was intrigued and surprised.

"I picked up the new document he gave me, got to the office, and looked at it locked in a cubicle in the Men's loos … James, they had a photo of Simon, Simon Hughes, an old friend of yours. The one who dated Clara and then all that mess happened."

James said nothing.

"James?"

"Oh God. I didn't want to tell you, but you're not going to let it go. It was him, it's him, the leak."

"So he's in your group too!"

James Nodded, and Luc went back to his thread, frowning. "Him? but, but why? … was it money?"

"He was angry, he lost Clara, his child and the Cause he felt, all at once, he wanted to hurt me. He leaked some of our member's names to their employers. Those people, our people whose names he leaked, they all died."

It was Luc's turn to fall to silence.

"They're after us Luc, I'm so sorry you know all this now!" James reproached himself. "But if I hadn't spoken to you, *I* wouldn't know all of this now, and it's bloody valuable. I finally know who it is: that Minister. And maybe, I can't believe it, maybe I have more than one mole ..."

"You mean Gemma? I can't believe that either, but every file went to her ..."

"Please go on, Luc."

"OK, well a few days before the evacuation, the Minister was furious with me for not coming up with anything, so he tried to force me to search Balthazar's desk -I searched Gemma's instead. They were all out that afternoon. That's where I found your name on a list." Luc took out his phone and brought up the picture of it. James scanned his eyes down it.

"Who are these people?" asked Luc.

"All members." James then looked about in frustration again, as if desperate to contact Mischa.

"I desperately tried to talk to you in person after I saw this list; I was worried about your phone being bugged if you were in trouble. But I just couldn't get to you. Then, as you know, I got very ill. Too ill to function. I had to pray that you were all right every day, I messaged you every day. On the day that I got better, today in fact, I went to that Mayfair club and broke into it, and I found this." He brought up the photo of the second list. "And a file with my photo in it and work/education history. So my gut was right, I knew I was in the shit as well."

"Luc ... this is all invaluable. I can't thank you enough. Don't worry ... we'll sort this mess out."

"What about all the names on the first list? Do you think they are OK?"

"It maddening!! I need to call everyone, and I can't, not until I can get some new phones! They might be tracking mine somehow … I switched it off in the alley."

Luc kicked himself for setting James off again, for he looked too pale now.

"Well if you weren't followed then you need to hide. There's no way you can go out again. I was going to suggest my apartment, but if they are sniffing at me, then that's not an option." Then Luc added, "… We've put Mer in so much danger."

At that moment, Mer returned.

"Your room's ready, James, if you want to lie down. Maybe you should, you know …"

Luc agreed with how unwell James looked. "She's right we've talked enough, we can talk more tomorrow," and then added, "there's nowhere else you can go tonight, I'll keep watch."

James bowed to his host's wishes, just as frail as she'd observed and rose to follow her, "Thank you so much, Mer," he said. On their way up the stairs, he asked, "So you've been staying here, Luc?"

"Yes, you know I became really ill the day we were meant to leave, and Mer took care of me."

"Ill, yeah you mentioned, I never realised it was so bad."

"Yes, Mer was a rock, and I stopped her from going to her spa holiday."

As Luc explained to James, both Luc and Mer felt like co-conspirators weaving a lie, although it was all true.

They settled James in his room, explaining to him how to reach the kitchen if needed, he too had an en-suite, in which Mer had placed fresh towels and then they left him there. Heading down the corridor, Mer looked back at his closed door wondering if James would glimpse her and Luc going into the same bedroom.

That room was as they had left it; Mer's side lamp was still on and cast a warm half-light, as if nothing had happened since they had left. Mer felt a distance between her and Luc, he seemed lost, pensive, as if he had taken a rowing boat alone and out to sea. He sat down on his side of the bed and rubbed his face, it had been a very long day. He then looked at her; she was hovering by her chair, regarding its fabric.

"Come here," he said.

It was as simple as that, and she looked so very composed as she went over to his side, but her heart bounded. She sat down, and he put his arm around her, bringing her in close and closing his eyes, and she was so pleased, so pleased to inhale him again, that sweet laced scent. He kissed her on her cheek and face, and then told her to sleep, then he dragged her green velvet chair to the window and sat down to face the street, keeping watch, she realised.

It took some time to be able to let go, and she anxiously glanced often from the bed at Luc, looking for any sign of alarm on his face. She even got up after a while and went to check on James, who sat up startled as she entered, and then she reassured him, that it was only her, and that Luc had seen and heard nothing. She saw that James was grateful for the reassurance.

Back in their bed, the passing silence marked by uneventuality, a few hours passed and at first Mer slept an exhausted dead sleep. As the slumber restored her, the sheer depth of the trauma, of what had happened that night began to seep in, so that she grew unsettled in her dreams and she awoke heart thudding in the black room, she thought she heard something and then she thought she saw a shadow by the window, her heart became wild so she forced herself to be fully awake, adrenalin pumped life into her and she lifted her head to see, then sat up and stared into the room as if daring on the darkness. There was nothing there, not even Luc by the window. She looked around wildly, and there he was, in bed by her side, the birds were singing even in the darkness for an oncoming dawn. She took a deep breath, waited, and then settled back down to look over at her lover, eventually there was more light in the room than she'd thought and she could see his face even in the blackness. She took her hand and swept it over his brow to move his hair off his face, in that instant, he started awake, as edgy as she was, and he took a moment to steady himself. He too stared at her in the dark, she did not take her hand away and stroked his temple, where James' wound would have been, as if trying to give it remedy. Slowly Luc grew more awake and came closer to her, he buried his face at her shoulder and rubbed his head there, as he came so very close, Mer realised for all the fear that had crept up on her, that it was nothing compared to what Luc was feeling, she could see that he knew far more than her, perhaps the length and the breadth of it and the burden was apparent; he had a serious glint in his eyes that she had never seen before.

Chapter 50

It was three hours after dawn that she woke again, Luc slept on mute; wiped out. It was an indistinct morning not yielding any clue to whether it was to be warm and sunny or not; they had all grown used to this summer, a tepid cloudy season would now be unfamiliar. The chill that had hinted itself in the night had multiplied in strength and sharply touched her face, so she pulled the covers closer in to herself, then she listened, remembering the foggy events that had taken place in her sitting room so recently, but there was nothing but her own breathing, rustling gently over the sheets that she had pulled up over her chin, Luc could not be heard.

Soon afterwards, she returned to her own bedroom and had a shower, she had not had nearly enough sleep, but it was a comfort to hear the familiar sound of hot rushing water and also to see the room lighten further as she progressed. Wet haired, she wandered to her wardrobe in an old deep blue bathrobe made of denser stuff than silk and pulled out a pair of black jeans and a soft blue t-shirt; she was aware of how she dressed now, having James in the house.

Feeling cleansed by the hot water, she went down to the kitchen to inspect the situation, it was remarkable how utterly quiet her house was at the best of times -it too had weight, gravity and now it swallowed each footstep to silence her as well. She noticed as she crept that no one had broken the seal of the house as the men had feared, no uninvited guest had bothered them yet. There was also no traffic outside now it was true, but the noise had never intruded; after her dense black front door had swung slowly shut, the world outside could not be heard and from her windows one could only see the tops of trees or the mass of green of Regents Park, and from the back, the undulating floral garden. She had glanced at James' door on her way down, his white door also blankly shut.

It was Sunday, they had to last another week, if that is, there were to be three of them staying there 'till then, even so Mer considered that it would be unlikely that all the supermarkets would suddenly open at 8am sharp on that Monday morning. All the workers and managers, they had to return to London first and then restock supplies, perhaps someone had thought of all this she hoped, someone who'd planned this very strange imposition onto London town. Her mind turned to Luc, asleep upstairs in another one of her barely furnished guest rooms, hair probably wild and messy, she mused intensely fond, which of course, led to an unsettled feeling. She took to putting away the washed dishes instead and then felt an exhilaration; whatever dark tunnel lay ahead of her, she could not escape what she felt for Luc, it was the kind of emotive passion that would stain her everyday actions and thoughts, as though marked with a red ink, touching the mundane with its intensity, like an anointment, or Hindu bridal vermillion. And as for James, whatever he was, it was still hard to view him as a criminal, or something worse ... If he were in a story book perhaps he would be an outcast hero she thought, it was true that she did not want rid of him, she was not outraged by him as she perhaps should be (and she did think herself perverse for this) but this blonde beaten man upstairs in her home, he was like the continued and piercing presence of a lightning strike, full of prospect.

It was at that moment that Mer turned around, and in the dim corridor that led into the kitchen stood the man last in her thoughts. James wore some blue pyjamas that Luc had lent him (Luc of course had never worn pyjamas since she had known him). James' blue eyes looked stark against a face that had lost much blood and his head wound although bandaged, gave the impression of an angry stamp of gore upon him, surely making his mind throb. For a moment Mer was startled, for she hadn't recognised him for an instant; his blonde hair streaked itself over his clean temple side and caught enough of the dim light to occasionally flash against the now alive blue eyes, pale face and turbulent bandages. It was him though, as Luc was to Mer like a boy who lived on a beach, an easy and giving spirit, James was to her …? Thus she tried to define James for herself as well…

First, it was a man that she saw in James and not a boy, from a city and not the country that was true, but yes, she had it, he was a gentleman from the past, but in modern day clothing. Deep blue jeans and a distressed leather jacket was how she had often seen him, but his air to her was of someone from the past who was preoccupied with seriousness; like a time traveller from the Wars, now confronted with a modern apathetic world, classless and dreamless, with worn and tattered aspirations and nowhere to go. Yet, James had still enough fight in him to fight the good fight, as if we were still in World War II and the dream of a better world was a real and tangible thing that lit up peoples' hearts. Mer believed that that quest had been alive in every British soul at that time; in order to survive for one thing, to live to see a better day and to fight for something, to fight for those they loved and to struggle for their freedom and to even see hope in a meagre ration of food or scant coal fire. Mer had only felt a glimmer of this in old war movies, and yet, here stood before her a man from this past, disguised in modern attire and mannerisms but alive with the quest; wounded by it currently, but here to behold.

James had stood still to face Mer as she contemplated him and as if he'd known, given her enough time to understand the sight of him and all that it meant to her; and for this she was grateful.

"Good Morning, James." Mer was not of course sure of what else to say.

"Sorry if I startled you. Just wanted to get some water, all seems OK …" he said looking about the house, and she knew what he meant.

"Luc kept watch for a good while, don't worry." Mer then smiled at him and took the small glass jug that he held in his hand, to refill it, his hand was freezing cold, she considered asking him how his head was but thought against it, it was obviously bad, it looked it. Instead she asked, "Would you like something hot to drink, some tea or coffee or herbal tea?" The varieties of which Christine had greatly expanded upon she thought, and she did not know what else to do but be polite, it felt too frightening and also a little absurd to ask if they were in grave danger, the house gave her no sign of breach.

"Oh, just some tea if you have it?" answered James.

It seemed that he was grateful for this offer and sat down at the wooden table as Mer asked him to. Mer prepared the tea looking perhaps more confident at the procedure than she was. It was simple enough, but as with all procedures in the kitchen that involved food, she shrank back as an alien imposter, she had no relationship with food or ingredients and they knew it immediately, shrinking from her touch, nervous to be handled by such a fraud, knowing that she had no understanding of their possibilities. She stirred James' tea looking down at the beige swirl, hoping she had put in the milk substitute correctly, or the right amount of it or not taken the tea bag out too soon, she considered apologising in advance to him about the state of the beverage, but felt of course that he had more important things on his mind. Before Mer had met Luc, and let him into her house she had not drunk traditional English tea with milk, she had had instead loose leaf jasmine green tea, for which the procedure involved taking a pinch of the crumbling, brittle, deep green leaves and casting them speedily to the base of a cup, upon which she then poured boiling water; thus the instant alchemy was out of her hands, the creation manifested itself and she liked how it made her feel, washed clean inside and uncomplicated.

They sat down to face each other and Mer politely smiled at James, he smiled back as a thank you although wincing soon after. It was hard to make small talk as of course, there was so much to discuss. So surprising herself Mer began directly yet pleasantly, "So, your grandfather started this group that you lead after the War. What did he do before that?"

James looked up at her from his mug of tea, looking startled as such matters were never discussed over breakfast, but Mer sat benignly, waiting for an answer.

"Well, it's not something I'm supposed to discuss, but I suppose it's a bit late for that … he wanted to go and fight in the War of course … but he was an advisor in the government and so instead worked quite high up, in the War Office."

Mer nodded, she went on, "Do you think it was then, because of that that he created or wanted to create …?"

"Yes, yes I do, he saw all the back room deals, the lies, but I think it was from his work before that, as during the War he told me that he felt they had been at least fighting for some sort of righteousness; they were just as corrupt, but at least had the backdrop of a seemingly just war. I think in those days the level of lies and cover ups was nothing, nothing as it is compared to now, yet still after the War ended and my grandfather went back to his old post, he saw everything return to how it had been and like many who had been through that war and the Blitz and the uncertainty, he didn't want to go back to the world as it had been, they wanted something better. So he spoke to his best friend who had been a journalist who then went on to own a paper, and told him that he would leak some scandals or some information about corruption, just to tip the scales he felt, and it started from there. His friend and him brought in a few others, lawyers, doctors, but all more importantly were first close friends, it would have been very dangerous to let just anyone know what they were doing, so it had to start with a small group of friends, most of these men had seen active service and witnessed the carnage and loss and destruction, they were ready to carry on the fight as it were …"

"It seems fantastical," Mer said to him wistfully.

"And yet, you believe me." He looked at her unflinching.

"I realise … that I do."

James nodded once, and looked grateful.

"So, you're not really a genealogist?"

"That's the thing, I am, no really, I really do it, enjoy it too."

Mer then felt it might be an opportunity to change the tone, to relieve her own stress if nothing else. "I'd love to know about myself, but I don't know if you can find out about people with an Indian heritage ... don't know if the same type of records are kept or any at that rate?"

"Well," James laughed, "it is surprising how much you can find out if you try, the thing about the British in India for whatever it was, they still kept notes and records as they do here, and so there are probably records kept from certain eras, and if there were any links to the British Army in India, then much can be found out ..." James explained, not adding that he knew indeed, all about her past.

"And so, Mischa is your lieutenant?" She asked James another direct question as though discussing the everyday, pleased that she had lifted some of his gravity but she had not noticed the figure approaching them from the corridor, it was still dull and dark although far beyond dawn, but light could seldom make its way into that passage placed as it was. As the figure grew near, the slow daylight that grew in whiteness at the window gave the figure, Luc, a halo about his face as he stood at the doorframe, hair streaked with light, taking in the scene before him.

"Good morning," he greeted them, although more stiffly than his character, everyone could tell that he hadn't forgiven James, not nearly.

Luc went about to make himself some tea but Mer rose from her chair, "I'll make you some tea?" she offered him, unusually he let her and sat down at the table in the chair next to Mer's, also facing James.

As Mer handed Luc a steaming cup she said, "I was going to suggest breakfast ..."

"I'll have a few sips and then I'll make us some," he replied, unable to contain a little dark mirth, as she was worried that she would have to produce edible food for her guests. She smiled a gracious thanks at him, trying to act as though no such underhand request had been made.

Luc sipped his tea eyeing James' wound. Silence slipped by.

"It's all right, I think it's healing," James said to Luc, Mer sat still, unsure as to when the exchange had begun.

"You think?" said Luc flatly, and then added, "I kept watch, nothing, I think you're OK here."

James nodded; Luc took another gulp of tea and then scraped his chair back, the noise rattling Mer, he set about to open the fridge and took out some eggs and then some bread from the freezer. She looked back at James who was looking down into his empty mug, sadly she thought, although it was not obvious. She wanted to ask him more questions, so she continued even though Luc had changed the tone.

"What will you do now?"

Both men turned to look at her, Luc straining away from his frying pan, James glancing up from his doleful cup of tea, there was such a sulk in the air she thought, it had been more pleasant before Luc had come downstairs.

Luc was looking directly at James now and James understanding said, "Mer, I can't impose for too long, this is, could be, dangerous …"

"Where will you go?"

Nobody answered her.

"There isn't anywhere, is there …?" she said.

In the silence that still followed, Mer's voice took over, "You can stay here, for as long as you need." A flush followed her pronouncement, but her decision was made. Mer went on, despite Luc's glare and admonishing vibes towards both of them. "I know you think it's dangerous, but because of the evacuation, it will be like looking for a needle in a haystack, and yes they may know, God forbid, that you and Luc are close, so they might look next door, but they don't know about me, not yet anyway, so it's the perfect place to hide, this cavernous house. We don't even have CCTV or security on the outside, there is no trail yet that leads to me... I believe they requisitioned this house during the War you know, so it played it's part then as well."

James also knew this last.

"But, Mer, it could be a while," James said concerned.

"There is plenty of room; you're not in the way ..."

This time Luc interjected, "There is also plenty of danger!" he said far too angry, an anger borrowed from last night, even though the men had resolved things a touch.

So she turned to Luc for the first time and spoke, "I'll have to live with myself if I throw him out. He should stay here." Mer as a new blade of steel, quivered after her delivery.

James then said, "Thank you, Mer, that is beyond gracious."

Luc glared at both of them and went back to his frying pan.

But Mer went on, "The only connection they have with me is Luc, and I have never contacted him through any phone or electronic or traceable device or been seen with him, only walked with him in the park."

"This is ridiculous, and there is a problem," said Luc, over the eggs.

Her cheeks grew red now.

Luc had not turned back to face them, he was emanating heat however, never mind the pan, he went on, "We need to keep James safe, so come Monday morning when I have to go to work, I can't be coming and going at Mer's anymore, as him and I are connected. In these seven days before Monday, I, too will be hiding here in a sense, until it becomes busy and I can creep back to my house, but if they're watching, we've had it, and if I get away with it, I can't come back here again as long as James is here. So on next Sunday night, when it is very dark, that will be the night that I will climb over the fence to my own garden and return to my home that way."

Mer grew alarmed; suddenly her own plan was turning against her.

James was shaking his head, and Mer had now a still, displaced look that hid that she was aghast, she had just told James he could stay for as long as he needed and she saw that that could be a long time … without Luc.

This time James spoke, "What makes you think you'll be safe at your flat? Remember what you told me you saw in the Minister's room today."

"That's my risk to take. I can't be where you are, and especially coming and going when you're staying with Mer. I'm sure you can have protection outside by Monday anyway?"

"Look," said James. "That's one night with no protection. We need to think about this. On Monday, in a week when one of you can get me a couple of mobile phones I'll be able to find out what's going on, and go from there, so hopefully I *won't* be here for long at all, I'm so sorry to do this to you both."

It was obvious of course that something had happened here between them, Mer and Luc, something more than a fling for whatever it was, it was palpable. James ran his hand gently through his hair with long tapered fingers that Mer noticed, and she felt at that moment that however much she did not want to be parted from Luc, that James' problems were far greater. And so, moved by a pure wave of pity, like a fresh benevolent tide, she let go of Luc and conceded instead to help this tall, dark blonde haired man in her kitchen; it was true that had he not been so picturesque, with blue eyes that gazed from a cast of the bludgeon as the wound bulged and asymmetrically framed his face, his situation may have taken a little longer to process; yes James was beautiful, but it was not his fault that it affected his case.

Luc looked very unhappy; he placed his culinary creation on a large plate for them to help themselves from and turned to put it on the table. And they sat, the three of them, so much changed, swayed and disturbed by recent events, now faced with breakfast and each other. Luc sat down crossly, more cross than Mer had ever known. But on Luc's cue, as he began to serve Mer on the plates that she had set out, they settled, her heart warmed as he put food in her plate first, she knew, as a mark of respect. Buoyed by this slight softening in Luc's annoyance, Mer resolved that she had to make the best of the days left that they had together, yes, she was determined to embrace these last few days, she did not want to face what that Monday would bring and so shielded her thoughts and emotions away from the subject; she knew, she knew that it may not be pleasant at all. Finally, she was satisfied with her decision as she did the washing up, and James brooded while Luc sulked at the table. Then, she turned to them, "James, is there anything we can do today to help you, or us? Do you think we should still keep watch?"

James sighed. "I think we are safe here, it's tempting to keep watch, maybe we should just be on our guard a little, they would have found us by now, I'm sure …"

"So, you really can't do anything 'till you get new phones to contact your people? No land lines?" said Mer.

"Oh, no way, I don't want to use your phone, Mer."

"But even if you ring them on a new number, your people's phones could be bugged, no?" she said.

"I know, don't worry, I'll have to be discreet, we have ways."

"So, so, there's nothing you can do till then?" Mer asked James again.

"I don't think so …"

"Well, then let's do something else, something random, distracting … um, so, would you like a tour of the house? …"

This caught both the men by surprise by its pure incongruity, Mer did not smile at the idea but looked at them expectantly, and then Luc said to James, "You know, she hasn't even offered to show me the house yet. She must like you."

Now Mer was caught off guard as she realised that the two could gang up on her in an instant, when she had thought they had been so divided. Never mind, she was undeterred by it, instead spurred on by the challenge.

"Well?" Mer asked, after the men finished with whatever spiked humour had just passed between them.

At that James and Luc rose, and James said with a smile that could have been a grimace when it reached his wound, "Lead the way ..." and so, epitomising the grace that she saw in him.

So she took them, room by room, through each floor, rooms that she never went to, that were not even heated in the winter. As she led them she realised that she too was a guest, not realising the splendour of her own house, she was as keen to see the hidden rooms now empty and quiet, with sometimes little in them except Regency flourishes and period features. She felt promise as she led them through rooms that she never visited and Luc too looked fascinated, admiring the history in the décor. James on the other hand knew, but so, said instead, "If this place was appropriated during the War, I can imagine British soldiers in army uniform at wooden desks here ..."

She took them up to the house's highest point; it was an attic, wooden and gloomy with just an old bulb to light the way. They stood there and admired even that, it was dusty and redolent with something old, the spirit of the past, things would have been stored here, boxes heavy with old muster, history embraced them and no daylight could enter there, they were quite silent as they surveyed it; Mer sensed that dull green-clad Army soldiers would have made it up here too, from what James had just told them.

Then she turned to them and said under the light of the gloomy bulb, "I know we can't go into the garden."

"No, I don't think so," said Luc, sending a wanton butterfly into Mer's stomach.

And so, they finally went back to their rooms, Mer still in her campaign for distraction, showed James the room where she kept her books, her art books and her story books and lots of old magazines such as Vogue and told him to feel free, she also offered for him to join them and to watch television in Luc's room or to go downstairs to watch it there.

James eventually chose to join Mer and Luc in their room, it was clear not wanting to be alone downstairs just yet; last night's assault still troubled his senses and made his entire body feel vulnerable, his head throbbed and after he took some painkillers from his bedside that she'd left for him, he made his way down the airy corridor to the lovers' door and knocked. Mer came to the door and led him in, he did not know it, but two new velvet green chairs had come to join the first, so that there were three, clustered near the window and facing the television, so too a little side table, where there sat two of Mer's books: 'The Bloody Chamber' and 'Wuthering Heights'. Luc was sitting quietly in the chair nearest the window, James, not knowing that Luc's usual position had been upon the bed, sat down next to Luc, and finally, Mer sat next to James. She seemed shy, yet enigmatic as if shyness were a glamour or lunar façade, thus a temporary mask; like an unnecessarily borrowed and melancholy beauty that eclipsed her, when he thought she was quite lovely in her own right.

The television was focused on the fact that food trucks would be among the first allowed to enter London, leaving at dawn like sentinels as well as the supermarket staff, so that they could be ready for the great influx. The television was listing strict rules for who would be allowed to enter London and when, they were trying to stagger the London districts, it looked, however, to all three of them, like a recipe for chaos. Luc himself was expected to be at work by lunchtime on that Monday, but there was leeway for those in his office who would run into difficulty, which it seems they were expecting; it was the Tuesday when all was supposed to run as normal again. As they watched, they braced themselves; it was coming whatever it was.

And then James realised- the phone!

He turned to Luc, too fast for his head, and asked, "Luc, do you still have the phone that you sent messages to Clara on? And did you keep it on all the time? Do you still have it?"

Luc opened his mouth as the same realisation dawned upon him as well, "Yes, on all the time, I've still got it."

"So if they knew about it, they haven't tracked you with it or anything, and if they will, well, I still have to act now, I have to!"

Luc got up and hurriedly brought the Clara-phone that had been on Luc's bedside, to James. James took a deep breath and let his fingers close upon it gratefully, then left the room, shutting the door behind him. Luc still stood where he was, staring at the closed door, and stationary after his friend's departure, but rooted more like, and unable to speak or move.

"Who's Clara?" then finally, asked Mer.

Chapter 51

"It's me, and the weather's dreadful!"

"James? You can speak, my phone is fine. I'm sure. I run Michael's gadgets on it all the time," said Mischa. "What's happened?!"

"I'm not fully sure that mine is safe, but it's urgent. Are you and Jelly safe?!"

"Yes, what the hell's happened?!"

And so James explained, he'd done it, be it dangerous for Luc and Mischa for using this phone. He knew from Mischa's quiet tone, and even his silences on the line that hummed with his white heat, that wheels would now be in motion … James' people could be moved from wherever they were staying, and Minister Sebold, had given them a target to focus on indeed.

The call ended, and James had to sit down upon the side of his bed, heart thumping. But now James' predicament was never more apparent, for there was nothing else to be done but to wait these next few days out, he was stranded, but at least safe. In the meantime he surreptitiously looked out of the window occasionally, and saw thankfully nothing: no shifting in the trees, or movement behind parked cars … Mischa contacted him often, letting him know if all were safe and plans or ideas for counter measures. Yet, there were still hours in the day to fill, and his wound often strangled his mind with the pain, and so, liking Mer's attitude and feeling his redundancy and needing distraction, he went to look at her books. Many were upon the History of Art as well as literary novels, he chose a big book on Pre-Raphaelite art, to gaze at the pictures and a copy of 'Brideshead Revisited' even though read more than once; he remembered how the book had begun or ended, focussing upon a great mansion requisitioned by British soldiers during World War II. With these clutched under one arm he made his way back to his room, too timid as yet to try out the living room downstairs, he laid down and first turned the pages of the art book, resting his eyes upon Rossetti's splendorous women, red hair and skin flourished with apricot hued cheeks, and adorned by flowers fit for the Gods; more beautiful than anyone could ever contemplate.

Even though his thoughts skitted here and there, as each member's name flashed into his mind as he worried about their safety, and he rose three times to look out of the window, where a summer's day looked abandoned, he was still finally able to calm himself somewhat by looking at the pictures, and only felt instead the rhythmic thud of pain in his temple. The medication he had been given by Mer then started to take its full effect, and before he knew it he was dozing and he slept, for a very long time.

*

When James woke, Mer was standing over him with her hand upon his upper arm.

"I'm so sorry, James, I had to make sure you were all right, because it's a head wound ... you know ... not in a coma or anything," Mer added, with a smile, though her eyes meant it. "Also, it's lunch time, make your way down when you're ready, if you want ..." And she handed him a glass of water. The book was still splayed open by his side, boasting divine feminine glory.

When James reached Mer and Luc downstairs, lunch was a roast chicken that Luc had defrosted earlier plunging into a sink full of cold water, and chips, also from the freezer, plus a bowl of verdant steaming peas. James took in the aromas gratefully, realising his hunger.

As the couple set the table, James watched Mer and Luc together in the kitchen, they were not like a normal couple, it was more than that; James suspected that Mer could not cook as Luc was in charge, but she helped him where she could, it was the fact that they orbited each other faithfully, whether it be in this quaint kitchen, busy city, or far off country; and James felt uneasy, for this seemed more than just a love affair …

"Are things under control? Others OK?" Luc asked him.

"Things are moving, Mischa and Jelly are OK." James nodded, as Mer and Luc stood still for his answer.

The latter took comfort from James' composure and then continued to try to have an amiable lunch, after which Mer ushered them to the living room for a change and Luc went away for a bath, there with James she said, "You seem a bit more relaxed?"

"It was a relief to speak to Mischa, I can tell you."

Mer nodded. "… You must have enjoyed growing up as neighbours, you and Luc?"

"Yes … Where did you grow up, Mer?"

"Here, very boring. In a big apartment near your own house actually."

"Where are your family? I mean are your parents still-"

"Well, they were visiting New York when the embargo happened and well, they're still there," she shrugged her shoulders.

James looked at her briefly, realising that she didn't want him to go any further, even though she smiled pleasantly, so out of politeness for the owner of his refuge, he did not.

"And you … and Luc …?" he asked instead.

"Well, yes … me and Luc," she said somewhat removed from herself.

It was a direct and personal question, but James refused to hold himself back about it, she seemed veiled somewhat, yet still had answered in an earnest way. He nodded. "You know, his mother died last year …" he added gently.

"Yes, yes it's awful … he doesn't seem to, to break down with it though?"

"I know, it worries me."

"Jelly and I, Anjelica- my sister, are concerned about this, he was an only child and his mother ... was wonderful, we know because we lost our parents a few years ago, so we know ... what it's like ..."

"I can't imagine." And she shook her head.

"And Mischa?" she asked. "What about Mischa, so he is your deputy, really?"

"Yes and a very good friend. He was unfortunate enough to literally stumble into it, after that I never wanted to inflict this life upon Luc, I wish he would understand that, did you know that Luc's grandfather was a spy for the Allies?"

"Yes, but not much detail?"

"Yes, he used to talk about it when we were young-"

"So you think he'd want it, your type of life?"

"Well you've known him for nearly two months, you tell me?" And he looked directly at her, blue eyes and gory bandage.

"Of course he would," she said, more to herself.

She faced him and then said, "I need to change your bandages."

James nodded, grateful for her help and followed her to the kitchen. Both of them were glad to be engrossed in the task. Looking at his dried blood and the debris of his assault, she let out a sigh, wrapping the old bandages in kitchen paper and then without warning sprayed antiseptic onto his gash, sending him smarting and to which he cried out a quick and brief, "Aaach!"

Then she redressed the wound with her slim fingers and he asked her, "Where did you learn this, Mer?"

"Well, I did a First Aid course in an in between summer at university."

"How come?"

"I wanted to be useful, it felt like such an affirmative thing to do, I suppose."

After James had been cleaned up he felt weary and wanted to retire and lie down, as he looked at Mer in her kitchen, he thought of Clara and his heart put up an immediate wall like a quick security curtain; they too had briefly had a cosy kitchen together, ironically during when she had been carrying another man's child. In that same kitchen that had had its windows smashed in over his head, Clara had put long stemmed dried flowers in empty water jugs and sun catchers to hang from the ceilings and refract blinking light when the sky allowed. Clara had made the house that had been left to him as a gift from his parents, their own. Where was she now? Safe, he said to himself as if to reassure himself that that was enough. He let Mer know that he was going to rest, as she seemed to have put herself therapeutically in charge of him and walked back to his new bedroom.

Left in the kitchen alone, Mer took a deep breath that took in the remnants of the antiseptic in the air and she appreciated the peace; living in this house she had noticed that people kept on arriving, she was not allowed to be alone there for long it seemed; and she had not minded being alone, she had very much wanted it, especially after Zafar had left. Mer stared at her garden from her window and took another deep breath; her Luc would soon be gone and she grimaced at the thought. She turned and made her way quickly up the corridor and the stairs to their room where she found him, sat on his side of the bed, watching the television. She shut the door behind her and they did not speak, she walked over to him, thinking about the little pieces of the past that James had told her about, little pieces of Luc that she had not known, but that she loved him for, she still did not know him, not fully she knew, and yet, she knew enough. She sat down next to him, her legs dangling over the side of the bed and for the first time just looked into his face and Luc held her gaze, he seemed not to be troubled by it.

A gateway in Mer had finally dissolved and she let him stare into her big brown eyes unmoving. Finally, after they had both had their fill, he reached his hand to her face and drew it down over one side gently as she closed her eyes. She did not bow her head to him yet, so he left his hand upon her cheek until she gave in and kissed it, moving her head gently to find it; she kissed it as if kissing a ring of allegiance, or as the fanatic kisses the ring of a pontiff, her whole being kissed his hand so gently, but with all her power. He pulled her to him and as he did so for the first time she smiled, as big and wide as a child, she had never done this before in all their encounters, Luc seemed to know that he had reached a hidden shore of hers, and kissed her back so gratefully.

*

The next few days passed with the three of them in rhythm with each other, each occasionally looking out of the window to see signs of threat, but otherwise as if they had all lived for years like this together. When James' phone rang, all knew that it was Mischa, and often held their breath, but James had yet been the only one attacked. And then finally, they were on their last day; that night Luc would leave them, and leave her. It was impossible; all three of them considered how on earth so many strange things had happened that summer. Tomorrow they would be closer to freedom, as the embargo of flights into all 'cleaned' cities in the U.K. would soon be lifted, but not immediately. It seemed a world away that place before, when London had had its opulent summer and no one was allowed to move, and Mer had a sense of nervous anticipation that she did not want to explore.

They had lunch together of what was left in the freezer, knowing that tomorrow the supermarket trucks would come galumphing in at dawn, restocking for the hordes. They were quiet and sat together afterwards in the living room. Mer strangely did not want to be alone with Luc; she did not want to be so close today. Yet after some time on the sofa, James needed to rest his head and so, left the two of them alone. As soon as he had gone from sight, Luc did not hesitate and took Mer's hand to lead her to their bedroom, he almost dragged her behind him as she could not keep up with his pace, but she did not protest and let him sweep her away. When he had taken her upstairs, behind the closed door, she could finally see in his hazel eyes and sun kissed face, something that had no place there: anguish. He had not given anything away since his own decision to banish himself, but now he looked at her like a sad youth; but she could not fix this (!) and was at odds with the responsibility. For the first time he looked to her and as she went to hold him, he could not see that she had become pale, suffused with his gravity, her head had begun to spin and thus she prayed that he did not notice; that she clung on to him as he clung on to her. They sat down upon the bed and he put on the television, and they held hands on either side of it as they watched the people in the camps preparing to come back, and as predicted, hulking food trucks stood ready and willing, piled up at the gates, ready to dive first into the yawning maw of the empty motorway. Mer felt unhappy with this, the niggle of anticipation now flourished into pure contempt; but it made no sense, it was bound to happen, this repopulation, but she didn't like it and held on tighter to Luc's hand.

They spent the late afternoon there and drifted off to sleep with the television still flickering quietly, until they woke in a darkened room unaware of the time. They could see light from the landing at the base of the door and then heard some footsteps. Luc tried to hurry himself awake by rubbing his face and then patting down his lightweight hair. Mer turned away from him onto her side and faced the wall; she pulled her knees up into a loose foetal position, and readied herself. She was glad that they were not too close now, she wanted to cry, she also did not want to leave their room. Of course, Luc abruptly switched on his lamp, which sent the nectarine shower gel that Mer had been staring at in the adjacent bathroom into a half form; it looked even more forlorn than it had done in the dark. Mer could feel that she may lose control of her emotions as she had done with him once before in the kitchen, but she tried her best not to, it would be a selfish act; Lucian Avium, a man that she hardly knew, who had lost his mother in the last year and whose best friend was in charge of a secret force, was struggling far more than her; and she, spoiled child that she was, would try to support him. It took her a few moments to gain composure as her emotions bled out inside herself, tears reabsorbed before any rupture, and when she turned to him she was paler than he had ever seen her but serene, and unfathomable, he stared for a moment caught by this, as though lost in the allure, and then asked, "Shall we go down?"

"Yes," she said, and at the same time she reached out her hand and lastly once more, flattened his hair.

Mer left the room as quick as she could after that and she left him to get dressed, her lip trembled as she walked down the staircase where no one could see and wiped her eyes, willing herself to stop the flow. She wondered when she would see Luc again. She then felt sick, and opened her mouth to breathe as she made the last two steps of the descent. As she turned around to face the kitchen corridor, she smacked hard into James. It was so abrupt and she had not heard him in the slightest, that it was a full body blow: her head hit his chest and her pelvis, his brown leather belt and so, she lost her footing. But it had not been such a shock for James, who caught her first at one arm then the other, not a painless experience in itself for her, and apologising profusely he helped her upright again, at which moment, he then pulled her in close and hugged her, pushing her face into his chest which she had just bounced off. She attempted to struggle against this for a moment, but she saw him glance upstairs and so, then she let him guide her, almost drag her, in to the nearest room, which was the living room. There, she thought he would let go of her, but he did not, so she tried to push against his chest with her arms, but he then clamped down. She could hear him speak then, "Shuuuush, Mer, it will be all right. Just take a deep breath, it will be all right."

She took some time to understand what he was saying and then realised that she was shaking and her face, thus his clothing, was wet. She controlled her breathing, they were ragged breaths, he was trying to keep them both very quiet and she knew why: for Luc's sake. They were still in the dark in the living room and he would not let her go, so she gave up and she clung on, putting her arms around him and sobbed as silently as she could, she rubbed her face upon his grey t-shirt and could smell pure James; what any woman would be able to smell if she were allowed to be so near. She didn't mind it, it was a concoction of his shampoo and traces of his leather jacket with a hint of blood, he was warm but vice like and she knew that he would not let her go, until he was sure. So she cried into his chest until she was truly still; he would know if she was faking her containment, so she did not try to. When she was better, he pulled her away and looked into her face and then wiped her eyes and cheeks with his own hands. This man was used to having a lot of authority she thought. But she was not one of his foot soldiers she also thought and looked back at him defiantly, but she was caught like so many others by his packaging; he looked like a brutalised angel and it was hard for many to say no to that. Yet, this was her house and he was a guest in it. She raised her chin, trying to meet his authority.

"Thank you, I didn't want to cry in front of him," she said.

"I'm sorry to make you hide, I agree, it would be unfair to break down in front of him, he must be scared," James whispered.

She rubbed her face to put some colour into it and his aroma had imbued itself onto her, it perfumed her, essence of James; she felt wayward, as if privy to something private.

James then looked at her and smiled, yet like a centurion, "Mer, I love my friend and I think he very much loves you, I wanted to protect him, from my life, from me, but now I've failed. Everything I do from this moment on is damage limitation … You like Luc don't you. You can see he's got such a good heart, I'll do my best to keep him from my affairs and he's not going to like it one bit, but I want to ask you and I am giving you the respect of asking you to your face, even though you have effectively probably saved my life -is there something you want to tell me?"

Mer said nothing.

"Mer, please don't be angry or throw me out, it's a testament to how much I care for him to even risk speaking to you like this, but please tell me what it is, there is something, isn't there?"

She shook her head, but he was relentless and brought his face in closer to hers, suffocating her with his blood tinged leathery scent.

"Mer, I know."

A freezing began in Mer's chest. But she had lost her voice.

"I know that you're married. Does Luc?"

Mer looked at him like a rabbit caught in the headlights. And then, shook her head.

James looked at her in the dark, she could feel his disappointment in her emanating, and then so she added, "No, James, please understand, I never thought it would become what it has, I didn't mean to trick him, I'm getting a divorce!"

James frowned, but considered her last.

Mer now grew urgent, "James, please, let me tell him. Let me do it, I just couldn't find the right time, don't you understand," she spoke plainly, "it seemed presumptuous … don't you see."

James' disappointment was like a horrible awakening in herself; Mer now knew that if she didn't tell Luc, then James would. Choosing her words, she added, "I love him, James … it … consumes me. I don't know what to do with it …" In the dark, it was not discernible how much it took for this admission.

There was a pause between them and then she confided in him, whispering, "James, how am I going to make this all right? How can I tell him so that he won't bolt in disgust? He trusts me."

James tried to run his hand over his hair but stopped in mid-air lest he break the wound and then lowered his arm. "Don't do it tonight, he won't take it well, he's under too much stress, but tell him soon, and dive in, fall at his feet if you have to."

"James," Mer shook her head. "I don't want him to go." Now playing the only hand that she had left. "Please help. If he goes you *have* to talk to him, please help me." She spoke calmly now and looked to him then with nothing but the truth laid raw and bare before her, with ragged curls, puffy eyes and pale face.

James nodded once.

With an unspoken agreement between them, she left the room first, to drink some water and then splash her face cold with it. Luc was thankfully taking his time to reach them. Now James knew everything and she felt sick and disgusted with herself, anyone else would have been able to digest the truth, understand that she meant no harm and that her marriage was over, but not Luc. She knew that he would look at her as if a stranger, as a duplicitous woman, not the woman that he'd let into his life. But why was this a problem, she raged inside. Because Luc will not accept it, and then she put herself in his position, and imagined herself falling deeply, sweetly in love with someone, someone wonderful and then finding out that they were married, even though it would quickly be added that it was over and that he was getting a divorce -she would see him with jaded eyes and thus, the serpent would have risen, and Eden found its end. Oh, why hadn't she told him!

They had dinner late, which she thought would have been a quiet affair, spaghetti again, but James and Luc made plans and strategies and more contingency plans, it was beneficial as it kept Luc occupied. As far as Mer knew, her part in it was that she was to buy another two Pay As You Go phones and Sim cards tomorrow and deliver them to James at her home, as Luc would take back his extra phone; she would do this before buying groceries she'd decided, the rest would then be up to them. Depending on what occurred, James would be able to leave immediately or stay a few days or in the worst case stay for quite a long time; while the men were sure it was the former, Mer was sure that it would be the latter and she drew some comfort in it, as though James could prevent Luc from leaving her, by sheer magnanimous force. They had told her what to tell Christine about James when she came back, Mer had completely forgotten about Christine. Christine was to be told that James was a friend who was having refurbishment at his home and was thus staying for the duration. Soon the endless plans became too much and she could feel her insides swirling. Once, James and she had caught each other's eye when Luc wasn't looking and he could not help her, although he could see the torment and anxiety within her.

Finally after dinner, when Luc went upstairs to collect his things, she came up as well and shut the door behind her. He didn't have much to put together as he had lived out of a bag for all of this time, but he mistook Mer's anxiety.

"It will be all right, I will see you soon," he said.

"Luc, I want to talk to you."

"Yes?"

"I want to say something, important ..."

He waited.

"Luc," she bowed her head "Luc, I don't know what's going to happen, I know that you and James are very confident, but frankly judging by the fact that James was attacked and nearly killed, I would say that we just don't know how things really are. So I want to tell you something and I want you to carry it with you no matter what happens, or what comes out. Luc ... I love you, it's the most

343

valuable thing I have to offer, please, please never forget it over the next few days, or weeks." She put forward her endearment only once, and quickly.

Luc's cheeks turned red and he embraced her gratefully, she had never given him so much and he was trying to speak, when she put her fingers gently upon his mouth to stop him.

"That was hard enough for me to say, you can have your moment at another time," she said.

So he kept silent, but kept his solid arms around her, his chest engulfing her face as James' had and in that crush she had the combined scent of both of them, pressing in upon her.

He kissed her on the cheek fondly and she felt so very awful, but she returned by kissing him on the mouth, in case it was for the last time and then they went down, where they met James at the foot of the stairs. They went to the living room and Mer unlocked the French doors, lovely cool night air suffused them, although James was careful to stay behind a curtain, out of sight of the garden. Luc had a step ladder in hand and looked at Mer for one last time, before going out into the garden, and then set up the small ladder by the fence, in seconds he had jumped over and was quickly up the stairs to his own French doors that he unlocked, and then he was gone. It was a fast disappearance, she closed the doors and locked them, drew the curtains and then sank slowly to her knees, James sat down beside her.

"I'm sorry," he said to her.

"Not as sorry as I'm going to be. He won't forgive me … for being a lie …"

James did not argue with her statement. She then rose, went to her own bedroom and curled up into a ball under the sheets.

Chapter 52

As Gemma slept, her mind was past dreaming, deep into a dark ether where little could penetrate, but the discomfort rose, raising her mind from a black dormant consciousness, and soon, she could hear unmistakably the dawn chorus, which was intensely vocal so deep in the countryside. And then there was something else, a sound so absent these last two weeks, that something inside her was forcing herself awake. She had sent her parents away to a hotel from this country house of theirs, and made them stay at it under a false name. It was definite that a car rumbled closer, and then it hit their gravel filled drive, far too close for her liking, so she fell to her side out of bed and reached beneath her bedframe, pulling out a double barrelled shot gun; quite fitting for their converted barn house.

Two car doors closed, and she grabbed her dressing gown, putting it on, and then barely shifted the curtain to have a look. She at least recognised who it was, but then; maybe her day of reckoning was indeed upon her. She ran to the hallway, gun in hand, her father had taught her how to use it, aged ten. But she then hid it in under a chair in the living room. She tried to flatten down her hair and waited.

Soon enough, the door knocker sounded through the house. And she gave it a few seconds before answering, as if stumbling there roused from sleep.

"Hello, Gemma." Mischa stood before her, no smile upon his face. And worse, Michael stood behind him.

"Mischa, Michael, thank God you're both all right. Is James all right?! Please tell me. Oh don't worry, I'll tell you everything! Just tell me if he is OK!?"

She could tell that both men were not sure of what to make of this.

But Mischa said, "… Yes, James is OK."

"I have a lot to tell you, I know, and please stop looking at me like a traitor 'cause I'm *not*. Come and sit down," she commanded this last, even if she was in her night clothes, and the men unsure, obeyed.

Gemma chose the chair under which she had stashed her gun. And Mischa and Michael sat down in chairs opposite, still not smiling, but not looking as severe either.

"I'll start at the beginning. You've got to hear me out," she insisted. "Just after we found out about the mole, Simon, Minister Sebold recruited me," both men shifted in their seats, as if ready to take her down. "I had no idea how far his arms stretched, how much he knew, he wanted me to spy on Sir John, if I went and told James I was worried that I would end up exposing him instead. Because if they knew about Sir John, why didn't they know about me? It could easily have been a trap. I was really scared to expose any of you. I decided to sit on it and find out as much as I could, before I knew it was safe to let you all know."

Silence.

"*Think* about it. What would you have done? I knew about the list, and the timings of the raids in London on some of our members' houses, it was a search operation, unless they found someone; I knew they would have all left London, but then Sir John told me that James had stayed at his house, so I called him at the last moment, I didn't want to risk exposing myself to the Minister but now I had to, thank God James is OK!"

"Gemma," said Mischa. "Surely, you could have found a way to let one of us know?"

"How?" she said simply. "I didn't know how much they knew, who was being watched or bugged, if they were watching me …"

"But you'd know if you were bugged-" said Michael.

"Yes, I know, Michael, the gadgets, but technology keeps evolving, I couldn't risk it … Please, I'm telling the truth …When you sent Clara to stay with me, I almost died, but it shows that they really didn't know about me-"

"So why didn't you tell us then?" asked Mischa.

"By then, I was in so deep, I wanted to find out even more to clear my name and also be of use, and still keep you all protected. Where is James anyway?"

Mischa Sighed.

"What are you going to do, Mischa?" She looked at him squarely.

Mischa looked at her, still with little expression, Michael the same.

"Is this what we're becoming now, Mischa? I want to speak to James!" Gemma turned red, her thoughts upon her gun.

Mischa shook his head. "Gemma, put yourself in my position-"

"Who put you in charge?!"

"I am in charge in James' absence," Mischa said calmly.

"Well then, the difference is that James would believe me!"

"You don't have much faith in me, do you?"

"Faith!? What would you need to bring Michael for then?!"

"Think, Gemma, if you had turned, then we would be expecting resistance, you would do the same."

At this she calmed down a touch, and now hoped they would not spot her weapon.

"Mischa, I've known James almost all my life …" she said.

"As have I," he replied.

"I'm no traitor. Think. If I was, doing away with James would have completely destabilised the group, left us floundering -I saved him, Mischa!"

Mischa sighed again, and looked at Michael, who said nothing. So he went on, "Gemma, you should have found a way to come to us, but unlike your suspicions we aren't going to 'do' anything to you …"

Gemma's hair was amok, and her cheeks burned.

"However, we're in serious trouble, and so, we're gonna have to keep you out of the loop-"

"You're excommunicating me!"

"No we're not, look at it from our side, we're just being safe, and it's temporary, I promise-"

"Temporary! You wait 'till Sir John hears about this!" she yelled. Then she stood up abruptly, went over to a side cabinet, and picked up a paper file. "Well this was hand delivered to my door yesterday, and I didn't give the Minister our country house address!" She thrust the meat of the papers inside at Mischa.

As Mischa looked at the first page, he saw his name, and Anjelica's, and James', and Sir John's, and Clara's and many many others in the group. Everyone who has direct contact with James, it wasn't everyone, but the list was forty people deep.

"The only name that isn't on it that should be, is mine!" spat Gemma. "They know, we're blown, you can cut me out, but I say again, *I'm no traitor*!"

Mischa handed to list to Michael.

"Michael's name isn't on it either," she muttered, regaining some control.

Mischa was still speechless, and staring at the depth of the list.

"Now, while you two manage to pull yourselves together, I say again, I need to speak to James!"

Chapter 53

Luc had passed a safe night, having slept little. It was odd to be dressing for work, in such a short time Luc had become unused to his apartment; it seemed more miserable now that he had stayed in Mer's great house, but he was grateful to be going out, he wondered how much he would miss her ... but no contact was safer he knew.

As he went into the office it smelled a little stuffy and everyone was busy at their stations, with eyes lit up by the reflected light of their monitors, Gemma, he saw once disappearing into Balthazar's office and then they both quickly left. At his computer screen, before him were reports and analytical summaries but, he longed to know if James was all right, or if he had received some answers, and also if Mer was all right ... and he missed the house; he knew now that it had been an enchantment of sorts to live there, a gifted seclusion.

The corridors and small kitchenette buzzed with talk:

"The food was surprisingly not bad at the camps ..." and, "I think it was quite a feat to pull off for the government honestly, and so well..."

Only Luc alone sat disgruntled. He kept his eyes out for Gemma or Balthazar all day, so that he too could speak to them candidly, but frustratingly, none returned. Finally, on his way home he thought of what he would say to them, now that he was in the know, and he was astounded by how many people there were, crushed into the tube, all over the streets, the noises of passing cars were like nasty droning alarms careering down the roads. As he approached the cream clad property that they called home, he looked up at Mer's windows through the gates, she wasn't there. Unhappiness flooded him, this was all he could have of her for a while, he also tried to surreptitiously look about to see if there was anyone watching them, it seemed clear, although there was a man who had just parked his car in the residents section that Luc had not seen before, the car was a flashy Mercedes, which was fitting for the place. As Luc made his way to his own front door, suddenly the new man was at Mer's door and turning a key in its lock, Luc did not realise that he had stopped and was staring, so the man also stopped and looked back at Luc.

"Hello there," said Luc, yet his heart was hammering.

"Oh, hello." The man looked brightly at him, "You must be a new neighbour?"

Luc nodded slowly without meaning to.

"I live here next door with my wife, I've been away for a while but you may have met her, Mehreen, I like to say hello to all the neighbours." And he smiled and approached holding out a hand to shake, but instead of giving his hand Luc said, "Mer ..."

"Yes, she calls herself that, my name's Zafar or Zaf for short," he said as he shook Luc's hand.

"Luc, my name's Luc, I live next door. Are you back then ... from being away?"

"Yes, yes I am," he said happily and then went back and opened the door, Mer and Luc's front door, to walk inside as if it was his to possess.

Luc felt cold in the evening sunshine and fumbled with his own key, he managed to reach his flat and then sat down upon his orange covered sofa, then he rose again and put his ear to the wall that he shared with her, he could hear nothing, but he would try again later on. He sat back down on the sofa and played with his thumb and forefinger by pressing them together; he could not think. Roughly an hour or more later after sitting and trying to make sense of it, he thought he could hear something and so put his ear to the wall again, it was distant shouting, but it soon diminished. He went over to the kitchen and poured himself a large glass of vodka with ice and then sat by his window waiting for the man to leave. Another hour passed and Luc had shallow breaths, the thoughts came to him then unbidden: it all made sense now why a young woman lived alone in that huge house, *he* probably owned it. Oh dear God another man's woman, it sickened him and what had he been to her he thought? She had only used him while her husband had been away, Luc became even paler, the vodka's acid intoxication was very strong and let him flounder within his sad sentiment, as he wondered if there was nothing good left in the world, from his best friend to the woman he loved and moreover ... his mother was gone. It was unbearable, he wanted to bang on the door, to see her face, to scream at her, what a fool everybody had made of him, and that man, her 'husband' was still not leaving.

Another hour passed by, it was approaching ten o'clock and Luc was still at the window watching, but by ten-thirty he gave up and retreated to his shower. The very hot water startled him, so he soon broke down under the torrent and started to cry whilst holding his head. There was no one he could call or to confide in ... He tried to pull himself together under the rushing sound of the water, and then, either naturally reached a safe equilibrium within himself, or perhaps a deity took pity upon him and gave him grace, so that finally, he steadied. He finished showering with an empty peace, a ragged sense of calm, however flawed, and went to bed; his new gift of mental absentia had allowed him to now leave aside his grievances, to be dealt with in the morning, or whenever he could.

But before he could rest, his Clara-phone beeped:

I can only give you one more week.

So, she really wanted to push him, to know who he was, well, Luc at that moment didn't care anymore. Do what you have to do, he thought.

It was not comfortable to wake the next day, he had slept but woken to realise that his fists and jaw had been tightly clenched and saw that the morning light was cold, like he had been used to enduring during his youthful days when he'd lived in Old Street. Perhaps the season had finally broken, it had been too wild a summer to last into September, not in the form that it had been in at least; Britain had been kissed by the searing sultry dragon breath of the East far past its ration, or what was considered enough. Perhaps now, late summer and early autumn would be more traditional; with icy mists and sudden frosts, as he had experienced in his childhood while on his way to primary school, when cold winds had slapped his face and he'd inhaled ice on the air, infused with the scent of mashed leaves and fresh earth.

He dressed unwilling to think, focussing instead on each practical task such as diligently doing up his shirt buttons; he was not as yet awake enough to reflect. Outside as he left the front door he glanced as casually as he could to the 'other' door and then round about to see if anyone was watching, yet it felt very clear, their premises had its own alcove in Regents Park so any change or disturbance could be easily felt, he hoped.

At work he looked about for Gemma, and there she was, ushering him to follow him from a distance, and so he did, right the way into Balthazar's office.

"Luc," she said. "We need you to go to Paris, and to run a trade delegation. Can you do it?"

She had not given Luc a chance to ask a single question; Balthazar sat behind his desk and said nothing.

"Well, um … of course," said Luc.

"Wonderful, you leave on Friday."

"This Friday?"

"Yes. Problem?" she asked.

"Ah, no. No. How long will it last?"

"As you can imagine after the embargo, trade is in tatters and people are ready to tear up treaties, we need to secure our ties. Not to mention certain countries are furious about us using the oil we were supposed to sell to them to survive this whole thing. So it's a bit indefinite right now, but your apartment here stays, is that sort of clear enough?"

"Uh yeah. Of course. Yes." He wanted to say so much more, but they only looked like his superiors now. Then he took courage, "Is James all right?"

"... He's fine," said Gemma, and smiled a little.

Luc looked at Balthazar.

"My boy, thank you. You've done us proud. Thank you for your help."

"Anything you need," added Luc, but he wanted to be alone with Balthazar, to ask about his days with his mother, but Gemma stood there like a centurion, and it became impossible to speak freely.

"Luc, it's a really important diplomatic mission, otherwise we wouldn't send you while the embargo was still on, and you'll be in and out of the British Embassy."

Luc nodded.

"I've got a full information pack for you ready, and it'll be on your desk soon. Thank you so much," Gemma finished.

As Luc walked back to his desk, he considered that this was not how he had wanted his meeting with those two to go, he had imagined something more intimate, candid, and familiar; for he'd imagined that he was now one of them.

He recalled that he was to leave on Friday, in three days' time, and in short: to leave Mer behind without an explanation. Departing suddenly without explaining would send a message to Mer, but was it the one he wanted to send? He knew that he was disgusted and furious with her, so then he said it to himself, "She's married", and his lip curled -what a fool he's been.

Yet, another part of Luc nagged at him to give her a fair trial. Surely he had come close to something of the truth of her, a core of sorts, he would have known a façade or a charade surely, at least it was worth finding out? He conceded that he did want to find out, to hear her out, even if it would be a humiliation and a great defeat for him and yet, in reality how could he? In the end he would have to leave and she would not know why. She was immoral, but he did not want to be, yet at present he had no choice.

Luc came home each day, looking up desperately at her windows, hoping to catch a glimpse and also fearing that it would be much worse if he did. He never saw her, and Friday afternoon approached.

That day, he arrived home with one last look up at her quiet blank house and packed, unsure of what to leave behind, unsure of his mission. He took many clothes but left behind all of his ornaments, even the picture of his mother; he would be staying in a hotel so he had packed enough for an extended holiday.

As his car doors closed, he looked nervously at her home for the last time, why hadn't she heard him or looked out of her window? Was she with her husband he thought, and it dawned on him finally, *that she may be*. His heart then sank to a squalid level of Hades and he purposefully called upon a deity, oh dear God he pleaded, he did not want to feel like this. The waves of fraught emotion rolled and knocked upon his bough, as he started his car and tried to steer himself away from them, and away from her. He was not to drive straight to the motorway yet, he had to meet Balthazar for a final quick briefing but at a different location, a private house in Hampstead, he had been told to drive into the garage which would be open, it seemed odd, but given the events of the last week he tried to take it in his stride.

It was a big, red bricked detached house with a long driveway, that lead into a garage who's door stood in open welcome to him, set past an ample front garden, neat and precise, nothing like his own, or Mer's. So he drove slowly in, hoping he had found the right house, and there became clear a figure inside the distant cover of the garage as Luc approached. Luc blinked a few times behind his glasses and then his face grew hot, he had to make a very quick decision for himself: to reverse very fast or to keep going, his feet hovered for an instant over the accelerator pedal and then something took hold of him, and so, he pressed down and on.

As Luc rolled in, at the back of the garage stood James in his jeans and jacket, next to him a small bag; he looked like a most apologetic saint but then again, also had a determined expression akin to that of Joan of Arc; he too had a mission. Luc watched and did not move, keeping the engine running. James came over to the car, opened the passenger door and sat down beside Luc, shutting himself soon inside and also saying nothing. Eventually, in the inert standoff, Luc switched off his engine.

"Luc, please don't be angry, we need your help. There are some things I haven't told you … There's more to the story. It's important, please listen. Somebody within our organisation betrayed us, you know, there's been some damage control, but maybe it wasn't enough, obviously not, but it's not so simple, Simon made, a mistake ..." James was finding it hard to make it sound credible even to himself. "He's extremely sorry, he was just very angry with me, with us, and now he's afraid for his life, they know he has more information than he's already given them and they want more, but he of course doesn't want to do that, he would have disappeared immediately were it not for the embargo, so I have to go to Paris, to get him out."

There was a pause.

"So, he's a traitor and we're going to save him?" said Luc.

"Yes."

"… And this is *all* because of Clara…"

"… I suppose, yes … In the end, human foibles, jealousy, anger, and vengefulness …" James shook his head, "They've torn us to pieces."

"I see Gemma back at work, all trusted and fine?"

"Mischa's excommunicated her."

"What?"

"Cut her out of the loop, she's furious and probably very hurt, but he just has to be sure."

"But she knows about me taking you to Paris," said Luc.

"That was unavoidable."

"... She did save you ..."

"I know, but she should have found a way to let us know more, she had been recruited by that Minister to spy on Sir John, a bit like you, but worse. She wanted to keep me safe, so she didn't say anything to us."

"Sounds plausible?"

"It does, but we, also have to be safe."

"But if she really was recruited by Sebold, isn't she important, don't we need her information?" said Luc.

"Of course we do, I don't imagine Gemma keeping anything to herself now, and if she's innocent like she claims, she'll tell me everything."

"Tell me more about the Minister, what do you know?" asked Luc.

"The businessmen who Simon had betrayed us to are all dead: Peter Armstrong, Dominic Burgess, and Michel Grimbaud, I think it's important for your own safety that you know their names. They all owned multinational companies. One or more of these men had spoken to their 'friend' in the British government before we found out about them. That man is Minister Sebold, and he'd started his own investigation into the little that Simon had revealed, as he knew that he would be implicated if things got out; he was very mixed up with those three corrupt businessmen. Once you alerted us to Minister Sebold, it was easy to make the connection between Armstrong, Burgess, Grimbaud and him, as we already have something on that Minister doing a shady deal with one of them, I just haven't released it yet.

"Gemma had been recruited by Sebold to spy on Sir John -we were incredibly lucky, if she's clean, they never knew she was one of us, but she says she could do nothing to help us or to let me know of her recruitment, she knew she could be under heavy surveillance -I just think she got in way too deep over her head. So she decided to save just me if it would come to that and called from a random mobile at the last minute. She did well in that sense, it had to look as if I had never been tipped off, and that she's achieved; to save her own skin if nothing else."

"The list ...?"

"Yes, everyone had evacuated London on that list of a few of my members that you saw, thank heavens, except me."

"That was why she was crying," Luc said absently to himself.

"Gemma is still a double agent until we find out exactly who is behind this, it may just be that one Minister that she is taking orders from, or it may go further, but we will neutralise this threat very soon, it has cost us too much."

"I wonder how he did it, how he found out about you at least?"

"I don't know, I would have been known to all three of my members who died but, but that connection would be hard to find as I barely saw them and communicated via very circuitous routes. They shouldn't have found me, I can't think of any other link."

"So, have you spoken to Gemma, personally?"

"No. Mischa's briefed me, I think he's just punishing her, he's also rattled, understandably."

"Also ... what do you mean by 'damage control' as you said earlier?" asked Luc.

There was a pause.

"... I'm not proud of it, Luc."

Luc blanched, he could not believe that this was James, his childhood friend, secret spy... and murderer? But at that he turned on the engine. It was time to go.

"Three of us were killed because of Simon, we would all be dead if I hadn't acted, you saw yourself that I barely survived."

Luc did not respond, his hands gripped the steering wheel more tightly than usual as he reversed, turned, and righted himself onto the road, driving on and on, to exit London and reach not Dover, but a remote Kentish port. There, they would take an exclusive diplomatic voyage to France, where Luc at least, diplomatic immunity temporarily or not, would be doused with cleaning agents and swabbed to make sure that he brought in with him no germs from Great Britain. It was planned that at that point alone, James would be in the car boot, as the guards on either side of the borders would still have no right to search it.

"Is there anything else I should know?" Luc asked finally, still looking ahead.

"I can't think of anything now, but if I do I'll let you know."

"You could have told me all of this, from the start, you could have trusted me from the beginning ... more than Mischa. You *could* have."

"I know. I'm sorry," said James simply.

Chapter 54

The sound of waves gently crashing upon a beach was a forlorn rhythm, the last gift of a lost melusine that stayed with Luc as he woke up; not sure if it was a memory or a dream. He scrunched his eyes into the shaft of sunlight glinting into the room from curtains that had not been pulled tight enough; but this was not his room and he remembered: he was in France, it was actually afternoon and his best friend was in the shower. The hotel room was pleasant; they were centrally placed so that Luc could reach the embassy and travel about town for meetings easily, although nothing was to start till Monday, not for him at least. They had arrived at three in the morning and had slept up till now and Luc was not sure what they would be doing today as James seemed quite calm.

When James came back into the room he was dressed and his hair was damp and flatter than usual upon his scalp. Luc looked up at him and said, "You're not going without me."

James looked back at him while stopping in his tracks, as if contemplating a million answers, but then nodded and sighed. "Hurry up then, we have to go."

"All right, so where are we, I mean did you contact, do you know-"

James shook his head quickly. He then looked at Luc pointedly and said, "We're going to a very popular café."

Luc knew that James was trying to tell him something, but couldn't help trying to recall all the popular cafes in Paris that he knew of offhand. "I'm going to have a shower, *don't* go without me," Luc now said pointedly himself.

It was the fastest shower that Luc had ever taken, he prayed that James hadn't already left; he held on to the fact that James would be tampering with the last vestiges of their friendship if he did so, but then realised that James had priorities and depths that Luc knew nothing of. So Luc hurried, scrubbing ferociously, in short he felt protective, finally, he almost burst back out of the bathroom door, towel around his waist and strangely half expected Mer to be there. Mer. It stabbed him, he had not discussed her at all as he had been too wound up with the concept of the 'damage control' that James had implied, and James also had been too preoccupied to bring her up. But James would know about her husband and her, he would know the truth -Luc needed to ask him but felt foolish and trivial to bring it up, it would have to wait, it didn't change the fact that she'd lied to Luc and used him, no, he sadly answered himself, it didn't change very much.

Luc drove James to their location; it was a small café in Belleville. In the car James explained, "Simon's been going to this café every day at 4pm in the hope of seeing me, or for an extraction. This protocol's been established as an emergency measure for all members, established by my grandfather and his friends, even I have my own extraction point in London, for me it's Mischa who knows about when and where."

Luc mused on the fact that poor Simon had been going to this café every day for a while, he hoped that he hadn't given up.

Luc felt excitement in its purest form, undiluted; for he'd never truly tasted down in the base-strata of his psyche, the real danger that faced James, even if James did have a gash on his head. In this sense, Luc had thought that it was one thing to watch a spy movie, but to actually be in one was a fanciful concept; like believing that the world could now possess in it, actual magic. Yet, Luc arrived behind James at the unassuming café and sat down with him at a table in the corner, his heart dancing in his mouth, his nerves now wild. Every time the door opened and someone came in, Luc looked up with more force than he wanted to, so he tried to control the inner dance and looked down at the table, forcing himself to breathe deeply and evenly. As he did so he noticed that it was a quarter past four, oh no, he was right, Simon had given up, he would have, he thought. He crossed his forearms upon the table and sat a little hunched over, when the waitress came over to them she gave Luc a tiny heart attack; it was as through a fog that she asked for their order, and Luc heard James reply back in perfect French; which he had honed by spending every summer with Luc at the beach in France, as far back as Luc could remember. The coffee was on its way, although coffee and stimulus was the last thing that Luc needed. At four thirty Luc sat up properly, disappointed, Simon was absent. James had been silently sipping his coffee and Luc did not bother him. Luc's thoughts drifted and he realised that he was starving, the sugar he had put into his café crème had been an elixir but had triggered his appetite most tremendously, it would keep him going however, although he wished for another staple. To keep his mind busy he thought of steak and some good wine, now that they were in France.

At that moment a completely unnoticeable man walked in wearing a dull dark blue jacket and blue jeans, he had a newspaper rolled up in one hand and James slowly put down his coffee cup; this small act pulled Luc rudely away from thoughts of French cuisine and into, he was not quite sure what. The man smiled at the waitress behind the counter, she said bonjour to him and he proceeded to look in their direction to find a table, at which moment everything about him changed, every pore in his body seemed to respond and he walked as normally as he could over to them, yet also as though his feet were made of clay.

The man came and sat down at their table and looked nervously at Luc, but they had met a few times before when Luc had visited London, at dinners at James' home, surely he remembered that? Luc wanted to reassure Simon that he had nothing to fear from him, but no one said anything.

"Have a coffee, then we'll go," James then said to Simon.

Simon nodded. He didn't speak yet. Luc imagined that he must be overjoyed.

"There's a ride home waiting for you." James told Simon in the same tone, quiet but not to be trifled with, and Luc remembered that Simon however small and inoffensive as he seemed now, had cost them three lives on this side and three lives on the other. This fact sobered Luc too.

Simon nodded again, opened his mouth to speak, and then closed it.

James signalled the waitress for another coffee, which Simon would have to drink.

"Also, before we go, I assume that you have it. I want you to place it under the newspaper; I'll keep it safe for you now." James whispered.

Simon took something out of his jeans pocket and placed it upon the table gently and under the newspaper. It was a mobile phone.

"James," said Luc. "Is this something I can keep for you? Think about it, it could be better ..."

"... Luc, you're right ... Thank you."

At that, Luc carefully placed his hand under the newspaper and then put the phone in his pocket.

"Right, let's go," said James. "Luc, I want you to go back to the hotel, Simon and I are going to the Rue du Faubourg Saint-Honoré."

Simon looked alarmed.

"I know it sounds odd, if we're compromised, but it is the best I have, anyway, Giles is a good man, and is going home for a bit, so you'll be hitchhiking as I did," James said to Simon.

Simon looked happier; Luc also understood the reference this time, that road was where the British embassy was, if he had understood it properly. They got up to leave and James patted Luc on the arm and said, "I'll see you back at the hotel."

Luc nodded all loquaciousness at a loss, he was pleased at least that James looked relieved, but Luc was not yet, perhaps it was an anti-climax but then he remembered that he was carrying an object and felt strange; he did not know whether to feel fear or excitement, as his mind could not accept the circumstances that he found himself to be in, as if he were only acting a part in a play. He tried to rise-

"No," said James, dead quiet, "wait fifteen minutes after we leave, order another coffee or a bite, and then leave."

Luc nodded again as his friend left him, he could not keep his eyes off James' back and his decreasing form once outside the café window; his gaze never leaving him, as a last act of protection and friendship that he had to offer. He glanced over at a hefty stack of patisserie behind the counter and now could not eat; he looked at his watch and then ordered a chocolat chaud.

The time passed but Luc was not bored, he processed fragments of what was happening and imagined how James would despatch Simon to this Giles: he must be a member and working for the British embassy here Luc thought, a useful and good placement for them, they must aim to be in places like this all over the world, and then he remembered that he'd been left out of this, in some way mocked, even though James had known how much Luc had worshipped his spy grandfather, James knew that Luc would have loved this; it hurt like a spike, right next to where Mer had placed hers.

He waited his allotted time and then made his way back to the hotel, where he placed his car in its own private parking, Balthazar had thought of everything. He went to his room and immediately ordered room service, enough for more than two; he ordered steak that would be strikingly rare and sweet fleshed langoustines in butter, plus an enormous sounding cheeseburger, grand and copious enough for a last meal. He felt some relief now and justified in his banquet treat, but the seconds ticked by and his food arrived decorously under silver domes, gawping redolently as he opened them, and he still had not seen James arriving behind the man in the corridor that delivered the room service, as he'd hoped. These things took time he thought; perhaps James was having an important talk with this Giles. He switched on the T.V. and opened another dome, the savoury aroma grabbed him thickly at the throat and he ate with the pleasure of a truly hungry man, while drinking perfect red wine as he had planned to do in Paris. He felt better, he left the cheeseburger for his friend and watched the television for some time until he noticed the shadows in the room extend as the sun waned; it had been too long and he knew it.

Chapter 55

It was still light and afternoon, but they had plunged into a tunnel; after retrieving a car that Giles had left for him near the cafe, James had decided for them to drive around Paris for a while, just to be careful. He glanced at his charge as Simon drove, and felt at least a small sense of achievement, that this loose cannon had been curtailed.

"... James ... how can I start to apologise, I don't even feel I can ... I *know* what I've done ..."

"I know you do, that's why I'm here."

"What's going to happen to me?" Simon asked.

But there was only sound, and metal tearing upon metal, glass shattering, a huge impact upon them like the blow of a final drum, and then once again, a noise hit them and tore their reality to pieces, everything spun and there was no time for speech, or comprehension and no time to take any other course ...

Chapter 56

"Are you all right?"

"I'm fine. And you?" asked Mer.

"I need to talk to you, Mer … were you OK during the evacuation?"

Mer said nothing, her husband, Zafar, sat before her in her sitting room, after having let himself in.

"I missed you," he said.

Mer said nothing again and remembered then that they were not alone in the house, far from it. Soon after, the inevitable happened and hearing voices James put his head around the door. Even though Mer suspected that it might happen she had hoped for some reason that James would see sense or hide -in retrospect she realised that it was probably very important for James to know who was in her sitting room. Still, when his pale face, blue eyes and flaxen mop -stamped with wound, appeared at an angle at the door, her stomach dropped a league and she felt light headed, a flush anointing her cheeks as if Luc himself were there as well; worse, with Luc gone, Mer had now lent James some of Zafar's clothes to wear!

"Oh, Zaf, this is my friend, James, he's staying here while his house has renovations."

Zafar got up to shake James' hand, as they did so Christine walked in holding Marina, and stopped in her tracks.

"Oh! Christine, you're here too?" said Zafar.

"Oh, hello, Zaf, I'll just, um …"

"Please sit down," he insisted.

And so, all sat down politely.

Mer said nothing about why Christine was in her house, then, in a rising quiet desperation she asked, "Everyone must be hungry, no?"

"I'll make some dinner." Christine rode to her rescue.

"I'll help you," said Mer, having no qualms about leaving the two men together, she knew James could and would, have to cope.

Mer did not know what they discussed, although she crept back through the corridor twice to eavesdrop: they were discussing their work, her husband spoke most and then James conversed about genealogy. James was asked how he knew Mer and if it had been from her work at the gallery, she froze on the spot, James explained that they had met at a creativity course, which was of course not true, and so she tiptoed back to where Christine was piously making them some rice. Christine did turn around at one instance and say to her, "Take deep breaths ..."

Christine of course had no idea about James, she had also been told the renovation story. Mer stood pinned to the door frame trying to stretch her ears to listen to the conversation in the other room and failed. Soon the meal was ready and Mer went to call the gentlemen to the kitchen, Christine had made plain rice and chicken in a white sauce with tarragon -wholly spontaneously concocted even Mer could tell, but well executed.

They all scraped their chairs back and sat, even baby Marina was ensconced in high a chair and given a bottle. Mer could see her husband going along with it all, as though in a strange waking dream. Mer tried to eat, although her stomach was absent. The pleasantries continued about what people did for a living, James at one moment caught Mer's eye while Zaf was looking down into his plate, and working hard upon the anticlockwise motion of a sauce gathering spoon; in that instant, her face burned and her eyes pled forgiveness, surrounded as they were by cheeks burnished with shame. It wasn't just Luc whom she'd lied to, it was plain for all to see that her husband didn't know her either; and Zafar looked less like a man who lacked in some department, and more like an innocent well-meaning chap, led to this sad incongruous dinner table by no one else but his wife.

Finally, and tortuously, the meal was over and James and Christine set about clearing up, Mer led her husband away, in the hallway she said to him quietly, "I'm sorry we couldn't finish our talk."

Whispering now, "I see you've been very busy here." He seemed no more a gentleman. "Who is he, Mer?! Is this it, is this the reason? Shame on you!"

"No, it's not! He's just a friend, you can ask Christine," she whispered back.

"Now I don't even want to know about that! Has she left your cousin? I've heard things ... What on earth has been going on here in my house?"

If Mer had been cowed and ashamed before, she was now quite instantly furious, but she said nothing.

He turned to travel up the stairs.

"Where are you going?" she asked surprised.

"To my room."

She followed him. "Which room is that?" she asked panicking.

"Which do you think?"

Rushing behind him, she wondered what he thought he would achieve by reaching their bedroom; as if by getting there first he would lay a stake to their marriage.

As he reached the doorframe of her bedroom not knowing that she had been sleeping in Luc's old room, she said "You're welcome to stay in this room if you like, but I'm not sleeping in here as well."

So he changed tack. "Mer, please at least talk to me ... we could see a counsellor?"

She let him walk into her bedroom and he sat down upon the edge of the bed, so, she did so as well and said to him with what had been interrupted downstairs, "You're a good man." She faltered, she was not sure that she was doing the right thing at all, but she did it nevertheless. "You're a good man. I don't know what to say to you ... but I can't do this anymore ... I'm so sorry."

"But we were only married for six months, how can you even know? You haven't even tried," he said openly bewildered.

"I've made a terrible mistake, I'm not proud of myself, I've been doing things to be someone else, you're all good in the things that you are, but we don't fit, and it's not even your fault…"

"But … you told me that you loved me. You were so *happy* on our wedding day."

"I thought I was."

"So you lied."

"It isn't like that," she said, but was it not? She thought to herself and she could see now his anger rising.

"Mer, none of this makes sense. I was giving you space, you'd become moody and we used to fight and then before I left, you just became depressed, it was awful. I thought if I went it would shake you up, make you realise that you were wrecking things, hell I thought you might even miss me, well I was clearly wrong about that!"

Mer braced herself.

"I honestly think that you need help," he continued, "we were married and then you fought with me *every* day, gave up in the bedroom and then went into a *huge* depression, so rather than bin our marriage, can't you see that maybe, open your eyes to these things?! I'm so sorry I left, it hasn't helped you at all."

"Zaf… you're right, maybe I do need help." She could not speak of the next part, about the bedroom and how she withdrew from him and his scent mixed with his aftershave which hinted of alpine tress and musk, that was strong, expensive and drove her away, she could not bear it; how could she explain such a thing, its meaning and ramifications. It seemed like such a trivial hiccup, but she knew now more than ever before that her revulsion to it elucidated the true nature of bonds, and of how and of what substance they are made, of what her soul actually needed; as when she thought of Luc, she felt

369

like their bond was capable of transgressing even the laws of heaven and earth. It would be impolite enough to ask Zafar to change his aftershave, but how could he alter his essence, it would be beyond a discourtesy.

"So, you will try? I mean, we can go to couples counselling, both of us," he persisted.

She shook her head, dealing him a hand that was blank.

He stood up to face her now. "Why are you so stubborn? Give it a try, give us a try. Do your parents even know?"

"No, not yet," she sighed, thinking.

"Have you considered what this will do to them?"

She looked at him, anger gathering inside her chest now and spoke in a voice that he had not heard before, "They will be fine."

"Fine about what? You seem to have this all worked out!"

"Zaf, I want a divorce."

He looked at her and then stated after a pause, "You've lost your mind." And he shook his head, as if she were planning on committing a crime.

"I've done my best to explain that this is not your fault," she said.

"What, like in a movie!"

"Yes, it is true, I want a different life."

"What life? What do you want? Have I ever stopped you from doing anything you wanted? Anything? Oh I understand now, I understand now, it isn't a different life, it's a different man!"

"Please keep your voice down."

"Why? In case he might hear us. Living in my own house, in my own house … and I've just realised, his clothes! How long then? I suppose this must have started a while back, it would explain things!"

"None of that is true. That is *not* true. I did lend him some clothes, but I can explain, that's why his house needed renovations, there was a flood-"

"During a heatwave?"

She said nothing.

"And, you became distant."

She said nothing again.

"I have a good mind to bring him up here and to beat him senseless."

She knew that that was not in his nature, so she sat still and continued to say nothing.

"Well, say something at least!"

"Zaf, I want a divorce, you'll be much happier without me."

"Happier? All these months, waiting for you, giving you time, happier! You whore! And in my own house!"

Although she could tell that he was bewildered and desperate, she had had enough, it was amusing to her that she didn't mind the abuse, it was something else that had flicked an errant switch once too often and so she stood up and spoke whilst swaying with the force of the expulsion, "This is my house!"

This stopped him for a moment; he looked at her, his face red and reddening further by the minute.

"This is my house," she repeated, in a whispered blow.

"Mer, this was our house, given to us together by your father, for us to live in as husband and wife." He was genuinely taken aback.

"This house is in my name, given to me by my father because he loves me, think about it Zaf, if what you just said was true why did he not put the house in your name too?"

"But, that's what it meant, to be a wedding gift …" he countered.

"You assumed."

He looked as though he had never thought that she would say such a thing to him and so he had little to say. "You're still a whore," he then added quietly.

She brushed her hair away from her face with her hand and displayed no sign of guilt for what she had supposedly done.

"… Mer, I've said some things today, I'm sorry. I'm asking you just to think about all the other things I've said and for us both to get some rest, I'll find another room don't worry, just think about it." And he turned to exit her bedroom.

He went upstairs to the second floor assuming that all the rooms on the first were taken, which was true, she supposed that he would go down and retrieve his bag later, she groaned inside, he was giving her what he called 'space' and hoping that she would see sense. At least tonight's brawl was over, she was exhausted and Luc was just a wall's width away, it was intolerable.

She walked around her now vacated bedroom for a while, unable to approach the bed and then washed her face with brisk cold water, making her smart each time that she splashed herself and brushed her teeth, somewhat in a hurry, put on her nightclothes and dressing gown and then peeped out of the bedroom door at the landing, it looked solemn, lit as it was by a light still on down below. She crept on tip toe to Luc's room and shut the door behind her. She crawled into his side of the bed and took one of the pillows to hold as she lay bundled upon her side, she put the television on at a low volume and was happy that no one could bother her here and she was comfortable too that if need be James would know where to find her, but not Zaf. She had her mobile phone at her bedside, now on all the time, which she looked at occasionally, mournfully, as if it would suddenly burst into action, into a shrill digital awakening, she so wished that it would.

She found eventually an old movie to watch called, 'Bell, Book and Candle.' It was about a modern day witch who fell, who used her powers to beguile a taken man in order to spite his fiancé, yet then, fell in love with him, and so lost all her powers. Perhaps it had been acceptable for the bygone audience of 1958 for the heroine to be de-witched as such, a fitting trade for love, especially as the hero was mild mannered and kindly, but Mer felt annoyed, why should the beautiful witch be stripped of her powers just because she loved a man? Mer wanted her to have both. But the romantic film did lead Mer to the formless realms of sleep, which considering the trials of the last few days, was not an assured a thing.

The next morning, Mer awoke to the faint scent of perfumed nectarines in the air, which had now an edge of torment for her. She rose, brushed away the scent and tip toed to the door once again to peep out at the landing and quickly went back to her own bedroom to get dressed. She had arrived just in time as there was a knock at the door and then it opened suddenly. Her husband surveyed the bedroom; both noted that the bed looked completely undisturbed.

"Are you having breakfast?" he asked her.

"I wasn't going to ... but very well," she answered and followed him down the stairs.

As they approached the kitchen it was obvious that it was already a very busy place, James was at the stove making scrambled eggs while Christine was trying to feed the baby; Mer was sure that this was not what her husband had had in mind and quite wickedly, wanted to snicker. For a moment Zafar had on a bewildered expression again, so James came to the rescue and asked him, "Would you like some scrambled eggs? I've made enough for everybody."

"I would," piped Mer, as her husband was not sure what to say. She then laid plates for all of them while the baby gurgled.

Seated, James served them individually and placed a plate of towering toast in the centre, he had even made Zafar some coffee. They ate as if they ate like this every day and had sat down with each other for years, making conversation as James remarked upon the weather and played with Marina. Zafar said very little. Eventually it was over and James and Christine again set about clearing things away, to leave Mer and Zaf with each other.

Zaf stood up and walked away, Mer followed him to the entrance hall where he turned to her and spoke, "I understand that you've made up your mind," he waved his hand towards the kitchen and said in a way that made her heart break with shame, "I have no place here."

To her surprise Mer panicked; she was about to get what she desired.

"I'm going. You can have your divorce," he said it gently, so as to create a fulsome blow.

She said nothing. He then turned to run up the stairs to retrieve his bag.

As Mer stood there, at the foot of her majestic stairs waiting for her husband to leave her house, she felt a heaviness about her face. He returned quickly, hammering down the stairs towards her and as he went past her towards the door she called out, "I'm sorry!" although her throat was constricted.

But he turned around and spoke, tears in his eyes, words which finally knew her, "Are you?" he whispered and then opened her giant door, and ran away as fast as he could.

After he left there was an enormous quiet in the hall, she knew she was upset but didn't want to go upstairs to those lonely rooms, so she went to her living room and sat on a velvet sofa and put her head in her hands, no sound came forth for many seconds and then she felt the heave of a sob, a beginning of many, but it was done she thought, and she hoped that the others couldn't hear her. She felt as though she had sinned and she wanted to call him up, her husband, but she would not know what to say to him; if he could not see who she was now, then how could she make him? Yet, it was true, that she didn't want him.

What had she done?

The marriage with all its colourful fanfare and expense, sense of great expectations and possibilities, had all been swallowed up by this house. When they'd lived here together, Mer had been full of wonder for each room, pondering upon its history but he'd only felt anxiety, the place had not suited him yet he'd been kind enough not to say anything or insist that they move out; instead however he'd irritated her by his lack of appreciation of it. Thus, because she had had no right, no just cause against him, she had become depressed, her last weapon. After this there came withdrawal, a most passive aggression that pushed him away without any effort, as now over a cliff, away from her and never to return.

She gained composure after crying quietly for a period. He would survive she consoled herself, they both had the rest of their lives in front of them to try and find happiness again, be it not from each other, it gave her peace this thought, but did not take away the feeling that something splendid had now been ruined. She recognised that her sense of personal morality consisted of exact theories and mental rhetoric but was not so evident in the expanse of her heart or in her bearing; this last she was digesting slowly.

That day, although she had had a trying start, Mer also saw some very productive results. She telephoned her old employer to ask simply if she could come back, and because she had been so wrung out from the morning she was brazen enough to have asked him in a calm manner that was quite appealing. She had been ready for any answer, so it came as a surprise when he said yes and then added that she could start as soon as the embargo was lifted and the world could begin again; he had been as endearing as ever. She sighed and then made another telephone call, this time to her mother. In the mood that she was in she was braced for more drama, although she did not want it.

Her mother answered in faraway New York, Mer had forgotten in her self-absorbed abstraction, about the time difference and that it was very early morning there. Her mother and father were woken up rattled by the phone call and of course assumed that something was very wrong, she calmed her mother down, but lost her courage and said that she just wanted to hear her voice and that she missed her and had forgotten about the time. She would have to tell them about the divorce later. Once again that nagging feeling, the one that mocked her strength sent her full of anxiety, as fluttering doves into a cave and she went off to find James.

He was in his bedroom and on the telephone she could hear from behind the door. She waited until he finished before she knocked and he looked as if it had been a very serious conversation indeed, so she asked, "Is everything all right?" without truly thinking.

He smiled at her and sighed. "No," was his answer.

"Is there anything I can do?"

"Well, harbouring me is contribution enough. But are you all right?" he asked her, curious.

She did not answer.

"Do you want to talk about it?" At this he reached out an arm ushering her to sit next to him on the side of the bed, her gentleman from another time.

She came and sat down, still mute.

"Has he gone, your-"

"Yes," she said quickly. "He's, gone. Really gone." She was sombre.

"I know it can't be easy to talk to me about this, but I'm sorry, if that is the right word."

"I don't know if it is. Sorry for him yes, maybe, but for me, I don't deserve it." Sitting so close to James, Mer thought of Luc and kept herself very still at the thought of him, lest she spill out wantonly all over the place.

"I wish this was over soon and so you could see Luc."

Mer nodded her thanks to James for understanding so much, and left him to it.

The next day was better; she awoke feeling glad that she would be returning to work soon and that at least there was no more drama awaiting her with Zaf gone. She made herself coffee as Luc would have done and felt determined to be practical, so decided to go and purchase groceries again, even though she had only been two days ago; as she left, she always looked up hopefully at Luc's windows when she was outside, although she knew he would be at work.

It was a mundane and practical thing to do and she enjoyed buying the ingredients for her house full of people even though she could still not do very much with them herself. There was nothing to pushing a trolley down an aisle as millions of others did, perusing shelves that were bare often due to the embargo, she watched the mothers with their children too young for school and the old men and women walk about as if nothing had happened, as if the evacuation and disruption had never taken place; everything was as it always had been, there was no change here to people's rhythm or sense of the world. She took her time, trying to prolong her enterprise not wanting to go home and be with only her thoughts. She lingered at the baking aisle full of wares and pretty things to create one's own cakes and confections with: nuts, cooking chocolate and candied peel sat in fat, bright little packets full of potential; she was fascinated by them.

It was there that she became aware of a tall gentleman in a suit that belonged in the City; his aura was amiable enough as his strong nose looked equally hard at the nuts and flour packets. He spoke, and Mer was not sure if it was to himself.

"I wish I could bake, it all looks so creative and productive," he said as he peered in closer at a packet of candied peel.

He waited for an answer.

"Yes ... me too. I can't bake either," Mer replied apprehensively.

"Please don't be alarmed. Or turn to face me. I'm a friend of Luc's. I am his boss; my name is Sir John Balthazar. You can look me up later to make sure. I know your name; I believe they call you Mer for short. Don't be afraid. I just want to say that for your own safety, please do not contact Luc *at all*, or of course James when he leaves. Yes, there's been a watch kept on you to keep you safe, I promise to do so, I chose to come myself to impress on you the importance of this and hoped you wouldn't run away, was worried I wouldn't get here in time ..."

Mer was very fixed at looking at the supermarket shelf. She did not move. Her chest however tried to dance to a rhythm of its own accord. She did her best to look normal. She wanted to ask if Luc was all right, but of course had no way of knowing if this was friend or foe. But she dared anyway to ask what she really wanted to know, "For how long?"

"I'm so sorry my dear, I really am, indefinitely, is the only answer I can give you. To keep all three of you safe."

At least by the answer she thought she knew that Luc was safe and then she could feel the tall man ebb away from her as she tried to understand what he had said. She dared to turn around and saw only the gist of him as he disappeared around the end of the aisle; she then looked down at her hand which was clutching the basket handle too tightly for a morning's shopping. She focused on releasing her grip and breathing again, trying to look interested at the goods as only a keen baker would and then she walked away, and wandered about aimlessly for five or six minutes in order not to shake nervously. She found herself at the checkout as a hollow person, scooped out, with just enough bones to move and skin left to enclose her nothingness; and also questions and howlings that could come up at any moment again and again, like the Hydra with so many heads.

She managed to return home, yet perhaps in a dissociative state, loading her goods into the kitchen bag by bag. Then, she turned suddenly, as if finally awake and scurried back up the corridor, somewhat slipping in her haste before yelling out, "James! ... James?!"

She did not quite scream it, but soon hurried footsteps could be heard coming towards her, rumbling down the stairs. "What is it? What's happened!?" he asked, his face white.

The story tumbled from her lips and she asked questions, of whether the man was credible, or was what he had to say of any worth, or if they were in far more danger than ever?

"What did he look like?" James asked.

She described the little that she knew and added in his manner of warmth and friendliness.

"Yes, that seems like him. Don't worry, he is one of mine."

"So then, I can't contact Luc at all?" she looked at James for an answer.

"Mer, no, not at present. Look I *will* do what I can to remedy this situation all right, I promise."

"But why did he come and tell me himself … I thought it could be one of the people who attacked you!"

"I know, I'm sorry, Mer. It's just that Sir John is doing all the work on the outside and getting the wheels set in motion, and as I'm stranded, sometimes he has to act before letting me know first. I think that's what's happened."

She nodded, still shaken and eventually went back to the kitchen, all the pleasure dissipated from her shopping trip. She decided to retreat then to her garden as she used to do weeks ago and sat there looking at the plants trying to be numb, yet unwillingly, sensed their colour and beauty as if sat inside a painting; it was little refuge, so she retreated up to her room and ran a bath, which she sat in hermit like, enveloped by hot suds and the weight of water.

That night she slept in her own room, after having been very quiet all evening. In an irrational rant with herself she felt that she had lost both her husband and her lover in twenty-four hours and so she felt afraid; her mother was so far away and tonight, finally, she needed her.

She awoke the next day with a start at 6am. It was far too early for her, and unpleasant to be awake, so she lay there drifting in and out of sleep, until there was a knock upon her door. James came in soon after and she looked at him from her bed, not caring about what she looked like.

"Hello, Mer."

"Hello," she said quietly.

"I just wanted to thank you so much," he said.

"For what?" she was blurry still, "oh, for staying here, that's all right."

"I'm leaving tonight."

"What?" She sat up.

"Yes, I have the all clear. I'll be out of your hair," he said.

"But, then I won't be able to contact you either?"

"No ... I'm afraid not. It hopefully won't be for too long." At her expression he sat down upon the bed and said, "I thought you'd be keen to get rid of me."

She sighed and looked so very sad.

"I'll make sure you can see Luc again, Mer.".

"Really?"

"Yes." He smiled. "I'm glad that he means this much to you," and he put his hand out to give hers a squeeze.

"You *will* say goodbye won't you, not just disappear?"

"Yes of course I will, but it will be late at night ..."

"Please make sure that you do." She looked him in the eyes as she said this, and then lay down again.

He nodded and rose to leave the room, looking back on her she was still as crumpled as her bed sheets, he added "Will you spend the day with me, Mer?"

She lifted her head, "Of course ... Where else would I be." And she smiled at him as best she could.

"So get dressed and meet me downstairs."

She came down to her kitchen wrapped in a cashmere over large red shawl, even though it was pleasant outside, and sat down. He made her a cup of tea and took a seat in front of her.

"Mer, I'm going to tell you some things if you want, but it's your choice if you want to hear them, I've made a decision that you deserve to know the truth."

"I want to hear," she said quickly.

"Very well. I'm going to France, we, I, have to get someone and something back from there urgently. I know you're thinking how with the embargo, well I need to go with someone with diplomatic immunity-"

Some dim awareness in Mer bristled.

"So I'm going in Luc's car ... with Luc ... He's been posted to Paris."

"Posted? For how long?"

"That is unclear," said James.

"Will he be really going? ... His flat?"

"Well you have a point, no his flat here will remain."

She nodded.

"Will you be safe?" she asked.

James cracked a devastating smile. "You're very sweet; I'll do my best to keep safe and him too. Will you keep yourself safe, Mer?"

To this she raised her eyebrows and thought to herself for a moment, "Am I safe, James? I'm thinking of the supermarket ..."

"I think you are, Mer, I do think so. Sir John's men are watching the place, no one hostile has been spotted since I landed at your home, I'm not even going to leave by your front door, and you and Luc never telephoned each other or connected through technology, or were filmed by CCTV, so there is no trail to follow ... It has been a pleasure."

"I'm never going to see you again, am I?" she said this with some emotion, clinging to the words like glue.

"Let's hope it doesn't come to that. Now, shall we do something to fill up the day, what do you say?"

She sighed, "Can't think of anything."

"Anything you want."

"Anything?" she asked earnestly.

"Well yes ..." he said mock warily now.

"I want to know things … I want to know all about Luc, how you grew up and I also want to know about you, all about you, your life, if you love somebody, everything." Something to be able to remember you by, she thought.

"Lord, woman, I don't tell anybody things like that," he said pleasantly.

"Yes, I guessed as much," and she smiled, although it was not such a happy one.

He studied her for a moment and then said, "All right, Mer, I *will* tell you. Hell why not," he shook his head to himself.

So he began and she was relentless in her own understated way, she was not going to let these two men leave her without having something of them as a token towards the sacrifice that she was about to make.

"Start at the beginning," she said, "when you were children ..."

She cradled her mug of tea that he'd made for her and sat forward to face him, this very beautiful man that was about to tell her everything.

Chapter 57

They had sat in the living room, all of them, after a very nice dinner of roast beef and roast potatoes that Mer had tried to help make. James was playing with baby Marina; she liked him as it was inevitable that she would, and Mer sat with a magazine that she could not read, as Christine watched the television. Christine and the baby had no idea that James was leaving that night. Mer looked about at this makeshift family of hers and felt unhappy that James was departing, but she was so full with the tales that he'd told her until lunchtime, that there was much to think about and she was looking forward to doing so once he was gone; although it would probably be painful.

Soon, too soon, Christine went to bed and carried her sleeping baby with her. When she was gone Mer looked at James and smiled, he looked worried, she realised that perhaps he had felt safe here and now he had to go.

"How will you do it?" Mer asked him.

"The same way Luc left. Our people have not found any surveillance going on here. So that's good. But I'm not going to chance going out of the front door anyway."

Mer and James sat with the television on until 2am, until it was time. Then he rose and so did she, switching the droning machine off. Facing her he looked very distracted, but wrenched himself back for a few moments, and then came towards her to take her up in his arms. She was surprised that he gave her such a fulsome hug that did not let her go for several seconds and so she held him to, retaining him for that moment; he had been her piece of Luc and now he was also something in his own right, someone she was fond of even though he had brought so much danger and separation and jaggedness to her life. Her blond haired hero whom now when she thought of, she thought of Clara as well: that mysterious, sleek, raven haired woman who sat coiled about his heart. James kissed Mer on her cheeks with force, indenting their softness and then he laid his hand upon her cheek so much like Luc used to, yet it felt very different, and said with all his heart, "Thank you, lovely lady. Be safe."

And then he left.

It was over too soon and then, James disappeared by climbing over her garden wall as Luc had done, while also managing to open Luc's back garden doors which were not locked. She watched him go and then an instinct made her run to the front of her house and to peep out from a corner of the curtains. There, there was a black Daimler sitting with its engine running, parked in front of Luc's door, it's nose sticking out sleekly, it made so little sound, a most polished deep hum, sure enough she heard Luc's building's front door shut and then witnessed James slide into the Daimler. The car hummed off and away, and she hoped that that black Daimler that bore him, was the right place for him to be. Her rooms and corridors were dark at that time of night, so she rushed upstairs, to her bedroom, where she had a desire to put a chair under the door handle as there was no lock. She was too tired and in truth too unhappy to think about either of them that night, so she went to bed but kept a lamp on.

The next day her mother rang as mothers do, as though through a telepathic primal cord and Mer buoyed by knowing a little about James' world, which had reduced her own problems into garden gnomes of paltry insignificance, finally told her the truth.

"Ma, I've been unhappy … Zaf left months ago … I'm going to get a divorce. I'll try and explain *everything* when I see you. Do you think you can tell Papaa for me?" the words tumbled out.

"Mer, darling, whatever it is we can sort it! I love you; now calm down … Where is Zafar? And for how long has he been away?"

"Ma, *please*, I would never tell you unless it was real. I can't explain on the phone."

"Well this embargo will be over soon, maybe in two weeks, nothing can happen till after then anyway, and yes … I'll tell Papaa."

"OK … thank you."

"I love you, baby. Bye bye."

Mer stumbled upon the phrase, that nothing could be done 'till after the embargo, this implied travel, which had no relevance to attaining a divorce, as all the divorce lawyers she needed were still in London as far as she knew. She bristled with suspicion, but at the time of the call had been too addled by emotion to place her unease. At least they know now, she consoled herself and then thought of her lost friends; James and Luc. So she then telephoned her boss at the gallery and said that she was coming in regardless, without pay to get a sense of what was going on until her work officially began. What could he do but say yes, although he added that it was all right but from Monday, which meant that she had the whole weekend to herself. Her one enjoyable task of going to the supermarket had been marred by her last visit, so she talked herself into going there again, to be strong.

The trip was manageable, yet her heartbeat elevated as she entered, she had little to buy having already been recently and too soon it was over, with no incident or mysterious men in dark suits to talk to, just blank looking people absorbed by potential purchases, and thinking about mundane things.

She came back home and looked desperately at Luc's first floor window from below, before going inside. She sat in her living room and switched on the television and rubbed her forehead, she then stood up abruptly angry and rushed to the kitchen, there, from a special cupboard she pulled out a clear bottle of vodka, which she poured and mixed with lemonade and ice, it was as strong as she'd intended and she went back to her sitting room after finding soft blankets to wrap around herself. She had drank a good gulp when she felt the heat of the drink course through her veins and the tolerable acid feel of it in her stomach as her limbs loosened and her mind unlocked itself. Soon she began to weep openly and she let herself; a box of tissues was nearby that was much raided. After this episode which lasted she did not know for how long, as time was of no use to her currently, she began to listen again in her mind to each of James' stories; each one a treasured jewel that she had claimed from him and was all that she had left now.

He had started at the beginning as she had asked him to, but during this personal recant the timeline meandered, as it was knocked about by her questions and enthusiasms for his tales of love, intrigue and betrayal and so, manifested finally into a swerving tale. She had learned too that he knew so much about her, more than she had known. At first, she tried to grasp and comprehend all the stories that he'd told her at once; as she had been given so much delicious information and it was as though her eyes feasted upon a banquet that she was poised to devour -but that led to confusion and a tangled mind; instead she had to take each course in its place and in order, with direction and purpose, as each bead on the rosary, one after next.

"Please don't be offended, it's my job you understand, but I've researched you, not just your life which's yielded few details, but the history of your family, where they came from and how your father or rather your grandmother claimed the house that you now live in ..." James had said and held her riveted, giving her a new sense of dark suspense, as even she had been 'researched'.

Her mind however then quickly turned to ideas and images of their childhood together: James and Luc, as it sounded idyllic, privileged in the scheme of things ... but, her attention then easily diverged and she remembered how at school she had secretly reflected that western children had no idea how different or easy their lives were, compared to the poor street children of Bombay's, or that of other poverty stricken places. She had been often taken to Bombay during school holidays, as her mother used to go home to see her own mother, and Mer had wandered room from room in that big marble floored apartment, in the dead still hours of the afternoon when everyone would take a siesta, except she, who could never sleep at that time. She had been taken once during these silent afternoons, by the servant, to her own tiny annex room where she lived with her husband and baby. The servant had been very keen for Mer to eat some plain noodles that she had boiled. Mer tasted them and they were awful, simply because they were plain and without salt. Mer was so young that she couldn't remember how she had declined from eating them, but did remember when a little older of trying to make sense of the episode, and felt that perhaps they hadn't been able to afford salt, and this fact then made her cry from pity. Now, in retrospect, she didn't know what to think, surely they could have taken some salt from the main kitchen which was their domain? Or it may have been a simple cooking mistake; but Mer never viewed that incident with that latter logic, she could not, the trauma she felt about that poor family, who had no salt in the small grey room, always stayed with her, buried, and resounded occasionally when she reflected upon her own opulence, or when people complained about their problems, then she always secretly thought of the East; it was to be deprived there to know what problems were she thought. But, she was just as guilty, culpable, as she did nothing to help those people either, apart from giving to charity as she was taught to do and she too dwelled indulgently on her paltry problems as she sometimes saw them, such as her marriage or her love life, when really she knew, that she had everything.

After these musings, Mer was directly led to think about her home again and that was a truly surprising story in itself …

"The house was once owned by a Lord," James had said, seated recently in this same sitting room, *"which is no great surprise, and his name was Lord Cavendish. However, he'd been posted to India for a time, not at all unusual, except that in his Will, for which lawyers had travelled all the way back to hot, sultry India for, he'd left the house to your paternal grandmother, Leila. It was only after Leila died that her son, your father, laid claim to it.*

"I don't think that Leila told your father until her last days about this house. I think, that she must have kept it a secret, the reason, I think, was that she must have had an affair with Lord Cavendish and a mighty great one at that for such a resultant romantic gesture, either that, or she saved him in some way. I found out when your father had come to claim this house, as there'd been some legal wrangling at the time. The house had been in limbo after having been requisitioned during the War, and couldn't go back to its normal owners as no one was sure who that was. Thank heavens for the steadfast and old fashioned continuity of law firms (!)" James had joked. "The knowledge about this Nash property had been passed down, and someone at the firm knew who its rightful owners were ..."

Mer's eyes had been wide when he'd told her this, as if enchanted by her own story. She herself had had to shake herself out of such fascination and try to be more observant and objective about what he was telling her. She had never expected stories about the deep past or about herself at all. But James knew so much, about her history and Luc's and even Christine's and he spoke and spoke, unburdening himself of the truths that he carried around in the solid citadel of his soul so that she worried now, as if perhaps she had been his confessor ... At one instance, she'd commented, "Lord Cavendish must have been a true romantic?"

"I agree,' James had replied. "Did you know that Luc's family name: Avium, descended back to Rome, -the last mention of which had been a woman named Aurelia Avium whose husband had been known to command ships to sail the seas as far as they would go, and that on Luc's mother's side there's also Tunisian blood, from the obvious involvement of France with that land."

Finally, James told her that Mer's mother's people, the Parsees had come to India from Iran, a Zoroastrian tribe and had made their home in the Gujarat; this last she knew well.

During Mer's recollections, the light in the room had changed and displayed in shadows the shifting of the day, Mer decided to vacate the living room in case Christine came home and found her drinking in the daylight. But before she left the room, she went to peek outside through the curtains, as if to be near the memory of the Daimler she'd seen, instead, only a tall man with curly hair was looking down at a map on the street. She went then to her bedroom, and continued to reminisce there until finally she fell asleep.

Much time later Mer guessed as the room was dim, there was a knock at her door and it was Christine, who came in unbidden after the preparatory knock. "Hello. Are you all right?" she asked.

"Yes, I'm fine."

"I can't find James, didn't see him this morning either."

"No. He had to go."

"So, he's gone ... just like that?"

"Just like that," said Mer.

"Shame, he was nice." Christine frowned to herself.

"Sorry, he means well, he had to dash," Mer added.

"All right. I won't ask. It sounds like you all want to keep a lid on something. Anyway, this came for you; I'm surprised you haven't opened it yet."

Mer eagerly took the envelope that she handed to her and struggled to open it, not wanting the paper to slice her finger. Christine stood to watch; she never did have any patience thought Mer.

"It's the college at Regents Park letting me know that the creativity class is starting again next Thursday."

"That's good, isn't it?" Christine asked.

"Yes," Mer sighed, disappointed. "I suppose it is."

"Mer ... have you been drinking again?" Christine asked her gently though.

"Yes, a little. Don't worry. It'll pass ... everything does."

At this juncture Christine walked over to her friend at her bedside and pulled her into an upright position, "Come on, up, up!" she commanded. "Mer, I know you're suffering, what's happened with you and Luc? Because something has, I can tell. The light's gone in your eyes. Also, I know that you've properly ended it with Zaf and that's good if that's what you want, but these things aren't easy, divorce in itself isn't easy, never mind falling out with your lover. What happened? Did Luc not know about Zaf, did he find out? Is that it?"

This was a brilliant idea and had not occurred to Mer herself, but it was a great excuse.

"Yes," Mer answered.

"So explain! Speak to him," Christine insisted.

"I can't, he won't talk."

"So, go over there. Force him to face you," Christine added militantly.

Mer was now regretting this tack as she had not calculated all these necessary details, so she added, "He's not there."

"What do you mean not there?"

"He may be staying somewhere else," Mer added.

"So keep trying. Do you want me to try for you?"

"No," Mer said quickly, but her friend's loyalty had warmed her heart and it was unpleasant to lie, yet she was tipping her hat to James for the moment; telling Christine the truth would have been unconscionable.

"It will be all right, I'll give him time, then I'll try," Mer replied earnestly and Christine at last desisted.

"Come on then get up, Mer, come and give Marina a bath. I insist, you're her family, come and play with her."

Mer soon obeyed Christine. Yet unwittingly -Christine had set ablaze an idea in Mer's mind ...

A week passed and in those seven days, Mer achieved a routine, she went to work although unpaid as yet, came home and tried to help with dinner and on

Thursday nights went to the creativity class, which had become a surreal experience; they had been asked to read 'Cider with Rosie' by Laurie Lee in that letter that she had received and she had already done so dutifully, many weeks back, as it had been on the reading list. Everybody had come, probably glad that the world was picking up where it had left off and the room, even though the blaze of summer had ebbed away to leave them the blank white clouded days of September, was still special, especially when the clouds burned away or parted and dappled sunshine lit up the rose coloured wood in spits and spots, nothing like it had been in heady July, but magical and playful for a few minutes, until the clouds came in upon the game and settled the room once again.

It was of course gawpingly apparent to Mer that one seat was empty and she glanced over to that chair often, in the hope that someone would suddenly appear. So much so that she focused less on what Mr Andrews said through his red bushy beard and instead pulsed in and out of his teaching, thinking about James and Luc and of what had happened to all of them this summer. The saddest part was when class ended and she walked home alone, head down, truly feeling the weight of absent friends. But the new idea that Christine had accidentally given her, still burned a quiet candle in her heart and when on Saturday it was announced that the embargo would be lifted in seven days, Mer began to give it real attention. Britons abroad had been advised to please stagger their journeys home as the airlines would not be able to cope. Of course, nobody listened and Mer's parents were booked on one of the first flights back. When Mer heard this news, she knew what it meant and her heart sank irretrievably; this strange summer would truly be over in seven short days and there was no other way to put it to herself; and yet it set her free, it set her free to go to Paris herself, and search for Luc, breaking every rule … Christine's fervour had placed in her this idea, and it only grew more insistent.

So she enjoyed this last week as much as she could as though everything would be gone in a week, including Christine and the baby's living arrangements and maybe even her own, although the house was hers she told herself and remembered the sight of legal papers and documents confirming this fact, and Christine surely wasn't going anywhere. Her routine was repeated much as the week before but with a degree of anxiety; she wanted each day to be completely hers and she hugged Christine often, surprising the latter and causing her concern, so too Mer often embraced the baby to kiss her eyes and face. How little she had appreciated them, her guests, and Christine had cooked Mer dinner almost every day that she had been there and had made sure that Mer had eaten as well. Mer attended her class diligently and tried to run through in her mind what might happen when her parents returned, perhaps they would want to see her and Zaf together, perish the thought.

*

Sunday arrived faster than necessary and her parents had landed from New York early that morning, she had arranged for their chauffeur to pick them up from the airport and waited for them at their St. John's wood apartment, finally excited to see them after all.

It was no sooner than they had arrived that her mother had tears in her eyes as she hugged and kissed her daughter, separated since the spring. Everybody settled in well enough and her parents wanted to take a siesta so Mer left them and went home, presuming that she would return in the afternoon, probably to face the music.

She tried to keep herself busy by re-reading her copy of 'Great Expectations', but concentration was scant. In the end she stuck her chin out, she wanted this divorce, there was no going back, she had no idea what she could possibly go back to besides; her marriage day, a loud and plush event, now felt as though a colourful circus spectacle that had been held in the last century, dusty and dated, inanimate and without life; in fact, her own singular new zeitgeist electrified her with the idea of danger and spies and the lost man that she loved; that in this modern day and age, she still could not reach.

In the early afternoon as she sat in her kitchen with her book, her doorbell rang, these days any surprise caused her an intense reaction, and she jumped. She went to answer and soon her parents were revealed behind the enormous door as it peeled itself open.

"Hello, Ma," said Mer; when alone with them spoke with a mild Indian accent, as perhaps she would have done when very young.

"Hello, darling, we thought we would come and see you." As they came in her mother added, "Is Christine here? Yes, yes I know about it," she added quickly and quietly. "I wanted to say hello and to see the baby."

"Yes, she is, I'll just call her." Mer knew that her mother would know that Christine was living with her and having marital problems, as word travels quickly in families and her cousin Rehan's mother, would have spoken with her. She hoped her mother did not know of every detail however, as Mer was very fond of Christine at the present.

"Wait, maybe we better have a chat first," said her mother, her face as pale as a lily's, yet skin pearly and dense as one of its petals with few lines and her father so different, much darker brown and angularly set, both dressed in smart western clothes yet both graced with the air of another country; as though they could never have grown up here.

"OK," said Mer.

Her mother and father found their way to the kitchen. Mer followed; not keen at all.

"So, he is not here, really?" her father asked in his usual quick to the point yet innocuous manner.

"No," replied Mer.

"Things must be very bad," he tried to say delicately. "I'm surprised you didn't move into our flat, this is such a big place to live in alone."

"I love this house, Papaa, it's wonderful."

"Yes but, alone, you are all right?" he asked.

Mer wanted to say yes, but instead she tried what seemed logical, "Well Christine has been here …"

"And that's another thing, doesn't your cousin think you are interfering, asking her to stay here, he is your cousin first you know …" he added.

"Well, she was my friend first also, Papaa, remember, but also, to be honest I didn't ask her, she just came."

"Oh, I see," her father nodded. Not seeing, but attempting to. Then added, "Darling, look, I don't want to interfere in your life, but I just don't understand this, you wanted to marry him. You *really* wanted to marry him. Has something happened? Did he do something?" her father asked so endearingly, as if ready for action.

Mer wished that Zafar *had* done something. "No, nothing like that Papaa, we are just …" and she squirmed, "incompatible."

"But, didn't you know that before?" he couldn't help but ask.

"Shezad." Mer's mother Nina, stopped him affirmatively. "I suppose these things happen …" she then added, nodding and looked at the empty cooker.

"Just like that?" quizzed Mer's truly baffled father. "But no one will tell me what has happened?" he protested, yet was still genial.

But the women of his family had closed ranks, so her father then sighed.

"So, you really want a divorce?"

"Yes."

"What will you do then? After you get it?" he asked.

"I have already gone back to work," Mer affirmed.

"And you'll come back to live with us." It wasn't really a question, more of a statement to himself.

"No," said Mer.

"No? So where will you live?" he asked.

"Here," Mer stated.

"With Christine? What about *her* marriage, at least give that a chance to sort itself out," he admonished.

"It has nothing to do with Christine, anyway, Papaa, that is not an issue right now, we can sort it out."

"Yes," said Nina. "Let it be, Shezad, you are getting obsessed with details now, don't upset her naah."

"Upset her?" He turned to his wife annoyed, but retreated upon seeing his wife's face and realised that this impending divorce was in fact a reality.

"Sweetie, go and get mama and baby, can't wait to see them," her mother instructed and Mer grateful, fled.

*

On Monday as Mer left for work, she saw again the same tall and curly haired man sitting in a car parked nearby as she passed. As she walked on, she felt the charge of a different atmosphere and looked habitually up at Luc's window to see that same blank dark stare, but things felt different. She noticed the odd airplane in the sky and felt a new tow, London was open for business; she felt excited, as if an unknown shackle had released itself and her breast was full of expectation, perhaps even hope as she took a deep breath wondering where this new freedom would take them now and possibly perhaps, if it would lead her back somehow, to her extraordinary lost summer.

Yet the days passed and there was no word, no clandestine message from a man in a dark suit or call on the telephone or even old fashioned letter; her lover and his friend the hero had dropped off the face of the earth. And so, the silence that Mer had so craved at the start of the summer truly mocked her now, she had been waiting and she had heard nothing, NOTHING from Luc. Not contacting him or James was one thing, but she had never expected such silence deep down, and the resultant feeling of complete banishment, or exile.

But she waited still, like a patient saint and went to work, enjoying its lack of structure; new art, old art, new buyers, expensive lunches with clients and open evenings wearing high heels for drinks and canapés at the gallery, which was a converted house in Notting Hill. She also went to her class diligently, as if still hoping to see Luc there. Six weeks passed in this way, London was on the cusp of November, to her mind that meant winter and on one Saturday morning she sat bolt upright in bed and said aloud to herself, "I'm never going to see them again, either of them!" And then promptly wept, like a woman at a complete loss. She soon heard her door open and Christine entered, took her in her arms, and did not ask any questions.

After that day Mer became quiet and subdued, she carried on her routine while a chasm began to open up inside her and she noticed that she carried it about wherever she went, as she sat at breakfast, as she stared at the baby, as she discussed a painting with a client and she never put up her hand up in class anymore, but as yet did still listen. Two weeks then passed like this, until finally she turned to the flame in her heart, her Plan B -if no one contacted her, and began to plot and plan in earnest … a voyage to Paris.

The season had changed just as Mer knew it would, it was cold as if summer was a far off thought and it was of course; winter had every right to be there, and who was she to condemn it? Her plan was to keep a watch on the British embassy in Paris, hoping that that would be where Luc worked. She knew that it was a ridiculous idea, he probably had offices somewhere else and it was a dangerous thing to do, she had only just escaped being able to be linked to either of the men. She didn't care, she was going to go to Paris, even if she had to dangerously dig for information as deep as she could, she had to go, to pursue Luc or the ghost of him.

She had considered calling his work to ask where he was, explaining that she was a friend, but then knew how many red flags that would send up, as that office was in league with James; but they weren't bad people she reminded herself and so that phone call was not inconceivable. She was determined to collate every scrap of information that she had on Luc, James and Mischa in order to find a lead; a way back to what she had lost. She considered using her own computer for this, but had gained by proxy enough knowledge to know that that would be a reckless thing to do, so she frequented different internet cafes, typing in the names of her quarry hoping that something would materialize and remembered that Mischa taught at Cambridge … his office number was easy to find.

"Hello, could I speak to Mischa Brearley-Jones, please," asked Mer.

"Ah, he's away on leave at the moment-"

"When will he be back?"

"Um … actually I'm not sure," said the receptionist. "Shall I leave your name and a message for you?"

"Uh, no I'll call back, thanks."

Mer thought that she could even drive herself there if she had to. She also traced Anjelica which had been easy enough as she was a psychotherapist and Clara as well, remembering that she worked for the U.N. in New York. She felt emboldened by all her leads, surely one would bear fruit if she tugged hard enough. But not one of these people were available, everyone was away 'on leave'. It was highly suspicious and worrying, and even though she knew she was in over her head she carried on collating, and read the newspapers for any sign of scandal or leak … or death -to see where she could find the hand of James' group, but she did not act quite yet, hoping still instead, that soon someone would come to her.

In this time Mer also saw her new divorce lawyer, to whom she had impressed the fact that her house was in her own name and that she didn't want to lose it. Apparently her ex had told his lawyer that the house had been a wedding gift, *to them both.*

Soon, it began to become very cold outside but the forbidding temperature itself did nothing to take the fire out of her grand plans. But, on December the first, Christine arrived with two delivery men and an enormous Christmas tree which was then hoisted up inside the living room -how could she leave now? Mer had thought, as she looked up at it, towering green and rooting her to the spot; Christmas was a time when her absence would be noticed -in the New Year, she told herself and this time she was certain.

And so, it was an empty season of goodwill for Mer, her work brought her revelries and parties and reasons to dress up, for which she did, sometimes helped by Christine, yet; she felt as though a corpse bride, mistakenly trying to wed herself to life. She played the part very well however and wore such things as a sleek grey dress that glinted a hidden shimmer as she moved, during her Gallery's Christmas party. People had looked at her, they could not help it, but Mer felt as though splayed open upon a surgeon's table, in this case her psyche the organ upon display as it were, and she had nowhere to look, so she looked at no one, as if her eyes were made of stone. For that winter season then, the glances that men and woman gave her fell short of the rule of the universe, of cause and effect, and they did not register with her, as she was not fully present at all.

However, during December an improvement could be felt, for no longer was she a stationary person, she had maintained her rhythm of continuing to work, study, as well as attend work related recreational excursions and so she dressed and preened as if ready for the world, that she sensed that she would be one day, as in her heart she clung to her plan to travel to Paris and to hunt for her lover there. She kept the scraps of information about her Luc and the people who knew him in a secret folder, concealed in her underwear drawer. As the season grew into hues of steel, iron grey skies, cold, wet and irritable, she thought of her file as a burning promise, although hidden, and then of the memory of the summer months that had been, now a cruel gift, as gloriously wondrous as she was left bereft without them.

As the New Year approached, her mother suggested, "Mer, darling, why don't you take a little holiday?" The suggestion caught Mer off guard, she had never considered leaving, it was as though she was maintaining a military post or manning a lighthouse, she felt anxiety; if she departed for a period and then returned, then surely everything would be too different and that summer could never find its way back to her; she grew gloomy knowing that human beings had no right to resurrect anything at all. Instead, Mer tried hard to contain her fear and expectation by taking herself to the nearest private club that boasted a large and decorous swimming pool. She submerged herself there as often as she could, and afterwards felt as though washed out and completely thrashed; as though all her fear and heartache had been beaten out of her by each watery stroke, or had been immersed in matter that was all consuming, so able to contain her and all that her burdened psyche brought with it. Inside the water was the first place that she allowed herself to abandon her mask completely, and so she swam lengths as if a driven thing, a water-creature much determined.

As the days counted down, her ritual in water had become a most devotional act and she always clambered out of the pool as a being experiencing the earthbound landing for the first time, her limbs protesting against moving into the burning air and upon matter that was not fluid; heavy muscles with a sweet ache wrenched from their watery frolics, stretches and pleasures. The heat of the shower she took as compensation for having left the enveloping pool, and she washed and lathered in an array of heady smelling things, careful always to avoid nectarine, and once dry skinned and damp haired she wore many layers, hiding her figure from the season and took the Underground back to her home. The Tube was sparser and empty now compared to the rush hour and some slept although it was not near late, or stared far off blankly as if alone on the trip.

Once, as she reached home, she saw again the tall man with curly hair on the telephone near her house, he must be a new neighbour she concluded and chided herself for seeing empty shadows.

By the time Christmas day arrived, Christine had turned the hall and living room into an old fashioned Noël spectacular. Even the kitchen boasted mistletoe hanging in sweet masses. It was again incumbent upon Mer to play a role and she acquiesced well in the Christmas duties, including a party that Christine threw at the house for friends and people that they both worked with. Mer had dressed up once more, now in burgundy silk and smiled occasionally until near midnight, when she looked out of the window onto the street, iron clad with cold and blackness and lit by a bulbous street lamp that cast its own beacon of yellowish light. Trees of the park hung behind like a spiky blanket, skeletons of themselves, their leaves vanished, so many stripped ominously bare. She thought at this moment, of where she was, exactly where she was, in this house, close to divorce, with an occupation that she liked and began to think, that this was all it was ever going to be, that this may be everything and nothing more, and that this was actually the reality of her life; the heady world that she had peeked into over the summer had perhaps closed its doors forever, and then, a vein in her temple throbbed.

She looked down at her hands, at her French manicure, and closed her fists at the sight, her plans must be realized she insisted to herself, but she knew that Christmas time was never a time to achieve anything and calmed herself with the promise of January, when the world would begin to stir again.

Christmas day itself was thankfully far more cosy; Mer's parents had come for Christine to cook them a feast. Christine had decided not to visit her own parents for Christmas, as Mer knew that Christine would have found it stressful; Christine had had to tell them the truth about why her own marriage was in disrepair, lest they blame her husband Rehan, and Christine had not wanted that horrid air of accusation hanging over her at her family's dinner table, as she was sure that it would; and so, they had not seemed to mind that she'd chosen to stay in London for the season of goodwill.

Instead their day was pleasant and jovial; Mer's mother doted over the baby and her father too had drunk some port and was pink cheeked. It was not their original custom to celebrate Christmas but they were happy to take part as was Mer, who very much liked to mark the occasion, as her upbringing in English schools had made her do so since she had been a toddler; from nativity plays to end of term Christmas feasts ...

She wondered as they sat around the kitchen table, what it would be like if Luc had been there as well, she knew since he'd left that she did not commit herself to anything with total emotion, and would not do so until she was sure that he was never coming back. She had never expected Christmas lunch to go so well and as it did, she was faced more and more with the idea that this, and only this, was her reality now; it always struck with a resounding blow; but one cannot strike someone who is not entirely present and so, her detachment became her armour while her campaign for Paris besieged her core; conversely protecting her from things that she refused to connect to.

Thus, by New Year's Eve, "I'm not going out!" Mer exclaimed, as she declined definitively to celebrate anything, insisting instead on babysitting for Christine; the latter had put up a great fight, but Mer had been adamant, she had had enough of celebration, it turned to ashes in her mouth. She was readying herself for her own mission and she did not want to falsely invest herself anymore; enough, was all she could think, so Christine retreated and Mer sent her away to a party.

After the baby had been asleep for hours and at midnight, Mer treated herself to a small glass of red wine, drunk from a half size table glass, and taken this time as communion, as well as a toast to both Luc and James.

New Year's day then dawned in cool sleek tones and weakened sunlight, gracing the beginning of a new time, and Mer woke up in her bed to see the baby sleeping on the other side of it, hemmed all around by white pillows; it was the sight of grace itself and Mer felt overwhelming waves of feeling towards the little life; the sight also set her spirit free, and she was truly ready to see Luc again.

*

The whistle for the train blew, and Mer gripped her arm rest. The train however left London slowly, as though they would only amble to Paris. She was ready, with maps, and a hotel for her near to the embassy. For the first time she realised, seated as she was ensconced in a heavy winter coat, with her red cashmere shawl bound about her neck, that she hadn't consulted her heart -her intuition, if this was the right thing to do -it had to be.

She had told her parents and Christine the truth, that she was going to Paris for a while, and had added, "To be alone", but that part was of course not true.

The train gained momentum at last and she wanted to pass the time, but all she could feel as the train powerfully gathered pace, was delicious and unbearable expectation; with each lurch and thrust, she had launched her own self she knew, and most likely there would be no going back.

Strangely, after an hour, her mind finally accepted where she was and what she was doing, and then she took a deep breath, knowing that she was definitely there and it wasn't a dream, so then, she drifted off; as the previous night it had been too hard to sleep, it had only been possible to sneak rapid glances at her packed suitcase.

Soon enough yet, French was being broadcast through the train, letting her know indeed, that she had arrived. Woken suddenly and faced with passengers already standing up and reaching for their bags she had no time to register any fear; but it was latent, making her actions jerky.

When she was in a taxi she thought about what she should do after checking in at the hotel, and decided to start her vigil as soon as she had laid down her bags.

On the large streets, she felt intimidated as she knew that she would, for the buildings in fine aspect, loomed above her in askance to her motives. But she scurried on, and found three doors down and opposite the British embassy, a café, as she had sought on the internet to make sure. There she brought with her: books, pens, paper and a laptop, to give her an excuse to spend her hours there.

She chose a good spot to view her quarry: The embassy doors, and knew it would be laborious, but she had come this far ...

She ordered a hot chocolate and a croissant. No one batted an eyelid, it was a good start. But, of course, nothing happened. Luc did not suddenly materialise, but she was too engrossed in her own passions to give a damn; it was now all, or nothing.

The day passed and she occasionally typed on her lap top, initial random nothings, but then after four hours a poem issued from her. But at 6pm, after a coffee and even a late lunch of hot soup and bread, she decided to quit for the day, her lack of sleep still not satisfied.

In her bed, as she lied down to watch TV and ordered room service, she was far yet from defeat. In fact, the air of Paris had given her an unexpected boon: a heady hopeful feeling, like a nudge to continue; as though the city of lights and lovers was very much on her side.

Three more days were spent like this. The café staff had become friendlier now, and suggested her hot chocolate as she entered before she asked for it. Mer even began an essay for her class, and looked up at the street after every three lines, in case, God forbid, she missed him.

On Friday, a freezing dusk was approaching although it was only afternoon, and Mer knew that it was unlikely that Luc would go to work on the weekend. Frustration filled her heart, where should she hunt! She had tried calling:

Anjelica, Mischa and Clara, all three more times and their leave seemed indefinite! Darkness hit the city, still yet clinging on to its dank frosty day, and the air of the weekend and frivolity rose up in the wake of it, making Mer feel even worse.

And then, she couldn't believe it: there he was.

Luc was walking on the other side of the road, towards the embassy, dressed in a suit and dark winter coat. Mer looked at all her paraphernalia and had not factored in this moment, so she just grabbed her handbag and said to the waiter (who was very used to her) in English, because she had no time to remember the French, "I'll come back!" Then she ran, out the door, and was hit by an icy blast. She was ready to charge across the road but the lights changed and the traffic looked ferocious. So she waited, watching Luc's every step, wondering if she had enough time before he entered the embassy and out of her reach.

Finally the lights did change and she was poised to sprint across the road. What hit her next completely blindsided her, and soon she was not only moving sideways, not towards Luc, but engulfed by a muscular stature far bigger than her own. She could not scream, so rapid was the attack, nor struggle to get away as the strength was unbelievable. Only her eyes cried terror and then he whispered quickly in her ear, "Don't struggle and don't scream."

Very soon she had been dragged into a side alleyway, where finally, he let her go.

She staggered back from him, and thought that that was it; her life was over, in a shabby alleyway what's more! But the man did not move, yet every muscle was tensed, both knowing that if she screamed, he would pounce.

Then, she saw it.

"You!"

"Mer, I'm sorry, I hope I haven't hurt you?"

"What? ... What? ... Why?" Mer couldn't yet be comprehensible.

"Calm yourself if you can ... Mer, my name's Michael, I work with James."

"You … you were near my house …"

"Mer, please breathe."

She was still standing hunched like a cornered animal.

"It's true, I've been watching you, it's nothing sinister which is why I didn't try to keep completely hidden, I wanted to look like part of the neighbourhood. James wanted his best man, namely me, to keep you safe."

Mer was trying to compute what the man was saying, "But then why-"

"Mer, you can't see Luc. A lot has happened. It's just too dangerous …"

"I know all about that, I don't care, look, I already know, it's not like I can find out now, I may as well be allowed to see him."

"But, what about him?"

"What do you mean?"

"Hasn't he made his decision? … Look, I'm sorry, but isn't it obvious?"

Mer opened her mouth a little, but no words formed.

"He's had time to think it over too, if he felt the same, wouldn't he have contacted you?" Michael asked.

"But he's trying to keep me safe …"

"He could have come to the same conclusion as you, but didn't."

"Well … I still need to know …" she said, yet Michael had planted an ugly seed …

"I know you do. But I'm afraid that's not good enough for me …"

"What do you mean? … You won't let me see him?"

Michael shook his head. "I'm sorry, no."

She gaped at him for a moment, trying to find a way out, but it became too cold to think. "… So, what now?" she asked instead.

"Now, you go home, young lady."

Tears of rage built up inside her, and she was more furious that she was going to cry in front of this large impediment. But she could not help it, her expectation and desire had exhausted her. In the freezing cold, she cried as she walked back to the café and shrugged off an arm he offered when she stumbled upon some rubbish.

Michael stood like a centurion outside her café as she went in and gathered her things, thinking how, if she could just lunge past him, across the road and into the embassy's open embrace, they would let her in; she had her passport on her and her driver's license, whereas Michael sounded Irish ... But she knew it was no good, and a huge, fat hot tear dropped from her face as she bent down while stashing her things away, hoping that the café staff could not see.

Upright and satchel packed, she looked at her overbearing guardian as he waited outside, she didn't care that her eyes were bulging and red. Now she hoped that perhaps Luc would exit the embassy and notice them on the opposite side just at the right time, but she also knew that if she dallied any longer, Michael would just come in and get her. She could scream and call the police and get Michael and everyone he was connected to into trouble -not a chance. So she walked on and out, into the dark icy air.

*

Seated once again on the Eurostar, there were no stars left in Mer's sky, and Paris pulled away from her and out of her grip. The pistons hammered and turned, each one burying its filthy nails into the coffin of her love affair. And there, sat right in front of her, was Michael, reading a magazine. He'd bought their return tickets that very day, and stood in her room as she'd packed.

Calmer now, as the hulking man sat serenely before her, Mer realised that perhaps her world now actually had more in it than previously, where she had no link and no news; for if Michael was to dog her, then wasn't he a constant link to James' world, and thus to Luc? And so, a new flame bloomed in her heart, for if Michael remained her faithful servant whether she liked it or not, maybe then, just his very existence paved a path for her return to Luc.

Chapter 58

Luc laid down a bouquet of flowers by the gravestone and then crossed himself; although there was no one else there, the action made him self-conscious. In summer this was a dusty place, with no spectacular headstones or ornate tombs as you would find at Père Lachaise in Paris. The sound of the sea could also not be heard, but the plain and simple expanse of the large plot, gave away that this was the graveyard of a small seaside town of no real importance; except that it was where his mother was from, and now laid to rest, and where his grandfather had lived, after winning so many medals during the War. And now he remembered his best friend; not quite a secret agent but on a similar hero's path, whose shadow contained the amount of lies that had to be told, to Luc and to others. He hoped that there would be no more lies now between him and James and the deception that had passed as an injury between them, would one day heal; neither though knew what aid they could give the rent to restore itself quickly or well, both relied on time and trust; the latter still an unstable concept. The other deceit had had far more a nasty sting; he had entered into a fancy game it seemed in London, with a woman who still yet despite himself ... entranced him. To this he had less charity; how very silly he had been to think that a woman who had so much money and grand abode, could ever be interested in a life with him. It bothered him, as he wondered if he had seen a mirage or had fallen in love with a delusion. He had been entertainment to her he conceded once again, and shook his head as it was not worth dwelling upon; he had far more important things to think about and far more drastic. Yet she lingered: *you are not being just,* a voice told him when he looked back at the waves in that town, it said to him: *let her speak* ... No, no, never he answered in his mind, as there had been too many lies now in his life.

He had come to visit his mother's town where he had spent so many summers with his friends and enjoyed so much happiness; it was gone now that time and his father was living in their tall terraced, white and blue trim home that had on it the house name: 'Demeter' -displayed in bright blue letters. Quite shockingly yet, as well as his father Vincent still living there, was Luc's mother's best friend, Isabelle, who was newly divorced. This had been a great surprise, enough to rattle Luc further considering the events of the past few weeks. Luc felt that he had no place to admonish his father and nonetheless, it was far too awkward. He had heard of this turn of events occurring after a death, of widowers marrying the friends or even siblings of a deceased spouse and he tried to be charitable, yet he could not stay there long and managed only two nights, in either event, he had to return to Paris.

Luc could not believe what had happened, events since he had moved to London were incredulous; but they were true, and he tried to reconcile his mind with everything that he had seen since then. For James' group as well he was sure, not since the War had anything like this happened to them; Anjelica was here now in France and Mischa had stayed for two weeks before he'd had to go back in order to hold things together ... Luc reviewed it all like a dream that happened weeks ago, that had now staked a claw into reality ...

That Saturday, after Luc had eaten his room service and felt eventually tight knots in his stomach from worry for his friend, the hotel telephone finally rang at 9.30 pm.

"Allo, is this the room of, Monsieur James Mackay?"

"Who is speaking please?" Luc decided not to speak in French, and let the heavily accented woman continue.

"I am a nurse at Jeanne d'Arc l'opital, Monsieur … I am calling you because we found this key card in his pocket, I 'oped that Monsieur Mackay was not in Paris alone …"

"Yes, yes this is his room … I am his cousin … what has happened?"

"Monsieur, please could you come immediately."

"Yes, what has happened?!"

"Monsieur James has been in an accident, I am sorry…" She pronounced 'accident' in the French way, and for Luc the room swayed.

He took down the address, pressing too hard with the pen. After putting the receiver down, Luc tightly shut his eyes and gathered himself, he then made sure that he tucked the mobile phone that James had made him take into his pocket, plus his other two, and quickly left. He took a taxi as he thought it would be safer and reached the hospital very glad now that he spoke fluent French. Again, he introduced himself as James' cousin, he wanted to say brother, but if they had wanted ID for anything it would have been a mistake. Someone then asked him, "Do you know who Monsieur Mackay had been riding in a car with this late afternoon?"

And Luc hesitated, he began to distrust the doctors, for why should they want to know that? Yet he made a snap decision and hedged his bets as well as he could, he said, "It was an acquaintance of James' called Simon, I think."

The doctor then asked, "Do you know this Simon?"

To which Luc responded, "Yes … but distantly."

"So you wouldn't know how to get in touch with his next of kin?"

Luc replied, "James' friend in London may know of how to do that, why?! What's happened?!"

The doctor paused and sighed. "Monsieur Simon has received catastrophic injuries from the accident."

The doctor then waited.

Luc did not understand, so the doctor had to add, "Simon is dead, I am very sorry."

Luc's breathing became shallow, his voice could not ask the next question, and the doctor continued, "Your cousin is in intensive care, he has a badly fractured skull, two broken ribs and a very badly broken leg and is in an induced coma. We cannot say yet anything about if he will recover; more can be said after he lasts a night or two."

He went on to request that Luc get him all the details of the next of kin of both men, "As there may be an embargo on, but the families still need to know, from the *hospital* ..." he added.

"I want to see him!" was all Luc could say.

And so Luc was then led to a private room, to see James for ten seconds. James looked as though besieged by machines and wires and bandages, lying flat, devoid of personality, an inanimate badly beaten man. Luc fought down a wave of emotion. As he was led away he demanded, "I also want to see Simon, please."

The doctor looked at him unsure.

"What if it is someone else? And not Simon?" Luc added. It was true that it was imperative that Luc identify the body before informing the family, in case they were wrong.

Luc was led to the lift and then through dull basement corridors, with over bright lights, to the mortuary, where lay Simon, also inanimate, and a bloody blue mess.

Luc said nothing, his heart in his mouth.

"Monsieur ...?"

"Yes, yes this is Simon."

The doctor nodded, "Please could you do me the service of getting the next of kin details?"

Luc agreed, after he thought, he spoke to Mischa and then Anjelica, yes, it would be done in that order.

"What happened? Do you know? What kind of accident was it?" Luc asked the doctor as they exited the mortuary, he had been kind enough to accompany Luc continuously through the hospital.

"I don't know, just that their car was hit by another when they were in a tunnel," replied the doctor.

"So were the other passengers hurt, in the other car?"

"Not that I know of ... in fact that is true, maybe they went to another hospital ..." he began to think to himself.

"Does that happen a lot, victims going to different hospitals?" asked Luc.

"Well, sometimes in big casualty cases, but this is very unusual ..."

Before Luc thanked the doctor and promised to return soon with the contact details, he asked him exactly which tunnel the crash had occurred in.

Luc had a plan, and could not make his way back to James' side until it was complete. First he made his way by the Metro to the tunnel where the collision had occurred. He walked up it as far as he could, it had been cordoned off, there were lights flashing from a stationary ambulance and police cars everywhere. From what he could see, there was only one car that was damaged and had crashed. After a period of looking about he leaned over a cordon and asked a policeman in French, "Will it be long to clear? How many cars were in the crash? It looks awful."

"Well, we think two."

"Yes I can see one of the cars, has the other been cleared already?" Luc asked, concerned.

"Well that is the thing, from what it looks like, one car must have hit the side of the other, sending it to hit the wall, but there is no other car," said the policeman.

Luc nodded.

"Sir, you shouldn't be here you know," the policeman added politely.

"Yes don't worry, I'll go. It's just awful." And Luc turned away to leave.

The policeman nodded, and watched Luc walk away.

Luc then quickly made his way back to the hospital and made his first telephone call.

"Hello, Mischa. Are you with Jelly?"

"No, what is it, Luc?"

"I'm telling you this first. Are you somewhere you can talk?"

"I can talk, I'm at home," said Mischa, with a note of alarm.

"There's been an accident. Simon's dead … James is in intensive care." Luc felt it best to be quick and direct, he knew that Mischa would understand.

"It looks like another car hit theirs on purpose, the police haven't found the other car, nor were there any casualties from it. I need Simon's family's details for the hospital …"

"I'll have to tell them first, Luc, can you wait half an hour before giving it to them?"

"Yes, of course. But I'm going to tell Jelly, Mischa," said Luc firmly, as though it was his own duty.

"Very well … Do you know … do you know if he'll be all right?" Mischa then asked, trying to keep his voice as steady as it had been throughout.

"I don't. The doctors said it depends on how he lasts the night." Luc then reeled off James' list of official injuries. "By the way, they know me as James' cousin."

"OK. Good luck to you, Luc, I'll be there as soon as the travel embargo is lifted. Please keep me posted, oh and tell me which hospital and hotel you're at, I'm going to scramble a protection team now."

"Are you going to manage Jelly? She might attempt something foolish, like trying to come here …"

"I'm going to drive to her house right now."

"Thank you, Mischa." And then Luc reeled off the addresses that Mischa needed.

"Thank *you*, Luc. I'm glad you're there," finished Mischa.

Next, Luc prepared himself to phone Anjelica.

"Hello, Jelly?"

"Oh hello, Luc, all right?"

"Jelly, where are you, love?"

"At home, why?" she asked pleasantly.

"There's been ... an accident."

There was only silence on the other end of the line, as if it reached a foreign, unwelcome land.

"James is alive," he added quickly, "but, he has some injuries ..."

"What injuries?" she asked rapidly.

Luc reeled them off again, feeling nothing but her dread.

Silence now from her.

He could tell without even seeing her, that she had tears streaming; that was how she cried. "The doctors won't say anything until the morning, but he *is* stable though, Jelly, and I'm staying here!"

"You are, aren't you," her voice shook.

"Of course I am! But there's more, and I need you to be brave."

"OK," she whispered.

"Simon did not survive the accident."

"What?!" she said much louder than before.

"Yes. He was also in the car. I've seen the body."

"Oh God. Oh God, Luc, you have to understand, you have to keep James safe. Oh God!" She had finally understood the full extent of what had happened and why.

"Don't worry. Mischa is on his way to you, he will start all the balls rolling. All right?" Luc tried to reach her.

"Luc, I have to come!"

"No! You can't Jelly. Don't you dare. You have to trust me! I know everything now. I know what to do. Stay put! I mean it. As soon as the embargo is over you can come, all right?"

"… OK," her voice shivered.

"Mischa will be there very soon."

"Thank you, Luc. Thank God you're there," and she kept saying it to herself.

"Anjelica. Keep a hold of yourself, think what James would do, would *want*."

Finally after fulfilling his mission to the old doctor, Luc was now free to sit in one of the hospital waiting rooms until the morning.

But then it hit him, that James may not last the night, or maybe the week. And so, he set off to find a quiet unused room and shut the door behind him.

There, he switched on Simon's last cargo: the phone, and first looked at all it's stored photos. Nothing. Then he played its recordings, and listened, his ear close.

"You want me to secretly supply free arms to any country you want to self-destabilise through civil war, uprisings or unrest?" said a man with a French accent.

"That is precisely what we would like you to do, Monsieur Grimbaud."

Luc's eye's widened; it was Minister Sebold's voice!

"But what would be the reason for us, why?" said Monsieur Grimbaud.

There was a pause in the recording, and Luc could hear a background muffled sense of a restaurant, or tea room.

"An exclusive contract with the British Government," answered the Minister.

Grimbaud ... Grimbaud, oh yes, he remembered James now telling him that name, he was dead of course. And then Luc also realised, that he held in his hand the missing piece of the puzzle; a way out for all of them -and Sebold's damnation. Luc felt a thrill, and then extreme protectiveness, -this recording must not be lost, and he also thought about if he should have Mischa release it immediately, to set them free perhaps. But he would wait the night before asking Mischa that, to see James' progress.

Luc went to his new spot outside James room, and chose to sit for a great part of the night in an uncomfortable chair. There was no way he could sleep even though the night was quiet; no one was present apart from the odd nurse. Then, during the small hours, knowing that Mischa had probably told the right people to help keep them safe, and that they could even be there or be arriving soon, Luc's eyes began to droop. It was then that a tall, slim man in a black suit, walked towards Luc, no moreover towards James' door. The sight was incongruous, such a neat black suit and at this time of night, when there were no visitors, the staff having turned a blind eye to Luc's presence. Luc quickly stirred and became fully awake, sitting up from his coiled slouch; the man, Luc could tell had almost stretched out a hand to turn James' door knob. Then it seemed to happen in slow motion, but it was very quick: Luc looked at him, and the man seemed to desist from fully touching his hand to the door knob, he looked back at Luc, straight in the eyes, then turned around and left. Luc's heart pounded out a machine gun battle rhythm. That was no normal or civil response, and so Luc took out his phone and dialled Mischa, to get progress on the security team; it was terrifyingly apparent to Luc, that they were not there yet.

After Luc quickly relayed what had happened to Mischa, and Mischa told him then to get off the line, Mischa texted back:

15 minutes.

Luc stayed awake and alert in his chair, then got up and opened James' door -yes he was still breathing, the tubes like his new appendages.

Half an hour later, a doctor and a male nurse walked towards Luc.

"Mischa sent us," said the 'doctor'.

Luc nodded, and waited to see what they would do next. The 'nurse' then went to the nurses' station, and the 'doctor' sat down opposite Luc, took out a clip board and notes and medical charts, and seemed to set to work before him. Luc was much relieved, and said, "He was tall, thin and sallow faced, and in a black suit."

The 'doctor' nodded.

"Get some rest, sir," he told Luc.

Luc could not rest or sleep, yet somewhere near dawn, reassured by the bodyguard's presence he must have drifted off. On waking in the morning, Luc found a different real doctor standing outside James' room, so he explained again that he was James' cousin and asked for news.

The doctor said, "It's a good sign that James has remained stable through the night, but his leg's in a very bad condition and it's going to need surgery, with most likely the insertion of some metal parts. We've scheduled the surgery for today, as the leg can't wait. You should go home, Monsieur, have a shower and please eat something. You need to be strong for your cousin. Come back at 2pm when the surgery will begin."

Luc had no intention of leaving, but then the 'doctor' spoke, still seated opposite him, with never ending notes. "He's right, sir. We have full scope of the floor. Please be assured."

Luc nodded and then once more, sought out now instead an empty store room, and phoned Mischa.

"What news?" said Mischa.

"He's OK, stable, surgery on his leg today, may add some metal parts. Docs say leg can't wait. It's at 2pm our time. Mischa, I've listened to Simon's recording, his last mission … It's Minister Sebold doing a dodgy arms deal with Grimbaud. Do you want to release it? Strike back, end this?"

"Luc, calm down. It's seriously excellent that you've got the recording. However much I want to act, we still have to know how deep this goes, so we need to see the Minister tip his hand further. I'm sorry, but do you understand?"

"Yes, yes OK. I'll keep it safe then."

"Good man."

"The docs want me to go home and shower, eat, but there's no way I'm leaving-"

"Luc, they're right, you need to keep your strength up. Philip and his team, they're our people. I have total faith in them. Go and wash up, the hotel is secure, come back fresh. I insist."

"Can we move to my aunt's flat in Nation, I want to get out of that hotel. Just give me an hour to move our stuff there." Luc gave Mischa the new address.

Luc left clutching the special mobile phone to his body and knew that he immediately wanted out of that hotel room, if nothing else but as a reminder of a terrible day. He had brought with him from London the keys to his great aunt's disused flat in Nation, that he used to stay in whenever he was in Paris, thinking that it might have been nice to stay there in case he hadn't liked his hotel.

It was true that he was due to go to work the next day, but as it was Sir John and Gemma that decided what his work was to be, he had free reign to be at James' side, and so, that is what he did for two solid weeks until the embargo was lifted, and then Mischa and Anjelica arrived as soon as was possible. Clara, having been informed of James' accident from Mischa, bothered Luc no more.

It was a relief to see them, James was improving but was not fully cognisant yet, he was in a lot of pain. So Luc had sat in a chair by his bed and read Wuthering Heights, while his friend coasted on a sea of morphine. Anjelica and Mischa took shifts to care for James, Luc had insisted that they all stay together in his three bedroomed flat and meanwhile, Simon's body came to be claimed by his parents to be repatriated.

That was a hard day indeed, they were all there that day and Mischa was the one who had to greet them solemnly and apologise for their loss. Soon, Luc was asked to attend meetings and liaise with French and European trade delegates, to fulfil his official function there. Thus, he experienced many gatherings set in hotel conference rooms or over elegant lunches, boasting rich and plentiful food, and an opulence that belied everyone's frustrations.

The weeks continued like this and Luc and Anjelica now took shifts between them to be with James, as Mischa had had to leave after two weeks; he had to take charge of the group and liaise with Sir John to collate all the information they yet had on their foe. A month passed, until finally one day as Luc sat reading in his usual hospital chair, James stirred, and so Luc looked up; James seemed to be looking for water which Luc quickly provided and helped him to drink it; in this small action alone everything changed, and a corner was turned.

"Hello, Luc, how are you?" asked James, in a croaky voice.

"I'm very well, how about yourself?" Luc replied, but with some tenderness.

"Oh well, you know, can't complain ... We haven't talked," James added.

"No, we haven't. Largely, because you've been in a coma, on drugs, or sleeping." Luc smiled then added, "The place has been swept; we can talk."

"Simon?"

Luc looked down at the floor; he had forgotten that this would be the first question.

"Luc?"

"James ... Simon's dead."

James closed his eyes.

"Don't worry, everything's been done, everybody's been told, Emily and George have already even taken the body home, they had a small funeral."

"Oh my God, I've missed so much," James said more to himself.

"Just that, nothing else," Luc insisted.

"And you've been here?" James asked him.

"And Jelly, Mischa came for two weeks in the beginning, he may come back depending on how you get on, but he knew the protocol as he put it, so he went back, he said it's what you would have wanted him to do."

"Damn right."

"James, you're still recovering. Be calm ... it's a lot to absorb."

"Don't you want to know what happened? Oh, and do you still have it?" James' blue eyes took on more focus.

"I've got it, it's safe. We've got Sebold on it. We can take him down, but Mischa wanted to wait ..."

"Mischa's right."

"OK, so ... do you know what happened?" asked Luc.

"Yes, well in part. That day, after I left with Simon, we didn't take a direct route, we drove about to be careful, then while we were in a tunnel we were rammed into the wall by two, four-by-fours. One after the other, to make sure we were finished. Simon was closest to the wall and he didn't stand a chance."

"... I keep it with me all the time, you know."

"Good, good ..." Then James laid down his head, and went back to sleep.

James' waking moments became more frequent after that and soon the physiotherapists got a hold of him as they do, and forced him to walk upon his reconstructed leg. This was easier said than done; Luc watched as two of them would hold James by the arms as he tried to take each shaking step. Progress was slow and Luc wondered if James would ever be able to walk properly again, in secret he asked the old doctor about this, to which he was informed, that failure was a possibility. Luc also wondered if James knew, that he may not make a full recovery, but never brought it up; instinctively knowing that for him such an attitude would be detrimental. Weeks passed like this, Anjelica had put her Practice on hold and her clients had been left to wait, for which most of them were good enough to oblige. Luc was glad that he'd made her stay with him in the flat at Nation, which as one of its quirks, had in it a small square bathtub, inside which one could only stand upright under the bulldozer of a shower; yet it was a cosy place, away from the tourists and the expensive shops and opulent museums.

One evening before Anjelica was about to leave to see James, they were able to speak, Luc was making sure that she ate something before she left and her mood was far more lifted than it had been of late, linked as it was to James' condition; which as he took faltering steps, seemed relatively bright in comparison to the past six weeks. For the first time she looked up from her plate and asked him, "How are you, Luc?"

Luc looked at her, not sure of her meaning.

"I mean, can you ever forgive us … for not telling you, did James make you understand?"

"Oh, that … yes he explained everything. I understand."

"No, you don't." Anjelica said, in gently mocking tones, her beauty and demeanour never disclosing her professional abilities, which of course made her an excellent reader of people. More so, she knew Luc better than he ever imagined, as she had observed all the older boys talk and play together while growing up, while she had only been seen as a small thing in the corner. She had watched both Luc and Mischa confide in James as teenagers, or during their low moods when they'd sat about with each other as youths, thus, she could stand testament and bear witness to all three of the men's development and inner circumstance. "Maybe one day you'll forgive us. I'm sorry, we've already cost you so much, and you've only known for a few months," she finished.

"Cost me?"

"The girl."

"The girl? ... You know about that?"

"Yes, James told me ... in one of his lucid moments last week. The one you all went to dinner with. It was important, wasn't it?"

"I thought it was," he sighed. "It wasn't you know, I was wrong."

"I don't understand, from what James said it sounded-"

"Yes I know, but it was a lie, Jelly. I found out just before I left that she was married, he'd just been away... It was a complete charade."

"Oh ... James never told me that," she said surprised.

"He doesn't know that I even met the husband! He shook my hand, while introducing himself to me outside our building."

"I'm so sorry, Luc," she said with a small frown of sympathy for him and also of confusion, she would realise later as she chewed upon the knowledge that something did not fit.

"It's all right. I don't dwell on it," Luc shrugged.

"Well that's because we've been so busy, for want of a better word." But the anomaly began to infiltrate. "It really doesn't make sense though, from what James described when he saw you together, he was so sad about taking you away from her, it had made him happy to see love like that -sorry to use the word. She can't have been that good a liar. Very few people are."

Luc looked at her, and then looked down.

"You haven't been able to speak to her to clear this up, have you?"

He shook his head and also shook it away, "Nor do I want to, honestly it's over, I shook her husband's *hand*, for God's sake, Jelly, its humiliation enough." His cheeks took on the hint of a flush.

"So it isn't a matter of whether or not she leaves her husband ... is it?"

"... No. She lied to me, used me. For some excitement I think. And he showed no sign of being near an exit."

Anjelica still frowned as she listened, her skills and instincts keen to solve the mystery and amongst all this death and sadness, restore what she had been told was a beautiful thing.

"You're going to tell him aren't you, that I met the husband," said Luc.

"Don't you want me to?"

He shrugged.

She then rose and gave Luc a big kiss on the cheek to say goodbye and he was left alone in the flat, keen to find a film to watch, a distraction, but it was too late ... Anjelica had taken down the veils and draped black cloths that he'd shrouded over Mer's image ... And so it began again ... whenever he thought of Mer, he thought of her flesh, not in any base way, but of the feel of her, her scent and cool calm warmth, that finally he'd seen open to him, as a lily in its last days of splendour; aching wide. Who had she been, if she could lie so well? She had seemed so kind and demure, especially in the way that she'd cared for James and taken such risks in letting him find a refuge with her. Yet Luc met him, the man who claimed her, as cheery and bright as though his wife was faithfully devoted to him. In any case, Luc had always believed that marriage was sacred and now, he had accidentally transgressed his own code. It must be shaken off, he was not interested in the truth; she could not redeem herself by it. He had shown her all the kindness in his heart, so he now took a black cloth again and painted dark swabs over her memory, erasing her from view, and so, only the sense of her remained; the scent of her skin, the cherished feel of her flesh, as if it was a sense memory, embedded into his very own living skin; and now, something which he could not accommodate. But soon, before he knew it, he was standing and ready to leave the flat, hospital bound, to speak to James.

It was ludicrous on all levels, the woman had betrayed him, but he still took one foot in front of the other to find himself knocking on James' door, where

Anjelica sat next to him, a smile on both their faces to see that Luc had come to join them.

By this time James had had the bandage on his head removed and it revealed an indelicate method of shaving some of his hair off; jagged markers in red and black disclosed where things had cracked inside. His feet had on soft slippers that Anjelica had bought especially for him, but were still very pale in the hospital light.

Luc sat down and listened to the conversation that they were already having, about when James could return home. James wanted to return as soon as was possible and to continue his treatment from London, but Anjelica wasn't sure about that at all, and instead of being overtly resolute, was trying a gentle tack by asking that he please stay put until the doctors thought it would be all right to move. Luc knew that inside she was actually adamant; she had looked after her brother with determination and fervour, and she probably felt that James was all that she had left. James did not have it in him to fight too strenuously, but he had made his feelings known, so that the proceedings could begin, as familial loyalty aside, he outranked everyone, and would and could play that card if he chose.

After this they fell silent for a time, idly listening to a French documentary on the little television that hung in a corner, so in this pause Luc took his chance, "I wanted to ask you a question, James, if you're feeling up to it?"

"Yes, sure, of course." James tried to raise his head, which he then lowered again, realising his mistake.

"Did you tell him, Jelly?" Luc asked her.

"Yes, I hope it's all right."

"It's fine. James, I wanted to know what happened, on that day when her husband came, Mer's ... - what happened then, did he stay? Don't worry -just tell me everything you know, seriously, I need to know everything, however it is." Luc readied himself.

"Nothing happened, Luc, it's over for them and she told him that, she asked him for a divorce," said James, meeting Luc's eyes.

"Really?" Luc sat further forward on his chair.

"Yes, really."

"… But he moved back in?"

"No, he stayed for one night, and then left. He slept in another room and Mer slept in your old room -every night."

"So, he left?"

"He went very soon, Luc, I'm so sorry that you didn't know."

"… But, it doesn't change anything." Luc stated in a final type of manner.

"It doesn't?" James asked him innocently.

"James, she lied to me."

"Yes … so? I lied to you … we all did."

"This is different," said Luc, unalterable.

"This is worse than the secret your best friends have kept from you, for your *whole* life?"

"Well, if you insist on depressing me …"

"I think, Luc's saying that her feelings can't have been true," said Anjelica.

To which James replied, "You should have seen them together, Jelly." His eyes blue liquid pools of memory, through which he tried to convey to her, the pure visceral sense of it.

"But none of this is relevant anymore, have you forgotten why I wasn't able to contact her in the first place?" said Luc.

Anjelica took it upon herself to intercede again, "That's the risk we all take. She knows about us, as do you, yes hopefully she's been saved from a connection to us, but if you really want her … it's a risk you'll have to take, for you both."

"It's not fair, to put her at any risk," said Luc, sure of it.

"Indeed," replied Anjelica.

"I don't want to say anything, but I think we have a degree of containment; we have some idea who was behind the attack on us, and we're just waiting to see if Minister Sebold has other allies, or a new hand to play. We've got the means to destroy him at least, with the recording you carry around, Luc. That was Simon's last mission; he'd posed as a waiter to record the conversation here in Paris, between the Minister and Grimbaud. I know because he'd let me know this before the embargo and his betrayal, I imagine that the Minister was no fool and knew that once Grimbaud and the others had been silenced, that everything may be known about his connection to them, and so, went after us ..."

"I still don't understand how they were able to find out about you and the few others in that first list I saw? The connection with Simon was just not visible enough, from how you make things sound," said Luc.

"Yes, I know, but I have a theory: Clara told me that there had been extra checks on her security in the spring, and I found out later that her file had been requested by another UN agency branch. She'd thought that it was me, keeping a check on her. I can only guess that Simon had kept a romantic record of her in some way, either something such as a letter, or more simply a photograph. Working relatively prominently as she does, a photograph of hers would eventually manifest in a data bank, as it may have done. So it was her, I think, and her link to both Simon and I, that brought them eventually to our door -but you can't *ever* tell her this. They must have found my previous connection to her quite easily, and once they'd found me, well, the rest came easily as well. Sir John hasn't acted yet; Michael has been key in letting him know who was behind the hit squad that attacked me and in helping him; Sir John now has the key parties under surveillance and would know if any more actions were planned. The Minister had used the evacuation as a good time to snoop on our home addresses, the few that he had, or in my case, to attack the source. They would be keen to get their hands on that phone of yours ... so we've been dormant for a while, no more leaks."

At that, the shadow of Simon's ghost hung over them briefly, as James continued, "And, things do seem contained, the other party probably knows that we're on to them, but they still don't know, thank heavens, that Gemma is one of ours, otherwise we wouldn't be here having this conversation, I've got protection on her especially though. We'll contain them properly, but once I know everything … and then I'll release the recording."

"Should I let Clara know now, that it was me …? She of course hasn't contacted me again since your accident."

"No, Luc," said James. "Not yet, let this all be finished, the less she knows the better … but my point is, is that I think we should live as best we can, it's up to you if you want to bring Mer into this."

As James said her name aloud it was like a brief verbal slash into the air; Luc did not like hearing it, it was a reality that he wanted to be diffuse and opaque, like the lost vestige of a dream.

That evening, as Luc and Anjelica left James, it was a freezing wintery Paris in January that greeted them on the street, and they took a taxi back to the flat as a luxury, both buoyed of heart from James' pep talk. Thankfully, Anjelica never mentioned Mer at all on the way home and once returned, let Luc simply fall asleep. He was exhausted enough to let his senses, that could not contain what remained in him of her, be overridden by slumber.

The next day, James phoned Luc and told him that all the plans were made; the three of them were to return to London, post haste.

Chapter 59

A large heavy bound book hurtled through the air and hit Maurice as he did not duck in time; so that even though his hands were up defensively, a visible open streak of blood now graced his temple. Every sinew in his body wanted to act, retaliate, but he stood still, hands still up and ready.

"And these!" The Minister slammed down on his desk a handful of small black things, like metal beetles. "I've had Jones in here de-bugging the place twice a day!"

At that Maurice glanced at a small device on the corner of the desk, with lights going up and down, gauging for bugs he knew. Maurice then lowered his arms and looked at the file he had set down moments earlier on the desk before the Minister, where Lucian Avium's photo still looked up at Minister Sebold.

Maurice' head hurt.

"All along! All along we've had Mr Avium to thank for this bloody disaster … Armstrong, Burgess and Grimbaud dead, my office bugged, that Clara woman disappeared, and James Mackay -the 'prize' you told me, got away from under our nose, twice!! No, three times because you failed at the hospital. And now, and now, you bring me a nice bit of 'proof', that the man you found sitting outside Mackay's hospital room, is Lucian Avium! Well I could have told you, that Mr Avium works in the same office as Sir John Balthazar, and has been couriering all our files, all our info back to him! That Gemma was useless; we had already started looking at Avium. And now the proof: Avium and James Mackay went to primary school with each other! And then lived next door to each other for almost their whole lives!!! Maurice, my dear, your reputation precedes you, but shouldn't you have found this out –months ago!"

"Sir, it was only by seeing Avium, could I have found that he had been staying with Mackay in Paris, and then I could research their history together, I didn't know who he was before that … and, sir, you had met Avium many months ago, surely you too could have-"

"That, Maurice, is not *my* job. It's yours!"

Maurice stayed silent, the open wound on his head completely ignored by the Minister.

"I want it finished, now. Find them all and finish it, even the girl, Gemma, not only was she useless, but she knows about me and my setup. She has to go. And do it yourself, outsourcing hasn't worked for you at all, that mess in Paris! And keep it quiet, there's a few people to get through and London's a busy place. I swear if you fail me now, Maurice, I'll make sure that you're finished."

"Yes, sir. It will be done."

"Well, what are you waiting for, get out!"

Chapter 60

Maurice listened to his own footsteps as he approached the house. *They never learn*, he thought, and looked back at the man sitting on a bench opposite the house. That man was stationary now, staring at what he was supposed to protect with eyes wide open. Maurice had simply sat next to him, and then pretended to drop his newspaper, on the way back from retrieving it he had used his favourite method of despatch: and quickly stabbed him with a small poison tipped weapon, so minute, that it was too late by the time the sentry knew what had happened. For, he must be a guard or sentry, someone to watch her house, keep it safe. No longer, and Maurice was also now in no mood for subtleties, as the burgundy and purple graze on his head attested. It was 6am, no one else was about.

He looked at the entry phone and smiled. Then he took out his gadgets and silver skeletal keys, each one jagged with testimony to Maurice's reputation. He entered the house, still, in the quiet morning …

His footsteps made no sound now, as he trod around the corner, to peek into the living room, and there she was, Gemma dear, sitting on the sofa; he thought he'd start from the bottom up of whatever annoyance of a group this was. He did not quite enter yet as he peeked; a steaming mug lay in front of her on the coffee table, and light suffused the room, glancing off the -he noticed- rather decorously huge mirror. He knew that if she turned her head to the left while he made these quick deductions, she'd see him. He had a silencer ready on his gun, but no … he wanted more than that. There were about five paces between the doorway and her, so when he struck, it would have to be fast. At last, she closed her eyes and yawned; it would be her last.

Maurice lunged, and soon grabbed Gemma about the throat; the hot mug as he had calculated hit the floor and shattered, unfortunately partially spraying his suit. She thrashed; he admired her spirit, for her eyes had not only that same old terror, but also great defiance, as if to admonish him: *how dare you!* they said. He dragged her by the neck so that he had her on the floor, and her legs put up such a struggle, kicking at the sofa, at the coffee table. At last Maurice could release some of the tension from this particular job; the Minister was right, these people, who confused him at first with their seeming ineptitude, had still eluded him nonetheless. Gemma's legs had a little less force in them now, and he knew he was close; it was then that he realised that he was posed in front of the giant mirror and paused for a split second, seeing himself as a black spider-like form, crouching over the young woman's body beneath him.

Thwack!

Something unimaginably strong, and unplanned (!) hit him about the head; as he looked up dazed, he saw her then, his 'beginning' -was she now his end? ... The woman in the photograph held aloft a cricket bat, and wore little else but a black silk chemise. Her hair was wild as were her eyes, and she looked paler than light itself in her fury; Maurice opened his mouth slightly, as though waiting for a communion wafer, and she inevitably swung, and hit him again. The blackness that ensued would still be curious he if could have registered it ... it was still her gift to him.

Chapter 61

Clara pulled Gemma out from under the slumped over man, his suit stained with tea and now his own blood. Her heart was racing but she could not hear it, she was moving too quickly.

She put her ear close to Gemma's mouth, and then let out a cry. "Gemma, Gemma, you're still here my love, come on, my love!" She rubbed Gemma's cheeks.

Gemma tried to breathe, and then rasped hideously instead. Clara let her try to sit up while she ran -she grabbed Gemma's car keys and their handbags and phones, but did not think to put on shoes. Then she pulled Gemma up, and dragged her fast to the car.

Seated soon and ready she first sent a text message:

SOS: BATTLESTATIONS

James would have to know what it meant. Then she started the engine and drove like a banshee, to nowhere else but St. John's Wood.

Chapter 62

Luc awoke as if someone had woken him, but there was no one else there. Once again, he took a moment to realise where he was: now in James' house, yes, he was back in London. They had arrived two days ago and he had stayed with James as Anjelica and Mischa helped to settle them in, and also stayed close in order to be ready for their next move; James had asked for Simon's phone back and the recording as soon as they had entered. As he lay there, Luc considered that Regents Park was so very close. And yet, he had done nothing. It had been months since he had seen her, perhaps it was best to let this ship sail away ... James had arrived in a wheelchair, and could not stand for very long at all, even though he now sported an elegant dark wood and silver topped cane that Anjelica had found for him in Paris. Luc saw Mischa look at James when he first arrived, and caught that glimpse of concern, at the state of their leader. Luc thought then, that if James could not continue in the same capacity, that then, well Mischa would have to take the responsibility ... but Mischa didn't want it, thought Luc. At least Luc was sure of one thing so far, especially after hearing the recording, that he was on James' side, not only out of blind loyalty and survival, but also he thought, that they must do some good.

At that moment, stirring and voices could be heard from another bedroom, and then the unmistakable gentle thump, thump, of James' cane came closer. Luc rose and walked nearer to the sound.

"Luc!"

James stood in the corridor, holding his phone.

"Call Mischa for me! He's downstairs."

"Mischa!"

At that Mischa could be heard running up the stairs, he had stayed over last night.

"Call Jelly! Tell her to get here, now!" yelled James.

"James, what's happened?" said both Luc and Mischa.

"Message from Clara." He thrust his phone at them. They each looked at the message she'd sent.

"I've been trying to call her and Gemma, no answer. Mischa, call Sir John, and call Michael! I want Michael here now!"

"James, we have protection outside, calm down," said Mischa.

"So did they!!"

Luc quickly went back to his room and looked at his Clara-phone, dormant.

Twenty minutes later, tyres screeching to a halt could be heard outside the front of the house and Mischa and Luc ran to see. Clara got out of the driver's side, in a short black slip, barefoot and seemed to be in a rush to get her passenger out and inside the house. Soon, Luc could see that it was Gemma that she was trying to retrieve, who looked-

Luc ran past James still hobbling down the stairs, but he was in Mischa's wake, who had already reached the women.

It was utterly freezing outside, but Clara moved as though her limbs were molten, Luc could see why: Gemma held one hand upon her neck, and Luc caught a glimpse of the red and purple trauma beneath. Strangling; a base and primal way to kill, he thought.

As all were ushered inside, Mischa whispered to James that Michael was at least an hour away, that he wasn't in Regents Park today. At that moment another car pulled up, and it was Anjelica who slammed her car door in haste, and came inside, to a picture of: Mischa on the phone telling member after member to get out of their homes, James looking furious, and the women; Clara still holding Gemma's side, and sitting her down on the sofa, soothing her constantly ..."It will be all right, my love, we're safe now..."

Tears streamed down Gemma's face. It was obvious that she could not speak.

"Get Osbourne here," said James.

"Who's that?" asked Luc.

"Doctor who's a member," said Mischa, and commenced dialling.

As Clara now knelt in front of Gemma on the sofa, she wiped away Gemma's tears as she continued with her soothing sentences, but then began to tell them all what had happened.

"... I heard the mug crash, but I was so deeply asleep, I just thought she'd broken something ... but then she must have been thrashing on the floor and against the sofa, there were more thumps, so I picked up her bat -I know she keeps it under the bed, as I passed her room, and then, oh God, James, I'll never be able to unsee it, he was just strangling her on the floor, just like that ..."

"What did he look like?" said Luc, and Clara looked at him unsure, making him realise that he was an anomaly.

"Luc's with us, Clara, please go on," said James.

"Luc, he was tall and thin, and ugly, sallow, but so strong!"

"What was he wearing?" asked Luc again.

"Wearing? ... A suit, black ..."

Luc nodded at James. "Same man, sounds like, that I saw at the hospital ... that first night."

The doorbell then sounded and everyone jumped. Mischa twitched the living room curtains to see. "It's OK. It's Osbourne."

"Luc, come with me," said James.

So Luc followed James to the back of the house to the kitchen and left the others in the living room to help Gemma and the doctor.

"I'm going to show you how it's done," said James, and opened his lap top.

"What are you going to do?"

"Release the recording, no more hands to play. Hopefully, it ends with the Minister."

"Just straight on to the internet? Won't they know it was you?"

"I won't be doing it directly. Watch ..."

James then telephoned someone called Ricky, and said to him, "Ricky? Wake up. Now! Ricky, it's time. Release it."

Luc looked at James.

"Ricky's one of our technical geniuses. I don't know what we'd do without them ... In a few minutes, Minister Sebold will be heard on the internet destroying himself beyond repair ... Luc, look at me."

"I know what you see," James said forcefully. "I look broken, I can barely move, I know. I'm sure I'll get stronger, but then look at Mischa- Do you know what I'm saying ...?"

Luc said nothing, reading James' eyes.

"... I need you, Luc. You've learned about us in the worst way, but I still need you. Mischa won't cut it; I think his heart wants to have never learned about us. You, on the other hand, you can do this."

Luc was a little dumbfounded.

"I'm not going anywhere!" said James hastily, "it's just if I deteriorate, or can't manage anymore, you- you and Mischa can do this."

After a pause, Luc nodded.

Luc then supported James back to the living room, he looked very white, his grip still fierce upon his cane yet.

"Osbourne?" asked James.

Gemma was lying on the sofa, Clara sat on another chair, covered now in a blue blanket, Mischa stood in a corner, still on the phone. "Sir John's been told," he said to James. At that moment Anjelica came back in the room, and looked at no one else but her brother.

But Osbourne then spoke, "Gemma will be all right. It was very close-Clara, you reached her just in time."

"Can she do without the hospital?" asked James.

"Well ... yes ... yes I think so. But I'll come and check on her a lot," Osbourne replied.

"Thank you so much," said James.

"Of course," said Osbourne.

"James?" said Anjelica.

"All right. Everyone listen. Gemma's been attacked, so I've released the recording. Osbourne, I'll fill you in later. It seems that Luc has seen her attacker before, a tall thin man in a dark suit-"

"So ugly!" hissed Clara.

"Michael is on his way, and we have protection outside who are on alert," James added.

Mischa then went upstairs to continue his phone calls, and soon just by the sight of him, Anjelica forced James upstairs as well to lie down, just for a short while. Gemma was given a sedative by the doctor, and left to rest on the sofa, while Clara, who'd now been given some men's pyjamas, set about in the kitchen, making toast and eggs as if she was the mistress of the house.

Luc left Gemma to rest with Osbourne still by her side, who was not daring to leave her yet, and went to the kitchen; they had left Luc redundant with nothing to do.

"I know, I know!" said Clara. "No one's going to want to eat anything, but I can't just sit there!" Her hands shook as she lifted a frying pan.

"I know what you mean ..." said Luc.

"Luc ... what I've seen this morning ... and Simon dead like that, the others dead, and now you, here with us ...?"

"It's a long story, Clara, not for now ..."

Clara nodded.

"But ... It was me Clara, I texted you to escape ..."

"What? ... You! ... You?" She stared at him and shook her head, then she came and kissed him on both cheeks. "Thank you ... The sandy haired one ..." she muttered now, understanding.

"You called me that, you said those words: the chestnut, the blonde and the sandy haired one, when we were fourteen."

She shook her head again. "I should have known ... and I'm sorry, I also had to know who it was ...I didn't want James to 'hunt' you down." She half smiled.

"We'll discuss it later, then?"

She looked at him and said, "James loves you though."

Luc nodded. He then left her to it, the strong aroma of coffee and toast meandered soon through the house.

Luc went back to his room, sat down at the edge of the bed and put his head in his hands. His mother had known them: James' father Edgar, Sir John or 'Johnnie' as she'd called him, Mischa and James and Jelly and Clara of course, maybe even met Gemma ... all of them in his mother's world, Luc marvelled; they were very good secret keepers. He thought then that if his mother Beatrice had known, found out by accident like Mischa, would she have told Luc about it? ... Yes. She would have Luc thought, and felt proud of her, for what she'd been; but would she want him to join? ... It was too late for that, and she was gone, and Luc did not want to look up towards the sky, as if her face remained there.

He got up instead and looked carefully outside the window. No one was there, no one was ever there; their protection stayed hidden. But then- No! Someone was, so close that Luc had overlooked it. Luc's voice caught in his throat, there wasn't time! he thought, to sound the siren. He grabbed his normal phone and pulled up the directory, as he then ran to the front door; he should have shouted for Mischa on his way down, but he was focusing on his phone, and now it was too late. He knew that Gemma was half unconscious in the living room, and the others were all over the house; he had to act, for no one else had seen.

Luc opened the front door and quickly closed it behind him. There, four paces away was Maurice, and to Luc: the man in the black suit. Luc had one hand in his pocket; maybe Maurice would think it was a gun.

"Monsieur," said Maurice in a lip twisted greeting; he looked dishevelled, and bloody about the face. "Quel courage, Monsieur. Do you really think you will be able to stop me? ... If you step aside, I will make it quick." He then smiled.

But Luc did not move; everything in his life had distilled down to this moment, like a trajectory set by everyone around him: his mother and her friends, his father and where he'd chosen for them to live, their summers by the sea in France that bound them so tightly, like a silent devoted oath ... And then, she was gone, Beatrice, who had made it so magical, so pleasurable, a childhood few could compare ... so he stood there, not only unwilling, but unable to move; he stood to guard so very much.

"Foolish boy!" Maurice lunged and Luc pressed his finger to dial.

Maurice stopped for a spilt second, as the phone in his own pocket rang. Luc still had his number stored, and had hoped now that this was indeed the Minister's man, who's number had been given to Gemma. But Maurice simply smiled and ignored the phone's clamour that had so temporarily stalled him, and began to approach again.

Luc decided to try and use everything he had; perhaps not only aim for the kidneys but also sweep his leg to trip the man up, he just needed to keep him from the door ... just another minute or two-

But as though without any warning -Maurice was upon him; Luc's strategy out of the window as Maurice had him before Luc had been able to speak with his fists. Maurice took him then as though a lover, and forced him up against the door, all the while pressing into Luc's side, a small and elegant dagger.

If pain could be exquisite, this was it, thought Luc. And yet, pinned to the door as he was, Luc still smiled now at Maurice, who raised an eyebrow to the audacity.

Luc tried to keep Maurice's brown eyes with his, breathing jaggedly through clenched teeth ... for, a true nemesis approached-

Before Maurice knew anything, Michael hulked behind him; he grabbed both Maurice's hands behind his back and held them there as though manacled. Maurice struggled manically but could not free himself; also incredulous at this turn of events.

"Luc, hold down the doorbell!" shouted Michael.

It was then as Luc and Maurice separated a touch, as Michael held Maurice back, that Luc witnessed the small blade in his side, and blood that bloomed about his nightshirt. Luc, even in his agony, turned around, and pressed his finger to the doorbell, not letting it go, until Mischa opened it.

At that moment, Maurice kicked out, Luc fell to the floor in the hallway and Maurice and then Michael fell heavily on top of him; the silvery blade in this ruckus, slipped out.

Luc heard Clara scream once, and then heard front door close. Then Anjelica screamed, "Oh dear God! Get inside!" at someone, maybe Clara.

"Get inside the living room and shut the door!" Luc then heard James say. But no footsteps ensued; instead, James' cane came in a rapid clunk.

All the while Michael struggled with Maurice, they both rolled off Luc soon, and then Clara and Anjelica screamed.

"I'm closing the door!" said Osbourne.

"Yes, do it!" shouted James.

Luc could see Clara's bare feet close to him. More furniture could be heard crashing, as Michael tussled with Maurice; Mischa came in holding a chair and brought it down on Maurice's back, and then Michael turned the beaten man over and put his hands around his neck.

"Michael! -James! No!" screamed Anjelica. But no one listened to her ...
Not long after, Maurice finally, was gone.

It was then that Luc could hear Clara; he smelled gardenias as she crouched down beside him, "Luc? ... Oh my God, Luc! James! Blood, there's blood! ..."

"Osbourne!!" Luc heard James yell and then pounding at the living room door. "It's safe, open it!"

Anjelica was now also crouching by Luc, as well as Mischa.

"He needs a hospital," said Anjelica.

"Let me through," said Osbourne. "... It's a small blade," he then added finally.

"Can you fix it?" asked James.

Osbourne sighed, "I could say yes ... but your man does need a hospital, James."

"All right."

"I have a friend at a private hospital, we'll say he had a kitchen accident, the knife was wet and slipped from his hands, you got that, Luc?" asked the doctor.

Luc nodded weakly, he was still prostrate upon the floor; the welcome mat now a sea of red.

"One of you girls, come on, come and pretend to be his girlfriend," added Osbourne.

Anjelica stood up, and together they managed to help Luc to the car; one of her hands pressing down on the bandages they'd quickly put upon his wound.

Anjelica drove and Luc drifted, the pain made him take shallow breaths; wondering if this was his last taste of his earthly journey, in the back seat of his friend's car, stabbed by a villain, and about to bleed to death.

Chapter 63

There were voices before, but they went away. The sun rose, and also went away again, and if there was night; it was only briefly glimpsed through medicated and dilated irises. The door opened sometimes, and then soon Luc was left in peace once more; a throb at his side, now less demanding. His eyes blinked foggily open, he tried to take a deep breath, and he felt it, the ghost of the dagger still in place; but yet he was free of it, and now could manage to turn and twist in bed with more ease. As he was stationary, he didn't know why but it felt like morning, probably from the condition of the flaccid light behind the curtains. Then, he realised that he was not alone, and there, sat on a chair by his bed was a quiet visitor.

"I hope I didn't wake you up," she said.

She was holding something in her hands, it looked like a photograph.

"No, Gemma, no you didn't ..." Luc's eyes flitted around the same spare room he had been staying at, at James'.

"How are you feeling?"

"I must be better, I know where I am ... but how are you?"

"I'm all right, Luc ... My neck and throat are OK."

"I didn't mean that," he said slowly.

Gemma half smiled. "You really are James' best friend ... I don't know how I am ... I nearly died, and you too ... eye to eye with that maniac, Maurice."

Luc nodded and didn't press her further, the memory of it shivered.

"They said it was OK for me to sit with you. Osbourne I mean, and James. James and Mischa are downstairs."

"How much time has passed?" asked Luc suddenly.

"You were stabbed two weeks ago."

Luc looked like he was trying to place and understand many things so Gemma added, "Your wound was luckily not too deep, but you had lost a lot of blood. They had to give you some more, blood I mean. They stitched you up and brought you back here, even though Osbourne wanted you to stay in hospital. But James wanted you here, where he felt we could keep you safe under one roof, I imagine-"

"Two weeks! So the Minister, the recording!?"

"Well, it hit the press pretty fast, and Minister Sebold tried to fudge it by saying that he was on a mission to try and trap Grimbaud on tape, that he was 'helping' MI6. Well, considering that Grimbaud is dead, well before his time, not only is it not true, but MI6 wanted nothing to do with it. Sebold was finished soon after that, out of his job and under investigation. Our protection continues, as well as surveillance upon anything we can connect to the Minister, but, well I hope, maybe that was as far as it went."

Luc nodded, looking relieved.

"Luc, I wanted to talk to you personally ..." Gemma looked into his eyes, and shared more of herself with him than she had ever dared at the office. "I wanted to show you this-"

She handed Luc a small black and white photograph, in it were three small little boys that he recognised, and another child.

"This is James and this is Mischa," she pointed as she spoke, "this is you, and this little girl, is me."

Luc looked at her with his mouth open.

"I'm so sorry to have to hide from you for so long, and I'm so glad I can show you this today. Look at the photo ..." The sea seemed to roll in the background even though the four children were captured still; at the seafront the three small boys were lost in their own world, but she was the one who looked vivaciously into the camera. "You held my hand every time we walked into the waves ... you've forgotten this holiday, haven't you?"

Luc blinked and looked harder at the photo. "... But I haven't forgotten it. I remember the sea ... and a lot of ice cream that summer ..."

"It was the only holiday or time we ever spent together; I don't expect you to remember me at all. But, I just wanted to show you the picture ..."

Luc nodded, and took his hand out from under the covers, to hold hers. He had been completely right about Gemma, and felt relieved that he could at least trust his judgement in that.

"What will happen now ...? With the group?" he asked.

"I think we will lie low, well if blowing open the scandal with the Under Secretary of Defence is lying low ... and then, well ... resume."

"Are you ... will you still ...?"

"More than ever," she replied, firm and steady.

At that, Luc filled with admiration for her.

"And you, Luc? I've heard James and Mischa muttering ..."

"Me? Oh, me ... I guess I'm in this now, aren't I ..."

"You don't have to be!" said Gemma, her eyes wide.

But Luc shook his head. "Gemma ... look at the photograph ..." And now he smiled at her, as electricity wound from his navel to his mouth and his stab-wound smarted, as though shivering with the ecstasy of the idea; and Gemma clasped his hand, as though promising never to let it go.

*

Clara was a beacon even in black; the hidden axis upon which so much of this tale turned thought Luc. There she stood on the other side of the room from James; as far away from him as she thought proper, Luc supposed. Her hair was characteristically short, shiny and fecund, and in deep winter, she was as pale as snow. She wore a black pencil skirt and polo neck which were sombre enough, but was yet elevated by glossy black heels, slick with glamour, as if she couldn't help herself, or perhaps it was an act of rebellion; a last streak of allegiance to the dead man that they'd come here today to respect. Next to her were her parents and other faces that Luc could not place; people of all ages, many were clumped together in family groups. On his side stood James and Mischa and Anjelica, and many other people young and old that Luc did not recognise. Gemma and Sir John made the rounds, talking and sympathising with people. They had erected a small white marquee in James' garden, so that the kitchen doors were stretched fully wide to create a new room filled with faces. Hot fiery burners stood at intervals around them, keeping them in bursts of warmth as the air made frosty mists of their breath. Most people wore black, some not, some wore suits and some even wore jeans. The programme had been set by Anjelica; music and speeches for a man that Luc was only too keen to remember, had cost them three lives. The glass door was rendered clear and fixed, with no imprint or echo upon it of the violence it had encountered.

After the speeches and music were played there would be food and drink: dark wine in proper glasses, hot steaming chicken and ham pies heated up by Anjelica in the oven, and marble cake in small squares handed about on thick red napkins, while layered terrines of salmon and asparagus also stood ready and elegantly sliced; one of the members was a caterer and she had done her best for the event. People would eat and drink and converse soberly, there would even be a laugh here and there; Simon had died just a few months ago, but enough time for the shock to have tempered itself.

James stood with his elegant cane, leaning heavily Luc noticed, and he felt sure that his friend would not walk properly again. Luc hoped that the preamble would not go on too long so that James could sit down; he did not have to worry for long, as everyone was now being seated for the service, ready to receive the communal balm.

Mischa began and Luc watched and listened; although Luc was a stranger, no one looked at him or eyed him with suspicion, he was visible and invisible and that gave him comfort.

"Thank you all so much for coming. James and I felt that we had to do this ... for ourselves and each other, but also for the man we lost, for in the end ... Simon was one of us," Mischa finished.

James now slowly stood up again, and turned to face his flock. "Thanks, Mischa. Simon, indeed was one of us, and put up with everything I threw at him, put up with very hard tasks, and came through, and moreover, put up with me ..."

Luc was not sure if it was only him, but he felt an undercurrent as James said those last words, as if they all knew, knew the truth about why Simon had betrayed them all, about how he wanted to hurt James, how he had loved Clara and lost her, and his baby ... but then, of course -they did know. Things were not kept secret from them, and yet ... they were all still there ... Luc looked about the room again, with a deeper resonance. It was then that Luc saw Clara, and it caught him what lay there; for it was a deep and penetrating melancholy with which she gazed at James, from the back where she had found a place to sit. She then softened and looked down, as though a child being reprimanded, so she knew she was the axis, thought Luc, she had taken it to heart, she blamed herself for all of this and so no longer looked at James, and instead with heartbroken eyes, took in his sermon as her punishment. And yet, after a few moments, in the end she returned to stare unflinchingly at James again, unaware or uncaring that Luc was her audience. Then some music began: it was 'Let It Be' by The Beatles, a few people cried or had tears in their eyes, but Clara did not break, not a whimper; instead she breathed in the song and let it's sweet melancholy douse her while closing her eyes to take it in. During the entire episode Luc was struck by her, she was obviously beautiful, but it wasn't only that, it was her -that the simple act of loving *her* had caused two men on the same side to go into battle with each other; resulting in abundant casualties everywhere, as James was a living example. Simon had attacked James in the only way that had been left open to him, by attacking them all. And so in the end, for all the might and high mindedness of this 'Army of Truth' as Luc had named them in his head, what ancient and primal things to be brought to its knees by: love, jealousy, pain and fury, had woven a powerful spell indeed.

Gemma and Anjelica now handed everyone a glass of red wine, as Luc took his, it brought the room back to him.

"… And so I ask you all to stand, and raise your glasses in honour of the man we lost: For Simon." All stood and murmured, "For Simon" and then James took a sip and so did everyone in the room, finally, they shuffled to sit down again.

More music now played, some form of Ave Maria, and people began to get up and walk about, the aroma of hot pies reached him and he too rose; not sure what he should be doing next. So he joined Anjelica at the kitchen table and helped hand out plates and napkins as people helped themselves to the beautiful fare.

"You don't have to, Luc," said Anjelica.

"I'm fine, it doesn't hurt much anymore, just no summersaults … I'm glad James is on the sofa though."

"Me too," she said.

Anjelica seemed more confident yet about James than Luc, and she had some colour in her cheeks from her efforts now.

The extended room was a hubbub of voices and people carrying wine and plates of food, many went to speak to James, marooned as he was on a sofa, now with a plate of food of his own that Mischa had brought him. Luc wanted to listen to what each member was saying to James, but hung back, worrying if his presence might cause them reticence.

Finally, people began to trickle away, and Luc walked about with a giant black bin liner to help the catering member, Gloria, tidy up. The sun was melting away so very early in the day as it did, and the icy breeze mingled with the hot air of the burners to surround him in wafts of warmth and ice while he watched Anjelica help take James upstairs, to make him lie down. Eventually, Mischa alone remained in the room with Luc, and as Luc looked at him, it was then that Luc knew what they both were: christened outsiders that yet now belonged; whatever choice they had had in the matter.

"... Do you think things will be all right?" Luc finally asked Mischa, as the sun was beginning to set behind them, streaking pink, early afternoon that it was in February.

"What do you mean?" Mischa asked.

"You know, I don't even know ... did you know him well? Simon?"

"I knew him, not well enough it seems." Mischa smiled sadly.

"Do you think it will happen again, what he did ...?"

"You mean, betrayal? ... No ... I don't *think* so, as however it happened, look how he ended up ... that'll stay with people, not that I think any of us would want to betray us, but, I could have said that of Simon once upon a time, he was a true believer ... things change, so I suppose it's not impossible, but as demonstrated, not advisable."

A shiver ran through Luc. He turned away to drag his full refuse sack and place it with the others, when he turned back he saw Mischa looking through a side window at the black silhouettes of the trees against the deep orange and streaking pinks of the early winter sunset, and there was a tinge of bonfire smoke in the air from a neighbouring garden. Luc then left the room, he didn't say goodbye, felt for his keys in his pocket, and exited James' house.

Out in the open air he felt the stinging winter chill; he took in a big lung full of it, however much it hurt his side to do so, and then finally, felt free. Without thinking he got into his car, prising her cold steel stiff doors open and settled into an icy cabin, permeated by puffs of his own breath that frosted into blooms upon the air.

He drove back there, where his home still stood, where he was always due to return, and the iron gates and cold alabaster walls greeted him coolly but graciously: *where have you been?* They would have asked him if they could, as he parked in his assigned place next to a Rolls Royce and a Jaguar. He made his way trying to focus on only the windows of his flat and felt very relieved to be where he had started; in the tumultuousness of these past few months he was glad that he would be returning to his old office and was now reassured to have back his old grey apartment; embellished as it was by orange throws and stout white candles half melted into glasses. As he walked stridently towards it, he had to take in very large freezing breaths -but it was impossible, what on earth had made him think that it would have been possible, to simply go home? And so, he turned from facing his own front door, and walked as a man possessed, with no thoughts, to the other -that stood black, mute and vast compared to his. He reached forward still without any thoughts at all and took hold of the freezing door knocker in his hand, ignoring the button for the doorbell, and struck it three times; his hand shook, now bitten by the cold as he waited with it back by his side.

It was blue-dark outside, although only a Sunday afternoon, Luc's fingers grew numb as he waited, his breath seeped away the warmth from his body and came out as long frosty mist, and soon, the hulking door began to slowly open.

And there she stood, in an emerald green silk dressing gown and bare feet, hair curled and disarranged, and also, mute. She became a picture and Luc too, stood still to stare at the vision before him. Her mouth opened a little but still no words came out, although her toes curled in a touch despite her inability to move, shrinking from the icy air. Luc did not dare to be friendly. So eventually, she spoke, and it was not what he expected.

"Luc! You're here ... I went to Paris ... to ... to find you," she said simply as her eyes shone, exhibiting in her countenance the true toll of the past months of exile.

Luc stood rooted, surprised.

"I went to Paris. I saw you ... I *saw* you. I'd researched where you might be working, *all* of you, so I could find a way to see you again ... but Michael stopped me ... Luc," she whispered, " he said that you'd made your decision ... so I thought ..." and she blinked. "And if you haven't, then you just left me after knowing all these things! As if it had all never happened, like it had been a dream, with no explanations." She stopped to draw in some freezing air. "But, you could've trusted me, I *already knew*, I didn't want to hide or to be kept safe, I don't care about being safe, do you understand? You can trust me; you could have always trusted me ..."

She took in another ragged breath, he could see that she was thrilled to see him, yet separation had not only taken its toll upon her, it had left anger as well in its wake. But her gaze did not waver, nor had her passion it seemed; she had never given up on him. And suddenly, moved by a wave inside, driven by everything he had been through, he cast away all his questions about an existent husband or not, and her errant behaviour, and instead regarded her as she stood there; her glorious female lamps emulated her deep green apparel, glinting gold flowered and bare bosomed, and so bolstered her frame, standing proud upon either side of her. Luc beheld Mer, and closed his eyes for a moment, before finally taking a step into her home, and so gave in to her plea; to trust her, with its sweet promising sound, he would give her this last request. As the door began to close behind him and as she stood there confused, he put his arms around her and closed his eyes again. And so, she embraced him and his wound, but he let the pain sing inside him, its own sad enchanted song. Perhaps it would be a stay of execution, perhaps in time he thought he was sure that he would be able to remove his distrust of her, of James and everything as he saw it now, as to lift away the vein running through the marble, like her dark strand that sometimes streaked her forehead … lift it out and away; or, see it as her mark of Cain and then choose to love her regardless, and without censure, as it should have been and with no restraint, as though it was still that sun-soaked enchanted summer. For she made him feel abandon, as though he were part of an endless sea, and so, absolute; as if he too contained the universe; whatever she was, she was still enough, she was everything.

Epilogue

As soon as Mer's divorce was complete, Mer and Luc were married in a small civil ceremony at Marylebone town hall; attended by Luc's father and new wife Isabelle, Mer's parents, Christine, Marina, and of course Mischa, James and Anjelica; who were unalterably close to the couple now. Mer had held a small bouquet of exquisite red roses tied with a black ribbon, and had worn a simple white silk dress; to grace the day in dark curls as she'd come as nothing but herself. Luc gave up his old flat to live with Mer in her huge house, where Christine and her child yet remained and where Luc still awoke on foggy, unclear mornings and wondered, how he found himself there ...

www.ingramcontent.com/pod-product-compliance
Lightning Source LLC
Chambersburg PA
CBHW021121260626
47169CB00005B/1385